She Walks In Power

Protectors of the Spear

MaryLu
Tyndall

She Walks in Power

Protectors of the Spear 1

© 2016 by MaryLu Tyndall

Published by Ransom Press
San Jose, CA 95123

ISBN: 978-0-9971671-3-9
E-Version ISBN: 978-0-9971671-2-2

Library of Congress Cataloging-in-Publication Data is on file at the Library of Congress, Washington, DC.

This book is a work of fiction. Names, characters, places, incidents, and dialogues are either products of the author's imagination or used fictitiously. Any similarity to actual people, organizations, and/or events is purely coincidental

Cover Design by Ravven
Editor: Louise M. Gouge

Ransom Press
San Jose, CA

Dedication

To those who yearn for the power of God in their lives

I say unto you, He that believeth on me, the works that I do shall he do also; and greater works than these shall he do; because I go unto my Father. John 14:12

Acknowledgments

All praise to my Father in Heaven for continuing to give me stories and for opening my eyes to the spirit realm. I owe so much to friends, readers, and fellow writers who help me along the way with much-needed encouragement and who also help spread the word about my books. Debbie Mitchell a.k.a Chappy, Michelle Griep, Rita Gerlach, Bonnie Roof, Karen Martin, Laurie Alice Eakes, Louise Gouge, Lora Doncea, Debbie Lynne Costello, and so many more! Also, I owe much to my early readers who leap at the chance to read my latest release! Thank you all so much!

Thanks to Shaleen Howard and Nicole Fremmerlid for your tips on archery!

And I simply must mention Anabelle, a young girl whose sister Amelia Allen begged me to make her a character in this book. So I did! Anabelle, you have a sweet, caring sister!

I so appreciate my online friends, too many to name, who offer ideas and support. And I especially am grateful to all my readers. Without you, my books would be quite lonely. Thank you!

But most of all, to God be the glory!

The night is almost gone, and the day is near. Therefore let us lay aside the deeds of darkness and put on the armor of light
Romans 13:12

Chapter 1

England, the Middle Ages

*A*lexia D'Clere slid an arrow from her quiver, nocked it in her bow, and drew back the bowstring. Wind whipped through the branches of the large maple tree above her, stirring a whirlwind of leaves and needles across the forest floor. But Alexia's gaze followed three men atop horses, accompanying a coach down an access road through Emerald forest—the three men who had ventured off the main trail and dared to penetrate the Circle of the Spear. To what purpose? She would have dismissed them as pitchkettled dolts if not for their attire and the magnificent destriers they rode. Now, as they came closer, she narrowed her eyes like a falcon on its prey.

Holding her breath, she tracked the first man with the tip of her arrow. Night was fast approaching as the sun withdrew its light through the maze of trees, making it hard to distinguish his features. She had no trouble, however, seeing the myriad weapons strapped to his hip—all manner of swords, knives, and axes. Not to mention the metal plates protecting his shoulders and arms. *The armor of a knight.* Oddly, he wore no protection on his chest, save a thick leather doublet. His chin was lightly bearded, his hair dark, and in place of a helmet, a hat sat atop his head, sporting a blue feather. His companions were similarly attired.

In the distance, a gray-haired man exited the stationary coach, nearly tripping on the black robe falling to his ankles. He uttered a blathering gush of complaints, most of which Alexia couldn't distinguish. Something about heat, hunger, disrespect, and incessant delays. She trained her gaze upon him, noting the gold-embroidered collar and blood-red stole draped around his neck. Potz! A bishop.

She shifted her eyes back to the men on horseback, narrowing in on the crest engraved on their rerebraces. *The Royal Crest.* Her breath caught. These men must be members of the King's Guard—elite warriors assigned to protect his majesty. What were they doing so far from court and with such a high-ranking member of the Church?

She pulled the bow tighter. As the Protector, she could shoot them all ere they knew what struck them. She had the right. The hemp whined beneath the strain as the feathers on the end tickled her ears. Still, the men came.

And still she did not release the arrow.

"Prithee, turn away," she whispered. "Or I shall make thee wish ye had." One well-placed arrow would bring the leader down and scatter the others.

The horses snorted. The leader sniffed the air as if sensing danger. She leveled the arrow at his unarmored leg.

The friar's words rose to stay her hand. "Concentrate, my dear. Hear the Spirit within. Let patience prevail."

A trickle of sweat slid down her forehead. The muscles in her arm ached.

Seek the light in others.

Willing her mind to settle, she closed her eyes and whispered a prayer. Two lights appeared where the leader and one of the men had been—barely flickers, but there, withal. The other man bore no flame. Two of these men knew the Father, one did not.

She opened her eyes. The lights disappeared. The leader turned his horse down a narrow path to the left. *Nay, not that way!* Still holding her bowstring tight, she stepped from the tree. A twig snapped, the faintest of sounds, barely audible above the chatter of bird and patter of wildlife.

The leader raised a hand. All three men stopped.

"What is it now, Sir LePeine?" the bishop complained as he mopped his brow with a cloth.

But the man made no reply. Instead, he turned and stared in her direction, his gaze weaving around trees, leaping over shrubs, speeding past boulders and fallen logs.

And penetrating straight into her eyes.

Alexia's heart stopped. *Surely, he cannot see me.* Not at this distance, and not with her attire blending in with the colors of the forest.

Still, he stared with those eyes as piercing as a wolf's, silent, unmoving as if he could not only see her, but read her thoughts as well. The intensity of that stare made her wonder at this man, this king's knight with the barest spark of light within his soul.

The destriers snorted and pawed the ground. The shadows deepened. An owl gave an eerie *hoot*.

One more step closer and she would be forced…

The leader nudged his mount forward.

Heart thumping, she drew the bowstring tighter, aimed at the man's leg, closed her eyes, and released the arrow.

It should have hit its mark. Alexia never missed. Yet when she opened her eyes, her arrow vibrated in the trunk of a tree, and the man was galloping in her direction. He pulled out his sword as he went, the chime echoing through the forest.

Flinging her bow over her shoulder, Alexia took off like a deer.

Horse hooves pounded behind her. Shouts echoed from

the other men. An angry whine of "Don't leave me here alone!" screeched from the bishop.

Not looking back, Alexia darted right, then left, around trunks and hedges, deeper and deeper into the Emerald Forest where horses could not tread.

A horse whinnied. More shouts and footsteps followed.

She dashed around a moss-laden boulder as darkness flung a black cloak over the forest. No matter. Her boots were sure and firm, her confidence high, her strength unfailing. She knew these woods like a servant knew the halls of a vast castle. She knew every tree, flower, fern, and pond. Every hiding place, cave, and den.

She knew—

A battering ram struck her and knocked her to the ground.

A breathing, warm battering ram who smelled of sweat and man. Alexia scrambled away on all fours, but he snagged her leg and pulled her back. Dirt filled her mouth. Flipping over, she kicked his shoulder. He released her with a groan, then leapt atop her. He was but a shadow—a dark, heavy shadow. More footsteps approached.

Fear soured in her mouth. Unusual fear. She could not be caught. She *would* not be caught!

She slugged him across the jaw. He shoved her shoulders to the ground, pressing her back against her quiver. An arrow bit her neck. She started to kick him, but he forced her legs down with his own.

"Who are you and why did you wish me dead?" he asked. His voice was deep, his breath hot and smelling of spiced wine.

His friends burst through the greenery. "In need of assistance?" one of them asked, his tone taunting.

"I have the matter in hand. 'Tis but a lad from the feel of him." The man atop her tightened his grip on her arms. Pain seared into her shoulders.

"I asked you a question, lad."

A cloud moved above him. Wind stirred the branches of the canopy. And for the briefest of seconds, light from a full moon shone down upon the scene.

Though she couldn't see her assailant's expression, she sensed his shock. Releasing his grip, he jerked from her and backed away. "'Tis a lady."

His two friends chuckled.

Alexia leapt to her feet, knowing it best to make a swift escape, but she couldn't resist a clever retort.

"Aye, 'tis a lady, ye clod. The Falcon of Emerald Forest at your service." Retrieving her bow from the ground, she swept her arm out before her, not caring that her hood was askew and her red hair tumbled loose. "And you will leave these woods immediately or next time I shall aim for your heart."

"Forsooth!" The man chuckled. "Any better your aim and you would have hit London!"

She kicked him, intending to strike his thigh but hit a softer part that caused him to double over with a cry of agony that made even *her* wince.

Laughter from the man's companions filled the air behind her as she fled into the night.

☙❧

Alexia dove into the bramble, shoved aside the prickly branches, and emerged onto the edge of the pond. Moonlight dappled silver over gentle ripples that spread from the waterfall toward a barricade of trees and shrubs protecting the secret place. She never grew tired of its beauty—day or night.

Drawing a deep breath of the sweet, musky air, she climbed atop the moist boulder to her right and slipped behind the curtain of water tumbling over the edge of a cliff above her. Droplets cooled her skin as she made her way to the narrow opening hidden behind the cleft of a rock.

Dipping her head, she entered the tunnel. She required no light to guide her down the dark, winding path, for this had been her home for the past nine years. A turn to the right, then left, and a light in the distance led her the rest of the way.

Pushing aside the wooden door, she entered the main hall of her abode. Not a cave, as one might expect, but a home built in stone, hidden beneath the ground. In fact, save for the odd way of entering and the lack of windows, one might think it a wealthy gentleman's manor perched on a hill.

Colorful tapestries decorated the stone walls, depicting scenes of courtly love and the life of Christ. High-backed wooden chairs boasting bright red cushions framed a hearth whose chimney led up to a hollowed-out tree above. A trestle table covered in white linen stood to the right, beyond which lay her sleeping pallet. To her left, shelves of books, all in disarray, lined the walls behind an equally disheveled desk. Candles flickered from iron spikes hung about the chamber, while above her a candelabra sent a golden glow over the room.

Alexia took a step onto the silk-woven carpet that covered most of the floor and listened for the friar. He couldn't be far. The candle on his desk still burned and his quill pen sat askew on the parchment as if its task was yet unfinished.

Removing her leather gloves, she stepped toward the fire just as Friar Josef entered from the back room. "Child, where have you been? You've been gone"—his thick brows rose upon seeing her face—"What happened?"

Alexia smiled. This man who had been like a father to her always knew when something was amiss. Flinging off her quiver, she set it and her bow down on a table and knelt before the crackling flames. "The King's Guard have arrived. A bishop is with them. An important one from the appearance of his coach."

"Indeed?" The friar pursed his lips as he approached, his

brown cowl dragging on the floor. "And what, pray tell, did you *do* to these men?"

"Not what I wished, you can be sure of that." She smiled and held her hands to the flames. "But the Guard? What are they doing here? They entered the Circle, hence I had no choice but to shoot one. Never fear"—she gave him a compliant smile—"'twas a warning only. I missed."

He chuckled, the corners of his eyes crinkling. "*You*? Miss? Forsooth, I cannot believe it!"

"Aye, and then he...oh, 'tis of no consequence." There was no need to cause the friar worry. She slowly rose. "I must be away to Luxley."

He bowed his head and uttered a sigh. Firelight reflected off the large wooden cross dangling against his chest as he folded his hands across his rotund belly. "What need? You were there yesterday."

"Where else would the king's emissaries be going?" Alexia started for the hallway that led to her dressing chamber.

"You make me regret allowing you to acquire a position there," he yelled after her.

Halting, she faced him. "I am eighteen, and you have taught me well. You must trust God to watch over me, for I have His work to do now."

He snorted. "That is what worries me. That you ignore His work and follow your own heart." Though his tone was incriminating, the love and care pouring from his eyes made her smile.

"I cannot abandon her," she said. "She has been unwell these past years."

"Should someone recognize you—"

"Alas, no one has. If not yet, they never will." Approaching him, she took his hands in hers. "I promise I shall be careful. I will but discover the mission of these men and return anon." Releasing his hands, she grabbed her gloves. "God's truth, they could be after the Spear."

He scratched the patch of gray hair atop his head. "Nay. What would have led them here?"

"That is what I must discover, dear Friar." Standing on her tip-toes, she kissed his cheek.

And as always, he swatted her away, face reddening.

In a small dressing chamber beside the main hall, she exchanged her shirt, tunic, and doublet for a plain wool kirtle tied around her waist with a rope. Removing her boots, she put on her leather slippers and strapped a knife inside a specially made slot in her garter. Next, she slipped on the leather wrist band that hid her mark, braided her hair, and then completed her ensemble with a plain circlet on her head that draped a netted veil down her back.

Pleased with her appearance as naught but a servant, she entered the tiny chapel beside her chamber, dark, save for a single candle atop the altar. Above it, the crucifix of Christ hung against a golden tapestry that glittered in the light. Kneeling before the altar, she lifted the glass top and retrieved the Spear from its silk pillow. It wasn't the entire spearhead, merely the tip which age had severed from the top. Still…to think of *where* it had been—of Whose blood it had touched. Holding it gently in her hands she bowed her head

"Holy Father, Almighty One. I pray your protection through the blood of Christ as I go forth this night. Give me thy wisdom, thy discernment. Grant me the wisdom to discover the treachery of these king's men and to protect Cristiana from evil. I thank thee for thine answer and for thine presence through the blood of my Lord. Amen."

She kissed the Spear, longing to bring it with her to ensure God's power and protection but 'twas too risky. God had ordained her as its Protector and she would never fail Him.

Chapter 2

*R*onar LePeine adjusted his position in the saddle in the hopes of alleviating the pain still throbbing through his groin. Dastardly woman! He'd never seen the likes of such a lady, wearing men's attire and traipsing through the forest shooting arrows at passersby! Tush! And at the king's men! She was obviously mad, depraved, mayhap even demon possessed. He shuddered at the last thought and shifted again as they made their way to the walled entrance of Luxley village, past an empty gallows, and over a bridge leading to the main gate. Torches perched on either side provided light enough to see the brook sludging beneath them, while an indescribable stench caused Ronar to cough and hurry forward.

A simple announcement of whom they were escorting quickly opened the gates. Children wearing more dirt than clothing emerged from the shadows shouting, "Sir, do you want a room, a bed? Sir, where are you from?" They reached to touch the horses, alarming the beasts, and Ronar had to rein in Penance to keep him from trampling them.

"Nay, little ones. Begone. We are on the king's business." Ronar waved them away while Jarin flipped a few coins in the air, sending them fighting like chickens for a scrap of seed. Behind them, the little urchins crowded the bishop's carriage, and Ronar turned to see the holy man drop the curtains to his windows with an annoyed groan.

Beyond the beggars, lights from the town square lured

them past a row of houses and inns with steeply angled roofs and then past several merchant homes, their shops closed for the night. Citizens poked heads from windows to see what was astir, and Ronar could hear their gasps and whispers. No doubt they weren't accustomed to receiving such an important visitor as Bishop Godfrey of Montruse.

Ahead, lights from within the Church of the Holy Trinity lit the stained glass windows in a collage of dancing colors while the bell rang in the steeple and a town crier sang his mournful report in the distance. Pigs and chickens darted across the street. An old woman, carrying a bucket of water, froze at the sight of them and ducked into the shadows. Those citizens still out after dark stopped their tasks to stare at the newcomers. Others, upon spotting the insignia of the king, ducked into homes and alleyways, while still others bowed toward the bishop's royal coach.

The bishop seemed to perk up at the attention, lifting the curtain and waving his jeweled hand out the window toward the peasants. Ronar huffed. The man had done naught but complain since they'd left the palace in London three days prior. Word was he was out of favor with the king who had sent him on this quest—one at which he must succeed or face banishment. Or worse. Alas, the poor man had been forced to sleep on the ground with the rest of them and eat whate'er the forest provided like a mere commoner.

And Ronar and his men had heard about the indignity—vehemently and relentlessly.

Flaming torches lit their way past simple homes made of wattle and daub. Smoke puffed from chimneys as the smell of sour pottage joined other unsavory scents that stung Ronar's nose.

He didn't much care for villages. Or for larger towns. Even in London, too much poverty and misery existed alongside wealth and excess. That excess now loomed above them from a hill in the distance. Luxley Castle—a dark, cruel master keeping an eye on its subjects.

A sense of dread rolled over him, heavy and ominous. Why? This mission was not unlike many he and his men had performed for the king. Save on one point, he suddenly realized—one very important point that gave him pause.

"Recovered from your joust with the wildcat?" Jarin, riding beside him, gave him a mocking grin.

Wildcat indeed. The Falcon of Emerald Forest, of all things. He blew out a laugh. "She would not have gotten the best of me if I hadn't granted her the favor due her sex."

"And she took that favor and made you eat it, 'twould seem."

"Indeed."

"A rather comely lass from what I saw."

A pair of eyes the color of jade fringed in thick lashes flitted through Ronar's mind. "Mayhap, but what good is beauty housed in lunacy?"

"Ah, but I do so like a challenge." Jarin winked.

"Then when we pass through Emerald Forest again, may her arrow be aimed at you, my friend." Ronar chuckled.

They rounded a corner, then ascended the hill to the castle. Lush gardens surrounded the entrance, whirling the sweet scent of lavender and roses around them and sweeping away the foul stench of the village. Ronar drew a deep breath as they halted before the gatehouse.

"Who goes there?" The shout came from above.

"Bishop Godfrey of Montruse to see Lady D'Clere," Ronar responded.

"That should get their attention," he said to Damien on his left. The man's stern features seemed even harsher in the torchlight.

"'Tis rare to have the king's special adviser at one's door," the knight replied, scanning the surrounding darkness. Damien, ever the staunch warrior. The best fighter Ronar ever had the fortune to battle beside.

"What is taking them so long?" the bishop spat from within the coach. "How dare they make me wait!"

Ronar exchanged a glance of disdain with Jarin. Ah, to be rid of his excellency's company—if only for a night.

"Mayhap they—" Jarin's reply was cut off as the gate swung open, and Ronar led them forward over a bridge into a small courtyard. Torches on posts cast flickering light over the inner bailey that was soon arush with squires, servants, and knights. Keeping his hand atop the hilt of his sword, Ronar slid from Penance and handed the reins to a stable boy. A knight started toward them. Dressed in chain mail with a sword at his side, he was a large, imposing man around whom the stench of alcohol whirled like a haunting specter.

"Walter DeGay, Captain of the Guard." His eyes flashed upon seeing the king's insignia on their forearms. "To what do we owe the pleasure of the King's Guard?"

Had the man not been informed of the identity of his guest?

The knight's hazy eyes sped to the coach where the bishop's page assisted him down. "Your Grace."—he stumbled toward him and then bowed clumsily— "We were not expectin—"

The bishop cut him off. "We wish to see Lady D'Clere immediately."

"Of course." Sir DeGay gathered himself and escorted them past the chapel and servants' quarters, through a set of large wooden doors, into the main hall of the castle where a tall middle-aged man with a commanding stride met them. A purple tunic covered with a vermilion silk surcoat threaded with golden filigree flaunted his high status. That and a jeweled broach positioned at his throat. Graying brown hair curled around his face, matching the thick brows dipping over cold dark eyes.

A chill coursed down Ronar.

"Sir Francis LeGode at your service." Ignoring Ronar and

his men, he approached the bishop and bowed himself so far to the ground, Ronar thought he might fall. "Your Excellency. Forgive me. We did not receive word of your visit."

"Rise." The bishop glanced around the great hall, empty now save for a few servants. Banners bearing the heraldry of various lords and knights draped from the ceiling high above them, while tapestries lined the cold stone walls. Shields and a battered Saxon war axe hung over the high seat above an immense hearth whose flames added light to the candles perched in wall brackets.

"What brings such a fine guest to Luxley Manor, your Grace?" LeGode inquired.

"Urgent business from the King."

"And these men are?"

"The King's Guard. My escorts."

Francis LeGode stared them up and down, respect and a tinge of fear in his eyes.

"We seek an audience with Lady D'Clere," Ronar offered.

Ignoring him, LeGode faced the bishop. "I fear 'tis impossible. She is quite ill, Excellency. I am steward here and attend all matters in her stead."

"Bah." The bishop growled and moved to stand by the fire, rubbing his pointed gray beard. "Very well. Is there somewhere private where we may converse?"

"Of course. But if you'll allow, Excellency. Surely you must be exhausted. I beg you to rest from your long journey." LeGode clapped his hands and several servants came running. "Escort these men to their rooms and draw a bath for his Excellency. I will have an evening repast prepared in your honor. Then when you are refreshed, we shall discuss business."

Ronar's stomach growled. A feast he could handle. Getting away from his Excellency, even for a short time, sounded better still.

❧

Ronar tossed his sack onto the cot and marched to the window. Behind him, he heard Jarin say something that made the servant girl giggle as she left. Damien lay back on his cot and placed his hands behind his head.

"What is amiss, Ronar?" he asked. "We are finally free of his *Grace* and will soon fill our bellies with warm food." He patted his stomach. "I, for one, could use something more solid than bird eggs and fish."

"In addition," Jarin added, his footsteps approaching. "We can have our pick of the pretty wenches who work in the castle. Though, I grant you"—he glanced over the room—"these humble quarters have injured my pride."

"Would that it would never heal," Ronar quipped, then swung about and took in the tiny room housing naught but three straw cots and a single table upon which sat a basin of water and two oil lamps. Modest, aye, but at least they'd not been put with the other knights. In addition, they were just off the great hall and had a good view of the inner courtyard, which would serve well to overhear anything that would hasten the completion of their mission. He faced the window again and watched stable boys, groomsman, knights, and all manner of servants hustling to and fro in the light of a full moon.

"And"—Jarin slapped Ronar on the back—"save for the pretty she-wolf—or rather *she-falcon*—who nearly killed you with her arrow, no band of brigands attacked the bishop on our journey."

"Would there had been." Damien groaned. "If only to stave off the boredom and drown out his relentless whine."

Withdrawing a figure from inside his doublet pocket, Ronar rubbed his thumb over St. Jude and stared down at the smooth gray stone. "Evil lurks in this castle. I sense it. The sooner we complete our mission and make haste back to London, the better."

"You worry overmuch, Ronar." Jarin crossed arms over his chest and leaned against the window frame. "'Tis a simple enough quest. I pray it takes a good while to complete. I could use a relaxing stay in such a place with women aplenty to sample."

Damien chuckled. "I hope there are enough to last our stay. For me, I could use a good fight ere I grow fat and lazy. If only the king would start a war somewhere."

Ronar turned to his friend. Fat and lazy he was not. As well muscled as the king's destrier and nearly as tall, Damien could land a punch with the force of a trebuchet. "You should have remained in the king's army instead of joining the Guard, Damien."

"And miss the chance to protect the king? To be counted among his elite warriors? 'Twas a miracle a man with such base beginnings as I was ever dubbed a knight, but this…my father would be proud. Were he alive," he added, the bitterness in his tone pricking Ronar.

Jarin stared down into the courtyard where a pretty maid passed by, a basket in her hand. "At least we shall not have to endure the bishop's blathering."

"He may be"—Ronar started to list a few unsavory names but caught himself—"*many* things, but he is still a holy man, appointed of God. He deserves our respect."

Damien snorted. "He will have to earn mine."

Jarin nodded his agreement.

Ronar raised a critical brow. "Have a care what you say against God's anointed. You think the king to be a harsh taskmaster. God will not forgive such an affront when you stand before Him."

Jarin fingered the tip of his short-clipped beard. "If God chose such a man, then I shall have a few things to say to the Almighty should He ever deem me worthy to stand before

Him." He pushed from the wall and strode to the basin of water. "As it is, I doubt I shall have the chance."

"I do not gainsay it, and that should worry you more than it does." Ronar watched his good friend splash water on his face and then shove fingers through his brown hair. With strong features, a perfect nose, deep-set, intense eyes and a dimple to charm the ladies, Jarin enjoyed far too much the attention he received from the fairer sex.

Grabbing a cloth, he faced Ronar. "I shall allow you to worry about my eternal fate, Ronar. Mayhap you could put in a good word for me."

"I always do, my friend."

Damien withdrew two knives from his belt and began sharpening them, the metallic rasp echoing through the chamber.

Ronar returned his gaze out the window and drew a deep breath. The stench of horse manure and pig slops made him instantly regret it. If only his companions would listen to him. His own lack of faith and pride had led to Ronar's downfall. One which he still did penance for and would continue until his debt was paid. He glanced once again at St. Jude in his hand. During Ronar's last crusade, the Archbishop of Jerusalem had given him the small statue. "Carved from Christ's tomb and then blessed with Holy water," he had said. No doubt 'twas true, for the saint had protected Ronar during one of the fiercest battles he'd ever encountered. He had carried it ever since. Another chill slithered down his back. He had a feeling he would need its power on this mission more than ever.

Chapter 3

*A*lexia slipped through the back door of the kitchen, basket of herbs in hand so as not to attract attention. Though her position in Luxley castle was minstrel for Lady D'Clere, she oft assisted with the gardening as well, in particular harvesting the herbs she loved so much. The room was abuzz with activity pantlers, butlers, butchers, cooks, dishwashers and maids dashed to and fro or worked before tables laden with all manner of food. The kitchen clerk shouted orders above the din. Pots and kettles steamed atop flames that crackled and spit from a fireplace that took up an entire stone wall.

Alas, the King's Guard *had* arrived, 'twould seem.

She was greeted by two scullery maids as she made her way through the kitchen and the pantry to the grand hall and scanned the room for her friend and confidant. With the arrival of guests, Anabelle would most likely be following Sir LeGode about as he spouted orders.

Alexia drew in a deep breath and attempted to settle nerves that always tangled into knots when she entered the castle.

You cannot discern the spirits when fear invades, the friar always told her. 'Twas true enough, but she had yet to learn how to control her rampant emotions.

There. Anabelle hurried down the grand stairs from above, a train of servants in her wake.

"Anabelle!" Alexia half-whispered, half-shouted, and upon gaining her attention, motioned her over.

Halting, the young lady gave instructions to the servants, which sent them scurrying off before she hastened to Alexia's side.

"Mistress Bregley, I didn't expect you till the morrow."

"Indeed, but I heard you have visitors from the king."

Sweeping blond hair from her face, Anabelle bit her lip. "The Bishop of Montruse requests an audience with Lady D'Clere."

"Montruse?" Alarm prickled Alexia. "The king's special confidant. Whatever does he want?"

"I know not, mistress. They will meet with Sir LeGode after the evening meal."

LeGode's harried shout blared from his study across the main hall, jarring Anabelle, who glanced his way.

Alexia gripped her friend's arm. "Then you must find out for me, Anabelle. Please say you will."

"I will try, mistress." Though Alexia detected a quiver running through her, determination shone from her eyes. Brave girl.

"How fares Lady D'Clere?"

"Worse today. Mayhap you could bring her some comfort."

Fear gnawed Alexia's gut as she smiled at her friend and headed up the winding stairs of the keep to Lady D'Clere's chamber. Creeping inside, she cringed at the creak of the door and set her herbs on the table, suddenly struck by the putrid order of illness, tallow, and smoke.

Something moved near the upper corner of the arched ceiling—a darkness, a shadow that disappeared before she had a chance to close her eyes and examine it. She had no need. She could *sense* what it was. If only she'd brought the Spear. A quick scan of the room revealed other shadows— fleeting, dark mists that shrank back and finally retreated.

With their exit, the light from candles positioned about the chamber brightened, revealing two carved chests, tables and chairs set before a hearth, and the large curtained bed on the right.

Seraphina rose from her spot beside the bed, giving Alexia a curious look. "What is amiss, my lady?"

"Naught." Alexia approached. "How is she?"

"She sleeps now, but she has been restless all day." Seraphina glanced around as if noticing the brightness in the chamber. "I always feel better when you are here, my lady."

"Do not address me as 'my lady,' Seraphina. Remember, my life depends on your discretion."

"Yes, of course. Forgive me."

Alexia stared down at the figure sleeping behind the gauze curtains. "I thank you nonetheless for your kindness to her."

Seraphina adjusted her plain woolen kirtle that did naught to hide her feminine curves nor diminish the beauty of her hair, the color of snow, tumbling down to her waist. "I am but her lady's maid and cannot offer much aid."

"You remain by her side day and night in my stead. Truly, I deem your kindness of no small account. And God's truth, you are so much more than a lady's maid. You are my friend." Alexia placed a hand on Seraphina's arm and smiled before she returned her gaze to the bed. "Night horrors?"

"Aye, they grow worse. She wakes up screaming things no lady should say."

Swallowing a lump of dread, Alexis swept aside the curtains and cringed at her sister's pale face. She took her limp hand in hers. "Her skin is hot. What of the apothecary? Has he brought medicines?"

"Yes, every day, mil—mistress."

"And Sir LeGode? What does he say?"

"He is worried...or so he *appears*. He has ordered the apothecary to administer new herbs."

Alexia glanced at Seraphina. "And yet a hesitancy simmers in your voice."

"As you know, mistress, I am not sure I trust him."

"'Tis but that crooked smile of his." Alexia shrugged. "Never fear. Sir LeGode was best friend to my father and mother. Faith now, he saved my father's life in the battle of Nain. And when Father died, he brought great comfort to my mother. Then, of course, he was here with us all when she herself passed away."

Alexia closed her eyes, forcing back the horror of that day, yet the wound still festered in her heart. "Mother wouldn't have handed the care of the manor over to him, made him steward because my sister and I were still too young, if she did not trust him implicitly. He has been a great overseer and done well here."

"Aye, mistress, quite well. For Luxley. *And* for himself."

Alexia frowned. "He has his own estate just ten miles hence. What need has he to manage ours? Surely it must be more burden than blessing." Alexia kissed her sister's hand. "Cristiana is lady of the manor and whoe'er she weds will be lord. What purpose would Sir LeGode have for staying here, save loyalty to my family?"

Seraphina flattened her lips. "Then why have you not revealed to him your true identity? If he is so dear and trusted a friend, mayhap he could assist you in laying bare the plot to end your life."

"'Tis my utmost desire, yet the friar has convinced me to wait. The truth would only endanger LeGode's life, as it also endangers yours." Alexia gazed up at her friend. "For which I am deeply sorry."

"No need." Seraphina's blue eyes grew moist. "I would gladly give my life to save either of you."

Cristiana moaned, and Alexia brushed curls from her face. Whatever illness robbed her strength, it had not stolen her beauty. Brown silken hair, streaked in gold, fanned across the white pillow in a lustrous bronze halo. High cheeks, a straight narrow nose, and well-shaped lips formed an angelic face. "Cristiana, I'm here."

Her sister opened her eyes ever so slightly, and a smile tugged upon her lips. "You came."

"I will always come for you."

"'Tis not safe for you."

"No one knows who I am."

Her sister's brown eyes, once so clear and sparkling, grew distant behind a haze. "I grant you, I barely recognized you when you first appeared. Seven years was far too long to believe you were dead."

"I am here now and will never leave you again."

The friar had caught Alexia sneaking into the castle when she was twelve, and she had suffered severely under his reprimand. "Someone at the castle wants you dead," he had said. "And they will succeed if you play the fool." The terror he had invoked had kept her watching her sister from afar for too many years. Until she learned that Cristiana had fallen ill on her fifteenth birthday. After that, Alexia's persistence finally persuaded the friar, who knew the kitchen clerk, to procure Alexia a position as one of the herb gardeners. That job didn't last long, for when Sir LeGode heard her singing as she crossed the bailey and saw its calming effects on Cristiana, he promoted her to the lady's personal minstrel— placing her right inside her sister's chamber. God was, indeed, amazing.

Yet now, as she gently caressed her sister's hand, she realized that was two years ago, and her sister was still abed with some mysterious illness.

A year younger than Alexia, Cristiana had always been a timid, nervous child. While Alexia had insisted on learning to ride horses, Cristiana knitted and sewed and kept to her chamber. While Alexia sneaked out of the castle at night to fence with the squires, Cristiana cuddled beneath her quilt, jumping at every sound.

As if reading her thoughts, Cristiana said, "My brave sister. You should not risk so much for me." She attempted to sit, but forsook the effort. "I still cannot believe anyone would want you dead. To what purpose?"

A question Alexia had been asking herself for years. At first she assumed it had something to do with her and her sister acquiring the estate after their mother died. Yet whether they married or not, they would each inherit half of Luxley. If both died, the land would return to the king. If only one died, the other would inherit all. Which would leave only her sister to profit. And with no suitors hovering about like vultures when they were but eight and nine, what would the villain have to gain by Alexia's death?

Mayhap he was after the Spear.

If so, how did he know it was in her possession? And why were there no attempts made to find it in the past nine years?

"I do not know yet, but I will discover the villain," she finally said to her sister. "And when I do, I will destroy him and return here to live with you."

With all the passing years and the rumors of her death a fading memory, she prayed whoever wished her dead had long since gone. But the friar insisted the threat remained. And he was usually right about such things.

"I believe you will, Alexi—" Cristiana snapped her mouth shut. "I mean Katherine. 'Tis been two years, and I still have trouble remembering."

"Me, as well," Seraphina added.

Cristiana lifted a hand to the maid. "God bless you for your loyalty to us."

Seraphina knelt before the bed. "How could I not, my lady? Your mother and father were so kind to take me in when I was but a babe—an orphan. They gave me a home, an education, and made me your companion."

"And we gained a sister." Cristiana smiled.

"Indeed." Alexia laid the back of her hand on her sister's cheek and cringed at the heat emanating from it. "What is this, dear sister? Alas, I saw you yesterday taking your supper in the hall at your proper place."

"The healing potion robs me of all strength." Cristiana closed her eyes. "But the apothecary insists it holds my affliction at bay." Her eyelids fluttered and her chest rose and fell. "They frighten me, Alex—Katherine." Her voice cracked.

"Who does?"

"The dark ones. They are everywhere. Shadows, here one minute, then gone, then reappearing again." She opened her eyes, stark with fear. "Am I going mad?"

Alexia gripped her hands and kissed them. "Nay. Never. You are too strong for that. You are merely ill, and you will get well soon. You have my troth."

The words seemed to calm her. But they did not have the same effect on Alexia. A storm brewed in her spirit at her sister's words. Something evil had invaded this place. When Cristiana first fell ill two years past, Alexia assumed it was but a simple fever, especially when her sister recovered quickly and went about her normal duties. But then she would grow ill again, then well, then ill. And of late, the dreams, the shadows, the fear that plagued her...could only mean one thing.

Something tormented her from the dark side.

Alexia turned to the maid. "Pen and parchment, Seraphina, if you please."

Rising, the lady moved to one of the chests, opened it, and returned with the items. Alexia set the parchment on a table by the bed, dipped the quill in ink, and scrolled the only thing she could think that might help her sister. Then dusting it with powder, she blew it off and handed it to her.

"What is this?"

"Read it."

Cristiana held it up to the light of a candle. "He that dwelleth in the secret place of the Most High shall abide under the shadow of the Almighty. I will say of the Lord, He is my refuge and my fortress: my God; in him will I trust." She gathered her breath and continued. "Surely he shall deliver me from the snare of the fowler, and from the noisome pestilence. He shall cover me with his feathers, and under his wings I shall trust: his truth shall be my shield and buckler. I shall not be afraid for the terror by night; nor for the arrow that flieth by day; Nor for the pestilence that walketh in darkness; nor for the destruction that wasteth at noonday."

Releasing a sigh, she sank back onto the pillows. "This is beautiful. Where is it from?"

"It is the Word of God from the book of Psalms."

Cristiana tossed the paper aside as if it would burn her skin. "The Holy Scriptures? 'Tis heresy to read it thus."

"'Tis heresy not to." Alexia picked it up and forced a softer tone. "The friar has been translating it into the king's English and allowing me to read it. 'Tis magnificent and full of wonders we are never told." Folding the parchment, she slid it beneath the quilt. "When you see the shadows, when the night horrors come, read this aloud. I promise 'twill help."

Cristiana gave her a skeptical look but nodded and squeezed her hand. "Prithee, sing to me before you go?"

"Of course." Alexia drew up a chair and began the tune their mother used to sing to them when they were little.

"As I lay on yule night
Alone in my longing
I thought I saw a fair sight
A maiden rocking her child..."

It had the effect she hoped as her sister calmed and quickly dozed off. If only Alexia could stay longer, sit by her bedside and pray. But the friar would worry.

"I will return anon." Alexia addressed Seraphina, but her gaze was on her sister's ragged breathing. Fear rose to taunt her faith-filled words.

"Worry not. I will give her the best of care, mistress."

Nodding, Alexia slipped out the door into the dark corridor and started down the stairs. So consumed with thoughts of her sister, she didn't hear the footsteps behind her.

"Mistress Bregley. You are here! Excellent."

Startled by the sound of Sir LeGode's voice, she halted and turned, careful to keep her eyes lowered as was proper for a servant. "I sang for Lady D'Clere, Sir."

"I am glad to hear it. She has been distressed of late."

"If that is all, Sir." Alexia started on her way.

"We have very important guests, and I request you sing for them at our feast tonight."

She halted once again. "Sing?"

"Aye, the sweet sounds that come hence from your mouth?" He teased.

"Of course, but … I am no troubadour, Sir. I fear I would bring you shame."

"Nonsense!" He started past her with a wave of his hand. "I shall expect you as soon as the meal is underway."

Sing!? How could she sing in front of the King's Guard? In front of the man she'd battled in the forest? Should he recognize her, her ruse would be up, the Falcon of Emerald Forest unmasked, and she'd be tossed into the dungeon to rot. Yet if she disobeyed Sir LeGode, 'twould cast equal suspicion on her that could lead to the same end. Now what was she to do?

Chapter 4

*R*onar popped one last piece of cheese into his mouth, took a swig of wine, and sat back in his chair before the high table in Luxley's grand hall. On either side of him sat Jarin and Damien, while beyond Damien perched the bishop, appearing none the worse for wear despite his long, arduous journey. In good sooth, he seemed quite in his element, surrounded by doting sycophants—Sir LeGode, chief among them. Ronar huffed. The steward fawned over every word out of the bishop's mouth—every word he could manage in between morsels of their delicious feast—stewed pheasant, venison boiled in almond milk, onions, and wine, baked apples and pears in sugar, a variety of cheeses, and an excellent spiced red wine. Quite a repast for so late in the day.

Not that Ronar was complaining. 'Twas good to have his belly full again. His soul, however, was another matter. Despite the good fare, pleasant conversation, warm fire, and festivities that surrounded him, he could not shake the foreboding that had assailed him upon entering Luxley castle. Even now, he scanned the great hall, seeking its source. If it hailed from a person, he or she would most likely be present. Nigh everyone, save the lowest of servants, were enjoying the feast—from the gardener, blacksmith, and messengers who sat toward the back of the hall, to the knights who sat before them enjoying more drink than warriors should. Why should they not when their commander, Sir DeGay, had long since dropped his head into his stew? Next came the reward table where the clerks, cofferer, marshals, and almoners sat, while the Lord's High table, the place of greatest honor, was reserved for Bishop Montruse, Ronar and his men, Sir LeGode, and his son Cedric, a fatuous fellow with the disposition of a jester.

No ethereal figure slithered about, no black-hooded men ducked into the shadows, no evil glints in narrowed eyes or sneers upon twisted lips. All seemed to be enjoying the evening. Ronar shrugged off the sensation. Alack, if such evil existed here, the bishop would feel it as well. Yet one glance his way revealed a man eating and drinking and laughing as if he hadn't a care in the world.

Ronar sipped his wine and drew in a breath of the sweet odor of lavender and rosemary herbs scattered across the floor, tainted by the scents of meat and spices, human sweat, and tallow. Candles protruding from spikes on walls and two large chandeliers provided a warm glow that flickered over the assembly like sunlight through trees.

To Ronar's left, Damien drank more than he ate, his listless eyes shifting over the crowd—always on the alert, always seeking the object of some ancient revenge of which the man would not speak. Ronar took no concern of his friend's inebriation. Damien had the odd ability to sober at will should danger advance. Jarin, however, was another matter. Seated at Ronar's right, he continued eating, drinking and flirting with the few wenches who kept his cup full of wine and his ego full of flattery. Though mostly young boys served the food, as was common, Ronar had to admit Sir LeGode's use of a few women offered a pleasant diversion. Especially after three days and nights sleeping beside naught but snoring, foul-smelling men.

Alas, now that they were nearly finished with the meal, Ronar longed to get to the business at hand, acquire a good night's sleep, and begin their task on the morrow.

A group of colorfully-dressed troubadours entered carrying various instruments—lyres, flutes, cymbals, and a viol—and Ronar huffed and grabbed his cup of wine. More delays. Jarin elbowed him, and pointed at a lady wearing a plain woolen kirtle walking alongside the musicians.

"Finally, some entertainment." His brown eyes flashed.

Damien took another sip and let out a belch, mimicking Ronar's sentiments at the interruption. Still, something about the lady caught his eye. Her back was to him, but 'twas her hair that intrigued him...the most lustrous shade of red, like fire...nay, like the color of flaming copper. The curled tip of her braid swayed over her waist as she walked. A flowered chaplet graced her head and spread a net over the lustrous strands as if it could possibly hide them. But nothing could dull their shine. She walked with grace, aye, but also with authority and power as if she were a princess and no mere peasant.

She turned, keeping her head down, and stood to the side of the musicians, who plucked and tuned their instruments, drawing the attention of the crowd.

Yet when she opened her mouth and the words to "Sing we to this Merry Company" came out in the sweetest, clearest voice Ronar had ever heard, he regretted his impatience. The song drifted through the hall on angel's wings, stunning the company to silence and eliciting sighs of comfort from all present. And Ronar felt his own tension leeching from his body as he sat back and closed his eyes to fully enjoy the pleasing melody.

When she finished, cheers filled the air, and Ronar opened his eyes to see the lady hastily pushing her way through the crowd as a juggler took her place and a new song began.

If she had continued on her way, face down, weaving around servants and guests, Ronar wouldn't have given her another thought. But the lady lifted her head and shifted her gaze toward him, their eyes locking for but a moment in time, ere she continued bounding forward.

And Ronar knew. He knew they'd just been serenaded by none other than the Falcon of Emerald Forest.

"Sir LeGode," he shouted loud enough for her to hear as he leaned forward to address the steward. "Pray, tell us who is this Falcon of Emerald Forest?"

LeGode's face twisted as if he'd bitten a lemon. "Alack, tell me she did not bother you and His Grace on your way here?"

"'Twas a minor incident with an arrow that nearly pierced my heart." Ronar dared a glance toward the lady and found she had slowed in her exit, her ears tilted in their direction.

LeGode faced the bishop, his voice edged in panic. "I pray *you* were not harmed, your Grace."

"Nay, my guards dealt with her." The bishop tossed meat into his mouth as if the subject bored him.

The juggler dropped the apples he was tossing, and the crowd roared in laughter.

Sir LeGode addressed Ronar. "I apologize for your inconvenience, Sir Knight, and I'm glad no harm came to you."

Damien chuckled, but Ronar elbowed him to silence.

"Pray, who is this fierce lady archer?" Jarin asked.

"A nuisance, a pest, nothing more. She hunts and provides food for the village."

"Against the king's command?!" The bishop sparked to life, finally pushing his trencher away and patting his belly. "'Tis the king's forest. She should be caught and hanged."

"Many have tried, your Grace, but she has proved"—Sir LeGode cleared his throat—"rather elusive."

"Elusive, indeed." Jarin smiled at the wench who filled his glass, then raised it to a toast. "Quick as a rabbit, sly as a fox, an archer with no equal, is the Falcon of Emerald Forest.

But knights beware her boot!" He chuckled, his eyes glinting playfully toward Ronar.

LeGode snorted.

"Who is this rebel who dares defy her king?" The bishop wiped his mouth with the tablecloth.

"As I said, no one knows, your Grace," LeGode replied, annoyed. "A peasant with a bloated ego, I expect. Never fear, we will catch her. And when we do, she'll hang from the gallows."

Ronar's gaze found her again at the edge of the crowd. She cast him one last glance ere disappearing out the door. He couldn't help but smile. The infamous Falcon of Emerald Forest posing as a servant girl in the midst of Luxley castle. Either she was the most courageous woman he'd ever met, or she was utterly and completely mad.

❦

"You seek *what*?" Sir LeGode turned from the narrow window of his study to face the bishop, who sighed and spread out the embroidered black robes of his vestment around his feet. Short-cropped gray hair circled an angular face whose lines were as harsh as the man's squinty brown eyes. During the past three days, Ronar had sought those eyes and that face for any semblance of the grace and kindness of God, but as yet, had not found even a suggestion.

Quiet, reserved, and obedient, his page, a lad of only fifteen, shadowed the bishop, attending his every whim.

Flanked by his friends, Ronar shifted his stance impatiently behind the bishop, most anxious for news of their quest. Instead, he found his thoughts returning to the Falcon of Emerald Forest. *Captivating woman.* To what purpose would she risk her neck by coming to the castle? And singing before LeGode and all the knights. Ronar smiled. Intriguing! He simply must know more about her.

The bishop's voice jerked Ronar from his thoughts. "The Spear of Destiny, Sir. Surely you have heard of it. And 'tis not I who seeks it but *your* king."

Sir LeGode grimaced. "Of course. Of course. Anything for the king. 'Tis just that..." He lowered to a chair. "The Spear that stabbed Christ?" His thick brows rose in skepticism. "'Tis but a myth."

"It is no myth, I assure you. 'Tis real and quite powerful, and the king has need of it to help fight his many enemies."

Cedric, LeGode's son, an odd-looking man in his twenties with wide eyes, a receding chin, and a face much kinder than his father's, grunted from a chair in the corner.

Ignoring him, LeGode snapped his fingers, and a young maiden who stood to his right poured them drinks from a decanter on a side table.

Damien licked his lips, while Jarin followed her every move. Ronar kept his eyes on LeGode. Something was amiss with this one. Where most men flattered and cowered in the presence of a man who had the king's ear—and the power of life and death that accompanied it—LeGode, contrary to his behavior at the feast, appeared suddenly annoyed with the man as if the bishop were but a servant interrupting his master. There was something else as well ...something vile lurking behind his feigned smile.

The girl bowed before the bishop and handed him a drink, then served Sir LeGode, Cedric, and finally Ronar and his men. If she'd lifted her gaze, she would have seen the grin on Jarin's face as he examined her pretty features.

"But why look for the holy relic here?" LeGode sipped his drink.

The bishop set down his cup and fingered the large gold crucifix hanging about his neck. "The king has been investigating the Spear for years. The priest who found it in Jerusalem when we took the city in the Sixth Crusade swore on his death bed that he gave it to a young girl living at a convent in the south of France."

Candlelight flickered over the man's age-lined face as he stared at the tomes lining the wall.

LeGode had the foresight to wait for the bishop to continue.

"*That* young girl we believe to be Lady Grecia D'Clere."

"Lady D'Clere!" LeGode balked. "Forsooth, I do not believe it."

"You do not believe your king?" The bishop's tone pierced.

"Nay, 'tis simply that I knew Lady D'Clere well. I was her husband's dearest confidant ere he died and then hers, until illness took her home. Surely she would have told me."

Bishop Montruse shrugged. "Mayhap the lady was sworn to secrecy."

LeGode rose with a nervous sigh and approached the brazier in the corner, wherein hot coals provided the only warmth in the small study. "If 'tis here, I know not where. I've been steward of this castle for nine years, and I've ne'er seen this Spear. Peace froth, 'tis a bit farfetched."

The bishop snorted. "What *is* farfetched is that the knights from Luxley win every battle in which they engage. Do you wonder why the king so oft enlists their aid?" Bishop Montruse waved an arm toward the main hall beyond the door. "I've seen naught here that would render them with superior training or prowess, naught but a besotted head knight and a host of squires still suckling at the breast."

Sir LeGode flattened his lips, anger simmering beneath the surface of his raging eyes.

"In addition," the bishop continued, "Were you aware that Emerald Forest is by far the most lush and plenteous of all the king's forests? Teeming with deer, rabbits, and wild boar, as well as an abundance of wild berries and herbs."

"What does that have to do with the Spear?" LeGode snapped, still staring at the flames.

"Wherever the Spear resides, the blessings of God follow."

"Mayhap our Lord is simply pleased with *me*." LeGode finally glanced at the bishop, his sickly-sweet smile instantly fading, followed by a look of resignation. "Of course, your Grace, search the castle and the grounds all you wish. My servants will assist you, and I shall assign my son to supervise. I have no doubt you will find him up to the task." He gestured toward Cedric, who was examining the fringe on his surcoat with great interest.

Bishop Montruse cast the lad a scowl ere rising to his feet. "Nay. I will take charge. Mayhap when Lady D'Clere is well, she will be more accommodating."

LeGode bowed before the bishop. "Forgive me, your Grace, if you have not found me so. Lady D'Clere takes her council from me. I will inform her of our meeting, and when she is well enough to receive you, you can hear her sentiments. Far be it from me to hinder the king's quest."

"Yes. Far be it." The bishop sneered. "There is one additional item the king wishes me to discuss with you. His Majesty has sent four suitors for Lady D'Clere, all men of title and honor, worthy of her station and two who would have improved upon it."

LeGode's expression twisted like a snake slithering through grass before a look of innocence prevailed. "I seem to recall messages about suitors, but alack, they never arrived."

"They were all killed by wolves not long after leaving their estates."

"Wolves? How sad."

Though Ronar could detect no such sorrow in the man's tone.

"You know nothing of this?"

"How could I?"

"Humph" The bishop turned to leave.

LeGode moved toward him. "If I can assist you in your search, your Excellency, I am your servant. But I fear what you seek is not here."

"We shall see." Bishop Montruse snapped at his page and the boy fell in line as his master headed toward the door. Before he exited, the bishop turned, his robes swinging about him. "If you are hiding the Spear from us, Sir, we will not only find it, but you will find the noose."

The last thing Ronar saw ere he followed the bishop out the door was Sir LeGode clutching his throat.

Chapter 5

He recognizes me. He recognizes me. The realization pounded through Alexia's thoughts and thundered through her heart as she left the great hall and made her way to her sister's chamber. She knew she should leave immediately before the surly knight sought her out, but she was desperate to check on her sister one last time ere she left.

However, now as she attempted to sing again per her sister's request, her voice emerged rattled and about as soothing as a cow's bell. But her sister made no complaint. Repeatedly, she smiled at Alexia as her breathing slowly settled.

Mayhap the friar was right to ask Alexia to stay away from the castle this night. Another day or two and the glimpse that dastardly King's Guard had of her in the moonlight would be but a fleeting memory.

Potz! Why had she glanced his way? Her curiosity had gotten the best of her. Along with her foolish courage and impatience. All qualities Friar Josef had warned her about.

Despite Alexia's jangled voice, her sister finally drifted to sleep. Sweeping hair from her brow, Alexia leaned and kissed her forehead, wincing at the heat and dampness she found thereon. A reminder for her to speak with the apothecary.

After squeezing Seraphina's hand and bidding her good eve, Alexia slipped from the room ere she changed her mind and stayed by her sister's side for good. Once in the corridor, she leaned back against the thick door and drew a breath, whispering a prayer into the darkness. Candles, waning with the night, shifted light and dark over the hallway as she started on her way. So immersed in her thoughts and prayers, she took no note of the body that stepped in her path until she was nearly upon him.

Her scream was instantly silenced by a firm hand on her mouth—a rough, calloused hand that smelled of horses, wood smoke, and wine.

"Softly, my cosset, softly," the man whispered.

Knocking his hand away, Alexia spun around in a move the friar taught her. But before she could shove her elbow in the fiend's gut, he pressed both her arms onto her chest and held them locked. No amount of thrashing, kicking, or struggling granted her an inch of freedom. Instead, it only caused her breath to heave and her annoyance to rise. He pressed her back tight against his chest as his warm breath wafted down her neck, followed by a sultry chuckle.

"A feisty little one, aren't you?"

"I'll show you how little I am when you release me."

"I would love the chance, but I find I'm quite enjoying this close exchange."

"Foul beast! I shall scream."

"Nay, you would have done so already. In truth, I wager that by now you know who holds you and what secrets we share."

Cursing her foolishness, Alexia made one last attempt to free herself, but the knight was steel against her back with arms of iron keeping her in place.

"Strong for one so lithe, but not strong enough, little one." The voice was deep, like the soothing purr of a lion, yet bore no threat of harm.

"Prithee release me, and I will not run."

The iron bands lifted, and she jerked from him and spun around.

Crossing arms over his chest, he leaned on the stone wall, a hint of a smile on his otherwise severe lips. "Greetings, Falcon of Emerald Forest."

Alexia frowned. "What do you wish with me?"

"We shall start with why you wanted me dead."

She huffed and looked away. "Your ego, Sir Knight. 'Twas not *you* in particular."

"Ah then, are the deer so scarce that you have need to hunt men?"

Alexia took a step back and studied the man—the only man—who had ever caught her. Twice in the same day. He stood a head above her, the armor on his shoulders and forearms doing a poor job at hiding the muscle beneath. Black boots rose to his knees where they greeted woolen breeches and then a tunic covered by a sleeveless leather doublet. A sword and various knives were clipped to a belt circling his shoulder. Brown hair hung loosely about his head, brushing over a manicured beard, while a jagged scar cut through his right eyebrow. But it was his eyes that lured her... deep blue and filled with sorrow and an intensity that made her squirm.

"'Twas merely a warning. If I'd wanted you dead, you would be."

At this he smiled. "A warning?"

"Aye, I protect the forest."

"Then you are under the king's commission? You may wish to enlighten Sir LeGode as he believes you to be stealing the king's meat."

She narrowed her eyes. "I provide for those in need. The king would surely agree."

"Would he? How presumptuous of a peasant girl to speak the mind of the king."

"I have many talents," she returned sharply.

"Alack! And a talented thief at that."

Uncomfortable silence yawned between them, and the look of interest in his eyes made her both nervous and gave her hope he would release her.

"I am no threat to you, Knight."

"Unless I enter the forest, 'twould seem."

"Indeed." She raised a playful brow.

"Why risk coming to the castle, Falcon?"

"I sing for Lady D'Clere. It soothes her."

He nodded. "Such a voice would soothe the demons in hell. Still, why risk it for one who would order you about were she well?"

Alexia bit her lip. "I do as I am told. Sir LeGode overheard me singing in the courtyard and ordered me thus." Those infernal eyes of his! They seemed to dig right into her very soul. "Will you give away my secret, Knight?"

He cocked his head as a flicker of candlelight shifted across his eyes. "Nay. But on one condition."

Dread consumed her. "Pray tell."

"You grant me a kiss."

☙❧

Ronar had no idea why he asked for a kiss. 'Twas something more akin to Jarin's intrigues. But the way the candlelight shone over the woman's moist lips, so soft, pink, and enticing...well, in truth, Ronar could think of naught else worthy of his silence.

The lady's expression hardened, and her eyes pierced like the bird for which she was named. But the moment passed, and her features softened... and a smile ever-so-seductive raised a corner of her lips.

"Very well," she said. "'Tis a small price to pay."

Oddly, Ronar felt disappointment at her easy acquiescence. Still, why deny himself?

Tilting her chin upward, she puckered her lips and drew close. Ronar's heart betrayed him with a leap whilst his blood heated and his body reacted even before their mouths met. He moved to greet those luscious lips, desperate to feel their softness....

When she plucked a knife from his belt and held it to his chest.

Her eyes seethed. "You foul, lecherous, ill-bred princock. You dare barter such favors from a lady?"

He smiled. Tush, what a fascinating woman. He glanced down at the blade leveled upon his heart. "Have you ever stabbed a man, my cosset? Even if you have the strength to pierce my doublet, you must penetrate a barricade of bone and muscle. And then you must know the exact location of the—"

"Silence!" She pressed the blade. "I have the strength, Sir Knight. Will you wager your life on it?"

"Would you wager yours? When all I require is a kiss?" A kiss he suddenly no longer desired.

She huffed. "Were I to grant your sordid request, you would betray me, withal, and I would be disgraced."

"Disgraced by one kiss?"

"One kiss given in payment, aye."

"Ah, a talented and moral thief. I'm intrigued."

"I am no thief, Sir." Her eyes, green as forest moss, flashed.

"The law argues, my little Falcon."

"Laws made by men, not God."

He chuckled. "Alas, a God-fearing thief as well."

"Back away." She pressed the knife, and he allowed her to move him aside. Why? He couldn't say, save he was enjoying himself. *Immensely*. A rare occurrence these past years.

"Here are my terms," she began as pointedly as if negotiating a treaty. "I will leave you with your life, Sir Knight. And you will not disclose my secret."

"And if I should do so after you depart?"

"I will return and slit your throat."

He smiled. "To see you again would be worth it."

Surprise flickered over her lovely features, swept away by fury. "You fool. The moment you see me again, 'twill be your last."

"I shall take the risk."

"You find this amusing?" Her lips twisted in a most adorable way. "You know not who you face, Sir Knight."

"The Falcon of Emerald Forest, 'twould seem."

She pressed the blade again. This time, it pieced his doublet. *Enough.* In one swift move, he grabbed her wrist and wrenched the knife from her grasp.

She pounded him with her other fist. "Release me at once!" Her foot struck his shin. Pain etched up his leg.

Sheathing the knife, he clutched her other wrist and held them locked together. Then backing her against the wall, he pinned her thrashing legs with his own. "Shh, my Lady Falcon."

Her scent of herbs and forest and woman filled his nostrils in a heady incense, spinning his thoughts. Bringing both her hands to his mouth, he placed a gentle kiss upon them.

She struggled, panting and groaning, but finally ceased with a defeated sigh. "What now, Sir Knight? Are you to steal more than a kiss?"

"You will find me too honorable for that. Nay. You may go, Falcon." He lifted her hands for one more kiss, and light flickered over a smudge on the inside of her wrist. Not a smudge. A mark, defined, detailed.

Jerking from his grasp, she cast one last seething glance his way ere she fled down the stairs.

Chapter 6

Thwack! The arrow split the tiny branch in two, firing splinters in all directions. Alexia drew another, nocked it in her bowstring, and pulled it back, this time aiming at a pine cone sitting atop a fallen trunk nigh twenty yards away. She imagined it was Sir Knight's tiny head housing his tiny brain. She released the string. Missing its mark, the arrow disappeared into the forest.

"You are not in the Spirit today, Alexia." Friar Josef stood beside her, a basket of nuts and herbs he'd gathered from the forest floor in his hands.

"They seek the Spear, Friar." She lowered her bow with a huff.

"At the castle, not here."

"'Tis only a matter of time. This Bishop Montruse knows my mother had it in her possession." On her way out of the castle, Alexia had found Anabelle waiting for her in the courtyard, and the young servant had conveyed all she had heard in LeGode's study. Alexia's worst fears were confirmed. The powerful Bishop Montruse and his three King's Guard had come for the Spear. And from what Anabelle had said, they did not intend to return to London without it.

Friar Josef smiled and glanced at the rays of the morning sun piercing the canopy in glittering beams of light. "Where is your faith, child? God will protect it."

"God expects *me* to protect it. Or so you've been telling me for years." She positioned another arrow, this time aiming at a closer branch, all the while desperately trying to evict Sir Knight from her thoughts. An almost impossible feat. *Infuriating man.* Arrogant boor. Demanding a kiss as the price of his silence!

"God will give you the power to do His will. What a lovely morn." The friar stopped to pick up another walnut then drew in a deep breath of the moist, loamy air. "Praise God for the beauty of His creation."

Alexia wasn't in a praising mood at the moment, nor could she understand why the friar wasn't more concerned. The King's Guard were not men to be trifled with. Lifting her bow, she took aim, this time striking her target. *Anger.* That's what she needed to keep her focus. Pure, raw anger. "He saw the mark."

"Hmm. Is that why your fury runs so rampant this morn? Holy saints, this Knight's Guard has you quite perturbed."

"How now, Friar? What makes you say so?" She taunted him as she drew back the string and fired at a distant tree. *Thwack!* It struck the spider she'd aimed for.

He shook his head. "Because the poor innocent trees, cones, and insects suffer so dearly when you are angry."

Lowering her bow, Alexia kicked a pile of leaves. "Did you not hear me? He *saw* the mark." She lowered to sit on a moss-covered boulder and examined the spear tip on her right wrist.

The friar shrugged. "What of it? He knows not what it is."

"He's no simpleton, Friar." Or a weakling. The man was strong. A warrior with reflexes of a cat. Wisdom had mocked her from his eyes. "He will figure it out."

"You worry overmuch. 'Tis a sin not to trust God."

"'Tis a sin to throw caution to the wind as well."

"Patience, child." The friar smiled down at her from a face so filled with peace and kindness, she wondered if he weren't one of God's angels. "God well knew these men would arrive. We must but follow His leading. And pray."

"I have been." Almost all night. Sleep refused a visit, so Alexia had spent the dark hours kneeling before the Spear, appealing to God for His protection and to aid her in her task. She'd felt His peace, aye. *And* His power. But there was something unsettling about Sir Knight that had kept her emotions awhirl. A formidable opponent, to be sure. But 'twas more than that.

A squirrel darted into the clearing and stood on its hind legs, staring up at the friar.

"Here you go, little one." He plucked a nut from his basket, knelt, and handed it to the creature, who scurried off with his treasure.

Alexia smiled. Her first one today. All woodland creatures adored the friar. She'd yet to see one run from him in fear. 'Twas the loving Spirit of God inside of him, he oft said. Which made her wonder why that same Spirit within her bore not the same effect.

He rose slowly, pressing a hand to his back, his cross wavering over his belly. "The creatures loved your mother as well."

"You loved her too."

"Everyone loved her. She had a gentle, kind spirit."

Sorrow clamped Alexia's heart. Memories of her mother had faded much these past ten years. "I am nothing like her."

"Not true." The friar's busy brows rose. "You are much like her. Yet different in your own way, stronger, more determined. God made you a warrior."

"But she was also charged to protect the Spear."

"Aye, for a different time than this."

Images filled Alexia's mind, images of a candlelit room, sobbing servants, a priest giving last rites, and her mother's frail body lying in her bed. Moist hair had stuck to her feverish face, the strands glittering gold in the candlelight as if they clung to the last spark of life leaching from her. "I remember her last day like 'twas yesterday…the fevers, the bleedings, the bitter stench of death."

Sitting beside her, the friar placed his hand atop hers. "She loved you immensely."

Alexia glanced up at the canopy of leaves fluttering in the wind. "The last time I felt her touch me, she slipped the Spear tip into my hand and closed my fingers over it. At the time I had no idea what it was. Then she motioned me forward and whispered in my ear, 'You are the Protector of the Spear now, Alexia. Guard it with your life.'"

Alexia fingered the mark on her wrist. "Then this appeared. One minute there was naught but bare skin, the next, the mark of a spear. At a mere eight years of age, how was I to know what it meant?"

The friar nodded, sorrow glistening his eyes. "She asked me to look after you." He set down his basket and breathed a sigh. "Less than a year after that, I heard of the plot against your life."

"I still wonder at the truth of such a tale." Anger surged at all the wasted years.

"I would not have stolen you away if I weren't convinced your life was in danger. Afterward, 'twas a simple task to spread the rumor of your death by wolves since you so oft snuck from your chamber at night."

"Yet we still do not know the perpetrator. Or if he is even still at Luxley."

"I have asked God to reveal the villain, but alas, He's been silent. He has only told me the threat is still very real." He gripped her hand, pleading in his eyes. "If you would but use the power God has given you when you are at the castle, mayhap you could discover the truth."

"I have tried, Friar." She fisted her hand and groaned. "I am too distraught over my sister, too nervous. I cannot sense things like I can here in the forest."

"You must seek the peace within. Trust God, and the sight will come."

She nodded. "I do sense something there. Evil, darkness." She looked at him. "I simply do not see the source."

"It will come." He smiled.

"It makes no sense." She rubbed her temples. "What threat am I?" A chorus of birdsong filtered down from above as if God were trying to lighten their mood. But how could Alexia find joy when she was kept from her home, from her family? "What threat is my sister?"

"How does Cristiana fare?"

"Worse. In truth, Friar. I fear she's being poisoned."

Friar Josef frowned and grabbed the cross hanging on his chest. "This is not good."

At the lack of his usual optimism and faith, Alexia's gut clenched. "You suspect someone?"

"Mayhap. But 'tis too early to say."

Rising, Alexia grabbed her bow. "I know you told me to stay away for a time, but 'tis been a sennight. I must see my sister."

"What of this King's Guard?"

"He knows only that I am the Falcon of Emerald Forest. I cannot...nay, I *will* not leave Cristiana alone. Not when she is ill. What if someone wishes her dead as well?" She flung the bow over her shoulder. "Besides, Sir LeGode will wonder at my absence, and I must discover how the search goes for the Spear—whether they take to the forest and we must be on our guard."

The friar gave a tilted smile. "You give many reasons for your disobedience."

Alexia kissed him on the cheek, luring a blush from his lined skin. "You have been a father to me, dear friar, and I love you dearly, but I must follow God's leading."

"I fear 'tis *your* leading you follow." His dark eyes held censure. "Remember patience, dear one, and listen to the Spirit."

"You have my troth. Now, see that pine cone?" She pointed to the one she'd missed before. Then, positioning an arrow, she pulled back the string and closed her eyes, seeking direction. Her senses woke, her spirit saw. She released the arrow.

The pine cone shattered into a dozen pieces.

❧

After a week of searching every crack, corner, and crevice of Luxley Castle, no trace of the Spear had been found. At least not the one they sought. There were spears aplenty, of course, along with crossbows, swords, armor, and pikes, not to mention dust, sewage, slop, and rats. But no spear tip. Would they even recognize it should they find it?

Now, as Ronar and his men rode through the muddy streets of the village, he wondered if the French priest had told the truth. Or had he merely been trying to relieve himself of the king's emissaries ere they chopped off his head?

Rubbing the sweat from the back of his neck, he exchanged a glance with Jarin, riding beside him.

"'Tis hotter than Hades out here." Jarin removed his hat to rake back his hair.

"Might as well be Hades for as miserable as I am," Damien remarked from Ronar's other side, holding his gut as his horse ambled along.

"Mayhap if you didn't take to your spirits every eve, Damien."

"What else to do? I tire of this search." He gripped the hilt of his sword. "Warriors sent on a lady's errand."

"'Tis important to the king," Ronar returned, though he quite agreed. Surely their skills could be put to better use. He'd signed on with the King's Guard because he wanted his life to count for something. He wanted to do good for once, to serve God and king, and to leave his mark. But after a week in Luxley, boredom began to set in, especially since he'd not seen a glimpse of Lady Falcon.

"There are many delights in the castle to entertain besides spirits, Damien," Jarin interjected, wearing a quite-pleased-with-himself look that always followed a night spent in female company.

Damien only groaned in reply.

Upon spotting the King's Guard, villagers parted the way, some casting cursory glances toward them, others dipping their heads out of respect. No doubt word of their mission had spread, and Ronar wondered if 'twould do any good to question them as the bishop ordered. Surely if someone knew anything about the Spear, they would have come forward by now to collect the reward.

'Twas the fear he saw in some of their eyes that disturbed Ronar most. He had no wish for anyone but his enemies to fear him. He had tossed the cloak of power away once and had no desire to wear it again. But 'twas well known that the King's Guards fiercely obeyed his Majesty's every command, no matter how harsh or cruel it may be.

They passed the wealthier homes made of stone and slate and came upon the smaller peasant cottages of wood and straw. Thatched roofs, made green by moss and lichen, extended down over walls to offer shelter from the rain and snow. Gray smoke rose from openings in roofs, while chickens and geese wandered about yards strewn with piles of firewood, privies, and various houses for hens, geese, baking, and brewing.

The *clank clank* of a blacksmith's hammer rang through the street, accompanied by lowing of cows and snort of pigs, and villagers conversing and haggling over wares. The odor of refuse, animals, and pottage pricked Ronar's nose as he lifted his eyes to gaze over the thatched roofs and beyond the city wall to farmland spread in all directions. Both men and women labored among the crops in the stifling heat, and a vision emerged of the bishop as Ronar had last seen him, lounging in a chair in the great hall while servants attended his every need.

They turned a corner and headed toward the parish church, where all important village business took place. There, shops lined the streets—the apothecary, spice monger, metalworker and leatherworks among them. Hawkers shouted from the front of stores and also from carts they wheeled about, carrying their wares.

"Hot peascods," one of them shouted.

"Rushes, fair and green!"

"Hot sheep's feet!"

A troupe of musicians played instruments while a man dressed in colorful attire danced. Children ran and twirled to the music, nearly bumping into two men playing draughts. On the opposite corner, a man in a cowl preached to a crowd.

Ronar was about to give the order to halt when several yards past the church, exclamations of glee hailed from a mob of peasants. A few of them shot gazes toward Ronar, and instantly their gaiety ceased and whispering ensued.

"What goes on there? Disband at once!" Ronar shouted as he urged his horse into a gallop toward them.

Shuffling sounded, followed by grunts and groans, and the group moved as one behind a cottage. Within minutes, the peasants reappeared and scattered over the street, none of them daring a glance his way.

Raising a brow toward his friends, who had also witnessed the oddity, Ronar halted Penance before the cottage, now abandoned by all but a mother sow sifting through a pile of refuge. Ordering Jarin and Damien to remain out front, Ronar dismounted and, with a hand on the hilt of his sword, crept around the side of the house toward the back. There, he found naught but an old woman washing clothes over a pot of boiling water, a small herb garden, and a litter of piglets wallowing in the mud. The woman gave him a toothless grin. The piglets began nibbling his boots. Shaking them off, he circled around front and gestured toward the door. With his men behind him, he pushed open the wooden slab that hung crooked on its hinges and entered the dim interior.

A woman and her children huddled in the corner opposite a cow chewing hay. A man stood in the center beside a trestle table and chairs, hiding something with his body. Ronar peered around him to two piles of hay that failed mercilessly in their attempt to hide deer carcasses lying near the back of the room. The smell of some type of stew rose from an iron pot over the fire.

"Where, pray tell, did you get that fresh meat?" Ronar asked.

The man cowered before him, not meeting his gaze. "I know not, Sir."

"The bucks simply appeared in your home?" Ronar snorted. "The king forbids hunting in his forest. You are to buy meat from those licensed to bring it to market."

The woman spoke, her voice quavering. "We cannot afford t' purchase it, Sir."

"Heed your tongue, Martha!" the man snapped toward the woman, and she retreated into the corner, her little ones diving into the folds of her skirts.

Ronar glanced around the tiny one-room cottage with its dirt floor, two straw mattresses, and scarcely any furniture. And he forced down the anguish in his heart. Not forty yards hence, the lady and steward of the castle lived in excess. How abundance mocked the needy. Yet hadn't he done the same in his youth?

Glancing at his friends, he snapped his head toward the door. "Leave us."

Jarin and Damien hesitated a moment, but finally did as he said.

Ronar faced the peasant. "Tell me who brought you the deer, and you will suffer no punishment."

The man kept his head down, his breath coming fast. The cow snorted, and one of the children whimpered.

"I wish 'er no harm."

"Her?" Ronar shifted his stance. "No harm will come to her either, you have my troth."

"'Tis…'tis the Falcon of Emerald Forest, Sir. She is good t' us. She feeds us when we 'ave naught else to eat. Prithee, leave 'er be."

"What is her common name?"

"I know not."

"When was she last here?"

"Only minutes ago, Sir."

Ronar sped from the hut and found his friends. "Question the villagers about the Spear and report back to the bishop." He mounted his horse.

"Where are you going?" Jarin shouted after him as he galloped away.

"To catch a thief."

Chapter 7

*N*o sooner had Alexia entered the village than whispers reached her ears that the King's Guard were riding down the main street, stopping to question villagers. Potz! Of all the times to come into town. Surely, they hadn't searched the entire castle yet? Did they even know about the secret tunnels and passageways? Mayhap not. But what did it matter? The object they sought was not there.

And would never be in their hands.

Several beloved villagers surrounded her—her friends— Gwendolyn, the widow and her five children, Fordwin the spice monger and his wife, Wimarc the butcher, Gerald the leather-worker and his wife Ada and their two children.

"Mistress, you must leave at once!" Wimarc shot a quick glance behind him. "The King's Guard are at the church."

Over their heads, she spotted the blue feather in Sir Knight's hat bouncing down the street.

"Take these two bucks and hide them in your home, Wimarc. Mayhap they will pass by."

"Gramercy of your kindness and good will; God reward you," he whispered in reply. The mob closed in to keep them hidden as the men unloaded the deer from her cart.

"Wait until they are gone and then divide the meat among the poorest of the village," she told the butcher.

Wimarc nodded.

"God be with you, Mistress," Gwendolyn said, her eyes moist with tears.

"God bless you," Gerald added.

"I will return with more when I can." She glanced over their grateful faces, then knelt and took the hand of three-year-old Emma. The child flew into her arms. "Thank you," she whispered into Alexia's ear, and Alexia embraced her tightly. "God loves you, Emma. Never forget."

"What goes on there? Disband at once!" That voice. She *knew* that voice. More angry than frightened, she ducked within the cover of her friends, dashed behind the row of cottages, where she climbed a tree and dropped over the stone wall with ease. She had hoped to visit her sister, or at the very least seek out Anabelle and learn of her condition.

But Sir Knight had ruined her plans.

Grabbing her bow and arrows from where she left them, she sprinted across the open field and within minutes, plunged into the forest, her heart pounding as fast as her feet, her anger rising with each step. The King's Guard had better not confiscate those deer! Surely, they had more heart than to steal food from hungry peasants. She'd not sensed evil in the one who'd caught her in the hall. In good sooth, he had not taken liberties, though he had the opportunity.

Horse hooves drew her gaze back toward the village, but the trees hid all from view. She hurried her pace. The cool mist of the forest showered away her sweat and livened her step as the sound of birdsong, pattering of creatures, and fluttering leaves combined to create a melody that always soothed.

A sound met her ears not of the forest—a footstep, a breath. She froze, plucked an arrow from her quiver, and turned slowly around...listening...listening... There it was again. The slightest of movements. She ducked behind a tree. "Who goes there?"

More footsteps. Pressing against the trunk, she crept around the side and aimed her arrow over the forest. The footsteps stopped.

"Come out or I shall kill you."

Sir Knight stepped from behind a boulder, much closer than she anticipated. How had he followed her so quickly? And why was his chest not heaving with exertion?

She leveled her arrow at his heart. "If you think to arrest me, Sir Knight, you will find it an impossible task."

"Arrest? Nay. If that were my goal, I would have done so already." He wore that same cocksure smile she'd seen on his face a week past. He took a step forward.

Her anger burned. "One more step, Knight, and I *will* shoot you."

His blue eyes pierced, his smile never faded, and, despite her warning, he advanced.

Alexia closed her eyes, sought the peace, and released the arrow.

The knight's shout echoed through the forest.

৩৫৫৩

Pain throbbed through Ronar's thigh. Not enough to topple him. Tush, he'd been wounded far worse than this. But as Lady Falcon dashed for him, a horrified look on her face, he crumpled to the dirt, keeping one hand on his knife on the off-chance he'd misread her.

He hadn't.

She dropped to his side, tossed aside the bow, and stared at the blood bubbling around the arrow protruding from his leg. "Alack, what have you done?"

Ronar groaned. "What have *I* done?"

"I warned you, Sir Knight. Did you not hear me?"

"Alas," he grumbled out. "Prior experience gave me no faith in your aim."

"Again, you underestimate me."

"Wait," Ronar said, as a vision of her firing at him cleared the fog in his mind. "You closed your eyes 'ere you shot."

She laughed. "Hogtoes, what madness you speak, Sir." Her panic turned to determination. "Stay here." Leaping to her feet, she searched the ground.

"I find I have no choice," he replied, admiring the way she filled out men's breeches and the feminine curves she tried to hide behind her dark green doublet. Leather belts crisscrossed said doublet wherein two knives were sheathed. The quiver of arrows hanging at her back did naught to hide the waterfall of bronze curls tumbling to her waist.

He cleared his throat and shifted his gaze. What was he doing? He should arrest her for stealing the king's game. And shooting the King's Guard. Not ogle her like a love-sick squire.

Using her knife, she sliced a vine hanging from a tree and returned to his side with a handful of peat and cobwebs. A stream of sunlight broke through the canopy, igniting her hair in glittering copper. Eyes green as the forest around her, save for tiny specks of gold, stared at him as if she had bad news to convey.

And he lost all sense of pain and discomfort.

"I'm going to remove the arrow now," she said softly. "I fear 'twill pain you greatly."

Precious lady. He forced back a smile. If she only knew the battles he'd fought. The wounds he'd sustained. "I trust you will be gentle," he replied a bit too tauntingly.

Suspicion flashed in her eyes. "You do not fear me?"

"I am at your mercy, Lady Falcon. One more well-placed arrow, and you could be rid of me forever."

"And why would I wish that?" She studied the wound.

"Three times you have attempted my demise. What else would I think? Alack, what better way to keep me from telling your secret?"

"Have you?" She set aside her forest treasures and pressed a light finger where wood met flesh.

"Nay, as I promised."

"I do not recall hearing your troth. Merely my threat to slit your throat."

"I do not gainsay it, Lady Falcon. The thought brought me great terror." He smiled.

She narrowed her eyes. "You are pleased to mock me, Sir Knight. But you will find that I am indeed one to fear, withal." She clutched the arrow.

"I have no dou—Ouch!" His flesh ripped. The bloody arrow flew past his vision and into the bushes.

Grabbing a handful of peat and cobweb, she pressed them into the wound, a flicker of fear passing over her expression at the blood soaking his breeches.

Pain rippled up his thigh, setting it on fire. He grimaced and took a breath. "A warning next time, if you please."

"It would have hurt more." Removing the blood-soaked peats, she grabbed a wineskin from her belt and poured it over the wound.

"Woman, cease!"

"Do you wish it to fester?" Setting the pouch aside, she applied more peat, then fresh leaves, and tied it all in place with the vine. The smell of blood and wine mingled with her scent of pine and woman, and indeed, his head spun slightly.

"There. The wound is shallow. That should last until you return to the castle and see the physician." Rising, she wiped her hands on some leaves and grabbed her bow.

But he didn't wish to return to the castle where he would dawdle away his time with feasts, fruitless searches, and the bishop's incessant whining. At least not yet. He longed to spend more time with this fascinating woman. He longed to discover her secrets—where she lived and with whom, was she spoken for, and most of all what madness caused her to risk her life to feed the poor, and even worse, serve in a castle at the risk of discovery? He found he must know.

"Alack, I am loath to attempt it, lest I bleed to death on the way." He winced at his pathetic tone.

She gave him the look of a mother to a naughty child. "And this from a king's man? Forsooth! 'Twould seem tales of the Guard's bravery have been greatly exaggerated." Planting both hands at her hips, she arched her auburn brows. "Find the courage, Sir Knight, for I bid you adieu." She made it to the edge of the clearing ere she spun to face him again. "'Tis in your best interest not to enter Emerald Forest, or I fear your other leg may meet my arrow as well."

He longed to wipe the smirk off those succulent lips of hers, but instead he did the only thing he could think to do in order to keep her with him. He fainted.

❧

Stooping, Alexia nudged the still body of the knight. Potz! She could not fathom how such a strong, virile man— one of the elite warriors of the kingdom—could faint at so slight a wound. He'd bled a good amount, but surely not enough to warrant swooning like a maiden. Now, what was she to do? One glance around the forest told her night was fast approaching. She couldn't very well leave him to be devoured by foxes or wolves. Grabbing her pouch, she poured the remainder of her wine on his face. Nothing. No twitch. No wince. No movement at all. Mayhap something else plagued him. She leaned close to his nose to hear him breathe. Slow and steady. His scent of wood smoke, leather, and man rose to taunt her with memories of steely arms holding her close and hot breath wafting down her neck— both of which had caused her to feel things no lady should.

Such a dichotomy in the limp man before her.

Rising, she paced the carpet of leaves and needles. She could sit here until he woke, but how long would that be?

The friar would be overwrought at her late return. The knight was too heavy to carry, and she'd left the cart she'd used to transport the deer at the village. Not that she could lift him into it anyway. Nor could she bring him there. An unconscious King's Guard with an arrow wound would certainly bring a death sentence to anyone who housed him.

"Wake up, you fool!" She nudged him with her foot.

An owl hooted from above, mocking her predicament. Would that she could join it in flight and leave this knight to his fate. But she couldn't. Enemy or not, he was one of God's children. Albeit a bit of a wilted reed at the moment.

She peered closer, examining him. A strong jaw and chin bristling with short whiskers gave the impression of nobility. His deep-set eyes seemed peaceful in repose, yet she knew they could pierce iron when opened. A thin mustache draped around either side of his mouth, forming a perpetual frown, while a red scar cut across his right eyebrow and etched down his temple. Wavy hair the color of rich earth surrounded a handsome face—if she admitted it—while a strand fluttered over his forehead in the breeze. She longed to brush it aside, all the while wondering at the odd attraction she felt. Mayhap 'twas because his biting tongue was finally still and the usual taunting smirk absent from his face.

Ugh! Dropping to her knees, she slapped him across that face. Hard. Nothing. Very well, she had but one recourse.

Chapter 8

$\mathcal{A}$s soon as the lady darted off into the forest, Ronar rubbed his face where she'd struck him. Seemed unnecessarily cruel to strike a sleeping man that hard, but then again, he supposed she was desperate. Now, if he'd judged her correctly, she either went to get help or find something to convey him out of the dangers of the forest at night. Either way, he'd surely learn more about her. And if she didn't return and left him to die, he would learn that he didn't wish to learn more about her, save where she hid so he could arrest her and bring her to justice.

He should arrest her regardless. He'd taken an oath not only to protect the king with his life but to enforce his laws across the kingdom.

Struggling to rise, he tested his injured leg. Sore, but not enough to prevent him from walking back to where he'd left his horse. And mayhap even to the castle if need be. He glanced down at the leafy bandage. The lady had not hesitated to yank out the arrow and tend his wound, even at the sight of shredded flesh and pooling blood. So unlike most women he'd known. But she wasn't like most women. Which is how he found himself in this predicament and, dare he admit, even considering defying the king's orders. Begad! What was wrong with him? He rubbed the back of his neck and gazed over the shadows dropping a blanket of gray over the forest. Above him, a bird squawked as night crickets began to chirp. He'd give her an hour.

It didn't take that long. Several minutes later, he heard voices. Those voices grew louder as he carefully positioned himself exactly as she had left him.

A man's voice, an older man spoke. *Her husband?* "So this is your knight? Holy Saints, what have you done to him?"

"He is not *my* knight, Friar, and I shot him as I told you. 'Twas but a shallow wound, which I tended, but then he swooned like a girl."

Ronar suppressed a groan at her comment even as surprise filtered through him. A friar? Odd company for a thief.

"I had hoped to find him gone," she said. "But alack, he not only swoons like a girl, he sleeps like a babe."

Ronar ground his fist in the dirt.

"A rather large knight," the friar said. "And quite handsome."

Ronar liked this friar.

"I hadn't noticed," she said with nonchalance.

The friar chuckled. "Alas, there's naught to be done but build a fire, tend his wound, and keep watch over him. We cannot take him home, and as you have told me, we cannot take him to the village."

"There is no need for you to sit with me, Friar. I can fend off predators."

Shuffling sounded. "I've brought food, healing herbs, blankets, and a Bible. What else have we need of? Besides, you should not be with him alone."

"I can take care of myself."

"'Tis *him* I worry about." The friar chuckled again. "What if he should awake and prick your ire once again?"

Ronar quite enjoyed the loving tone of their banter, and he wondered if the friar were her father. His own parents had been distant, austere, believing that expressions of emotion were naught but displays of weakness.

Within minutes, the crackling of a fire met his ears, and smoke drifted past his nose. Heat from the flames instantly chased the chill from his body, for darkness had long sense robbed the forest of its warmth. How difficult it was to remain still. Yet, he must keep up his charade as long as possible if he were to garner the information he sought.

Footsteps thumped. He sensed someone hovering above him, felt his knives plucked from his belt and his sword pulled from his sheath. And it took everything within him to keep from grabbing the wrist of the offender. No one relieved Ronar LePeine of his weapons without his permission. No one but this lady, apparently, as she then laid a blanket upon him. Odd, but the sentiment warmed more than his body.

"We should dress his wound 'ere he wakes," Lady Falcon said.

Ronar wished he could protest. The throbbing had finally subsided from her last ministrations. Girding himself against the pain, he remained still whilst they unwrapped the injury, peeled off the leaves and peat, and washed the gash again with wine. Relief began to take root at the hope of a conclusion to this mad intrusion upon his flesh when a cold, stinging paste was applied to his leg. It smelled of juniper, rosemary, and lavender, and once the throbbing ceased, the scent soothed him.

Another scent soon drove him to distraction. 'Twas some kind of meat roasting on the fire. It tickled his nose and stirred his stomach into a low growl of protest. Yet he remained quiet as the dead, while the lady and friar partook of their meal with much laughter and conversation. Naught was discussed of particular interest—the summer's progress, the abundance of deer, the friar's chastisement of the risks Lady Falcon took—save one topic that pricked Ronar's ears. Something about an object of great interest to them both. Lady Falcon asked if the friar had brought it, and he replied "'Tis safe where it should be."

Afterward, they prayed, both out loud and unashamedly. Ronar had heard many prayers before, most of them in churches and cathedrals uttered in Latin by men of the cloth, or in the whispered pleas of the devout kneeling in the pews, rosaries in hand. But these prayers were different. For one, they were not in Latin, for another, they were simple and forthright as if God Himself sat around the fire with them, conversing as a friend.

Ronar found it both disturbing and yet, comforting.

Finally, the friar began reciting words from a book—at least Ronar assumed 'twas a book—the most comforting, sweet words he had heard in a long while. Words that stirred something in his soul.

"In the beginning was the Word, and the Word was with God, and the Word was God. He was in the beginning with God. All things came into being through Him, and apart from Him nothing came into being that has come into being. In Him was life, and the life was the Light of men. The Light shines in the darkness, and the darkness did not comprehend it."

"I love that passage," Lady Falcon said.

"'Tis one of my favorites as well."

"I love that His light scatters all darkness."

"Aye, we need His light more and more these days for the darkness grows bold," the friar returned. Then, he must have tossed a log on the fire, for crackling filled the air.

"'Tis heavier than ever in the castle," Lady Falcon added.

"Hmm. All the more reason for you to stay away." Shuffling sounded and another log was tossed on the fire. "Now, what of the verses you brought to memory?"

Instead of speaking, Lady Falcon began to sing. Her voice was even more beguiling echoing through trees than it had been off stone and wood. The dulcet notes swirled about him, calming his spirit and tantalizing his soul with words that spoke of a love freely-given that had always seemed out of Ronar's reach.

Comfort, hope, peace—sensations so foreign to him—began to settle within the deepest parts of his soul when… alarm pinched every nerve! *Heresy! 'Twas the Holy Scriptures.* It took all Ronar's strength to not leap to his feet, grab his weapons, and drag them both before the bishop to stand trial. 'Twas his duty for God and king.

Thankfully, the lady ceased her singing, and they soon bid each other good rest. After several minutes, the deep rumbles of sleep filled the air, and Ronar remained still, contemplating his next move.

Something dropped on his chest. A leaf? Too heavy. Acorn? Nay, it began to crawl. Terror stole his breath.

Jerking up with a start, he batted the enormous spider away, watching it scamper under a bush. When he spun back around, it was to the tip of a knife pointed at his throat and Lady Falcon's victorious grin beaming at the end of the handle.

❧

"Afraid of a little spider, Sir Knight?" Alexia laughed but kept the blade leveled at the fiend's throat. She'd suspected from the beginning that he feigned his benumbed state, though she'd admit to believing it for a while. What warrior takes a strike to his face without retaliation? Yet after the friar fell asleep, she'd watched the knight closely…and movement behind the lids of his eyes gave her pause. 'Twas then that a grand idea had occurred to her.

Seemingly unmoved by the knife at his throat, he frowned. "*You* dropped that hideous creature on me?"

Hideous creature? She wanted to laugh. "How else to wake you from your ruse?"

"Ruse, what ruse?" He reached for his head as if to feign another spell.

She released an impatient sigh. "You did not swoon, Knight. You tricked me, though I know not the reason." Her heart tightened. Had she and the friar said anything about the Spear? She could not remember.

"I am cut to the quick you would say so." Mischief flashed in his eyes.

"You *will* be cut, Sir Knight, if you do not tell me what you are about." Remembering the last time he snatched a knife from her grip, she backed away.

Confident blue eyes followed her as if *he* were the one holding the knife. He moved against a tree and leaned back on the trunk. "In truth, I am feeling a bit light-headed."

"Light-brained would be my guess."

He smiled, drew one knee up, and placed an arm across it. The insignia of the King's Guard taunted her from the rerebrace.

"What is it you want of me, Knight?" Could he possibly suspect her of harboring the Spear? Nay. There would be no reason.

He glanced at Friar Josef, snoring on the other side of the fire. "Your father?"

"My father is dead."

"We have that in common, Falcon. And your mother?"

"The friar took me in soon after she died." Why was she telling him this?

"And the friar's home is in the middle of the king's forest?"

She lowered to sit on a rock, keeping the knife pointed his way. "His home is with me, and I with him. That is all you need know."

The fire crackled and spit as he assessed her.

"I could arrest you both for heresy." He spoke the words as calmly as if they were merely exchanging news at market.

"So you *were* awake."

"Enough to hear the Word of God spoken in blasphemy." There, the first glimmer of mal-intent appeared in his eyes. Somewhere a frog croaked its displeasure.

"Blasphemy?" She huffed. "Have a care, Knight. You call God's Holy Word blasphemy?"

"When it is read and interpreted by those not appointed by God."

"*All* are appointed by God. And we do not interpret it, merely read and feed on the bread that fills our soul."

He studied her, shifting his position. "The Scripture is so far above the mind of common man, how can we know its intent? If everyone from the lowest peasant to the highest king had access, the precious Words of God would be trodden underfoot and deprived of their holiness and power."

"So you have been told."

He cocked his head. "Do you not agree with the Church?"

"I follow the teachings of God. You would be shocked how many edicts of the Church are not found in the Holy Scriptures."

"I will not hear your heresy," he spat and tossed a pebble aside. "I follow the rules of the Church and the king."

"Not God's?"

"God has anointed both."

"God may anoint, but man distorts and perverts, some not knowingly, others for power and wealth. You, of all people, should know that, being so close to the intrigue at court."

A breeze rustled the leaves and stirred the tips of his hair. He flattened his lips. "What I know is that straying from the teachings of the Church, disobeying the dictums of king and Society bring naught but tragedy."

Again, the same sorrow she'd sensed in him earlier reappeared—a wave of pain spilling from an ocean of agony in his eyes. He lowered his gaze.

"Laws should be followed when civil," she acceded.

"And the king's gaming laws are not?" He fingered the whiskers at his chin. "You spoke of being a protector. What are you protecting?" One brow arched.

Alarm rang. She picked at the moss covering the rock, then rose and moved to a pot hanging over the fire. "The village, of course. I feed its starving people. Pray, do tell me kindness and mercy aren't against the king's law as well?"

He offered no reply, merely dropped his eyes to her wrist where the band protected her mark. She must be careful. He was not dull-witted, this one.

"Would you like something to quench your thirst? The friar made lemon-grass tea." She knelt by the fire, opened the friar's satchel to her right and rummaged until she found the vial she sought.

"Aye, thank you."

Discretely slipping the contents in the pot, she stirred the tea, ladled a cup for Sir Knight, and then grabbed a hunk of meat left over from their meal. Knife still in one hand, she offered him the food and drink.

He bit off a chunk of meat, then sipped the tea, as he studied her with those eyes of his—piercing, authoritative, yet curiously interested. And she longed to close her own eyes and seek the Spirit's wisdom on this man. But she couldn't risk it. Instead, she practiced what the friar had been teaching her, blinding herself to the temporary world and opening inner eyes to the real one.

She calmed her breathing and sought the Spirit. After a few moments, the scene before her remained, but another scene took form and overlaid upon the first. Flowers spread throughout the forest in vibrant colors, sparkling in the light from a moon far larger and brighter. Colorful birds and graceful creatures meandered from behind trees and shrubs trimmed in emerald lace. Fearlessly, they grazed on grubs and moss. A glittering ribbon of silvery-blue water bubbled across the clearing, tossing diamonds in the air and laughing as it went. Butterflies, dipped in silver, fluttered above their heads.

Three men appeared, glowing as bright as the sun, immense in stature and armed with swords and shields. She'd seen them before—guardians sent from God. The one most familiar to her nodded her way. The other one stood by the friar as he slept. But the third took a stance beside Sir Knight, who was sipping his tea and staring at her curiously.

Light appeared in the knight's belly, a thin beam that shone up through his head and into to the dark sky. She scanned the area around him. No shadowy, large-eyed entities lurked among the trees. This man belonged to God, though his light was small.

"You are a good man, Knight," she finally said. "I see your heart."

He laughed. "Then why point a blade at it?"

"Because I fear you do not yet *know* your own heart."

"I am called Ronar LePeine." He took another sip of tea. "Since I have made the acquaintance of your arrow, mayhap that has earned me your name?"

"You may call me Falcon."

He frowned. "Very well, Falcon, what else occupies your time aside from feeding the village, singing for the Lady of the castle, shooting knights, and practicing heresy?"

"You make me sound so adventurous. Yet, I assure you, I am no one of import."

"And yet I have a feeling I have only scraped the surface." He finished the tea and set down the cup, giving her that grin of his that could disarm an army.

She looked away. "Pray, what is the punishment for my crimes, Knight? The dungeon? The stocks, or mayhap burned at the stake?"

"I must turn you in, of course. 'Tis my sworn duty."

"As I feared."

Sweat formed on his brow. He blinked and rubbed his eyes.

"I cannot allow that, of course," she said.

"If you think one little knife will stop me, you are wrong, Falcon."

"Knife?" She tossed it, and it stuck point first in the trunk above his head. "But that tea... well, that is another matter."

The briefest flash of alarm passed over his eyes, followed by a glimmer of understanding... ere he groaned and toppled to the dirt with a hearty *thunk*!

Chapter 9

"*What* have we here?" Jarin chuckled, gesturing toward Ronar's leg. "Lady Falcon topples the great Knight LePeine yet again? Ha Ha, I am a poet!"

Ignoring him, Ronar removed the leaves and peat, washed out the wound with the water the servant had brought, and upon smelling no infection, bound it with a clean cloth. "She had an advantage," he grumbled out, his mood as dark as their gloomy chamber.

"Yet so rarely do you give anyone such," Damien remarked from his stance by the fire.

Outside, thunder rumbled across the dark sky as rain pounded the courtyard. Not only had Ronar woken lying in the dirt, feeling as though he'd been trampled by horses, but rain as heavy and thick as syrup slapped his face. By the time he dragged himself to his horse and back to the castle, he was sopping wet, shivering, and angrier than he'd ever been. At the wench, aye, but more than that, at himself.

"She used trickery. I will not be fooled again." He stood, tested his weight and donned his breeches and boots. How could he have been so half-witted? Accepting tea from a known thief and heretic. A beautiful thief at that. Beautiful and witty and clever. And—as he remembered her tending his wound—kind and merciful.

"At least you had an eventful night." Damien crossed arms over his thick chest. "Boredom threatens to undo me."

Sitting on his cot, Jarin expertly flipped a coin betwixt his fingers. "Surely the bishop will soon forsake this futile quest. In good sooth, there is nowhere else to search."

But the bishop had no intention of quitting. Not yet, anyway, as Ronar discovered just minutes later when they were summoned to the great hall. There, they were forced to endure a barrage of insults from his Excellency as he paced before the huge fire.

"The King's Guard and not one of you can find a tiny spear! Not one of you can either induce, threaten, or bribe it out of those who possess it!" With a growl that scared a rat out from hiding, the bishop flung an arm their way. "Why, you couldn't even frighten a crumb from a mouse!" His long black robes swirled about him like demon wings. Immediately Ronar chastised himself for the thought as another wave of dread washed over him, the second since he'd entered the hall. What was it about this place? He glanced up at the banners hanging from the tall ceiling, then to the colorful tapestries lining the walls. Thunder shook the stones, only increasing the foreboding saturating the air around him.

Jarin and Damien stood at attention, their faces stoic masks, save for the tiny twitch on the right side of Jarin's lips and the tight grip Damien had on the hilt of his sword.

"We cannot produce something from nothing," Damien said a bit too harshly, and Ronar prayed his friend's temper would not inflame and put a quick end to all their careers.

As it was, the bishop's searing eyes leveled upon the knight.

Thankfully, LeGode intervened. "Surely it is not here, Excellency." He gripped the carved wood of a high back chair and moved to the stone hearth, his face a twist of frustration. "You have searched the castle twice, and if one of the villagers had the Spear in their possession, they would have come forth to receive such a grand reward."

"Silence!" Bishop Montruse roared and gripped the gold jeweled cross around his neck as if it held the answers. "It must be here." He swallowed hard and stared into the spitting flames, and Ronar almost felt pity for the man who could not return empty-handed to the king when his position—and mayhap even his life—were at risk.

Cedric, LeGode's son entered the hall and bounded toward them as if he strode into a market square for a day of games. Halting, he swirled a gold-embroidered sash through the air. "Why all this pother over a spear? The king needs no talisman to win his battles."

Ronar cringed at the man's foolishness even as the bishop charged him, his face mottled in red.

Sir LeGode stepped in front of his son, and Ronar gripped the pommel of his sword, his one thought to protect the bishop, as was his duty. But a female voice hailing them from the grand stairs prevented the catastrophe.

"Can you men not cease your fighting for a single day?"

Every eye turned, including the servants flitting about the hall, to see a vision of beauty descending the steps, an equally-stunning vision following behind her. The first woman had brown hair dappled in honey and walked with the grace of a goddess. The second woman bore the face of an angel surrounded by lustrous hair the color of the moon. The men simply stared for a moment until LeGode approached the first lady and took her hands in his. "Lady D'Clere, you are looking well. How fare you this day?"

"Better. So much so, I grew weary of my chamber and wished to finally greet my guests properly." Her brown eyes scanned the group, hesitating on Jarin, ere she approached the bishop.

"Bishop Montruse, what a pleasure to have your Excellency grace Luxley." She bowed before him, the other lady holding her elbow lest she fall.

The bishop extended his hand, and she kissed the jeweled ring on his finger, his anger of but a moment ago dissipating beneath her charm. "I am pleased to see you well, my lady. Word of your illness has reached the king."

LeGode elbowed his son and nodded toward Lady D'Clere. It took the lad a moment ere he approached her and proffered his elbow. "Pray, do not tax yourself. Come, sit by the fire, my lady."

Refusing his elbow, she offered Cedric a gentle smile and allowed him to lead her to a chair.

Cedric tripped, laughed at himself, then bowed toward her. "You look lovely as ever."

But the lady wasn't listening. Instead, she turned and whispered something to her companion and both of them smiled toward Ronar and his friends.

Only then did Ronar notice that Jarin had not taken his eyes off Lady D'Clere. Tush. Could not the man seek casier—and less dangerous—prey?

"I'm most anxious to meet the King's Guard," she said, and Jarin needed no further invitation to approach and take the lady's hand.

"Jarin the Just, ever your humble servant, my lady." His lips lingered overlong upon her hand as their eyes met. 'Twas no shock at Jarin's interest in a comely lady, but 'twas quite a shock at her response. Brown eyes, alight with flecks of gold, flitted betwixt Jarin's for what seemed several minutes as a smile graced her lips.

Jarin returned the smile, still clinging to the lady's hand until the bishop cleared his throat. Releasing her fingers, Jarin dipped his head once more and moved aside, allowing Ronar and Damien to introduce themselves.

Though comely, the lady's thin hand and pale complexion bespoke her illness, reminding Ronar of how Lady Falcon's singing soothed her during her feverish bouts. Not that he needed reminding of Lady Falcon. She had consumed his thoughts since he'd awoken that morn.

"My companion, Seraphina de Mowbray," the lady introduced her friend to the gentlemen and each dipped their head before her.

"Now, what is this I hear of the Spear of Destiny hidden away in my castle?" Excitement tinged Lady D'Clere's tone.

"Aye, my lady." The bishop folded his hands before him, his tone condescending. "Every trail the king has followed for the past several years has led us to Luxley."

"I am all astonishment, your Grace."

Sir LeGode snapped at a passing servant and ordered mead brought for his guests. "My lady, we have searched both the castle and the village and not found a trace of it, withal."

"You say my mother may have been in possession of this holy relic at one point?"

The bishop gave a sickly-sweet smile. "That is what Father Aurand told the king's messengers."

"Hmm." Lady D'Clere shook her head. "If she did, she made no mention of it to me."

Bishop Montruse gave her a placating nod. "Hence, 'tis why I intend to search beyond the village into the Emerald Forest."

Damien huffed. "Unlikely you will find anything but trees and deer."

"And Sir LePeine's notorious Lady Falcon." Cedric joked.

Ronar frowned.

Lady D'Clere faced him, her eyes sparking interest. "Ah, Sir LePeine, pray tell, do you know this Falcon of Emerald Forest? My knights have been trying to catch her for years."

"I had an unfortunate encounter with her on the journey here." Ronar gave his friends a look that told them to be silent.

Servants returned with cups of mead set upon trays.

"This lady thief irks me." The bishop snorted, taking a mug. "We must catch her. Who better to know if the Spear resides within the forest? She may even possess it herself." He lifted his chin as if such a glorious idea could only have hailed from his own brilliance.

Cedric downed his mead, grabbed another cup and began kicking rushes across the floor.

LeGode glowered at his son.

Seraphina leaned to whisper in her mistress's ear. Whatever she said caused the lady's breath to increase, but so slight that most would not have noticed.

"Whatever you wish, Excellency. We have naught to hide." Turning, Lady D'Clere reached for her steward's hand, and he immediately grasped hers as she addressed the bishop again. "You should know that Sir LeGode has been an exemplary model of Christian kindness and charity. With my sister"—she hesitated before continuing—"gone and my illness, I have been unable to manage things properly. I trust he has extended you every courtesy."

"Indeed, my lady"—the bishop tapped his chin—"However—"

The great wooden door creaked open, and a boy rushed into the hall, a blast of rain-spiced wind swirling in behind him. He halted before the bishop, hair and surcoat dripping on the stone floor. "A message for Bishop Montruse from the king."

A momentary flicker of fear crossed the bishop's eyes as he took the parchment, broke the seal, and waved the boy off.

His expression softened, and he swung to face the lady. "The king sends another suitor, Lady D'Clere. The son of Lord Hadrian Falk of Kent. A good man, I make bold to say. A great benefactor of the church, wise, and lord of a substantial estate."

Ronar could not help but notice the alarm that rolled over Sir LeGode's face.

Lady D'Clere sighed and exchanged a glance with her companion. "I am surprised the king indulges me yet again and doesn't find me accursed. Mayhap this one will survive the journey."

A thought galloped through Ronar's mind, fleeting, yet as dangerous as if he'd been assaulted. Could Lady Falcon have something to do with the death of these suitors? Nay. They'd been eaten by wolves. Besides, what purpose could she have for keeping Lady D'Clere from wedding?

From behind the lady, Sir LeGode stared intently at his son. "How difficult it must be to consider marrying a man you've never met."

Cedric rushed to a servant, grabbed a cup of mead, and brought it to her.

Thanking him, she took it, but barely spared him a glance.

"Whatever the king wishes. I am of age and fast becoming a spinster." She smiled, and Ronar found he liked this lady's devotion to the king.

Bishop Montruse nodded his agreement. "The king will be pleased to hear of your loyalty, Lady D'Clere."

The pinch braiding LeGode's lips instantly softened into a smile. "A feast! We must celebrate your renewed health and the impending arrival of Lord Falk."

Bishop Montruse lifted his cup in the air. "And on the morrow, we shall renew the search."

Ronar groaned inwardly, a battle waging within him. Should he disclose his knowledge of Lady Falcon, as was his duty? Yet, what knowledge did he possess? Merely that she was a heretic and good with the bow. Naught to aid in finding her. Nay, he would wait until their paths crossed again, gain her trust if possible, and discover for himself if she had knowledge of the Spear. Then he would arrest her for heresy and thievery. No matter how intriguing he found her, a traitor to the crown could not be tolerated.

Chapter 10

The feast was near to an end, and Sir LeGode's imbecile son had not yet captured Lady D'Clere's attention for more than a second. Aye, he'd flitted about like some deranged bird, bringing her fruit, drinks, and sweets and even telling her fanciful stories which brought naught but a placating smile from the lady.

"You dolt!" LeGode sneered, resisting the urge to slap the boy upside the head as they stood to the side scanning the guests who were still laughing and eating. In the corner, a minstrel thrummed a happy tune. "Can you not do a single thing right?"

Cedric pouted and fingered his fur collar. "I've tried everything, Father. You've seen. She harbors not a single shred of interest in me."

"Because you behave the fool! Act like a man. Quit catering to her every whim."

"Peace, froth! I thought you wished me to cater to her every whim." Cedric shifted his silk shoes across the floor then examined his nails. "May I have your leave to return home, Father?"

"So you can whittle your time away playing Skittles, Ring-Toss, and other foolish games? Nay, you may not! You are a handsome lad, well formed, with a pleasing face, and heir to a meager, but successful estate which sits beside Luxley manor. A fine catch. Any lady would be pleased."

"I don't want a lady, Father. I find a serving maid on occasion is more to my taste, for I have no desire to marry."

"You *will* be married"—LeGode ground out—"and to *this* lady. Think, man, think! This match will triple our land and fortune. Not to mention elevate your position. Quit being so selfish and think of your family."

"But how to make her take note of me?" Frowning, Cedric gestured to the lady in question, who leaned her head toward the arrogant King's Guard, Jarin the Just. More like Jarin the dust when LeGode was through with him.

"I cannot compete with a man such as he," Cedric whined.

"Yes, you can and you will. He has naught but a fine physique and handsome face. No land, no title, and no brains. She will tire of him soon enough." Or LeGode would have to intervene. "Return at once to her side. I sat you beside her for a reason. Not so you could stand here talking with me."

Huffing, Cedric started on his way.

"Think of something clever to say, for God's sake, boy," LeGode whispered after him.

But an hour later, as the guests dispersed and Lady D'Clere returned to her chamber, Cedric had not managed to lure more than a glance or two away from the libertine knight.

Enraged, LeGode tore from the grand hall—ere he tore his son in two—and descended the tower stairs toward the dungeons below. Round and round he fled down the rough stone treads until he was dizzy and sweaty and madder than ever. He needed help and he needed it fast. How was he supposed to carry out his well-laid plans when the king's bishop and his knights were right under his nose searching the entire manor, nook, cranny, and hall? *Devils Blood!* Lady D'Clere was finally well enough to attend a supper, and his impotent son couldn't attract a fly if he were covered in manure. LeGode should admit it. He had an unambitious clod for a son, and there was naught to be done about it.

Well, mayhap something.

He reached the bottom, grabbed a candle from a post on the wall, and crept down the narrow tunnel, groping the cold, moist stones as he went. Finding the crevice he sought, he slid his fingers down the jagged rock to the latch at the bottom. *Click.* He shoved and the wall became a door. Slipping inside, he closed it behind him.

A dank chill invaded as he was assailed with a foul smell—a mixture of vinegar and sulfur with a hint of moldy orange. He covered his mouth with his sleeve and searched the shadows. An iron pot hung over hot coals encased in brick in the center of the room. Gray smoke curled and twisted upward through a dark cone-shaped hole in the ceiling. The carcasses of bats and rodents hung from the ceiling alongside various dried herbs. A table to his left was crowded with mortars, alembics, braziers, sieves and bowls, while shelves of books and two chairs perched to his right. More than a dozen candles attempted without success to push back a darkness that LeGode sensed was more than mere shadows.

One of the shadows moved. Drogo materialized. Hair that looked more like gray straw hung about his face, matched by a long, frizzled beard. The black band wrapped around his head starkly contrasted with a white tunic ornamented with oddities that made LeGode wince—bird wings, animal feet, amulets, and trinkets of various sorts. Even a small book that looked as old as the warlock himself. Drogo stared at him with eyes so small and pointed, LeGode could never guess their color.

A shiver ran through him. He hated coming down here. Hated begging favors from this warlock. But what choice did he have? He'd come to realize long ago that there were powers at work in the world, in this very castle, powers that were against him, powers for which he possessed no weapons to defeat—none but what this man offered.

"Ah, LeGode, a pleasure." Drogo sneered.

LeGode dared a step forward. "Things are not going as planned."

"Do tell."

"No doubt you are already aware." As naught escaped the warlock's attention.

Drogo stared at him with eyes devoid of light.

"The Bishop of Montruse is here with the King's Guard searching for the Spear of Destiny," LeGode offered.

For the first time since LeGode had met Drogo, fear made a brief appearance on his face. *So, he does not know.*

"The Spear of Destiny!" he roared.

"Aye, the Spear that pierced—"

"Do not say that name!" Drogo waved his hand, and LeGode's tongue clung to the top of his mouth as if someone had nailed it there. "Never say that name!"

Terror sped LeGode's heart into a frenzy. He nodded his assent and Drogo snapped his fingers.

LeGode's tongue loosed. He clutched his throat as Drogo walked to the pot and peered in.

"It is not here, I assure you. I would know."

"Alas, as I have been telling the bishop," LeGode coughed out. "But the pompous puttock won't listen to reason and insists on searching the manor and even Emerald Forest on the morrow for some insolent lady thief."

Grabbing a bottle from which puffed white smoke, Drogo poured it into the pot, then stirred and stared within. "They will not find it."

"I would rather they do and be rid of them!" LeGode drew a deep breath and instantly regretted it as the stench of rotten eggs saturated his lungs. "Alack, can you at least tell me when they will leave?"

Drogo shook his head. "That is unclear."

LeGode frowned. "The king sends another suitor."

A rare smile lifted Drogo's pale lips. "Indeed? And what would you have me do to this one?"

"The same." LeGode took up a pace, fingering the ruby brooch at his neck. "Wait. Mayhap that would cause the king to cast suspicion my way."

"There are many wolves in the land. The deed will not bloody your hands."

"These suitors are not weak, feckless men, Drogo, to be so easily overcome by wolves."

Drogo laughed, an evil laugh that never failed to sour LeGode's stomach. "You do not know my wolves. Never fear. When Cedric and Lady D'Clere announce their engagement, the king will be so glad to have the matter resolved, he will give no thought to his losses."

A rat skittered across the floor, halting LeGode. He swung to face the warlock. "It will be done, then?"

"It will be done." Drogo mumbled, still staring into the pot. "There is something else…something which disturbs the darkness."

"Pray, what now?"

With his bare hands, Drogo grabbed a handful of burning coals from beneath the pot and scattered them over an iron table to his right.

LeGode's palms began to sweat as he waited for the stench of burning flesh to greet his nose. Though he had witnessed Drogo perform this feat a dozen times, it never failed to disturb him.

The sorcerer stared at the coals intently for several seconds. "There is another suitor. He is near to Lady D'Clere. She will choose him unless fate intervenes."

"Devils Blood!" LeGode raged. "That vain wagtail of a King's Guard! You must get rid of him for me."

Unmoved by LeGode's outburst, Drogo continued staring at the simmering coals. When finally he raised his gaze he replied, "I cannot. He is protected."

"Protected! By who?"

Such hatred twisted Drogo's features, LeGode regretted the question and thought to make a quick escape. Instead, he appeased the warlock with, "Never mind, I will handle Jarin the Just. But prithee, give me something to keep Lady D'Clere abed. That should keep the coxcomb away for now."

"You do well to remember that I have kept her ill for two years now." Drogo turned to search through myriad bottles scattered on his shelves.

"And I thank you for it. When the little whelp celebrated her fifteenth birthday, she thought to run Luxley herself— send me scurrying back home as if I were naught but a servant boy! Devil's Blood!"

Selecting a vial, Drogo turned and handed it to him. "Your debt to me grows, LeGode."

"I have already pledged my son after his wedding. What more can I give you?"

"We shall see." The warlock grinned and dismissed him with a wave and a look that made LeGode question whether the man's price would be too high for him to pay.

❧

Alexia dashed behind the waterfall, down the winding tunnel, and barreled into her home. The friar was just placing steaming bowls of porridge on the table, the scent of rabbit, onions, and carrots rising to tempt her to stay.

But she couldn't.

"Friar, the king's men are searching the forest."

"Sit and eat, dear."

"Did you hear me?" She scanned the room for her bow and arrows, which the friar had insisted she leave behind when she'd claimed a need for fresh air. "There are dozens of them. The castle knights join them."

Pouring wine into two cups, the friar took his seat. "Come pray with me."

"There is no time! They look for the Spear. Why are you not alarmed?"

"God is never alarmed, dear one. He is patient and wise, not rash and driven by fear. And so must we be." He gestured toward her chair, the peace on his face casting shame on the torrent brewing within her. "Pray with me. Let us seek His wisdom."

Against everything within her, Alexia plopped into the chair, her breath and heart refusing to calm. "You've forbidden me to leave this place for two days. The village needs food and now danger is near. I've done enough praying. 'Tis time for action."

"There is never enough praying." He took her hand and squeezed it, then breathed out the most eloquent prayer she'd heard him speak, praising God over and over, then asking for His wisdom and will. Silence settled her heart as they waited for God's answer, the Spirit welling within her, filling her with indescribable joy and a love of which she would never tire. Then came the strong sense of affirmation, the knowing that they were in God's will, and the friar continued his prayer asking for angelic protection over her as she went forth.

Alexia opened her eyes, met the friar's, and nearly cried at the love pouring from them. She sipped her wine, then leapt to her feet and planted a kiss on his cheek. He blushed as usual as she gathered her bow and quiver, strapped on her knives, and headed toward the door.

"I'll return anon, Friar. Never fear."

"You are in God's hands now, dear one."

Once past the waterfall, Alexia took to the trees as was her way in battle. Though she tried to cling to the peace of only moments ago, the fear returned. She'd thwarted bands of warriors before, drove them out of the Circle, but never when they purposely sought the Spear.

Strapping the bow around her shoulder, she leapt from branch to branch, tree to tree, making her way to the last spot where she'd seen the knights. Birds, long since accustomed to her presence in the forest, greeted her with tweets and squawks and happy tunes. Squirrels darted. An owl flapped its wings, angry at having its sleep disturbed. Though 'twas midday, low hanging clouds shrouded the forest in gray and lured a mist from the ground, coating everything in moisture. Good. 'Twould make her harder to see.

Halting, she flattened against the trunk of a tree and listened. Voices and the thud of heavy footsteps alerted her to their position. *Within the Circle of the Spear.* Not good news for them.

With a balance honed from years of practice, she dashed down a thin branch, then hopped to another tree, sending two wrens from their nest in a tizzy of feathers and screeches. Leaping to another tree, she landed hard on a high branch and stopped to catch her breath. Through a web of leaves, she spotted five men beneath her. No, six, seven…more came, all having abandoned their horses and now creeping through the forest, weapons drawn.

Did they expect the Spear to simply appear, lying on a fallen leaf or atop a rock? Or mayhap dangling around the neck of a rabbit? She suppressed a laugh at the thought. No doubt they hoped to find a woodsman's home or hunter's lodge to search—or better yet, torture the inhabitants for any news they had of the holy relic.

Or mayhap they searched for her! Though she'd been a wanted criminal for years, never before had anyone ventured into the forest to find her. Which was a blessing since they surely would have noticed the change that had taken place since the Spear had arrived. More game, milder weather, an abundance of fruits and nuts. The trees grew ever taller and fuller. The waterfall that hid her home had been naught but a trickle dripping into a puddle before the Spear. In truth, the entire western section of the forest had become a mini-Eden.

The crunch of leaves sounded as the warriors moved beneath her. Three more emerged from the greenery. The leap of her heart betrayed her at the sight of Sir Ronar LePeine—all leather and man, and moving so stealthily with his two companions, she barely heard them. How could men so well-muscled make such little sound?

More knights followed, spreading out in a long line, combing the forest like a giant sieve.

And heading straight for the Spear.

"Father, grant me thy grace," Alexia whispered.

Then pulling an arrow from her quiver, she nocked it, leveled it on one of the men, and closed her eyes. The temporary world faded, the real one appeared—all glitter and glory and wonder.

The knights moved as either shadows or light.

She released the bow at a shadow.

Chapter 11

*T*he scream spun Ronar around, his sword drawn ere he completed the turn. Rushing toward the sound, he shoved aside a branch, and came upon one of the castle knights on the ground, an arrow in his thigh. Before Ronar could lift his gaze to scan the foliage, another arrow sped past his ear and struck another knight, expertly aimed between the upper and lower armor shielding his arm.

The knight stumbled backward, plucked out the arrow, and uttered a curse.

Dashing for the nearest tree, Ronar flattened against the trunk, directing Jarin, Damien, and the others to do the same. More arrows rained on them from above. He craned his neck and scanned the canopy but could not spot Lady Falcon. Forsooth, it had to be her! Leaves rustled, a branch creaked, and he thought he saw a shadow leap from tree to tree before more leaves swallowed it up. Sword still drawn, he dashed in that direction just as wails of agony filled the air.

He circled a large boulder and saw two more knights pierced by arrows, three more darted for cover, and the head knight, Sir DeGay, swayed in place as he stared in puzzlement at the leaves above him. Grabbing his arm, Ronar yanked him out of the clearing and shoved him beside a tree.

"Have a care, Sir Knight, or you may be next."

"Where, how? He attacked from nowhere."

A cloud of alcohol enveloped Ronar. "She." He sheathed his sword and withdrew a knife.

More knights burst into the clearing. A hailstorm of arrows shot from the sky—at least five of them in such quick succession, 'twas hard to believe they came from one bow. Two of the knights were hit. Before they even struck dirt, more arrows assailed them from the south.

Mayhap Lady Falcon *did* have help.

"We have to split up or she'll shoot us all!" Ronar shouted. "Sir DeGay, assist your wounded out of danger, then divide your remaining knights in groups of three and send them in different directions. Tell them to keep low and fast. Jarin, Damien, with me."

He didn't wait to see if the besotted knight complied. The man's incompetence was not Ronar's problem. Though how his knights won so many battles was becoming more and more suspect. Mayhap this Spear of Destiny truly *was* close.

Wiping sweat from his forehead, Ronar took off in a sprint, keeping low to the underbrush—brush that was dense and verdant. As were the trees and shrubs. Even the moss covering trunks and rocks was the most beautiful shade of green he'd ever seen. Water dripped from leaves like diamonds. Patches of wild flowers sprouted here and there. Why had he not noticed how lush the forest was before?

Mayhap because the last time he had ventured within, Lady Falcon had shot him in the thigh.

Ducking from tree to tree, shrub to thicket, Ronar followed the screams of pain as the phantom archer wove a trail through the forest toward the north—back toward the village and castle. She was leading them away from someone or some*thing*.

Ronar would not play her game. He gestured to Jarin and Damien to make no sound, attempt no engagement, and follow the archer. Both men nodded their understanding, and all three proceeded forward, quiet as a summer breeze and eyes peeled to the canopy. More than once they lost her trail, halted and listened for the wails of her victims or any creak of branch or sudden flight of birds disturbed from their nests. Mist curled up from the ground, chilling the sweat on Ronar's back as ever-increasing shadows made it difficult to spot anything in the trees above. Finally, after an hour, they had followed her north, northeast, and then south to west again. All grew still and quiet. Even the forest creatures hushed as if in reverence to this Falcon of the forest.

Ronar inched west toward the last sound he'd heard. Night approached, darkening the gray skies even further. The gurgling of water drifted past his ears... then a splash, ever so slight. He crept forward, held up his hand to halt his men, then knelt behind a thick hedge and moved aside the leaves. There. Lady Falcon in her breeches and leather doublet, quiver at her back and bow over her shoulder, leaned by a creek and cupped water to her mouth. A tumble of red hair spilled over her like a cloak of fire.

Ronar smiled. He gestured for Jarin to circle around the creek to her right and Damien to her left where they could trap her when he forced her forward. They nodded and as soon as Lady Falcon rose and started on her way, the three of them did the same.

Ronar kept at least ten yards behind her, training his eye on her every movement, her confident gait, the sway of her feminine hips, and the way she wove effortlessly around trees and bushes as if she were one of the forest creatures who inhabited this verdant paradise.

Two times she halted and turned. Both times, Ronar enjoyed the vision of her comely face searching the foliage. Both times she proceeded on her way.

Finally, the thunderous rush of water grew louder. The lady shoved through a thicket and disappeared. Kneeling, Ronar peered through the leaves. Water careened over a ledge of stone into a large pond. The lady strode directly to the falls as if she would dive into the powerful deluge. Instead, she halted, turned once more to scan her surroundings, then ducked beneath the water and disappeared.

He kept staring, expecting her to reappear, but after several minutes, there was no sign of her. He didn't have time to ponder where she'd gone when Damien appeared beside him, stealth as ever. "I circled around and tracked her here. Where is she?" he whispered.

Soaring on the wings of her victory over the knights, Alexia begged and begged the friar to allow her to venture to the castle to determine how her sister fared. He finally agreed she could bring game to the village and seek news from her friends. But she was to go no farther. 'Twas something at least. She understood his fear. Sir Ronar LePcine knew her face and was surely seeking revenge for slipping the potion into his tea. God's truth, the man was not one to cross. He may have already revealed her identity and alerted the castle guards to be on the lookout for her. Especially after she had won a victory over him and his men in the forest. In good sooth, he was most likely the one who had sent the knights after her in the first place.

Pride surged through her as she realized she'd routed over thirty warriors—including the infamous King's Guard— away from the Spear and back to the castle, injuring over half. She did, indeed, feel a morsel of guilt over the latter. She took no pleasure in causing anyone pain, but her task was simple: Protect the Spear at all costs.

Why the knights had not since returned to the forest she couldn't say. Mayhap they were plotting another way to trap the elusive Falcon.

The villagers welcomed her with happy smiles and grateful words as she delivered her load of deer and rabbits. After the game was taken away and hid, they begged her for a few verses from the Holy Scriptures. Regardless of the danger to herself, how could she deny those who were so starved for God's Word? Hence, she perched on a bench outside Wimarc's home, a mob of children at her feet, while their parents huddled behind them and recited Psalm Eighty-One from memory. The people soaked in the Words with rapt attention, oohs and ahhs, joyful smiles, and sighs. And Alexia grew even more angry that the Church kept such hope and comfort from the people who needed it the most.

Grendale, the village washer woman, darted up to her just as she was finishing. "Falcon, I have a message for you." Her eyes shifted from the crowd back to Alexia, urgency firing from her face.

That message had sent Alexia sprinting home to don her kirtle, inform the friar, and retrieve a *certain* item. Her sister had grown ill again, this time far worse. And regardless of whether Sir LePeine had betrayed her secret and she walked into a trap, she could not leave her sister to die alone.

Now, as Alexia made her way through the village to the castle, she patted the pocket she'd sewn into her chemise. The touch of the Spear brought her comfort. And also a twinge of guilt that she hadn't told the friar she'd brought it with her, for he would certainly protest. He'd protested well enough at her venture to the castle. But after the evil she'd sensed upon her last visit, and now with her sister fallen ill again and the great threat to Alexia, she needed its protection more than ever.

And so did her sister.

With the friar's protests along with his prayers still sifting through her mind, Alexia slipped through the back gate into the courtyard, careful to keep the hood of her cloak over her head and her face down. Hard to do when the yard was full of knights, bow and arrows in hand, firing at targets strung along the stable walls.

"Fire!" Sir DeGay shouted, and ten knights released their arrows. *Whish!* They flew through the air... some hitting the target, others striking the wood, others flying over the walls. *Eek!* Alexia hoped they wouldn't find a mark in human flesh.

Regardless, she suppressed a laugh. What she wouldn't give to teach these knights how 'twas done, to grab a bow and split one of their well-placed arrows with hers. Wouldn't that show them? Potz! There went her pride again.

"Imbeciles!" Sir DeGay shouted. "Again!"

All this for little ol' her? Smiling, Alexia drew her cloak further over her head and moved along the outer edge toward the kitchen. The *clank clank* of metal caused her to peek beyond the archers where two men fought bare-chested with swords.

Ronar LePeine and one of his men.

She should look away. She should, she should, she should! Just continue on, slip unnoticed into the kitchen, not risk revealing herself. Instead, she froze, watching, admiring the graceful yet powerful way Ronar wielding his blade, his swift, elegant moves expertly aimed, the muscles rounding his arms, rolling across his back, and rippling down his firm belly.

Hot-blooded pigs' feet! She should not be staring at him. Though 'twould seem she wasn't the only one, as several kitchen maids and even the old washer woman had stopped to watch. Sir LePeine's friend was equally skilled as their blades met and rang across the yard. Shoving Ronar's sword back, he gave a mischievous grin and motioned Ronar forward. Ronar circled him, breath heavy, sweat moistening his hair.

He swooped down upon his opponent, the hiss of steel crackling the air. His friend met his blow, and the two struggled hilt to hilt, muscles flexing, faces grimacing. Ronar jerked his blade back and brought it swiftly to bear on his friend's leg, but the man leapt out of the way and laughed tauntingly. "I know you too well, Ronar."

"Not well enough," Ronar replied. Jerking hair from his face, he circled his friend once again.

Alexia shrank further into her hood, peering out from the corner.

Ronar snapped his blade to the left, luring his opponent, then spun around and caught him from behind. "Do you surrender?" He taunted.

"Never," his friend replied, though he was clearly beaten. Leaping aside, their blades clashed yet again.

She had promised the friar she'd avoid Sir LePeine, but here she was staring at him. One glance, and he would surely recognize her. *Foolish woman!* Tearing herself away, she ducked into her hood and made her way to the kitchen. If only she could use the secret tunnel, but the wardrobe was too heavy for her to move by herself As it was, cooks and serving boys greeted her with their usual nonchalance. Good so far.

Overwhelmed by scents of venison, boiled wine, onions, and stewed pheasant for the noon meal, she hurried through the pantry and buttery, then made her way up the stairs, forcing a slow pace so as not to attract attention.

Breathing a sigh of relief, she finally slipped inside her sister's chamber. Seraphina, ever the faithful companion, sat by Cristiana's side, while a maid hurried out with chamber pot in hand. The foul stench of sickness wafted over Alexia as the woman passed and closed the door.

Seraphina glanced up. Shadows lingered beneath her eyes. A sudden chill rippled down Alexia, twisting her insides. Attempting to calm her spirit, she searched the room, seeking the source… peering beyond the natural.

Take a deep breath, Alexia. Seek the peace.

A slithering cloud of black emerged from the corner. An elongated mouth screamed silently at her from beneath two malevolent eyes. Other shadows flitted about the room.

"Out! In the name of my Lord Christ Jesus!" Alexia shouted with authority.

She could have sworn she heard the large creature growl before it and its friends instantly disappeared.

Alexia pressed a hand on her heart to still its mad thumping. She hadn't been completely sure what the friar had told her to say would work. But he'd been right as usual. The name of the Son of God, along with the Spear, thwarted *all* evil. Yet—she forced down another burst of terror—what was it about her sister's chamber that lured such beasts from the underworld?

Seraphina approached, following Alexia's gaze above. "What just happened?" She hugged herself.

"Naught to worry about. How is she? You poor dear, you haven't slept." Alexia peered into Seraphina's red, puffy eyes.

"Do not vex yourself over me. 'Tis Cristiana who suffers. She's worse as you can see."

"What happened? Last I heard, she was well again."

"I know not. She was indeed recovering, supping in the great hall, conversing with her guests. And then within days, she took back to her bed. This time with night terrors and vomiting."

Alexia sat at her sister's side and took her hand in hers. Cold, moist, limp.

"Cristiana, 'tis me. Prithee wake up."

Moaning, her sister pried open her eyes for a moment. A tiny smile flitted across her lips as she squeezed Alexia's hand, but it soon faded.

"What has changed?" Alexia asked Seraphina. "Something she's eaten? Did she have a new visitor?"

"Nay. She hasn't been able to eat anything in two days. Before that 'twas the same food she's always eaten—the same food served in the great hall to everyone." Seraphina's expression crumpled. "Only the apothecary and the physician and Sir LeGode have been to see her. Oh"—she gestured toward a bouquet of flowers sitting in a pot on the side table. "Sir Jarin the Just sent flowers and a note that wished her well."

"The King's Guard?"

"Aye, very handsome," Seraphina said. "And quite taken with your sis— Lady D'Clere."

Alexia couldn't help but smile. "Who wouldn't be? Cristiana has the biggest heart of anyone I know. What of her medicine?"

"LeGode ordered a different potion be administered, and the apothecary has been mixing it up and delivering it every day."

"Does he say what it is?"

"To me? Nay. But Lady D'Clere has not drunk her full measure this day." She gestured toward the table where a vial sat, half full.

Alexia picked it up and sniffed. The strong scent of nutmeg, rosemary, and something else not so pleasant, burned her nose, but brought her no alarm.

"When was her medicine changed? Before or after she grew ill again?"

"After."

Alexia drew the vial to her mouth.

Seraphina reached for her. "Pray, my lady, what do you intend?"

"I'm going to drink it. If 'tis what causes my sister's illness, we will soon find out. If not, it will do me no harm." Tipping the vial to her lips, Alexia gulped it down.

Chapter 12

*D*rawing water from the basin, Ronar splashed it on the back of his neck then scooped another handful onto his face and chest.

"Forsooth, I've never seen a more inept group of knights in my life," Damien commented from behind him as he tore off his sweat-laden tunic.

Jarin chuckled. "More court jesters than knights, and the chief among them Sir DeGay." He glanced out the window, folding arms over his chest. "A week of practice and most could not find a target if it were pinned to their behinds."

Grabbing a towel, Ronar faced his friends and dried himself. "Nor would they find Lady Falcon flying through the tree tops like the bird for which she is named."

Damien threw a fresh tunic over his head. "She was within our grasp. I cannot believe we lost her."

"*I* lost her, you mean," Ronar said as he donned a linen shirt, hearing the shame in his voice.

Jarin glanced his way and grinned. "'Twas unlike you, I'll grant, but I believe you've met your match in this lady. She outwits you at every turn."

"Tush! A woman equal to me?" Easing into his leather doublet, Ronar began tying the laces. "Never." Then why hadn't he told Damien that she'd disappeared behind the waterfall? If he had, they could have gone after her and mayhap be closer now to finding the Spear and leaving this cursed place—or at least relieve the king of one less thief. Ronar had cursed himself a hundred times since then. In truth, he *had* opened his mouth to speak the words, but his throat had closed so tight, he could barely breathe. By the time he could, his admission would have cast too much suspicion on his silence.

Alack, if he were honest, he did not wish to see the lady tossed in the dungeon, pilloried, and then hanged for her crimes. Not for merely feeding hungry villagers. Though that would surely be the punishment enacted by LeGode, as was his right.

Pulling St. Jude from his pocket, Ronar rubbed the tiny statue. If ever there was a lost cause, it was Ronar. If ever he was in need of intervention by St. Jude, 'twas now, for he feared this Lady Falcon was making him weak, luring him away from the straight path he'd vowed to take.

Nay. He would *not* allow her to bewitch him. Now that he knew where the lady hid, he would seek her out at the right moment, gain her trust, and discover the whereabouts of the Spear. Smiling, he slipped the statue back into his pocket. How pleased both the bishop and the king would be when he presented them with the Spear of Destiny—earning yet another notch in his belt of penance.

He sat to tug on his boots when a chill scraped his arms— a common occurrence since he'd arrived at Luxley. Still, it never failed to set him on edge. Aye, there was darkness in this keep, heavy and thick like fog made of tar. Mayhap he should seek the bishop's advice on such spiritual matters.

His glance took in Jarin, still staring out the window, absently flipping a coin through his fingers.

"How fares your lady?" Ronar asked to lighten the mood.

Jarin gave a sad smile. "Still ill, I fear. Would that they'd allow me to see her."

Ronar stood and strapped on his belt and short sword. "If such a visit were proper, I have no doubt you could make the lady well by your smile and flattery alone."

"Alas, if you truly wish to see her, we could sneak you into her chamber," Damien added. "'Twould be of no account."

"Tempt me not, dear friends. It may come to that, withal."

Damien sheathed a knife in his belt and laughed. "The poor lady might die of fright should she open her eyes to find your ugly face peering at her."

Ronar chuckled. "Mayhap I should go in your stead, to ensure her heart be tuned to true love."

Jarin snorted. "Begad! Your face, Ronar? Such a sight would surely prompt the lady to join a convent!"

Damien raised his brows, eyes full of mischief. "To his point, if your history with Lady Falcon is any indication."

Ronar's resolve to capture said lady only grew stronger as he and his friends endured the wrath of both the bishop and LeGode at the noonday meal. Their initial inquiries into how the training was going and what information Ronar and his men were able to glean from the villagers transformed into angry accusations the more the wine flowed. Ronar had learned to endure raging censure in silence over the years, for it seemed that those who do nothing are the angriest at those who do all. However, keeping Damien's temper in check was quite the feat. Thankfully, Jarin had been blessed with the gift of ignoring buffoons, though his current lack of flirtations with the serving wenches gave Ronar pause.

"I assure you, your Grace, we will find this Lady Falcon and bring her in," Ronar finally said when the bishop's rage had run its course.

"Alack! I shall believe that when I see it, Knight. Or mark my words, the king will hear of your incompetence."

Aye, Ronar had no doubt the king would see it as such. Regardless of his friendship with Ronar, his Majesty would believe his favored bishop.

A young boy darted into the hall, searched the crowd, then headed for LeGode.

"What is it, lad?"

"Sire, I fear the news is grave."

The bishop bit off a piece of venison, then leaned to listen.

"'Tis Lord Hadrian Falk of Kent. He is dead."

"Dead? How?" LeGode shouted a bit too forcefully, though neither surprise nor sorrow tightened his expression.

"Fell off his horse, Sir. Struck his head and then devoured by wolves."

Bishop Montruse laughed. "Another dead suitor? Sir LeGode, if I didn't know better, I'd think the lady cursed."

"She is *not* cursed, your Grace." LeGode visibly restrained himself. "'Tis simply fate or God's intervention. Mayhap she is meant for another."

Putting aside his shock at the bishop's pleasure at another's death, Ronar kept his eye on LeGode. Something was amiss with this one.

"Meant for another, you say?" The bishop tossed a cherry in his mouth. "She is *meant* to be taken to bed to produce heirs. Any coxcomb could do that."

Ronar cringed at the crude remark.

Jarin, however, slowly rose, and before Ronar could stop him, he faced the bishop. "The lady deserves your apology, your Grace."

"Apology!" The bishop sprayed wine on the table. "You dare speak thus to a man appointed of God? She is a woman and deserves naught but my pleasure in seeing her." His eyes seethed as he stroked the red silk stole around his neck. "You do well to remember 'twas Eve who caused the fall of man. I would watch my tongue, Knight."

"Forgive him, Excellency." Ronar stood and bowed toward the bishop. "'Tis been a trying week full of disappointments. By your leave." Then taking Jarin by the arm, he dragged him down from the dais and across the crowded hall, gesturing for Damien to follow.

"Becalm your temper, Jarin," Ronar whispered as they walked. "Or 'twill be your head he'll be tossing into his mouth next."

"He dares insult Lady D'Clere and then blames it on God!" Jarin hissed.

"'Tis not our place to judge." Though the bishop was making that difficult of late.

"Why do you defend him?" Damien spat.

"I defend God and the Church."

"Are they not one and the same?"

A fortnight ago, Ronar would have said yes. Now, he was not too sure. "'Twas the wine and the bishop's fear of our king that loosens his tongue."

"I should run him through with my sword," Jarin slurred.

"If you wish to lose your head, by all means." Ronar was nearly at the door to the outer bailey when LeGode's woman servant ran up to him. "A moment, if you please, Sir."

He handed Jarin off to Damien. "Take him outside. Mayhap the fresh air will revive his good sense."

After they left, the woman moved Ronar to the side, then glanced around as if expecting an army to appear.

"What is it?"

"'Tis…'Tis a friend in need of help." Her eyes sparked with fear.

"What friend have I here?" Save the two who just left.

"I beg you, Sir. If you'll follow me"—she glanced at LeGode—"but at a distance."

Against his better judgment, Ronar nodded, his curiosity piqued. The lady left and ascended the stairs of the keep.

A group of minstrels began thrumming their instruments while a jester—bells sewn into the bright red and green fabric of his attire—sped through the hall, teasing people and playing the fool. At the command of its owner, a dog followed the jester around and leapt and danced beside him. The crowd roared in laughter.

Ronar wandered toward the pantry, keeping an eye on the bishop and LeGode. Thankfully, both men's attention was elsewhere—the bishop's on the entertainment and LeGode on his stew, which he stared at, sulking.

Halfway up the stairs, the woman met Ronar and then led him further up, past several halls and chambers, finally stopping before a door lit by candles on either side.

"What's this now?" *A trap?* He gripped the hilt of his sword.

Opening the door, the woman urged him inside, quickly closing it behind them.

The chamber smelled of sickness, tallow, and bitter herbs. Darkness inhabited the corners as if waiting to reach out and drag a hapless victim to his death. *Cold.* Why was it so cold? A bed draped in gauze sat to his right, a woman lying within. But 'twas another woman who drew Ronar's gaze, her dark shape lifeless on the floor. He took a step forward.

Lady Falcon.

❦

"You owe me." Drogo entered the dank, misty dungeon from his chambers beyond, white robes fluttering like vaporous spirits.

"So, 'twas your doing, then?" Sir LeGode stepped back as the warlock swept past, leaving behind a trail of putrid odors and hopelessness.

"Who else? You asked me to do the deed, did you not?"

"Aye. Another eaten by wolves," LeGode said more to himself, hiding the shudder coursing through him. "You command these barbaric animals?"

"Not the animals, the demons within." Drogo stopped, started to pace again, stopped, stared at whatever brew bubbled in his pot, then glanced up at the ceiling.

"Would that you could command them to catch a certain *Falcon.*"

"The forest thief is naught to me." Drogo waved him off and continued moving about the chamber as if the floor were too hot to stand upon.

"She may lead us to the Spear," LeGode offered.

"I care not for"—his expression knotted and it almost seemed as if smoke emerged from his mouth. He fingered his gray beard and continued storming about the tiny chamber.

LeGode watched, his fear rising. Normally the warlock was calm, controlled, in command, frightening in his hatred and rage. This…this behavior bordered on hysteria.

"Obtaining the Spear will send the bishop and the King's Guard scurrying back to where they came from, which is good for us both," LeGode dared to say. "Can you lead us to this witch of the forest? Or better yet, to the Spear itself?"

"If she were a witch, I could find her." Drogo's breath came hard and fast as he increased his pace.

"What is amiss, Drogo?"

Halting, Drogo grabbed a handful of hot coals. But before he could scatter them on the table, his scream shook the very walls of the chamber—not an ordinary scream, but a shout that was sharp enough to slice steel. A row of bats above them added their own screeches to the cacophony as they flew up the cone in a mad dash to escape whatever otherworld creature made that hideous sound.

Drogo dropped the hot coals and instantly plunged his hand into a bowl of water. When he withdrew it, bubbling, red flesh covered his skin.

He lifted his face and roared into the darkness. "I cannot see! It hinders me."

"What hinders you?"

Drogo lifted both fists to his temples and squeezed as if he could ground his head into ash. "The Spear. It's here in the castle!"

"I didn't know who else to summon, Sir Knight." Lady D'Clere's companion glanced up at Ronar from her position beside Lady Falcon. The servant who had brought Ronar stood against the door as if she could keep others from entering.

Kneeling beside Lady Falcon, Ronar took her limp hand in his. "What happened?"

"She came to see her..."—the companion raised a hand to her mouth to catch a sob— "to comfort Lady D'Clere with song, and she accidentally drank her healing potion."

"Accidentally?" Ronar huffed and pressed a hand to her cheek, feeling the rising heat of a fever. A tumble of copper-colored hair, shimmering in the firelight, spilled about her head over the white-knotted carpet. Ragged breaths tumbled from her lips, followed by a slight moan.

"I've tried to awaken her, Sir, but she seems to be getting worse."

"Why summon me? Am I not her enemy?"

The woman instantly dropped her gaze.

"Come now, we both know who she is."

"I don't know what you mean." The companion shared a harried glance with the servant at the door.

"She is the Falcon of Emerald Forest, is she not?"

The companion breathed out what seemed like relief. "And you have not disclosed her secret, which gave me hope that you possessed a heart of mercy."

"True enough, I have not told anyone. Hence, she is in no danger. Why not hail the physician and have her put to bed or brought to the village? Her presence here is not uncommon."

"But her sudden illness is, Sir Knight. It proves someone here in the castle is poisoning Lady D'Clere."

"It could be anyone." The woman at the door wrung her hands. "We know not. But should they discover that...that...she drank the potion to reveal the truth, they may attempt to ensure her silence."

"Alas, 'twas no accident then?" He raised a brow toward the companion.

She glanced at Lady Falcon and shook her head.

He followed her gaze back to the woman who had caused him naught but trouble these past weeks. And now to discover she risked being poisoned merely to help another. Ronar growled and ran a hand through his hair. Why did this lady touch him so?

The companion's blue eyes pleaded with him. "We haven't the strength to carry her to the village where she can recover in safety."

"Will you help us, Sir Knight? Or will you turn us in?"

Ronar rose and studied the still shape of Lady D'Clere behind the gauze curtains of her bed. Such a sharp contrast from the comely lady who'd graced them with her presence nigh a sennight ago. Could someone truly be poisoning her? And to what end? Yet the proof lay before him. The Falcon of Emerald Forest, de-fanged and de-clawed. He could easily call the guards, turn her over to the bishop and LeGode, and take full credit for her capture. Mayhap God had shown Ronar mercy for all his blunders.

He debated while gazing at the woman, so frail, so weak and helpless lying there. Not at all like the Falcon who had defeated thirty knights—the thief with a soul kinder and braver than any he'd known.

She may have the Spear. The voice was ever so slight within him. Why turn her in now when he could turn both her *and* the Spear over to the king and receive a much bigger reward?

"Aye, I will help you," he said and instantly regretted it as the thump of boots thundered through the castle. *Many* boots.

LeGode's servant, eyes flashing with terror, slipped out the door. Seconds ticked past like minutes as Ronar strode to the window seeking a way of escape. But they were too far up.

The door opened and the servant entered. "They search every room for the Spear. We are trapped."

Chapter 13

*B*ootsteps thundered up the stairs and echoed down the corridor. Ronar grabbed the hilt of his sword, trying to come up with a plausible story should the knights burst through the door and find him where he should not be—in Lady D'Clere's bedchamber. The truth would win out, but Lady Falcon's life would be forfeit.

And oddly that thought disturbed him more than fear for his own fate.

Alarm screamed from the companion's eyes. Her chest rose and fell as she glanced at her mistress, still unconscious in her bed, then to Lady Falcon and finally to Ronar.

The footsteps grew louder. Shouts ensued.

"There is a way," she finally said. "Come." Moving to the hearth, she pressed the side of the mantle. The creak of wood and grinding of stone echoed through the room.

Fists pounded on the door. "My lady?"

The companion pulled aside a tapestry on the wall to reveal a door, slightly ajar.

Ronar didn't have time to ponder the secret passage. Kneeling, he scooped Lady Falcon in his arms and squeezed through the opening.

"Follow this until you can go no farther," the woman said, her eyes darting to the chamber door where fists continued to pound. "Take the path to the right down a set of stairs. It will end in a wall with no way out. Press the stone and it will move. It opens to the maids' quarters. From there you can exit into the courtyard. Hurry."

The tapestry fell into place. The door closed. The last thing Ronar heard was the castle guards bursting into the chamber.

Darkness cloaked him, thick and heavy. The sound of his breathing mingled with Lady Falcon's tortured breaths. The drip-drip of water, along with the scampering of rats, sent a chill down him as the bitter smell of mold and rot filled his lungs.

Using his shoulders, he groped his way along the moist walls, step by step, breath by breath, longing for a flicker of light, a hope that he wasn't descending into the depths of hell. The lady in his arms moaned. Heat from her body leached through his doublet, driving him onward. He reached the end, turned right, and carefully navigated uneven stairs that led further downward. A cloud of damp, cold air chilled the perspiration on his forehead and caused his fear to rise.

His gut had said to trust the fair-haired companion. But his gut had betrayed him before.

At the bottom of the stairs, he pushed against what felt like solid rock. It gave way slowly, the sounds of scraping and grinding echoing into the void. A sliver of light chased away the darkness. Teeth clenched, Ronar groaned and shoved with all his might, straining against something positioned behind the door. Finally, it gave way to a gap large enough for him to squeeze through. The chamber was small and modestly furnished with several straw cots, tables with lamps and basins, and a wall filled with all manner of tunics and cloaks on hooks. A scream alerted him to a maid at the far end of the room.

"I beg your pardon, and your silence, Miss. I am on the king's business." Laying Lady Falcon on one of the cots, he shoved the wardrobe back in place, then hoisted her in his arms once again and rushed out the door.

Night had consumed the courtyard, empty save for a few squires and servants scurrying about. Thanking St. Jude, Ronar kept to the shadows and headed for the stables. There, a few coins in the hands of a stable boy bought him the lad's silence, his help saddling Penance, and then assistance in lifting Lady Falcon up to Ronar once he mounted.

He settled her gently in front of him and tugged the hood of her cloak about her head as he rode through the village. She'd garnered so much love and respect from the people, he couldn't take the chance some of them might recognize her and challenge him.

Once in the forest, he found a clearing wherein to leave Penance to graze. The destrier would stay close and come at Ronar's whistle when he had need of him. Moments later, the lady grew heavier in his arms, her groans louder, her fever hotter, but he finally found the waterfall behind which she had disappeared. Taking care not to scratch the lady's skin with a sharp branch, he navigated through the brush surrounding the pond and stepped onto one of the wet rocks bordering the falls. He leapt onto the next rook, slipped on the damp moss, and nearly fell into the water, but finally regained his balance long enough to duck behind the cascading water.

A magical world appeared—glistening rock, moss, and lichen covered with tiny violet flowers—all protected by a wall of water through which the world beyond seemed mystical and surreal. A fine mist coated his face as the scent of lavender, damp earth, and life brought a sense of peace over him.

Lady Falcon's moan prompted him to the back of the small cave where he dragged his shoulder along the rocks, seeking an opening. There, hidden behind a cleft, a dark hole appeared. Without hesitation, Ronar carried the lady within and began descending yet another dark passage. This one, however, was not as long, and it soon ended at a thick wooden door. Ronar tried the handle. Locked. Breathing heavy, he hoisted the lady up and knocked.

Moments passed. He was about to heft his shoulder against the wood when a "Who goes there?" shouted from the other side.

"Sir LePeine and your Lady Falcon."

Something banged against the thick wood, and it swung open to warmth and light and the friar's frightened face. Ignoring Ronar, he stared at the unconscious lady, gasped, and moved to show Ronar a straw-stuffed pallet to his right.

Ronar laid her gently upon it while the friar slammed the door shut and hoisted a huge bar across it.

"You need not fear," Ronar said. "No one followed me."

The friar gave him a skeptical look as he moved to kneel beside the lady. After making the sign of the cross, he took her hand. "What has befallen her?"

"I'm told she drank Lady D'Clere's healing potion."

Oddly this information effected no surprise on the friar's expression, only fear spiced with a hint of reprimand.

"And you know not what was in this potion?" He gazed up at Ronar, his bushy brows colliding.

"How would I? I was merely summoned by Lady D'Clere's maid to bring her to safety."

Rising, the friar moved to a table, dipped a cloth in a basin of water, wrung it out and returned to Lady Falcon, placing it on her head. "The fever is good. She fights the poison." Then clutching the large cross around his neck with one hand and laying the other on Lady Falcon, he began to pray, at first in Latin but then transitioning into English.

Ronar took a moment to examine the room, which appeared like a hall in any gentleman's home, complete with hearth, desk, pallets for sleeping, a trestle table and stools, and a wall lined with books. Tapestries decorated the walls, while tightly-woven rugs added warmth to the stone floor.

Who built this place? And how had they accomplished such a task beneath the ground?

What better place to hide the Spear of Destiny?

A smile formed on his lips at the kindness of Saint Jude. If the Spear was here, Ronar would find it, for who was there to stop him save an old, meek friar and a sick lady.

When he turned to face the friar again, it was to the sharp tip of a rather long knife pointed at his gut.

"Now, Sir LePeine, tell me how you found this place before I am forced to kill you."

Alexia was having the most outlandish dream. The friar was attacking Sir LePeine with a knife—the favored long knife he kept hidden in the folds of his cowl.

Sweltering heat roasted her from within. Why was it so hot? And why did her head feel like a thousand crows pecked her brain? Her stomach fared no better, beaten, bashed, and scrubbed like a tunic on a washboard.

In her dream, she pried her eyes open again, ever so slightly, to see the knight raise his hands, wearing that cocksure grin of his.

"The Falcon led me here. I followed her a sennight ago."

Aye, definitely a dream. Nay, she would never have allowed the pitch-kettled knight to follow her home.

"And you have not told anyone nor come here since?" The friar poked Sir LePeine with the knife, his tone one of disbelief.

"As I told you, nay," LePeine replied sternly. "Beware, Friar, I do not relish having a blade at my belly. Nor do I wish to inflict harm on a man of the cloth."

The friar chuckled. "'Tis fortunate for you that your wish will be granted."

In a flash too fast to see, Sir Knight shifted aside, plucked out his own knife, and slashed at the friar's hand. But the friar, a grin on his face, leapt out of the way in time. The two men circled one another, blades drawn.

Alexia smiled. Men always underestimated the friar. He'd been a knight himself ere he dedicated his life to the Church.

"Ah ha," Sir Knight said. "You hide a viper's bite beneath your lamb's wool."

"Be ye wise as serpents and innocent as doves," the friar quoted from Scripture.

Sir Knight eyed him. "I mean neither you nor Lady Falcon harm. I brought her here to protect her."

"And yet, were you not out in the forest seeking her capture merely a week past?"

"On the bishop's orders."

Friar Josef waved his knife before the knight. "Mayhap you are here now on the bishop's orders."

"If so, you both would be bound and on your way to Luxley Castle." Sir Knight lowered his knife. "Come now, let us cease this foolishness."

The friar charged, but the knight caught him by the wrist and spun him around, leveling the blade at his throat. "If I'd wanted to capture her, I could have done so at the castle."

Alexia longed to see how the dream ended, but the ceiling began to spin, and her breath fled her lungs. She heard herself groan, and the hand she raised to her forehead met skin so hot and waxy, surely it did not belong to her.

In an instant two faces swirled above her. One was the friar's, wearing his familiar look of concern, the other was Sir Knight's handsome face bearing the oddest expression. *Care?*

"I'm dreaming," she mumbled.

"Nay, you drank poison," Sir Knight said.

Her stomach vaulted. A sour taste filled her mouth. She attempted to rise, and Sir Knight flung his arm around her back to assist her. Pushing him away, she frantically searched for the chamber pot, all the while trying to restrain the volcano erupting up her throat. Too late. She tossed the contents of her stomach onto his boots.

She rather enjoyed the horrified look on his face before everything faded to black.

The next time she awoke, voices, muffled and distant, floated around her too far out of reach. Sir Knight's and the friar's. She couldn't make out their words, but there was neither challenge nor anger in their tones. Instead, she thought she heard laughter before she faded away again.

Alexia was in her beloved forest. Above her, a full moon laced leaves and trunks in milky white. She hurried her pace. Friar Josef would worry that she was out after dark. Leaves crunched behind her. She swung about. "Who's there?"

An owl hooted from above. A raccoon scrambled across the path.

Alexia's breath settled as she turned and proceeded on her way. A growl, low and deep, rumbled across her back, prickled up her neck, and buzzed over the crown of her head. Halting, she reached ever-so-slowly for her bow. It wasn't there. Another growl, fierce and threatening…closer this time. She spun and searched the shadows. A wolf formed out of the darkness, a beast nearly half her size with malevolent red eyes and muscles that bulged across its back as it slowly approached. Fangs longer than her fingers gleamed white in the moonlight.

Alexia backed away. So this was to be her fate? *Jesus, help me.*

The wolf leapt.

Alexia jerked awake, breath heaving.

"Shh, shh. 'Twas but a dream, Lady Falcon." A voice that sounded like Sir LePeine's spoke far too soft and caringly for the gruff knight as a strong hand folded around hers.

Memories too real to be a dream rose—Sir LePeine and his friend sword fighting in the courtyard, her sister feverish in bed, the new potion. *She'd drunk it!* 'Twas the last thing she remembered, save the nightmare that Sir Knight was in her home.

In her home? She pried her eyes open to see the man in question holding her hand and leaning his forehead against it, lips moving as if he were praying.

She jerked from his grip. "What are you doing here? How?" She tried to sit, but her head felt as heavy as armor.

"Never fear, Lady Falcon. You are safe."

Had his voice always been that deep and soothing? His scent so intoxicating?

She tried to regain her breath. "'Tis true then. You followed me here. Potz, how did I not sense you?" She could hit a target at forty yards with her eyes closed, but whenever Sir LePeine was around, her senses spun into mayhem.

Grabbing a nearby mug, he eased an arm behind her back and helped her sit. She barely tasted the warm wine for the strange sensations rippling through her at his touch.

Pushing the cup away, she sank back onto her pillow and rubbed her aching head. "Are you not afraid I will lose what you offer me on your boots again?" She should be ashamed at the memory and even more mortified at mentioning it to this man, this knight. But at the moment, she'd say anything to replace the look of admiration in his eyes with disgust.

"I have recovered from the incident." Oddly the admiration remained as he set the mug down. "Now, pray tell, Falcon, why did you drink Lady D'Clere's potion when you knew it might be poisoned?"

Poisoned, aye. No doubt remained that someone wanted her sister dead. Or at the very least weak and bedridden. She returned her gaze to the knight. Light from a candle enhanced the scar running from his forehead through his right eyebrow, making her wonder how he'd received it. "'Tis my duty to serve the lady of the manor," she finally answered.

"To your death?" That scarred eyebrow rose.

"If need be."

"I've rarely seen such devotion among nobility, let alone a peas—"

"A peasant? You may call me so. I find no dishonor in the title."

He gazed at her as if he found her a curiously delightful creature.

She closed her eyes to erase the vision and relished in the crackle of the fire and rush of the waterfall in the distance— familiar, soothing sounds. "Why did you bring me here? 'Twould have been easier to simply turn me over to LeGode."

He leaned toward her so close she smelled the friar's special ale on his breath, all spice and honey. "I'll admit to a weakness for a lady in distress."

She pushed him back. "I am no longer in distress; hence you may leave."

"The friar refuses to let me go until he decides whether to trust me." His shrug reminded her of a little boy's, but his smile was so alluring, so full of mischief, it did strange things to her insides. 'Twas the fever, no doubt.

"We both know you can leave any time you wish. Even now, whilst he sleeps." The friar's snoring could be heard across the chamber as Alexia's words muffled in her ears and her head grew heavy.

The Spear. He must be searching for the Spear! Desperation set in, and she fought to stay awake. Wait. She had it in the pocket of her chemise. *Didn't she?*

"I wished to see you well, 'tis all," he said. "Do you find me such a brute as to not have a care for a lady's welfare?" Firelight lit those blue eyes of his as they searched hers so intensely, she feared he'd uncover her secrets.

"Your charm has no effect on me, Sir Knight." She managed to mumble out, perceiving darkness creeping across her vision. "And as soon as I am well, I shall …I shall reacquaint you with the tip of my arrow."

She saw him smile before oblivion once again took hold.

Chapter 14

*A*fter Lady Falcon drifted off to sleep, Ronar spent hours searching for the Spear. The strange underground home consisted of three chambers—one that must be Lady Falcon's dressing room, full of her clothing, comb, soap, lotions, and other womanly-items; the other was a small chapel, complete with a candle-lit altar positioned beneath a crucifix hanging on the wall; and the third was the main living hall. Whilst the lady and her friar slept, Ronar peered beneath rugs, behind tapestries, shuffled through chests, searched under trestle tables, on the mantel, and even rifled through each drawer in the friar's desk. He opened up every book on the shelves, carefully flipping through hand-written pages, amazed at the friar's collection. He even scanned through the parchment atop the friar's desk, but as soon as he saw that the man was copying the Holy Scriptures, Ronar backed away. He would take no part in heresy.

Now, as he knelt before the fire and gazed at the simmering coals, he ran a hand through his hair and sighed. These two may be heretics and the lady a thief, but they were not in possession of the Spear of Destiny. And that was the only reason the king had sent him and his men to Luxley. Not to punish a lady who fed a village from the king's forest or sang to comfort the lady of the manor.

Or who drank the lady's healing potion for no other reason than to prove it to be poison.

Why take the risk? For a liege who would barely take note of her were she well. Besides, what would the knowledge gain Lady Falcon? No one would listen to a servant, and it could only put her in danger from the one who wished Lady D'Clere harm.

Which was another matter altogether. Evil was afoot in that castle. Could Ronar trust anyone with the information that someone was poisoning Lady D'Clere? And how to prove it without involving Lady Falcon?

He moved to sit on a chair beside her and laid the back of his hand atop her cheek. 'Twas warm but not fiery hot as before. Her breathing had settled as well, and she appeared to be sleeping soundly. He should leave and not sit staring at her like a besotted fool. He'd finished what he'd come here to do. But...candlelight flickered over the lady's face, casting shadows from her thick lashes over flawless skin. Her full lips, that normally bore a rosy color, were slightly parted and looked so soft, he licked his own in a desire to kiss them. Coppery hair as fiery as the lady herself, haloed her head, while her tunic clung alluringly to feminine curves. Long slender arms lay by her side— strong, firm arms.

The arms of an archer.

His gaze drifted to her wrist where a scar marred her creamy skin. Careful not to disturb her, he picked up her hand and brought it into the light. Not a scar—a mark of some sort. The same one he'd seen before. Odd, but it appeared to be a...

"Did you find what you were looking for?" The friar's voice caused Ronar's heart to vault, though his training forbade him to jerk in surprise. Slowly, he lowered the lady's hand.

"I did not," he answered without emotion ere he glanced at the man.

"Humph." The friar folded hands over his brown cowl. "Unfortunate."

"For you or me?"

He smiled. "Come, sit, I want to read you something."

Reluctantly, Ronar left the lady and sat on a stool before the fire while the friar took the high back chair, a book in his hands.

He opened it and began to read. "If thou shalt confess with thy mouth the Lord Jesus, and shalt believe in thine heart that God hath raised him from the dead, thou shalt be saved. For with the heart man believeth unto righteousness; and with the mouth confession is made unto salvation. For the scripture saith, Whosoever believeth on him shall not be ashamed."

Ronar took in the strange words, allowing them to penetrate his soul, wisp through the dark places, and dare to strike a spark—*Wait.*

He leapt from his seat. "Silence!"

Unmoved, the friar looked up. "I have read this entire book. 'Tis magnificent, holy, and full of life and wisdom. Its words tell the sad tale of mankind, how we came to this earth, why we are here, our fall, and God's plan of redemption and rescue from our enemy, the evil one. I have not found any of it too complex to understand nor have I been struck down by lightning for reading it."

Ronar huffed. "Give the Almighty time."

"In truth, I haven't found so much as a word or phrase about such things as penance and indulgences and the worship of saints. Nor that the Pope is divine and speaks for God."

"Blasphemy!" Ronar backed away and glanced at the door. He should leave before God smote him dead for listening to such lies.

Closing the book, the friar caressed it lovingly. "God's word tells of salvation through faith alone, faith in the Son of God and His sacrifice on the cross. It says naught about works, save those which we perform to please Him and help our fellow man, those which prove a changed heart within."

Ronar shifted his gaze to the hot coals, trying to scatter the heresy from his mind and send it to hell where it belonged. Yet…he swallowed a burst of longing…salvation through faith alone? It could not be, for that was too simple, too wonderful to believe.

"There will come a day," the friar continued, following Ronar's gaze to the fire, "when this book will be made available to all, from the lowliest peasant to the king himself." He brought it near to his chest in an embrace that bespoke of adoration. "At first people will delight in it, reading and cherishing every word. Its truth will set many free and bring many to salvation." Sorrow claimed his features, and Ronar could swear he saw tears moisten the friar's eyes. "But afterward, man's religion will rise yet again, and though this great book will be available to all, people will not read it and will instead listen only to those who claim to speak in God's name. Then great deception will once again entrap the multitudes."

Ronar gaped. Either the man was unbalanced in the head or he believed every word he said. "How do you know this?"

"God reveals things to me," the friar said as if it were an everyday occurrence.

"I pray to Saint Jude." Ronar retrieved the tiny statue from his pocket, unsure why he disclosed such a thing, save he suddenly felt the need to justify his own spirituality. "Given to me by the bishop of Jerusalem, hewn from our Lord's sepulcher."

"The saint of hopeless causes." The friar's eyes glittered. "Is that what you think of yourself?"

Ronar frowned.

"And has Saint Jude answered your prayers, young man?"

"Aye."

"Or mayhap 'twas God." The friar patted the book in his lap. "God's Word says those of us who follow Christ are *all* saints. It also tells us to pray only to God, for there is one God and one mediator between God and men, the man Christ Jesus."

Shoving Saint Jude back in his pocket, Ronar grimaced. "Enough of this. I must go."

"And yet I sense you want to hear more." The friar clutched the crucifix hanging at his belly.

"Do not pretend to know me, Friar."

"I know you are a man of conviction, a man of strong faith. And"—he studied him until Ronar felt so uncomfortable, he turned to leave—"a man loaded down with a burden of guilt."

The words sliced across Ronar's back. Bad cess to the man! How could he know such a thing?

"Will you betray us, Sir LePeine?" The friar's voice followed him to the door.

Halting, Ronar glanced at Lady Falcon, so peaceful in her sleep. "She steals the king's game. My duty is"—Ronar faced him—"You must make her stop, Friar. Ensure me she will no longer hunt game in this forest."

"That I cannot do." The friar chuckled. "As you are aware, the lady has a mind of her own."

Aye, so he'd noticed. A foolish, stubborn mind.

"If the lady ceases hunting, you have my troth I will keep silent. But if I find she has filled the villagers' bellies yet again, I fear I will have no choice but to capture her and turn her over to Sir LeGode to receive her just punishment."

❧

Sir Walter LeGode stood before the narrow window of the treasury and gazed down upon the gardens outside the castle wall. There, Lady D'Clere—much improved since he'd withheld Drogo's potion—strolled on the arm of his son, Cedric. The numb-brained oaf finally managed to entice the lady out for a walk through the gardens on this fine spring day. Now, if he wouldn't muck up the conversation and instead shower her with the flatteries and witty remarks as LeGode had instructed him, the lady might show some interest. Yet, as he watched them weave around a stone statue of the Virgin Mary, the lady looked terribly bored. Cedric, himself, gazed about as if he wished he were anywhere else.

Mayhap the distraction LeGode had arranged would give the couple a little shove in the right direction.

Activity drew his attention down to the inner courtyard where several knights removed their armor, chainmail, and leg chausses and then donned the common tunics of peasants and farmers, hiding swords and blades beneath their cloaks. 'Twas the bishop's latest plan to capture Lady Falcon and hopefully the Spear, since Sir DeGay's incompetent knights could not master archery in time. If only LeGode had been able to infiltrate more of his own knights among Luxley's guard, but thus far, he'd only managed to bring a few from his own estate. More, however, were on their way.

He swept his gaze back to his son as the couple passed a flowering bush of pink primroses.

"Pick her a flower, you imbecile!" LeGode seethed.

Instead, Cedric leaned over and said something to the lady which bore no effect on her languid expression. LeGode clamped his hands into fists and directed his gaze to the village. There. Finally. A horse-drawn wagon raced down the center of town, spitting up mud and stirring screams from villagers who leapt out of the way.

One quick glance back to Cedric brought a smile to LeGode's lips. At least the lad had directed Lady D'Clere back onto the main path. Now, for the gallant rescue that would win fair lady's heart. Or at the very least, soften it a bit toward his son.

The wagon tore out of the village and careened over the wooden bridge, bouncing so high, hay, fruit, and pottery leapt from the back and landed splat in the mud.

"Out of the way!" the driver shouted. People, chickens, and pigs scattered before him. The wagon whisked around a corner. One side tipped and wheels flung mud and manure into the air. Still, the horse galloped onward, wide-eyed and nostrils flaring.

As planned, Cedric left the lady's side for but a moment to pick her a flower. Hearing the approaching danger, she glanced up just as the horse dashed around the corner and headed straight for her. She had but moments to leap out of the way, moments in which Cedric was supposed to hoist her in his arms and bring her to safety. Instead, he stared dumbfounded at the wagon as if it were an advancing army.

Lady D'Clere did the same. When the driver finally realized the plan had gone awry, he attempted to slow the horse as LeGode had instructed, should his son fail—yet again.

Out of nowhere, Jarin the Just darted to the lady, swept her up in his arms and leapt to the side of the path just as the wagon sped past... finally stopping mere yards away.

Jarin set the lady down. She began to falter, and he held her close, wiping wayward curls from her face and gazing down at her as if she were the queen herself.

She smiled and must have thanked him, for he dipped his head, then lifted her back in his arms and carried her over the bridge, past the gatehouse, and into the inner bailey.

All while Cedric stood there staring after them like a gorbellied donkey whose last meal had just been stolen.

LeGode growled. "Idiot!" He marched from the treasury, stormed down the stairs, and finally slammed into his private study where Annabelle was laying out his afternoon tea.

"Tell me, how can such a prominent man as myself have such a pribbling puttock for a son?"

The pretty little thing gulped and stared down at the floor. "I know not what you mean, Sir."

Such lovely hair, a dark golden shade that shimmered like silk. LeGode swept his gaze over her and licked his lips, then approached slowly so as not to frighten the timid fawn. He ran a finger down her neck.

She jerked from him. "I have brought your tea, Sir. Will there be anything else?"

Grabbing her by the waist, he pressed her curves against him. "What else are you offering?"

"Not what you think." Blue eyes, stark with fear, met his as she pushed from him. "You have a wife."

"She's an old hag, Anabelle, not young and fresh like you. When will you give yourself to me? I can make your life *very* comfortable."

He leaned down to kiss her, but she jerked from his grasp and fled out the door.

LeGode slammed his fist on the table.

Chapter 15

*H*is mind awhirl with the friar's words, Ronar left Penance with the stable boy and headed across the courtyard just as Jarin entered through the main gate, Lady D'Clere in his arms. The sight would have shocked Ronar if it had been anyone else, but when it came to the ladies, Jarin possessed a special gift. The evidence of which was written all over Lady D'Clere's expression—one of thankfulness and admiration, not horror at being carried so intimately by a common knight.

Ronar met them at the entrance to the grand hall. Acknowledging Ronar with a smile, Jarin set the lady down at the foot of the stairs per her request, just as the lady's companion descended to greet them.

Though flushed, Lady D'Clere fared much better since the last time Ronar had seen her—abed with nary a breath to stir the air about her. *Poisoned.* Should he tell her? Inform his friends? Nay. Not until he gathered more proof and sought out who might wish her harm. He had to be sure before sending his men on a quest that would no doubt cause the villain to withdraw. Or worse.

Lady D'Clere spared a glance toward Ronar ere her focus returned to Jarin. "How can I ever thank you, Sir? You saved my life."

"'Twas nothing, my lady. It pleases me I was close at hand."

"I don't know what came over me. I found my feet unable to move."

"'Tis no doubt caused by your recent illness which has drained you of your strength."

"Then I thank you for lending me your rather impressive strength, Sir."

Ronar coughed to squelch a chuckle at the ridiculous dalliance.

"Come, my lady, you must rest." The lovely companion pleaded, while her questioning eyes bore into Ronar. He nodded in the affirmative in reply to her unspoken question of Lady Falcon's safety. Still, he must seek the companion in private, ensure that she prevented Lady D'Clere from drinking any more potions. Surely she knew that already.

Lady D'Clere offered her hand, and Jarin placed a kiss upon it, then gazed up at her as adoring as any gallant. "You may call upon me whene'er you have need of my strength again, my lady."

She smiled, an alluring yet innocent smile that would make any man melt. A gown of crimson wool draped to her feet, trimmed and girdled with golden ribbons embroidered with white lilacs. Her rich, chestnut hair had been braided and bound with threads of gold while a golden circlet embedded with pearls sat upon her head.

"A generous offer, Sir Knight," she said. "One which I shall be happy to accept." Then giving him a coy smile, she turned and ascended the stairs, her companion at her side. Halfway up, she gave Jarin one last glance ere she disappeared from sight.

Jarin faced Ronar, a grin on his face. "And where, pray tell, have you been all night?"

"Searching for the Spear." Ronar replied as he started for a sideboard in the hall for a drink.

"All night?"

"I fell asleep." 'Twas not really a lie.

"In the forest?"

"Is that so strange?" Ronar poured himself a cup of mead from a pitcher and took a sip.

Jarin shrugged. "Did you happen to run across your nemesis, the elusive Falcon?"

"I find her as elusive as always."

"Unfortunate." Jarin bit into an apple and leaned back against the high table. A servant girl passed, casting glances toward Jarin, but the libertine never once turned his head. "'Twould have saved us from spending days wandering about the village," he added.

"What's this you say?" Ronar stared at him.

"'Tis the bishop's new plan," Damien said as he marched into the room. "Discard our knightly garb for peasant cloaks and hide among the villagers until our charitable lady arrives with fresh game. We begin on the morrow."

Ronar forced down a chuckle. "She is far too clever to bring meat so soon after our encounter in the forest. No doubt she is hiding away until we and the bishop are gone." At least Ronar hoped the lady had more sense than she had thus displayed.

"Not if she learns that Bishop Montruse has ordered the confiscation of all the village livestock. I imagine the peasants' cries of hunger will find their way to the benevolent Falcon's ears."

Ronar sipped his mead and stared at Damien, waiting for him to start laughing. Instead, the staunch warrior poured himself a drink.

"The bishop would never order such cruelty," Ronar said.

Damien huffed. "Your unwarranted trust in anyone who wears the chasuble astounds me."

"Where is he?"

"Taking his afternoon rest, I imagine. I wouldn't disturb him if I were you."

Staring up at the banners hanging from the high ceiling, Damien gulped his mead and uttered a curse. "May we find this infernal Spear soon. I grow to hate this place."

"I find I heartily disagree." Jarin tossed his apple core into a pail across the room. "'Tis your quest for the man who ruined your family that drives your impatience, Damien. I have no such lure to return to the palace. In truth, quite the opposite."

Damien shook his head. "Not sampled all the maids yet?"

"How can I when there is one who has stolen my heart." Jarin placed a hand on his chest and shared a glance with Ronar.

"Jarin smitten by love?" Damien laughed. "Never!"

"I do not gainsay it." Jarin shrugged and gazed up the stairs where they'd last seen Lady D'Clere.

"Leave her be. It will come to naught, and you know it," Ronar said more sternly than he intended.

Damien raised his brows at Jarin. "I am intrigued."

"Well then, Sir Intrigued and Sir Smitten." Ronar raised his cup toward his friends with a smile. "I will call you whatever you wish as long as we find the Spear—and soon. Or I fear the king's displeasure will rain down on all of us for months to come."

Yet...the thought of never seeing Lady Falcon again....Ronar frowned and cursed his weakness. Tush, he didn't even know her name. She'd done naught but bring him trouble, cause him to entertain the thought of disobeying his king and God. *Women.* They were the devil's tools to distract men from their Godly callings.

Taking leave of his men, Ronar stormed the hall, crossed the courtyard, and slipped inside the chapel. The door creaked shut, leaving him in darkness, save for two candles on the altar and a rainbow of sheer light angling in from a small window of colored glass. The scent of mold, aged wood, and heartache filled his nose as he strode toward the front of the small room, crossed himself and knelt on the cold stone. He tugged Saint Jude from his pocket, wondering why no chaplain inhabited Luxley. There were things he must confess, things not meant for the bishop's ears. Guilt assailed him at that last thought, for surely even *that* was a sin.

He kissed Saint Jude and gazed up at the wooden figure of Christ hanging on the cross.

As much as he had tried not to listen, the friar's reading of the Holy Scripture refused to vacate his thoughts. Surely God required more than a simple confession and a heart belief? Then even the worst of mankind could be saved—without paying for all their many evils inflicted on the innocent. Nay, 'twas heresy pure and simple.

As for himself, he had more good deeds to accomplish in order to pay the penance for his past evils. And he would not allow a woman—a thief and heretic—to bewitch him into a life of disobedience and heresy.

"Holy Christ, forgive me, for I have sinned." He continued reciting the prayers he'd learned over the years. But after an hour, he still felt empty. Mayhap he should pray to Saint Jude. After all, he had many requests which seemed naught but hopeless causes—finding the Spear, Lady Falcon's safety, discovering who poisoned Lady D'Clere.

After uttering more prayers and feeling no better for it, Ronar stood and replaced Saint Jude in his pocket. Rays of sunlight filtered through the colored glass, sending dust swirling in its path. The hollow *clang* of a blacksmith's hammer chimed through the room, along with the muffled voices of servants, squires, and knights in the courtyard.

A shadow moved in the corner. Ronar rubbed his eyes. He'd not slept all night and was no doubt seeing things.

One of the candles flickered. He jerked around. The door remained shut.

A cloak of ice settled on him.

Another shadow slunk along the floor—a black fog twisting and turning around the altar and chairs.

What devilment is this? Hand on the hilt of his sword, Ronar backed away, swallowing down his fear. The dank air grew icy still, prickling over his skin. A foul stench arose. He held a hand to his mouth. The flames of both candles sizzled out as if someone had smothered them with two fingers. Smoke curled upward. A sense of foreboding draped over him. Finally, he spun on his heels and barreled out the door into the sunshine. Drawing a deep breath, he soaked in the light, dispelling the darkness, but was unable to dispel the hopelessness that had invaded his spirit—a hopelessness that told him his future was filled with naught but danger and defeat.

Chapter 16

"*W*hat choice do I have, Friar?" Alexia stuffed her gray kirtle into her sack.

"You always have a choice. Seek wisdom, my dear."

"This is the wisdom I know—my sister is being poisoned, and she is defenseless, the bishop has stolen the villagers' only means of putting meat on their tables, and I am the only hope for both."

One of the friar's bushy brows rose. "Have you taken the place of the Almighty now?"

"Of course not." Flinging the sack over her shoulder, she gathered her knives and slid them into her belt. "But I am His chosen protector."

"Of the Spear. That is all."

"The Spear is safe." Alexia patted her breeches where the relic remained in the pocket of her chemise.

"You should not have taken it." The friar offered her his usual look of censure. "Nor should you have it now."

"If I hadn't, Sir LePeine would have found it."

Friar Josef merely stared at her with those wise eyes of his, eyes that pleaded with her to see reason.

In good sooth, she *did* see reason. Only 'twas *her* reason, not his. "'Tis no longer safe here as you well know. I do not trust that bothersome knight to keep our secret."

"There is good in him—the Father's light. You have seen it as well."

"Aye, but 'tis a mere flicker. Ergo, he is not to be trusted." She glanced around, heart plunging at the thought she had to vacate the only home she'd known for the past nine years. "While I am gone, you must take only what is necessary and move to the woodsman's cottage deep in the forest. Give me your troth you will do so."

"Is this to be my lot? Ordered about by the child I raised?" He huffed. "What if you are caught? What if they find the Spear?"

"They won't."

"You are not ready, dear one." His tone softened. "Your powers fail when fear, worry, and sorrow abound. As they so often do when you visit your sister. Your faith needs more training, your emotions more control."

"I'm eighteen, Friar. Mayhap 'tis you who needs faith that you have done your job well."

"Holy Saints, 'tis that very thing which keeps me up at night."

Alexia smiled. "I must do as the Father commands. He will be with me. The Spear will protect me."

"Ah, the plight of a father…to worry so about his child."

Standing on tiptoes, she kissed his cheek. "How can one so worried teach me to not do so?"

He sighed and closed his eyes as if seeking a way to make her listen. "They look for you in the village."

"They will not find me. And when I get to the castle, I shall proceed directly to Sir LeGode and tell him all. He will know exactly how to discover who is poisoning my sister."

Alexia peered from beneath the hood of her cloak and suppressed a laugh. Did the castle knights think her bird-witted? Regardless of their common garb, she could spot each one of them as they slunk around the village, pretending to tend to various tasks, conversing with each other, or lurking about the market square.

Not to mention that the villagers gave them wide birth. Outside the village wall, it had been a small task to distract the guard posted there with a pitcher of ale offered by one of the village maidens Alexia had recruited from the fields. Once the man could see naught but the girl *and the ale*, Alexia hoisted the game she had caught—two deer, four rabbits, and a duck—over the wall with a rope.

Then, all she had to do was bend over like an aged woman and enter through the front gate carrying a basket of beans, peas, and parsnips, as if she'd just harvested them from the fields. She had abandoned her breeches at the edge of the forest for her simple kirtle and belt, and now, with head down, proceeded along the main street. One glance over her shoulder told her the maiden had entered as well. She nodded toward Alexia ere she proceeded to Wimarc's to inform him of the game.

Keeping close to the buildings, Alexia passed the villeins' simple homes, then the leather workers shop, the apothecary, and the scrivener's. She hobbled past the church and market square, keeping her gaze from the castle knights loitering about everywhere. Sir LePeine's two friends leaned against a post before the weaver's shop, looking beyond bored. Though the handsome one's eyes grazed over her, he went on conversing with his friend. What if LePeine was in the village as well? Of all the guards, he would be the most likely to recognize her.

As if the thought of him could conjure up the surly knight, she spotted him helping a young maiden carry pails of milk, his authoritative bearing unmistakable even attired in his peasant garb. The light-haired milkmaid gazed up at him with adoring eyes, and an uncomfortable feeling swirled in Alexia's belly at the sight.

At that moment, as if he sensed her presence, he looked up, and Alexia jerked her face forward again, head down, body bent.

"Fresh pheasant pies!" a man yelled from his cart.

Other sounds met Alexia's ears, the shout of laborers, the distant cry of a babe, the clang of hammer on anvil, children laughing. Absent was the cluck of hens or snort of hogs. She passed the wealthier homes made of brick and noticed chickens no longer pranced across the Jenfray's yard. Potz on Bishop Montruse! What sort of man of God would see these people starve?

She dared not look to see if Sir LePeine followed until she slipped through the back gate of the castle grounds and was halfway across the courtyard. Thankfully, he was nowhere in sight.

Releasing a sigh, she entered the kitchen, where she deposited her basket, then sped through the pantry into the main hall and made her way to Sir LeGode's study. As a mere servant, she should not enter unannounced. Yet after today, she would no longer be such—at least not to LeGode. Halting at the door, she smiled, excited to finally relieve herself of the burden she'd carried all these years. Especially to a trusted member of the family. A man who had been closer than a brother to her mother and father and who cared for her sister as if she were his own.

The door flew open and Anabelle appeared, carrying an empty tray. She bumped into Alexia, her expression transforming from shock...to glee...to fear. "What are you doing?" she whispered, trying to drag Alexia away.

"I must speak to him. 'Tis important."

"On what matter?" Anabelle glanced over her shoulder and bit her lip. "Prithee, reconsider. He is not in a good humor."

"What is all the commotion, Ana?"

"Merely the minstrel, Sir."

"Announce me." Alexia gripped her friend's arm and nodded her head in assurance.

It did naught to reassure Anabelle as she reentered the room, her face awash in fear. "Sir, she wishes to speak to you."

"Devil's blood! Whatever does she want? I have work to do. Very well, see her in."

Moving aside, Anabelle allowed Alexia to pass, giving her a look of dismay.

LeGode busied himself with several parchments spread across his desk, quill pen in hand. Sunlight speared through two narrow windows behind him, one stabbing the desk, the other Sir LeGode's back. Dust coated rows of books sitting haphazardly on a shelf. Coals simmered in the brazier, offering a modicum of heat while two crossed swords, a map of England, and a painting of LeGode himself hung on the walls. The scent of tallow, ink, and smoke drifted past her nose. Alexia took a step onto the silk woven rug and tried to remember what the room had looked like when her father was alive. She couldn't.

She cleared her throat.

With a huff, Sir LeGode lowered the pen, grabbed his wine, and sat back in his chair, examining her with eyes full of angst and frustration. Before she could wonder why, he snapped at her. "Well what it is, girl?"

"I have important news for you, Sir." She glanced toward the open door. "Personal news."

"Ana, fetch me some cheese and bread and close the door."

After Anabelle left, Alexia slid the hood from her head, removed her cape, and laid it on a chair. 'Twas the first time she had given him a full view of her face, and she hoped he would recognize her. Instead he drank his wine and stared at her as if she were an annoying rodent. That annoyance transformed into appreciation as he continued to take in her features, and she thought she saw a flicker of desire cross his face. But that couldn't be. Rising, he wove around his desk, a smile forming on his lips. She braced herself for what surely would be a tight embrace of one thought long lost.

Instead, he eased a finger down her cheek and drew even closer. His warm breath on her neck elicited a shiver of unease.

She moved away. "Someone is poisoning Lady D'Clere." She hadn't meant to blurt it out so bluntly, but she could think of no other way to halt his advance.

His eyes narrowed. "Peace, froth! Madness!" he blubbered and headed toward the door. "Acquit me at once!"

"'Tis me, Alexia, Sir LeGode. Lady Alexia D'Clere."

He halted as if he'd struck a stone wall. Moments passed in which the only sound filling the room was the simmer of coals in the brazier. Finally, he turned ever so slowly, his face pallid, his eyes wide, an indiscernible emotion brewing within them.

"I am not dead, as you assumed." She stepped toward him, desperate for a warm welcome from her old friend.

Instead, the breath seemed to flee his lungs, and he stumbled away from her, hand on his chest as if his heart would burst free from the shock.

Taking his arm, she led him to a chair by the brazier. "Pray, forgive me for telling you in so abrupt a manner, but I knew of no other way to garner your trust."

"How?" He gazed up at her. "Alexia?"

"Aye, 'tis truly me." Taking his hands in hers, she knelt before him. "Friar Josef stole me away when he discovered a threat against my life. I've been living in Emerald Forest these past nine years."

She thought she saw a streak of hatred, mayhap even anger dash across his eyes, but then it was gone.

"Threat? What threat?"

"I know I should have told you then, but Friar Josef forbid me to return to Luxley."

"Oh, my dear sweet child." He squeezed her hands. "If I could only have known you were alive." His voice emerged in a wail, yet no tears formed in his eyes. "The hours of agony it would have spared me. And your poor sister!"

"She knows. At least she has ever since I began to sing for her."

He drew her hands to his mouth for a kiss. "All this time you were right here at Luxley, and I didn't recognize you. How could I have been so blind?" His dark eyes searched hers.

She smiled. "I've changed much over the years."

"You have become a comely woman." The prurient tone of his voice reminded her of the way he'd looked at her earlier. Not in the way a married man advanced in age should look at a young maiden. Surely she'd mistook him, for he seemed genuinely happy to find her alive.

"I have much to tell you, Sir LeGode, but the matter of my sister is most urgent. Her welfare, her very life, is why I have revealed myself to you." She rose. "Someone wishes her dead. Mayhap the same villain who wished me murdered. Though I cannot know why. Which is why I must beg for your aid. While I remain hidden as a servant girl, I have need of someone in authority who can help me find the culprit. You are the only one I trust."

Sir LeGode stood, his mouth twisting, eyes shifting. "I am honored, my lady."

"You were a dear friend to my mother and father, and you have assumed the managing of Luxley whilst my sister has been ill. I know full well the sacrifice you have made on my family's behalf, and I intend to compensate you fully."

"Think no more of it." He waved her away, the sleeves of his silk cote flapping. "I do my best to love others more than myself. Is that not one of our Lord's commands?"

His statement put Alexia at ease, and she smiled. "Indeed."

"Forsooth, poison?" He circled his desk with a huff. "I can hardly credit such news. The physician informs me that your sister has a tender digestion and is merely weak of disposition. Hence, all she requires is bed rest and extra care."

"You have been misled, Sir. I drank some of her healing potion and became very ill. Aye, 'tis poison to be sure." She approached his desk. "Pray, say you will help me find the villain. Once he is brought to justice, I can take my place as lady of the manor alongside my sister. And you can finally return to your own estate. I am sure it has suffered neglect all these years."

"Nay, my son manages it quite well," he replied, gazing down at the parchments on his desk with a grimace. "Very well, my dear, I will assist you. We shall uproot this brigand together. Never you fear." Yet his tone lacked conviction. No doubt he was still stunned by her resurrection.

"If you would allow my identity to remain a secret for now, I shall better be able to move about unnoticed."

"Of course. As you wish." He leaned both hands on his desk and finally met her gaze. "God's truth, 'tis so good to have you back. And alive! 'Twas too much to hope for."

Then why did his smile never reach his eyes—eyes that remained dark and empty. Odd. Closing her own eyes for a moment, she sought the Spirit's guidance. Surely light would blossom from within this kind, Godly man, and angels would appear by his side.

Instead, she saw nothing but a dark void.

She shook it off, berating herself for once again being too overcome with emotion to see clearly.

Still, a heaviness fell on her as he led her to the door—a weight that hooked her soul and tugged it down like an anchor tossed overboard.

"Now, my lady, I insist you go tend your sister. I have no doubt, your very presence will sooth her. Meanwhile, I will begin our quest by speaking to the physician—discreetly, of course." He winked.

"I knew I could count on you, Sir LeGode, as my parents did before me."

Then why did a blast of cold air envelop her as she left the room?

Chapter 17

" *How* could Alexia D'Clere be alive and serving in this castle without my knowledge?" LeGode raged across the cold stones of Drogo's lair. "And how could you not know this as well? I thought you knew all that happened here at Luxley."

Drogo's lifeless eyes followed LeGode like an insolent hawk.

"You told me she was dead! Devoured by your wolves," LeGode continued, unable to stifle his fury. He should have killed her in his study. A quick snap of her pretty little neck and she'd no longer be a problem. He ground his teeth. Weak fool! He could not bring himself to do it. Not yet anyway. He must think…think. The lady must meet her demise in a way where no blame could ever be cast his way.

Drogo remained in place, gray hair stringing about a face devoid of emotion. And LeGode knew he must curb his temper and tread carefully, or this emissary of satan would turn him into a toad. Or worse.

"She is protected by the light," the warlock finally spat out. "Even now, I sense her in the castle, but I do not see who or where she is. Nor can I read her purpose here."

"Then why did you tell me she was dead?"

He shrugged. "My wolves returned gorged with blood. How was I to know 'twas not hers."

"And you, the all-powerful one," LeGode seethed.

Drogo hissed and a mist burst from his mouth. "There is but One whom I cannot overcome. And He protects her."

"Can you not put out this light of His?"

"He *is* the light." The warlock's tone sliced.

"So you cannot kill her, and you cannot curse her or make her ill?"

Drogo shook his head.

Groaning, LeGode stared at the floor. A spider crawled from beneath a chest and scrambled across the stones. Above, a bat screeched in its sleep, and a glorious idea took root in his mind. Smiling, he raised his gaze to the warlock. "Then give me something that would prove she is a witch."

Drogo studied him for a moment, then moved to a wooden chest perched in a corner. Lifting the lid, he withdrew several objects and placed them in LeGode's hands—an amulet, candle, potion, a clay figure, and an incantation scrawled across paper. "This will convince them."

LeGode dropped the items in a pouch. "Good. You better hope this works. The woman must die, or our bargain is off and you will never have my son."

⚬⟡⟣

Ronar entered the main hall of Luxley castle, happy to be summoned away from the tedium of wandering about the village. Jarin and Damien, equally pleased, strode on either side of him, while ten castle knights followed in their wake.

The bishop sat on the great chair, his robes flung about him, his lackey at his side, and a jeweled staff in hand as if he were God Himself at the final judgment. Sir LeGode stood before a small table, looking like a fox about to devour its prey.

Halting, Ronar and his men bowed before the bishop. "Your grace."

"Go to Lady D'Clere's chamber and arrest the red-haired maiden who sings for her."

Ronar's throat closed. It took a moment ere he could ask as nonchalantly as possible, "On what charge?"

"Witchcraft!" LeGode pointed a crooked finger at a candle, parchment, a vial and other items scattered over the table. "I discovered these crafts of the devil in her possession. She has been casting spells on Lady D'Clere!"

The bishop crossed himself and began to pray in Latin.

Ronar huffed, drawing LeGode's suspicious gaze.

"What do you know of her, Knight?"

"I have no knowledge of any witch, Sir."

His narrow eyes seared. "Alack, the proof is before you."

Ronar scanned the items. He'd never seen such things on Lady Falcon's person, nor in her home with the friar. Yet...did she not read the Holy Scriptures in defiance of Church law? Alas, he'd allow that she was a heretic, but what devil worshiper reads the words of God?

His insides clenched. *Foolish lady! Why return here?*

Jarin cast a frown his way.

"Witches are known to have supernatural power," the bishop added. "Hence, bring these knights with you. Once you have her in hand, bring her to me. I will question her and determine if she is a witch. If so, she will be burned at the stake immediately."

✺

"My lady." Anabelle rushed into Cristiana's chamber, her chest heaving and her face a portrait of terror. "You must leave immediately."

"Whatever is wrong, Anabelle?" Alexia rose from her sister's bed where she'd been holding her hand and telling her all would be well, though her sister remained unconscious.

"He is saying you are a witch. He intends to have you arrested for casting a spell on your sister."

Confusion spun Alexia's thoughts. "Pray, who would spew such nonsense?"

"Sir LeGode." Anabelle glanced out the door.

"LeGode? Nay...he wouldn't—"

Anabelle shut the door. "You must go! Even now, he could be summoning the guard."

"I don't believe it. I will speak with him." Alexia started to leave.

"Nay." Anabelle gripped her arms and led her away as Seraphina rose from her chair by the window.

"You told him?" the companion asked, alarm ringing in her tone.

"Aye. And he promised to help discover who is poisoning Cristiana."

Seraphina gasped. "What if 'tis him?"

Alexia could only stare at her, terror threatening to obliterate her peace. She glanced at her sister, her brow dotted with fever, her breath coming far too fast.

"Nay. He loves my sister and me as if we were his own."

Seraphina approached. "My lady, you know I've had my suspicions."

"As I have," Anabelle added. "Whate'er you believe about LeGode, you must believe the bishop intends to see you arrested. Prithee, leave ere 'tis too late!"

The sound of men's boots thundered up the stairs.

"Now, my lady!" Anabelle pressed the latch on the side of the mantle and the scrape of wood on stone filled the room

Alexia dashed to kiss her sister on the cheek. "Take care of her, Seraphina." The lady nodded and squeezed Alexia's hand as she dove into the tunnel and the door scraped shut with a thunderous crunch.

Darkness pressed in on her, confusion followed. Sir LeGode...poisoning her sister?

She couldn't think of it now, nor deal with the pain etching across her heart—nor what a fool she'd been to tell him all.

Nay, at the moment, she must escape the castle or all would be lost.

Ronar didn't know whether to feel relieved, angry, or ashamed. Mayhap all three.

"Imbeciles!" Sir LeGode raged across the great hall, his furious bellow echoing off the tall ceiling. "You lost her!"

Jarin crossed arms over his chest. "We can hardly lose someone who wasn't there in the first place."

Sir LeGode let out a string of curses that raised the bishop's brows. "If you please, Sir!" He slammed his staff on the ground. "Control your tongue."

"Forgive me, Excellency."

Ronar shifted his gaze, guilt winning over a brew of other emotions. No doubt the lady had escaped through the secret tunnel. He should say something. And fast. They could catch her before she crossed the courtyard. Yet…still…he hesitated.

As he had done in Lady D'Clere's chamber when the companion's silent plea screaming at him from her eyes had held his tongue.

"I know what to do." Sir LeGode stormed into his study beyond the hall, muttering to himself.

Tush! Ronar stared after him. What was it about this Falcon that made him defy orders, made him sin against God and king? He could put an end to it right now. Elevate rather than diminish his position in the Kingdom of God. What was she to him anyway? What if she really was a witch? 'Twould explain the way she had bewitched him into doing her will and keeping her secrets.

Nay, a witch would not drink her own poison. A witch would not feed a hungry village nor tend the wound of a fallen knight.

The bishop released a sigh and stared at the jeweled ring on his finger as if disappointed there would be no one burned at the stake today.

Ronar wished he would release him and his men back to the village. Every moment he remained was another moment he kept silent when he should tell all—another moment for his guilt to grow and, thus, his debt owed to God to mount.

LeGode returned with a cloak in hand and gave it to Sir DeGay. "This has her scent. Give your hounds a good whiff and then go find this witch!"

Unwelcome fear gnawed at Ronar's gut. Lady Falcon was swift and stealth, but she could only be moments ahead of them. "Why not let her go? Witch or not, surely she will not dare set a foot inside Luxley again."

"She poisons Lady D'Clere!" LeGode howled. "Forsooth, she will return to finish the task, I assure you."

Jarin gasped and then suppressed it with a cough.

"Why would a witch want to poison Lady D'Clere?" Ronar made bold to ask LeGode.

The steward grunted like a pig. "That *witch* is Alexia D'Clere, the lady's sister. And her purpose is to inherit the estate herself."

Several servants stopped to stare. Ronar forced a placid expression though his insides churned. Lies, lies, lies! Had the woman ever spoken a word of truth? No peasant was she, but the lady of the castle. Biting his tongue ere he spill all, Ronar shifted his boots, hoping the bishop would release them.

"I thought she was long since dead," Damien offered.

"So did I." LeGode snapped. "Apparently she's been hiding whilst plotting her sister's demise."

When she was entitled to half? Ronar made no sense of it. Was she really so vile as to murder her own sister to gain the entire estate? If so, why not just stab her in her bed and be done with it? Nay. That she had lied to him, he could not deny. Many times. But this...a murderer and a witch? Was he so bad a judge of character to be fooled by one so evil? His thoughts drifted to Idonea and Brom.

You've always been a gullible fool, his brother had mocked him.

Scattering the memories, Ronar faced LeGode. "We will find her," he said. Though he meant *he* would find her and discover the truth. If she was even capable of telling it.

"Nay." The bishop said with a yawn. "She is none of our affair. We are here for the Spear. Though mark my words, Sir LeGode, the king will hear of the devilish discord at Luxley manor."

Out in the courtyard, Ronar watched the knights mount their steeds as the squires held back hounds that already had caught Lady Falcon's scent and were barking and straining on their leashes.

Jarin stormed toward him. "If this witch is indeed poisoning Lady D'Clere, I say we find her and bring her to justice. The poor lady." He glanced up the tower to her window. "Thank God this sorcery was discovered in time. Her own sister." He shook his head. "What ails you Ronar?"

"I have something I must do." He started for the stables.

"Another secret mission?" Damien called out. "We will join you. I could use some excitement."

"Nay, 'tis a risk only I can take," he shouted over his shoulder. "Watch over Lady D'Clere. Whoever is poisoning her, 'tis no witch."

Chapter 18

*A*lexia made it past the village walls before she heard the hounds barking, the horse hooves pounding, and the knights shouting at the villagers to move aside. Potz! She'd forgotten about LeGode's dogs, the sound of their fast pursuit only confirming his betrayal. Her heart ached at the thought as she tore off her tunic, exposing the breeches she wore beneath, and pumped her legs as fast as she could across the open field, dark now in the thick of night. The splat of mud and huff of her hard breath rose to mingle with the howling behind her.

All this time 'twas LeGode!

Leaping over a boulder, she entered the forest and reached inside a hollowed-out tree for her bow. In one swift move, she tossed the quiver and bow onto her back and dove into the thicket.

LeGode was poisoning her sister. For what purpose?

She wove around a tree and took the path to her left. Thanks to a moonless night, she dove deeper into a darkness she prayed would hide her from her pursuers.

But not from the hounds whose barks grew ever louder.

LeGode was the one who had wanted her dead. She'd trusted him!

Her heart shriveled as she leapt over a fallen tree, unimpeded by the dark night. She knew this forest, every tree, path, boulder, and creek. Swiping aside a prickly thicket, she jumped onto a low hanging limb and grabbed the branch above her, then swung up onto the next branch and the next, higher and higher until she was well out of sight.

What a fool I am! The friar was right. She hadn't been ready. Her rampant emotions had stifled her powers of discernment.

The barking grew louder. The sound of horse hooves was soon replaced by boots and shouts of men.

Alexia laid a hand over her thigh where the Spear was hidden. "Father, protect me. 'Let all mine enemies be ashamed and sore vexed: let them return and be ashamed suddenly'," she quoted from Psalms. Then taking a deep breath, she leapt onto a limb of the next tree and thus, flew through the forest, aided by the stars above and the Spirit within.

Why would LeGode wish her and her sister dead? The question kept raging through her mind.

Minutes later, out of breath, she stopped, leaned against the large trunk of a maple tree, and glanced behind her. Flickering lights bounced up and down through the forest, appearing and disappearing through leaves and trees like malevolent fireflies. Hounds growled and snipped. They were close. *Too* close.

Heart in her throat, she closed her eyes. Shadows, black and empty crept along the forest floor, hovering over leaves and dirt, oozing over rocks and logs, slinking around trees, leading the men directly to her.

Father, help me. She touched the Spear and shook the vision away. "In the name of Christ, you shall not catch me."

Pushing against the trunk, she pulled an arrow from her quiver and nocked it in her bow. Mayhap, she couldn't outrun the dogs, but she could injure the knights. And the fools were making perfect targets of themselves with their bright torches.

At least ten hounds burst through the brush and halted beneath her tree. Whining like demons deprived of their meal, they sniffed the ground then leapt onto the trunk, clawing the bark and growling as if they hadn't eaten in weeks.

And she was their last supper.

Alexia pulled back the string, waiting…waiting…eyeing the bobbing torches.

A knight crashed through the leaves, then another and another.

She closed her eyes and released her bow.

A guttural moan echoed through the darkness. One knight went down.

"Douse the torches!" another ordered, and within seconds the lights disappeared and smoke curled into the night. A dozen footsteps pounded toward her as the dogs continued to howl and jump on top of each other in an effort to be the first to dig their fangs into her tender skin.

Alexia blinked, nocked another arrow, and closed her eyes.

Nothing. *She saw nothing!*

But she heard something—the sound of someone climbing up the tree.

Returning her bow to her quiver, she grabbed hold of a branch above her and hoisted herself up and up, seeking a sturdy enough limb from which to leap to the next tree.

The knight was a good climber, much faster than she would have thought. His grunts and groans filled the air, along with the creak of wood beneath his weight. Terror threatened to undo her.

Forcing it down, she swung up onto another bough. Then holding her arms out for balance, she plunged through a web of leaves, praying the branch was sturdy enough to hold her.

The man's breath filled the air behind her.

"Come hither, witch. Unless ye can fly," he said with a snicker.

She suddenly wished she could, for the next tree was nigh two yards away and the limb beneath her feet grew more thin and wobbly with each step.

The dogs growled and yipped.

"She's to your right, Gerald!" one knight yelled up to his friend.

The branch trembled beneath the weight of the man.

Alexia had no choice. Whispering a quick prayer, she dashed across the limb and leapt in the air for the next tree.

Arms and legs flailing through the darkness, she reached for a hold, *any* hold. But found none. Her fall was broken by a lower branch that sliced through her bodice. She groped to hold on, but her grip loosened, and she tumbled down again and struck another bough...and another...ere she landed hard on the ground.

She jumped to her feet to run, but pain throbbed in her ankle. Her legs buckled beneath her.

A pack of dogs leapt on her as if she were a slab of meat. Teeth dug into her arm. She screamed. Hot breath and saliva sprayed her. Dark masses slithered around her. The dogs' faces, fangs extended and dripping were suddenly yanked back as the knights pulled them from her.

One of them jerked her to her feet. Pain burned in her arm. A thousand blades stabbed her ankle, and she nearly fell.

"Let's get the witch back to the bishop." She recognized Sir DeGay's voice, though she couldn't make out their faces in the darkness. The dogs continued to bark, angry at being restrained from their meal.

The sound of metal rasping against leather met her ears. A groan. A thud.

Uneasiness drifted over the knights.

"Tucker?"

No reply.

Shuffling ensued, a grunt, and a splat.

Sir DeGay shoved Alexia toward another knight and ordered him to watch her as he drew his sword. His men followed suit, separating from each other and peering into the darkness.

Should Alexia dare hope God had sent a rescuer? The knight shoved her against a tree and leveled his blade at her chest. Unable to bear weight on her ankle, she sank to the dirt.

Metal rang against metal and mayhem exploded before her. A shadow—nay, a man—wielding a sword fought two knights. *Clang!* He met one of their blades high, then shifted to his left and swung in low to slice through the man's leg. Screaming, the knight fell. The other knight charged him as his friends, blades drawn, did the same. Six knights against one man. Impossible odds. Blood dripped down Alexia's arm, along with her hope.

Instead of running, her rescuer flung his sword through the air as if it were a whip, striking one man after the other—swooping down on one blade here, slicing an arm there. His movements were lithe and swift. He was there one minute, vanished the next, only to reappear somewhere else. She'd never seen the likes of it.

Another scream wrenched the air. One more knight down. The stranger appeared out of the foliage to her right and knocked another man over the head with his sword hilt. Sir DeGay toppled to the ground.

Three knights swung about, growling and sneering like the dogs still straining at their leashes.

The man met the first knight's blade then thrust low in a counter-parry. She had a good view of him now. Dressed in simple leather breeches, boots, and vest, he wore a black kerchief around his head with two holes for eyes.

The hiss of steel filled the air as he swiped metal on metal then swung to the right and met the next knight's attack. He fought with such skill and speed, it seemed surreal, and she wondered if he were a warrior angel sent from God to protect her.

He thrust his blade forward, striking one man in the thigh. The three men holding the hounds tied them to a tree and entered the fray.

"Behind you!" Alexia shouted. The man guarding her slapped her across the cheek. Blinking through the sting, she watched as her rescuer spun just in time before the first knight ran him through. Caught off balance, he attempted to jump to the side, but another knight sliced through his arm. Growling, the rescuer shoved the man back with his blade then slugged him across the jaw. He toppled backward, struck his head on the tree, and slumped down to the dirt.

The dogs continued barking.

Another knight joined them and three knights circled the stranger, blades leveled.

Alexia could hardly breathe. The man guarding her shifted nervously from foot to foot. If she could but grab his blade...

The knights attacked with ferocity. Her rescuer skillfully fended off each blow, but they drove him backward. One of them managed another slice to his chest. He kicked him backward, but the knight quickly resumed his attack.

Another man in a mask marched into the clearing as if he owned the forest and took on two of the knights, quickly dispatching them both.

The man guarding Alexia lowered his blade. Fisting her hands together, she leapt toward him and knocked it from his hand. Momentarily stunned, he went to retrieve it, but she kicked him in the groin. He doubled over. She grabbed the sword and held it to his chest. Someone chuckled behind her, and the fallen knight glanced in that direction, cursed, then scrambled to his feet and dove into the thicket.

Spinning around, Alexia found her rescuers—two of them now—engaging the remaining knights with both sword and knife. Hoping for a quick escape—or at the least a slow, hobbled one, she dropped the heavy sword and shrank into the shadows. But the two strangers made quick work of their enemies, sheathed their blades, and headed her way. Without a simple by your leave, the first one grabbed her, flung her over his shoulder, and marched into the forest, leaving behind a pile of moaning knights and growling dogs.

"Took you long enough," the man holding her said to his friend, who walked beside him, her bow and quiver in his hands.

She'd know that voice anywhere. "LePeine, you beast!" She pounded his back

"You seemed to have things in hand," the second man replied, humor in his tone. "Besides 'twas fun to watch."

The moss and needles of the forest floor transformed to grass, embroidered in silver from the starlit sky above.

Horse hooves thumped and Sir LePeine lowered her slowly down to the ground. Their bodies slid against each other so intimately, she couldn't help but feel the gorged muscles beneath his doublet still twitching from battle. Heat swamped her as an odd ache formed in her belly. She tried to step away, but pain shot up her leg and she stumbled.

"Easy there." He grabbed her waist and held her close, then tore off his kerchief and shook out his hair. Rescuer two did the same, and as she suspected 'twas Sir LePeine's larger friend, Damien LaRage. Sounds drew her gaze up to Jarin the Just, who led three horses toward them across the clearing. The men no longer wore the knightly garb of the King's Guard, nor boasted the Royal Crest on their shoulders.

She drew a deep breath, head swimming. "Bravo, gentlemen, you have saved me from LeGode's knights. Now, if you don't mind, I shall be on my way."

Dismounting, Jarin handed the reins of one of the horses to LePeine. "Not very grateful is she?"

"I have never found her so," came Sir LePeine's reply.

"What do you intend to do with her?"

Damien snorted. "I say we take her back to the bishop."

Alexia gave a lady-like growl.

"She's no witch," Ronar glanced her way. "She's Lady Alexia D'Clere." He gave a bow, and though she could not make out his expression, she sensed mockery in his tone.

She struggled against his grip, but to no avail. "All the more reason to release me. I am lady of the manor and should not be treated like a common wench."

Jarin chuckled. "Ah ha! This lady is your Falcon, is she not?" He circled her and whistled. "I would never have thought so, but I find myself of the sudden opinion that all women should wear such tight breeches."

Alexia grimaced. "Reserve your sordid gaze, Sir Jarin, for your strumpets."

Damien rubbed his chin and snickered. "This little sprite is your fearless Falcon, Ronar? The one causing you so much trouble?"

"I am no one's Falcon. I am—" She intended to reiterate her station to these buffoons, but Ronar picked her up by the waist and placed her atop his horse as if she weighed no more than a sack of corn.

"What are you doing?" She swung her legs on the other side, intending to slide off when he leapt behind her and wrapped arms of iron around her waist.

"We must not delay. LeGode's knights may awaken and come after us."

Damien mounted his steed. "Enough of this troublesome woman, Ronar. Falcon, witch, or lady, 'tis none of our affair. Keeping her from LeGode will not bode well for our mission."

"Our mission is to find the Spear, and she may know of its whereabouts. Besides, we each took a vow to protect helpless ladies in distress," Ronar said.

"There you have it, Sir Knights. I have never been helpless, and I am most definitely not in distress. Ergo, you may release me at once!" Alexia attempted to pry Ronar's arms off her.

"She has a point, I'll grant you," Jarin said. "This helpless maiden *did* nearly kill us a sennight ago."

Ronar tightened his grip. "Would you have me turn her over to those who would see her burned at the stake? Besides, there is something evil at Luxley, and I believe LeGode is in the center of it."

"Where will you go?" Jarin asked.

"Rivenhall."

"We will join you."

Ronar's horse snorted and pawed the ground. "Nay, 'twill draw too much suspicion. Return to Luxley. Tell the bishop I am on the king's errand and will return in a few days. In the meantime, I will discover this forest sprite's secrets. If she has the Spear, I will return with it anon."

Alexia tried a new tactic and shoved her body backward against Ronar, attempting to hit his head with hers. Her back struck steel, her head a rock, and pain thundered through her already battered body. "I have no secrets and I'm not going anywhere with you!"

Jarin mounted his horse and stretched out his arm. Ronar gripped it. "Watch over Lady Cristiana. Whoever is poisoning her is still at the castle."

"'Tis Sir LeGode!" Alexia hissed. "And she is *my* sister. I will protect her!"

"Impossible to do, my lady, whilst burning at the stake."

"I will guard her with my life," Jarin said.

"Stay away from her, you frothy varlet, you..." Alexia shouted, but the wind stole her voice as Ronar galloped away.

Chapter 19

*T*he more the lady struggled in front of him, the more Ronar enjoyed himself, and the more he'd have to repent of that enjoyment later.

"Hush, be still, my lady," he whispered in her ear. "You are safe, now."

She elbowed him in the gut. "I need not your protection, Knight. Release me at once!" Her voice was lost to the wind as they galloped across an open field with naught but stars to light their way.

Those stars soon disappeared behind thick, heavy clouds. Thunder rumbled in the distance, and Ronar slowed Penance to a canter. Still the lady struggled. He tightened his grip around her waist. He would not lose this forest minx again. She might be the most skilled archer he'd seen, a benevolent caretaker of the poor, and quite good at hiding her many identities, but she was a fool when it came to her own safety.

And he would not see her burn.

In truth, if he admitted it, he would not see her harmed at all.

He'd caught up with LeGode's knights just as they were pulling the hounds off her. Would that he'd been there a second earlier, for the sight of her bloody arm sent him into a rage. He surprised himself at the anguish he'd felt, the fear for this lady who had done naught but lie to him. Yet, at that moment, he would have gladly taken on the king's army by himself...

If only to save her.

Tush, what a fool he was! Even now, taking her to Rivenhall, a place he'd vowed never to return to again—a place and a time he longed to release to the graveyard of forgotten memories. Yet 'twas precisely because of those forgotten memories he took her there, for no one knew of the place, save his closest friends.

A drizzle began, cooling his face with moisture. He drew in a breath of air filled with the scent of loamy earth, horse, the spice of rain…

And woman. Ah, the sweet scent of a woman. And this one in particular—all rich moss and pine.

The lady settled in front of him, but he would not be fooled. She was wise, this one. No doubt she waited for his defenses to lower, for his grip to loosen so she could fly away like a falcon. Though how far she thought she could get on her wounded foot puzzled him.

"Why have you stolen me?" She broke the silence with her sharp tone.

Ronar tapped the reins, turning onto the King's Highway. Though the road was well traveled, there would be few out on this stormy night, and it was the quickest way to Rivenhall. "Because you appear to have no concern for your safety," he finally said.

"My safety, Sir, is none of your concern." She hesitated. "Though I thank you for your help. However, I had no need of it and had things well in hand."

He chuckled. "If I had not intervened, your flesh would either be shredded by LeGode's hounds or sizzling atop a roaring fire."

At this, a shiver ran through her, and he realized the lady *did* have a smidgen of natural fear. Or was it the sudden cold wind that blasted over them? She turned her head slightly, her cheek brushing his chin. Her hair whipped in his face, and the scent of honey and herbs tantalized his nose. "I wish to return to the friar," she spoke so sweetly, he thought he'd captured the wrong lady. "You have fulfilled your knightly vow to protect the fair maiden. What need have you of me now?"

The rain came harder, tapping a cadence in the mud and on the leaves of trees and shrubs lining the road.

Ronar didn't answer. Mainly because he couldn't answer her with anything that made sense. He told himself and his friends 'twas the Spear he sought. But when this lady was present, his mind was not on the Spear at all. Though this vixen had done naught but distract him from his mission and send his life into a hellish spiral, he longed to know more of her, found himself enchanted by everything she said and did.

Rain splattered atop his head, and he realized he'd forgotten his hat. Thunder quivered the puddles forming on the ground. The lady trembled, and Ronar drew the reins and halted Penance. Keeping one arm around her waist, he opened his pouch attached to the saddle, withdrew a cloak, then flung it around her shoulders.

He thought she'd resist, but instead she tugged it around her neck and thanked him.

'Twas something at least.

Smiling, he nudged Penance forward again, listening to his hooves slapping the mud. So dark the night, he could barely make out the grassy hills surrounding them, nor the thick forest he knew they soon would reach. Rain slid down his forehead. At least the trees would give them some respite from the storm.

Pain burned his right arm where a blade had penetrated, and he eased his grip on the lady, knowing she, too, was injured.

Leaning, he whispered in her ear, "Are you indeed Lady of Luxley manor?"

"Along with my sister, aye."

They entered a copse of pine and maple, and the droplets transformed into a mist. "What need of such deception?"

Moments passed ere she answered. "Years ago, after my parents were dead and I was but nine, the friar discovered a plot against my life and stole me away. My mother and he were good friends, and she had charged him with my care."

"And he never discovered 'twas LeGode?"

"Nay. And he forbade me to ever return." The sorrow in her tone convinced him she told the truth. For once. "When I learned of my sister's illness, I begged him to allow me to serve at Luxley where I could be close to her."

"And he conceded?"

"As long as I vowed to not tell a soul my true identity. He sensed a danger still present."

"Seems the old friar was right. How did LeGode discover your identity?"

"I told him."

Ronar groaned. "For what purpose?"

"I thought he could help," she shot back, but then her tone filled with pain. "I trusted him. He is...*was* a close friend to my mother and father."

"And now he accuses you of being a witch."

"I've been such a fool." She turned suddenly, and he felt her breath on his chin. "You don't believe him, do you?"

"You are many things, Lady Falcon, but a witch? Nay." Releasing her, he raked his wet hair back. "Alack, no one is as they seem," he added sadly. Especially this lady who now leaned back against his chest as if resigned to her fate. A titled lady, nonetheless, flitting about the forest with bow and arrow. *Amazing!* "Lady of the manor, Falcon of Emerald Forest, hunter for the village, and maid in Luxley castle." He pulled back the collar of her cloak and pretended to peek inside. "Any other people hidden in there you wish to disclose?"

She tugged it back, but said naught as raindrops tapped laughter on the canopy above. Laughing at him, no doubt, for believing anything this lady said.

"Where are you taking me?" She sat up straight, sending a wall of chilled air between them.

"Someplace safe where you won't be found." Where Ronar could determine his next move and more importantly discover what was truly going on at Luxley.

"I will be safer with the friar."

"If Sir LeGode has wanted you dead for these many years, do you think he will allow anything to stop him now that he knows you are alive?"

"It matters not. I cannot leave my sister. She's in grave danger."

"Jarin will watch over her."

"Not like I can. He does not have access to her as I do, nor does he care for her welfare. Please, let me go!" She began squirming again and attempted to pry his arm from her waist. But 'twas the appeal in her voice that almost made him turn Penance about and grant her wish. Almost. But he would not allow her to bewitch him again.

They exited the wooded area to a blast of wind and sting of rain. She ceased struggling and shifted to look at him. What he wouldn't give to see those eyes of hers, such an exquisite shade of green and so sharp and yet soft all at once. "I don't understand you, Knight. I do not want your protection. I have no more secrets for you to discover. Why, when I've lied to you, deceived you, and even poisoned you, do you wish to save me?"

He chuckled and wiped wet hair from her face. "Ah, yes, how could I forget the tea?"

Lights flashed up ahead. The Crooked Billet Inn. Good. Just another hour of riding and they'd be at Rivenhall. He urged Penance into a gallop in order to speed past the tavern lest the lady decide to draw unwanted attention.

She did. In the form of a scream so loud it would wake a man who'd been in his cups for a week. He shoved his palm atop her mouth and sped past the two-story inn. Horses neighed from the stables, and a lad peeked out from the window. But no one followed.

He leaned in to say, "Your efforts are fut—" when a sharp pain stabbed his hand.

Alexia was cold, wet, her arm hurt, her back ached, and her ankle throbbed. And now she tasted blood—the knight's blood, salty and metallic. Releasing her teeth's grip on his hand, she glanced over her shoulder. The lights of the inn flickered and disappeared. No shouts, nor neigh of horse, or any commotion at all, save the tapping of rain. Potz!

Ronar shook out his hand. A growl rumbled from his throat to match the thunder overhead—a growl of fury that set her ill at ease. She'd seen this man fight, felt his strength even now in the arm across her waist and his rock-hard chest. He could break her in two with one move. Was it wise to anger him so?

"Did you consider, my lady," he ground out, his mouth so close to her face that his breath burned her cheek. "That the devil you know is far better than the devil you don't?"

"If you refer to yourself, I quite agree. As to the rest, it depends on what you wish to do with me." Since Ronar—when had she begun to think of him by his Christian name?—had already questioned her about the Spear and searched for it among her things, she could think of no other reason why he would take her against her will. Save one. The friar had attempted—in a rather blundering way, she might add—to explain the ways of men and women. She smiled even now as she remembered him so tongue-tied and red of face. Finally, he asked one of the village women to step in.

Hence, Alexia was not some naive maiden, ignorant of the desires of men.

He shifted uncomfortably in the saddle. "I have no ill intentions toward you, Lady Falcon. Rest assured. I am an honorable man who abides by God's laws."

"The Church's laws, you mean, and I've seen how some twist those to serve their own purpose."

Still, from what she'd seen thus far, this knight possessed an integrity not found in most men. He'd protected her, kept her secrets, and now had saved her life.

Aye, she'd admit to that much. She'd also admit to experiencing real terror for the first time when LeGode's knights and hounds had surrounded her. Her mind had shifted through a plethora of scenarios for the best escape—there had always been an escape—but she'd found none. In the treetops, armed with bow and arrow, she could easily defeat ten…twenty knights, but not on the ground, unable to even walk.

God had answered her prayer. The Spear had saved her by sending Ronar and his men to her aid. Yet what confused her now was why God allowed this beast of a man to steal her away. Every gallop into the darkness took her farther away from her sister, farther away from protecting her from Sir LeGode.

They emerged from the trees to pellets of rain that pasted her hair to her skin and slid into her eyes. Wiping away the moisture, she drew the knight's cloak tighter about her neck. His scent rose from the fabric and filled her nose. Not an unpleasant scent, but one that was distinctly his—all leather and steel and musk.

A brisk wind made her tremble and brought him close to whisper in that soothing, deep tone of his, "We are almost there, my lady." His breath on her neck sent a chill down her that had naught to do with the cold.

And very much against her will, her anger toward him subsided, replaced by an odd comfort in his presence. Much needed after her harrowing night and the shock of LeGode's betrayal.

Nay! She chastised herself. She must not be taken in by this man's charms. At the first opportunity, she would escape and make her way back to her sister.

Ronar said not another word, and soon they came upon a massive iron gate framed by stone walls with a blazon overhead she could not make out in the darkness. After dismounting and opening the gate, which screeched in complaint, he gained the horse again with one leap and urged them down a long winding path lined with ancient trees that seemed to reach for her with crooked claws.

Thunder roared, distant and muffled, and the rain lessened to a drizzle. Alexia wiped water from her lashes as they rounded a corner and descended a hill to a scene that must be beautiful during the day, but in the dark appeared as black mounds of land with a walled-in manor perched in the distance.

She could feel Ronar tense behind her as they moved toward the structure. The sound of sheep baaing and cows lowing joined the patter of rain sliding from leaves onto the wet ground. A cloud moved ever so slightly, allowing a sprinkling of starlight to penetrate the storm. It landed on a castle atop a hill beyond the house—a large, imposing structure, gray and black, all sinister sharpness and deep gloom. Then it was gone, swallowed by the night once again. An odd sense of sorrow came over Alexia, though she couldn't say why.

Ronar led his charger through yet another gate into a courtyard before the manor and dismounted. Before she could attempt to slide off the horse, he reached up, took her in his arms, and carried her to the front door, which opened to reveal an older man wearing a night tunic, a candle in his hand, and a look of utter shock on his face.

"Lord Rivenhall! I did not expect you."

Lord Rivenhall? Alexia pushed against Ronar's sodden doublet. "Let me down. I'm no invalid."

"No need to fret, Bridon," Ronar replied as he carried her through the dark house, down a hall, and into a room cloaked in shadows. "I did not expect me either. Light a fire and wake Cook. We'd like some mulled wine. Oh, and have James attend Penance."

"Aye, my lord." The man's shadow scurried about the room, tearing white sheets from furniture. "Pardon my attire, my lord. I hadn't time to dress properly."

Ronar set her down on a cushioned chair. She immediately rose in defiance, but pain speared up her leg until she feared she would cry out. Huffing, she sank back into the chair. Why did the servant address Ronar as "my lord"?

Flint struck steel and a spark lit up the old man's face for but a second. Then another and another and soon a tiny flame glimmered from the fireplace. Kindling and wood were added and the flame grew, crackling and spitting as if angry at being awakened so abruptly. Light revealed a large room filled with cushioned chairs, tables, a desk, and shelves of books.

A coat of arms hung above the hearth depicting a shield bearing a red cross with a sword laid across it. It was framed by two dragons breathing fire, while on top perched two birds, a dove and, oddly, a falcon.

The old man rose from the fire and smiled at Ronar. "Good to see you again, my lord. I'll see about Cook."

"Thank you, Bridon. And bring some blankets, " he shouted after him.

Alexia could only sit and stare, her mind and heart overwhelmed with far too many surprises for one night.

Ronar, hair dripping, tore off his wet doublet and knelt before the fire, holding out his hands. Blood marred the front and sleeve of a white shirt that clung to his rounded muscles. Wounds he had received when saving her life.

"My lord?" She asked with sarcasm.

Rising, he dipped his head in her direction. "Allow me to introduce myself, Lady D'Clere. I am the Ronar Meschin, Earl of Rivenhall."

Chapter 20

"*You* are an earl," Alexia heard herself say, though she meant to keep the words cloistered in her thoughts—thoughts that refused to settle into reason. "With an estate of your own?" she added absently, unable to take her eyes off Ronar. Firelight shifted over the right side of his face, accentuating the scar slicing his eyebrow. He stared at her with those sharp blue eyes of his. The playful gleam within them faded as sorrow clouded them, and he turned, hands on his waist to stare at the flames.

"Do you find it so surprising?" he said.

She did. Yet...of a sudden, nay, not as she took in the regal way he stood, heard the authority in his voice, remembered the commanding way he moved and held himself—as a King's Guard, aye, but as a man also accustomed to giving orders. Why had she not seen it before?

Rain dripped from the tips of his hair onto his shirt. A few dark strands hung over his stubbled jaw, suddenly so stiff.

Stooping, he tossed a log onto the fire, and the heat finally reached her. "Why?" was all she could utter.

"Why do I present myself as a mere knight in the King's Guard?" He faced her with a sad grin. "A tale for another time."

The old man hurried back in, dressed in a presentable livery this time, his arms full of blankets. Ronar took one and flung it around Alexia. Despite the instant warmth, she could not stop trembling.

"Mulled wine will be ready anon, my lord."

"Thank you, Bridon. I will need vinegar, thread and needle, bandages, and Mistress Yonk's mint and yarrow rub."

"Aye, my lord."

Hefting one of the wooden chairs, Ronar placed it before the fire. "Come sit and warm yourself." He approached to help her, but Alexia held up a hand. "I am quite able."

But she wasn't able. Her ankle throbbed, and the slightest attempt to stand forced her back to her chair.

Sliding his arms beneath her, Ronar lifted her without effort and placed her on the chair. Flames crackled and instantly cocooned her in warmth. The shivering lessened, and she suddenly felt self-conscious in her wet attire with her sodden hair matted to her head and falling to her lap like seaweed. Especially before this man who was an earl—one of only twelve in all of England.

"Seems I am not the only one proficient at deceit," she said, drawing his gaze and a glimmer of a smile.

"You never asked if I was an earl."

"You never asked if I was Lady of Luxley Manor," she returned, garnering another smile, and hating herself for the warmth flooding her at the sight.

"Mayhap neither of us are what we seem." His glance lowered. "Take off your boots. I must check your foot."

"You will do no such thing!"

"Your foot could be broken, my lady. I can and I *will*. We need tend your arm as well." He gestured toward her ragged, bloody sleeve where the dogs had bitten. In all the excitement, she hardly felt the pain anymore.

"You are wounded as well, Sir Knight, and worse than I."

"I am accustomed to it. You are not."

She raised a brow. "Might I remind you, I am the Falcon of Emerald Forest and not some pampered lady of the manor. Unlike you, I was not raised in such luxury." She glanced around at the polished oak, silk-woven rug, and rich tapestries.

He smiled. "Ah, yes, the wild forest sprite who lays her head on a mossy nest amid squirrels and hares." He gave her a pointed gaze. "We shall still attend your wounds first, withal."

The old man entered, tray in hand. "Your wine, my lord." Steam rose from mugs, filling the room with the scent of pungent grapes and spices. Two jugs also sat upon the tray, along with strips of cloth, a needle, a small jar, and a plate of cakes that smelled of butter and cream.

Alexia's stomach rumbled.

Ronar stood. "Thank you, Bridon,"

"Very good, my lord. Will there be anything else?" His hooded gaze sped to Alexia. "One of the gowns in your—"

"Nay!" Ronar's tone sent the poor man back, brows raised, but then in a softer voice he added, "That will be all. You may retire, Bridon."

The man scurried off as Ronar knelt before Alexia and tugged on her boot. Only then did she notice her breeches were torn clear up to her thigh, exposing her stockinged leg.

Her nerves heightened. "Is there no lady to tend me?" She'd never allowed a man to see, let alone touch her leg. Well, save for the friar, of course.

"I keep no servants but Bridon, Cook, a scullery maid, and stable boy."

"Then why did Bridon mention a gown?"

He yanked on the boot. Agony sped up her leg and emerged in a shriek from her mouth.

"Apologies." He handled her stockinged foot with the tenderest of care, pressing gently and then turning it ever so slightly.

"'Tis sprained, not broken. With rest, it will heal in a fortnight."

"A fortnight?" She couldn't possible stay here that long.

"Now, let's see to your arm."

"My ankle you have seen, Sir, I mean *my lord*, but I will keep my shirt on, if you please."

"I do not please." He gave her a devilish grin, which quickly faded at what must have been fright in her eyes. "Never fear, you may retain your modesty, Lady Falcon." Before she could protest, he grabbed her sleeve and ripped it asunder, exposing two rows of bloody teeth marks. The sight soured her stomach, and she placed a hand over her wet bodice and attempted to breathe.

"'Tis not as bad as it looks." Grabbing one of the jugs, Ronar poured vinegar on a cloth, then knelt beside her once again. "This will hurt." He gazed up at her with eyes so blue and full of concern, she swallowed a burst of emotion.

She nodded her assent and in the process shocked herself by realizing she trusted this man, this King's Guard, this *earl* who had saved her more than once.

He hesitated, his eyes peering into hers as if seeking out her very soul. He smelled of wet leather and smoke, and she looked away, uncomfortable.

He touched the cloth to her wound. Pain radiated through her arm, and she bit her lip, not wanting to scream, not wanting to reveal her weakness. Pulling back, he gripped her hand and held it tight as he continued. His hand was warm, rough, callused and twice the size of hers, and his strength and care brought her more comfort than she dared admit.

Burning spasms rippled up her arm. She closed her eyes and sought the Spirit, praying for relief.

Ronar continued his ministrations for what seemed an eternity, tending her wound with a tenderness in sharp contrast to the brash, brave warrior she'd witnessed earlier that night. Yet each time he poured vinegar on her arm, it took all her strength to not cry out. But she wasn't some weak female who swooned at the sight of blood. She was the Protector of the Spear, a Warrior of God.

Finally, he placed a sweet-smelling salve upon her wounds and gently wrapped them with strips of cloth, tying them off at the ends. Before she knew it, he drew her hand to his mouth. She opened her eyes just as his lips touched her skin, igniting her in a vastly different way than the vinegar had done.

A strand of hair fell across his scar, and she resisted the urge to brush it away.

"All finished now. It should heal nicely," he said.

She tugged her hand back. "Thank you, Sir Kni... I mean, my lord. I cannot get used to your new title."

"Call me Ronar, then." Gathering the bloody clothes, he rose and set them on the table, then picked up mugs of mulled wine and handed her one. "I fear 'tis not too warm now."

He sipped his and sat on a stool before the fire, and she wondered at the sorrow she sensed in him since they'd arrived at this place. She wondered why he hid his title and why this vast estate sat in ruins.

"Now 'tis your turn." She gestured to his arm and chest.

He glanced down at his bloody sleeve. "It will heal."

"We both know 'twill need to be stitched."

"I will attend it later."

"I will attend it now." Setting down her mug, Alexia rose on her good foot and hobbled toward the table.

Ronar was at her side in an instant. "What are you doing?"

She turned and found him within inches of her, his eyes adoring her as if she were a king's ransom and not a criminal who had caused him naught but trouble. But that couldn't be. She looked away. "Getting the needle and twine your man brought."

"What do you know of such things?"

"I have stitched wounds before." Only once and it was a squirrel, but he had no need to know that. "Take off your shirt."

"Very well." He poured more wine into his mug and returned to the fire.

Heart racing at the thought of stitching human flesh, Alexia retrieved the needle, twine, cloth, and vinegar. When she turned around, she suddenly wished she hadn't ordered him to remove his garment. *Sweet gracious saints.* Waves of iron billowed over his stomach and continued over arms of rounded metal. A bloody slice marred an otherwise perfectly formed chest sprinkled with black hair. Rubbing his bearded chin, he gave her a grin that told her he knew exactly the effect he had on her and he was enjoying it immensely.

"Forsooth, is the Falcon of Emerald Forest blushing?" Ronar teased the lady as an unmistakable red hue crept up her neck and blossomed over her cheeks. Huffing, she averted her gaze from his chest and approached.

"You flatter yourself, my lord. 'Tis merely the heat from the fire." She busied herself threading the needle, then doused a cloth with vinegar. Her trembling hands, along with the harried rise and fall of her chest, made him suddenly question his safety.

"Mayhap I should have Bridon attend it on the morrow."

She cast him a wry glance ere forcing him to sit and kneeling before him to examine his arm.

Firelight turned her skin to shimmering gold and her hair to a waterfall of flaming red trickling down her back. Her scent of pine and wet earth and a hint of lavender stirred his senses as her nervous breath warmed his skin. And he suddenly had the urge to kiss her, especially as she licked her lips and parted them ever so slightly.

Tush, but the lady was alluring. And enchanting and intriguing. *And stubborn and infuriating.*

As if sensing his scrutiny, she lifted her gaze to his. Firelight brought out golden specks sparkling across her green eyes like nuggets on a field of moss. Their faces were but inches apart, and he could control himself no longer. His gaze dropped to her lips, and he advanced.

She slapped the vinegar-soaked cloth on his wound.

Pain speared through his arm and stabbed his shoulder.

"If you brought me here to make me your mistress, *my lord*, you shall find yourself sorely disappointed."

"If I had brought you here for that purpose," Ronar said through gritted teeth. "I would have done so already."

Pouring more vinegar on the cloth, she moved to clean the gash on his chest.

"Ouch! Gentler, if you please."

"A knight who is afraid of spiders and has no tolerance for pain?" She smirked. "And you thought *I* was weak. As it is, Sir, the only wound for which I have no tolerance is a libertine assault."

"Assault?" He feigned indignation.

"You were going to kiss me, were you not?"

"The thought occurred to me."

"Well, un-occur it at once. I am no serving wench to be taken advantage of."

He smiled.

"You find this amusing?"

"Only slightly." He teased her. "Very well." He sat up straight, chin out. "On my honor as a knight, I vow never to attempt a kiss again."

She flattened her lips and released a sigh.

"A truce? Ere you put a needle through my flesh."

"Very well." She frowned and returned her gaze to his wounds. "The one on your chest will not require stitches. But this one." She peered at his arm. "'Tis too deep." Drawing a breath, she pinched the wound with one hand and slid the needle through his skin with the other. The metallic smell of his own blood bit his nose, and he wondered at the strength of this lady who didn't hesitate to pierce raw flesh.

He kept his gaze on her, the determination in her eyes, the tight line of her lips, the way her lashes cast shadows on her cheeks—anything to avoid feeling the pain.

Within minutes she was done. Ronar dared a glance at his arm. Though the stitch was a bit jagged, it would do nicely. "Well done, Falcon."

She offered him a nervous smile as she dabbed salve on the wound, then wrapped his arm with a cloth. Sitting back, she took another sip of her wine. No doubt the ordeal had unnerved her more than she let on, for she took several more gulps, then rose to refill her mug.

Ronar stretched his arm, testing the wound as she returned to her seat and stared at the flames, her thoughts elsewhere. He longed to be privy to them, to understand this fascinating woman who stitched up wounds after nearly being eaten by hounds and captured by knights. When every other woman he'd known would have taken ill to their bed by now.

Setting down her cup, she squirmed uncomfortably and stared at him, one hand on the laces of her bodice. "Avert your eyes, Knight. I wish to remove this wet garb."

He did as she asked, though surely she could not expect him to obey entirely. Grabbing the jug, he faced the fire and drew it to his lips, peering from the corner of his eye as she removed her stiff bodice and laid it upon the hearth to dry. Beneath she wore a modest cream-colored tunic that would normally not have been revealing, but damp as it was, it molded to curves that made his blood warm.

He would have to keep his eyes elsewhere. Mayhap he should have Bridon show her to one of the chambers above. *And soon.* It had been years since he'd felt such desire for a lady. After the incident with Idonea, he'd nearly taken a vow of celibacy. Would have if not for the call of the Crusades.

But this lady, this wonderful lady, had the uncanny ability to make null and void every vow he'd ever taken.

"'Tis been quite a distressing night, Lady Falcon. You must be tired." Part of him hoped she'd take the hint and demand to be brought to a chamber. Part of him never wanted her to leave his side.

Drawing her knees to her chest, she crossed her arms over them. "Distressing? Is that what you call discovering that the man I trusted with my life, the man in charge of my estate, is poisoning my sister and wants to burn me at the stake?"

She paused and took a deep breath.

"Is that what you call being chased by my own knights, attacked by dogs, whisked away against my will, and kept from my sister, who is in grave danger? Is that what you call distressing?"

Her tone pricked his guilt, and he took a swig of wine, then handed her the jug. She drank deep and heavy, then set it down and leaned her head sideways on her knees to look at him. Bronze hair glittering red in the fire fell down to her feet in waves. Seconds passed as the flames crackled and the wind whistled against the stone walls. And for the briefest of moments, she let down her guard, and he saw naught but a frightened little girl who bore a weight too heavy for one so small and young.

"Why do you not think me a witch?" she asked.

He tossed a log onto the fire. "Because you are too enchanting to be anything but a child of God."

At this she smiled, and her gaze dropped to his bare chest, lingered for a moment, ere she snapped it back to the fire. "I am a warrior. A protector."

"And what is it you protect?" Ronar grabbed his shirt and tossed it over his head. Though he quite enjoyed her reaction to him, he did not wish to cause her discomfort.

She didn't answer. Instead she rubbed her temples and started to slip from her chair.

Dashing toward her, Ronar caught her fall and placed her on the floor, then plopped down beside her and drew her close.

"I'm so tired, Ronar. So very tired," she mumbled and leaned her head on his shoulder.

"I know." He brushed hair from her face. "Rest now, my little forest sprite, rest."

She was asleep within minutes, her deep breaths soothing Ronar's nerves. How long he sat there, relishing the feel of her as she snuggled against him, muttering in her sleep, he couldn't say. But finally, he realized he had better put distance between them.

Rising, he drew her in his arms and carried her out of the hall and up the stairs. With each tread he took, agony reclaimed portions of his heart—portions that had grown numb over the four years he'd been absent from his home.

He shouldn't have come back. He shouldn't be here at all.

Kicking open a door, he carried Lady Falcon inside. Though no moonlight drifted in through the window, he knew exactly where the bed was. Where it had always been. 'Twas his chamber, after all.

The one right beside his sister's.

He laid her on the bed, covered her with a quilt and left ere he changed his mind and laid down beside her as he longed to do.

❧

Sunlight stroked Alexia's eyelids, coaxing her from sleep. Somewhere in the distance, a bird warbled a happy tune that should have soothed her—if her head didn't feel like it was being plowed by oxen. She attempted to raise her hand to rub it, but the movement caught her arm on fire. Moaning, she forced one eye open.

The first thing Alexia noticed was that she was not in her home with the friar. Nor was she at Castle Luxley. Nor in Emerald Forest. Instead, as she took in the rich wooden chests, chairs made of polished wood, an array of weapons housed in a cabinet, and a rather imposing wardrobe from which spilled male garments, she realized she was in a man's bedchamber.

Ronar!

Memories of last night's events peeked out from hiding. The brutish knight had taken her to his estate. Terror flipped her heart, and she glanced down at her attire, afraid of what she would find. But beneath the quilt she found her breeches, tunic, and stockings still in place. Relieved, she tossed off the cover and swung her legs over the edge of the large four-poster bed. An ache spiraled up her back as nausea brewed in her stomach. Pain drew her gaze down to her right foot, swollen beneath her stockings. Potz! She would not be able to walk on it today.

Nor should she go anywhere with her breeches torn so high. She'd be discovered as a woman and add to her already mounting troubles. She felt for the Spear in the pocket of her chemise. Still there, thank God.

Bracing herself, she slid off the bed onto her good foot, then hopped to the window and peered out. A brisk wind entered, swirling about her with the scent of grass, horses, and sunshine. Two floors down, a wall of stone surrounded a courtyard open to the rising sun. A wooden gate led to farm land beyond. Nay, not farmland, but rolling hills of green, dotted with wildflowers and sheep. Below in the courtyard, a young lad led a horse from the stables and began brushing it down. Only then did she notice the condition of the buildings. Stones crumbled on the walls, chipped and rotting wood formed the entrance to the stables, weeds broke through cracks in the steps leading to the front door, and brambles as tall as Alexia grew from what once must have been a garden.

Sorrow weighed upon her heart, making her wonder, yet again, what had happened in this place. What had happened to Ronar?

Pushing from the window, she made her way to the wardrobe and flung open the doors. Tunics, breeches, capes, and doublets spilled onto the floor, leaving behind similar items hanging within—all smelling of Ronar. The scent stirred something within her she dared not admit—could not admit. Not when her sister's life was in danger. She scanned the clothing. There, just what she needed. A pair of linen breeches. As speedily as she could with only one good foot, she stepped out of her breeches and into the new ones, then stuffed her tunic inside. The breeches were large enough to fit two of her, and she quickly found a belt and tied it around her waist, then donned an equally large leather doublet, which she laced up as tight as she could. If she were to make any progress, she'd have to hide her sex and keep off the King's Highway. Now, to retrieve her boots from the hall, her bow and arrow from the stables, and steal a horse.

Alack, steal wasn't the correct term. *Borrow* sounded better, for she would surely return it. But for now, what choice did she have?

Creeping, or rather hobbling into the corridor, she made her way to the stairway, noting how dark and quiet the house seemed.

The stairs proved more difficult than she expected, and more than once, she put too much weight on her foot and stifled a cry of pain. Finally, down in the hall, she found her bodice on the hearth where she'd left it.

Red coals simmered in the hearth, and she hesitated, remembering the tender moments she'd shared with Sir Knight, with Ronar—the gentle way he'd tended her wound, the way he'd looked at her as if she were a treasury full of gold.

She smiled. An earl, of all things. A well-bred man of title and fortune. She spotted the jug of wine. Had she drunk too much? What had she said as the night progressed? Naught to be done for it now.

Sitting, she tugged on one boot and shoved the other one beneath her arm. She'd have to wait for the swelling to go down ere she attempted to put it on, or she feared she'd not be able to silence her howl of pain. Hopping out of the hall, she passed through the entryway and slowly opened the front door. A newly risen sun barged into the dark foyer, scattering dust into glittering specks and bringing a welcome cheerfulness into the gloomy home.

She hobbled onto the front porch.

"Where do you think you are going, Lady Falcon?" Ronar's voice penetrated her hope. "And wearing my breeches!"

Chapter 21

Sir LeGode sifted through the parchment littering his desk, the numbers blurring in his vision. Tossing down his quill pen, he strode to the narrow window where a brisk wind entered, spiced with rain. It did naught to cool the angst burning in his gut. Nothing was going right. His inept knights had crawled and hobbled back to the castle looking as if they'd fought against a horde of thousands. How could one woman thwart ten of his best knights? The cowards claimed they'd been attacked by a demon, a specter from Hades with the power and skill of twenty men.

Bah! 'Twas just an excuse for their incompetence. He could have sent thirty of them, and the results would have been the same. Soon, however, more of his own knights would join these ill-bred Luxley minnows, and at least Alexia would have a force to reckon with. As it was, the joint-heir to Luxley manor was running about the countryside, no doubt plotting her return to power. *And his demise*. But what to do?

His door creaked open, and he turned to chastise whoever dared disturb him, when the bishop entered in a flurry of black robes and gold-embroidery, wearing his usual pious smirk—one that had begun to grate on LeGode of late. No doubt the bishop's fare at the noonday meal had not been to his liking, or mayhap 'twas too cold or too damp in his chamber, or the chamber maid had resisted his latest advance, or only God knew what other complaint longed to leap from the man's dry, thin lips.

LeGode rushed forward, bowed, and kissed his hand. "Your Grace. Forgive me for not attending the noon meal. I have not been feeling well."

"Nothing serious, I hope?" One gray brow arched, though LeGode detected no concern in his tone. The bishop dropped into a chair and waved at his assistant who had followed him in. "Do fetch me some of that sweet mead we had at our last meal." The boy bowed and started off. "And a bowl of those sugared peaches," he shouted after him.

The door closed and the bishop examined the room with the usual look of disdain.

"What may I do for you, your Grace?" LeGode folded his hands in front of him, lest he do as he longed and strangle the man.

The bishop snapped his droopy eyes toward LeGode and grinned. "'Tis my belief we can help each other."

LeGode held back a sigh of frustration. He hadn't time for this. He must find and kill Alexia D'Clere or force her sister to marry Cedric before she returned. *And* before the king sent another suitor—or worse, an inquiry to determine why five men had died on their way to marry the lady. If LeGode failed, these past nine years of hard work and sacrifice would all be for naught.

"How is that, your Grace?" He smiled.

"I understand you wish your son to marry Cristiana D'Clere."

An icy breeze tore in through the window and sent the candle flame sputtering. LeGode tried to hide his shock.

The bishop brushed dust from his vestment. "Yes, yes… I am quite observant. 'Tis part of my calling from God. I see things others do not."

Suppressing a snort, LeGode sat on the edge of his desk. "'Twould be a good match. They are suited, and Cedric adores her."

"It would be a good match for *you*, you mean to say." The bishop chuckled and glanced at the sapphire ring on his finger. "Cedric is the son of a mere knight, and the lady the daughter of a baron. The prestige of the title and all of Luxley would be Cedric's upon the union."

Heat stormed up LeGode's neck. Fear followed. "If you mean to imply…" he began to bluster.

The bishop held up a hand. "Tsk Tsk. Calm yourself, Sir. I am no judge of good-hearted ambition. 'Tis what runs the world."

Despite his relief, LeGode studied his opponent, unsure of how to proceed. "What are you suggesting?"

Thunder rumbled in the distance. The bishop rubbed his eyes and sighed. "I wish to leave this meager estate and return to my proper place by the king's side. But, alas, he has sent me on this futile mission with orders not to return without the Spear of Destiny."

"But what can I do on that account?"

"The King's Guard abide by a certain moral code." A sinister twinkle filled the bishop's eyes. "If you understand me." He steepled his hands before him. "There are things they will not do, methods they will not employ."

"'Tis unclear what you mean, Excellency. I have granted you the use of Luxley's knights in your search for the Spear."

"Aye, as was your duty." He waved him off. "Though, by all accounts, the village milkmaids could have done a better job. Alas, I have sent for fifty of my best knights whom I expect to join us in a fortnight. Then, mayhap some progress will be made." He stroked his golden crucifix and eyed LeGode as if they shared a secret. "In the meantime, I speak of other means to find the Spear. *Darker* means."

Alarm halted LeGode's breathing.

The bishop grinned. "As I said, I know *all* that goes on in this castle."

And he took no issue with a warlock? Nay, surely he was not aware of Drogo. LeGode forced a placid expression. "'Tis possible I *could* help you, but the risk would be high." High if this was a trap and the bishop burned him for sorcery. High if Drogo's fury was pricked, and he turned LeGode into a gnat.

"What if I give you my troth that when I return to London, I will advise the king to appoint Cedric to marry Lady D'Clere. He will listen to me, I assure you. But alas, I must have the Spear first in order to return to the king."

LeGode pursed his lips. *Curse that blasted Spear!* How could one piece of ancient metal have so much power? If so, mayhap he'd keep it for himself and use it against this pompous windbag. LeGode rose, approached the bishop and bowed. "I believe we have a bargain, your Grace."

☙⊙❧

Ronar leaned back against the cold stone outside his bedchamber and watched the light from the sconce cast dancing shadows on the wall. A single narrow window at the end of the corridor admitted but a sliver of sunlight into the dark hallway he knew was not only full of dust and cobwebs, but nightmarish specters from his past as well. Through the thick wooden door, he heard fabric rustling and the faintest of moans. Good. Despite her ardent protests and her insistence, she preferred men's clothing, Lady Falcon was donning the cote and surcote Bridon had fetched her.

"Potz!" chimed from within the chamber, eliciting a smile from Ronar. Something he'd been doing overmuch of late, though it still felt foreign on his face. Oddly, he longed to assist the lady, but not for the obvious reasons. Surely 'twas difficult to don all the layers required of the fairer sex with only one good foot to stand upon.

Pushing from the wall, he began to pace and shook his head. Brave, foolish lady! Attempting to escape when she could barely walk. And in breeches that if given half a chance would have slid to her ankles before she was even aware. He chuckled, picturing the anger flashing in those green eyes when she turned to face him, the groan of frustration....

The defiant line of her lips as she said, "You won't keep me here forever, Sir Knight."

And then her frown at his reply. "Nay, merely as long as I desire."

The door creaked open, flooding the corridor with light and with this woman—this sprite who sparked life into his heart long since dead. That new life jolted in pain as memories flooded him at the sight of the ruby red cote she wore, trimmed and laced with silver and garnets that also decorated the girdle at her waist. A golden circlet lay gently on her head from which a netted veil flowed down over her hair.

She was the picture of feminine beauty just like sweet Idonea had been, and agony wrenched his gut.

Gripping the door frame, she studied his reaction, understanding simmering in her wise eyes. She stumbled toward him, and he instantly shook off the past and gripped her elbow.

"Why risk invoking what is obviously a painful memory of one of your many trysts? I was quite content wearing your breeches."

Along with the sarcasm, he found an odd care in her tone, invoking emotion that burned his throat. Swallowing it down, he hoisted her in his arms, deciding humor was the better response. "And when those breeches sank to the ground, I fear your contentment would have vanished, whilst my enjoyment would have only risen."

"Then I am happy for the gown," she retorted. "For surely whatever memories it harbors will keep you at bay."

He doubted it. Smiling, he carried her down the stairs and set her in the hall where Bridon had laid out a feast of bread, cheese, yogurt, and fruit to break their fast.

She pushed from him. "No need to carry me about like a child. I shall heal, Sir Knight, and you will wake one morn to find me gone."

He led her to the table. "I have no doubt, Lady Falcon."

She lowered to her chair and glanced over the fare. "At least you treat me as a guest and haven't tossed me in the dungeon."

"The day is young, my lady." He took a seat across from her

She narrowed her eyes. "What do you want from me?"

"As I said, merely to protect you."

"If that were so, you would have let me go. Your vow to rescue fair maidens has been fulfilled, but I doubt that vow includes keeping them against their will." She studied him. "Or, mayhap from this lady's attire your man so readily brought me, it is."

Ronar poured hot cider into their cups, unsure he wished to respond to an accusation that would surely incriminate him.

"Or is it this mystical Spear you seek?" Her voice taunted. "Ah ha, forsooth, your pretense of chivalry has been discovered." She bit into an apple, and he enjoyed the way she ate, not delicately with small bites, but as a woman accustomed to hunger and appreciative of food.

"I admit I have my duty to perform." Unable to do naught else, he gazed at her with an admiration, dare he say affection, he could no longer hide. "Yet, if that is all you think this is, you are not as wise as you pretend."

She lowered her lashes and picked at her bread.

Sunlight streamed through the window, transforming the skin above her neckline into golden silk as it rose and fell beneath her breaths. Ronar swallowed. The forest warrior had transformed into a lady, and one he was having trouble resisting.

She sat back and sighed. "Sir LeGode wishes me dead. All along he wanted me dead so his son could marry Cristiana and inherit our estate."

"Aye." Ronar tossed cheese into his mouth. He had come to the same conclusion during the long night as he lay by the fire unable to sleep. Whether 'twas being surrounded by haunting memories that had kept him awake or being so close to this enchanting woman, he could not say. Either way, he'd risen early to go over the accounts with Bridon.

Alexia huffed. "What he doesn't know is that Cristiana thinks Cedric a whey-faced bore. She will never agree to marry him."

"Mayhap not in her right mind." His sober tone brought her gaze back to him.

She nodded sadly. "'Tis why he poisons her. To keep her mind addled." Gripping the table, she struggled to rise and winced. "I must be with her, Ronar. She's not safe."

Warmed by her use of his common name, Ronar resisted the urge to help her and instead spooned peaches into his mouth. "LeGode won't kill her. He needs her alive to marry his son."

"He's making her so ill she can barely move! I cannot allow it."

"And what will you do? Limp into Luxley, bow and arrow in hand, and demand he cease at once? He has everyone, including Bishop Montruse believing you are a witch." Setting down his spoon, Ronar grabbed his cup. "Not even *you* can defeat fifty knights, especially if you can't fly through the canopy like a falcon."

She stared at him, anger flaring from her eyes. But finally, after a few moments, she melted back into her chair. "I must do something. I will not sit idly by while they poison my sister."

He sipped his cider. "We are not sitting idle. We are planning our next move. Whatever special talents you have, my lady, 'tis not wise to allow sentiment to dictate your course."

She flinched as if he'd struck her. "And what is your plan, Sir Knight? Storm Luxley with your steward, cook, and stable boy?"

Ronar wanted to laugh at the woman's impudence. "If it comes to it." Setting down his cup, he leaned back in his chair. "I will devise a plan, rest assured of that. For now, you will rest and heal your ankle, or you will be of no use to your sister *or* to me. Now eat and regain your strength."

Defiantly, she bit off a piece of bread. "*I* will come up with a plan, Sir Knight. I fear I am not very good at waiting."

"On that we can agree."

♾

Alexia wasn't accustomed to taking orders. Not since the friar had given her more freedom at age sixteen. Yet the pompous earl-knight had a point, well, mayhap two points—one, her feelings had gotten her into more trouble than she cared to admit, and, two, she wasn't much use hopping around like a maimed bird. If only she could sprout wings and fly away, land on her sister's window ledge, if only to ensure she was well.

Regardless, she would soon do just that. Minus the wings, of course.

But for now, she was no match for an elite King's Guard with the strength of a lion, the wealth and title of nobility, and the wits of a fox. At least not while injured and without her bow and arrows. Nay, she would appease him for now, wait to heal, and then take the first opportunity to flee. Not that she wasn't enjoying the man's company. He certainly was pleasing to gaze upon, and she found their witty banter entertaining. Most of the time. Then, of course, there were those moments he gazed at her like no one ever had...as if he....

Nay, he was only after the Spear. She must remember that. Ronar LePeine was a man who knew naught but duty to king and God—in that order—and she couldn't see him compromising for the fleeting emotions of an *affaire de Coeur*.

Yet...she could not deny there were moments she found him fascinating and longed to discover his secrets. More of which were revealed when later that morning, he hoisted her up onto a bay palfrey and mounted his own horse in preparation to inspect his lands. With no other choice but to accompany him—due to his grip on her horse's reins—she settled back and enjoyed the splendid scenery. She'd never traveled past the Emerald Forest and Luxley village, and she found the rolling hills surrounding Rivenhall magnificent. Sheep, cows, and flowers of every color, dotted the carpet of green that was only interrupted by clusters of thick forest and quiet lakes that mirrored a blue sky laden with puffy clouds.

Ronar was pensive as they traveled, his gaze scanning his estate, his thoughts seemingly miles away. And she wondered what happened to make him turn his back on all this beauty. They exited a copse of trees to a stiff breeze that smelled of earth, sage, and sunshine. Reining in their horses on top of a hill, Ronar studied a village that sat in the distance below the castle she'd seen last night. Farmland circled it like spokes in a wheel, spring crops peppering the dark soil, along with the peasants who worked the land.

"All this is yours?" Alexia dared ask.

He simply nodded and started toward the village.

A thousand questions raced through her mind and a thousand more as they entered the open gates of the town. No doubt they'd been sighted in their approach, for Alexia heard a crier shouting, "Lord Rivenhall! Lord Rivenhall is here!"

Though smaller than Luxley, the village still boasted a market square, to which Ronar now led them, past several shops—a blacksmith, weaver, cooper, metalworker, and spicemonger among them, indicated by the painted drawings hanging above their doors. Geese, chickens, and pigs dashed about, as well as peddlers hawking their wares.

A crowd mobbed them as Ronar brought the horses to a halt. Peasants reached toward him, bowing, and exclaiming. "My lord. You've returned, my lord. Good day to you, my lord."

Dismounting, he greeted them all and even knelt to embrace small children clambering to see him.

Alexia could only stare at the adoration beaming from their faces. Alack, most of them at least. A few stood at the edge of the square, scowling. One of them pushed through the throng.

"Where 'ave ye been, milord?"

"Away on the king's business," Ronar replied as he assisted Alexia from her horse. Curious eyes followed her as they crossed the square, weaving through people and livestock.

They entered a building that served as part barn, part courthouse, from what Alexia could tell. Several of the wealthier peasants entered while the rest scattered to their duties. Ronar led Alexia to a chair and then proceeded to address the crowd, answering their questions with patience and keeping order when too many spoke at once. Alexia had never seen a lord speak so kindly to his villeins and tenants. Forsooth, most rarely spoke to them at all. But this King's Guard listened humbly to their complaints, nodding his head in understanding, and dispelled their fears with promises she knew he meant to keep. She couldn't take her eyes off him, attired not as a knight or King's Guard, or even as the Lord of a castle, but in naught but breeches, tunic, simple doublet, and leather boots. His dark hair fell in waves to just beneath his collar and his eyes repeatedly found her as he conducted his business. He was a leader of men, this Ronar LePeine, Earl of Rivenhall, wise and humble. And she found her admiration for him rising more than was safe for her heart.

By the time they started back for the manor house, the sun had sunk behind the hills, transforming the grass into waves of gold and the trees to amber.

"Who protects the people in your absence?" she asked as they rode side-by-side. "Are there knights at the castle?" A chilled wind whipped over Alexia, and she hugged herself.

"Nay. The castle lies empty since my mother's death." He seemed to be searching for something in his pack but gave up. "The king attaches his name to Rivenhall. Hence, no one dares attack."

"He must consider you a friend."

"My father knew him well."

'Twas the first mention of his father, and though Alexia longed to pry, she bit her tongue, wondering at this man's close association with the king. What other secrets did he harbor?

"And what of the wealth generated from the land?" she asked.

"A small sum goes toward the upkeep of the manor and the rest to the Church. I have no need of it."

His voice was curt and somber, and she thought it best to attempt no further conversation.

Once back at the manor, he carried her inside—despite her protests—and brought her to his chamber, wherein she found a basin of fresh water, lavender soap, and a towel.

"Refresh yourself, Lady Falcon. I shall return in an hour to escort you to our evening repast." Then without so much as a glance her way, he left and shut the door.

Not feeling safe without her clothing, Alexia hurriedly dabbed a wet cloth over her body in an attempt to dislodge some of the grime. Once dressed, she oscillated from sitting, to hopping, to staring out the window, restless with thoughts of the friar and her sister.

The sun dragged away its light and a sliver of a moon dared peek above the horizon as myriad stars speckled the night sky.

Alexia's stomach rumbled, reminding her the last meal she'd eaten was early that morn. Had Ronar forgotten her? Opening her door, she peered out, but saw naught but darkness, dust, and a distant rushlight perched on the wall. She staggered toward the stairs, keeping an ear out for Ronar's voice, then gripped the banister and hopped down the treads. But instead of heading toward the hall in which they normally sat, curiosity lured Alexia down another corridor to her right and around a corner. There, lit by wall sconces on either side, stood two closed doors that surely must lead to the great hall of the manor.

Gripping the handles, she yanked. The thick doors rattled but would not budge. She pushed. Nothing. Finally, after one more tug, the aged wood creaked in protest and started to open. Darkness as thick as mud slapped her face, along with the smell of mold, aged wood, and something foul.

She was about to stumble inside when footsteps alerted her to someone approaching. Before she could react, that someone shoved her hands from the door handle, then slammed both doors shut with an ominous thud.

"What is it, Ronar?" Candlelight sparked fury in his eyes.

"You are never to go in there." His harsh tone bit her as he turned and strode away, leaving her to hobble after him. What happened to the chivalrous knight?

"Why? I don't understand."

"That room is to remain shut forever."

"Ronar." She caught up with him and tugged on his arm. "Tell me why."

"Because 'twas in that room that I murdered my sister."

Chapter 22

Cristiana D'Clere gripped her stomach as yet another pain rose to steal her breath. Beside her bed, Seraphina patted her brow with a cool cloth and whispered words of comfort. But Cristiana would not be comforted. 'Twas not only the sudden reappearance of her illness which caused her torment, but her fear for her sister's safety. A witch! Ludicrous. Madness! How could Sir LeGode ever believe such a thing?

"There, there, drink." Seraphina held up a mug of sour wine which always seemed to ease the pain during a bad episode.

The bitter taste puckered Cristiana's mouth and burned her throat. She coughed and fell back onto her pillow, her breath coming hard.

"You must calm yourself, my lady." Seraphina placed the cup on the table and took Cristiana's hand in hers. "It does no good to worry so."

"How can I remain calm when my sister is being hunted as a witch?" Tears burned in her eyes. "She could already be caught, for all I know."

"Nay, Anabelle would have told us. You know your sister. She is no doubt hidden away somewhere safe."

Cristiana tried to laugh, but nausea threatened to dislodge the wine. She swallowed it down and drew a deep breath. "Hidden? Safe? The lady who walks unafraid about a manor in which someone wants her dead?"

Seraphina gave a sorrowful smile. "To your point, my lady."

"She will come back. I know it. She is foolish enough to return for me. And she'll get caught and be burned at the stake." Tears spilled down her cheeks as another pain struck her, and her thoughts became vaporous clouds as they usually did when the spasm subsided.

"Do not think of such things. God is with Alexia, and He is with us."

Cristiana wanted to say that she believed God had abandoned them, but a rap on the door prevented her from speaking doubts she would later regret.

With a squeeze to her hand, Seraphina opened it and stepped into the corridor, giving Cristiana time to think before she could no longer do so coherently. As soon as Anabelle had informed her of the hunt for her sister, Cristiana had donned her best gown and gone to see Sir LeGode. Despite her discomfort and an exhaustion that threatened to drag her unconscious to the floor, she had tried her best to reason with him. But he refused to listen, and instead showed her the articles of witchcraft he claimed to have found in Alexia's possession. Surely such evidence, he informed her, along with the fact that Cristiana's illness began with Alexia's appearance in the castle, proved that she'd been poisoning her.

"I'm sorry, Lady D'Clere. I know this comes as a shock." He had laid a hand on her shoulder as she sat in the chair in his study, his face folded in such genuine concern that it caused her to doubt her own sister for the barest of moments.

"But why?" she had muttered. "Why would she do that to me?"

"For the estate, the manor, land, wealth. Clearly she wants it for herself."

She had studied him then, seeing the evil in his eyes for the first time, the slight sneer on his lips, the deception written across his wide brow. And she realized what a devil he was. For the devil was a master of lies, just like this man before her. If Cristiana knew one thing about her sister, 'twas that she cared naught for wealth or land.

At that very moment, she had opened her mouth to call the captain of the guard to arrest LeGode and lock him below, and then to hail the bishop and defend her sister... but her head had suddenly felt too heavy to hold up, and all air rushed from her lungs.

"You poor dear." LeGode had leaned over to peer at her, and all she remembered were those eyes, dark and cold as coals not lit for years, swirling in her vision. "You are not in your right mind. Best leave these things to me." And she knew that neither her knights nor the bishop would believe her.

Seraphina reappeared and closed the door behind her, moving quickly to Cristiana's bed, a new sparkle in her eyes.

"What is it, dear friend?"

"'Twas a squire with a message from Jarin."

"The knight?"

"Aye, my lady. He wishes to arrange a meeting as soon as you are well. He has urgent information he must relay to you at once."

Two days later, when Cristiana's mind finally started to clear and her strength returned, she was able to rise from her bed, get dressed, and meet Sir Jarin at the secret spot he had requested—the chapel, vacant now for two years, ever since their chaplain had abandoned them without a word. 'Twas the perfect place to meet, for anyone seeing her enter would assume she went to pray. Not that many would be wandering about the castle at well past the midnight hour.

Arm in arm with Seraphina, Cristiana leaned on her friend more than she wanted as they made their way down the winding stairs through the great hall, and out into the front courtyard. A quarter moon greeted them from above as a dog lifted his head to watch them pass. Movement at the gatehouse shifted her gaze to a guard, who, upon seeing them, turned back to his post.

The chapel door squealed on its hinges, and they were met with a rush of chilled air that smelled of aged scrolls, mold, and tallow. A single candle sat upon the altar flickering in the breeze that swept past them through the door.

It had been a while since Cristiana had been in the chapel, due both to her illness and the missing chaplain. Yet she wondered at the chill that suddenly gripped her, causing her heart to tighten. She'd always felt at peace here, as if God Himself passed through on occasion and left some of His love behind. But that sensation had been replaced by one that made her skin crawl.

Clinging to each other, the two ladies approached the altar, searching the shadows for any sign of Sir Jarin the Just.

One of the shadows moved, and out stepped the figure of a man, a large man, who instantly held up his hand. "'Tis me, Jarin, my lady."

Another shadow emerged and Sir Damien LaRage appeared, his dark eyes drifting over her and landing on Seraphina.

Finding her breath again, Cristiana released Seraphina and bade her remain as she drew closer to Jarin.

"Lady D'Clere." Removing his hat, he dipped his head. "Thank you for meeting me." Deep brown eyes assessed her with care, sparkling in the candlelight. He shifted boots over the stone floor and scanned the room once again. What was it about this knight that made her feel safe? Mayhap 'twas his broad shoulders, the knives lining his belt, or the sword at his side? Nay, 'twas his very presence, a strength, a commanding power which made her feel as though he'd protect her at all costs.

Foolish woman. What silly romantic dreams were these? She hardly knew the man.

"Tell me, Sir Jarin, have you word of my sister?" she finally asked, unable to wait another moment.

"Aye, I have. But I must first tell you that you are in danger," he said bluntly.

"Me? What of Alexia? She is no witch!"

He nodded, set his hat on the altar, and took her hands. "I know. Never fear. She is well. Safe."

"Where is she?"

"With Ronar...Sir LePeine."

Finally, she was able to breathe. "Thank our Holy Father in Heaven."

"My lady, someone is poisoning you."

"I know." Cristiana glanced over her shoulder at her friend. "Seraphina told me what happened when Alexia drank the elixir." She swallowed. "I have not drunk it since, and yet I am still ill." As if confirming her words, the room began to spin, and she closed her eyes.

Flinging an arm around her waist, Jarin led her to sit on a bench. The strength and power of his touch, along with his masculine scent, both settled her mind and excited her heart.

"Mayhap the poison takes some time to leave your body," he offered.

Damien moved to stand beside Seraphina.

"I hope you are right." Cristiana offered him a smile, then drew a deep breath. "'Tis our steward, LeGode. I could not force myself to believe it at first. But alas, I am sure of it now."

"Aye," Jarin said. "Alexia believes so as well."

She stared up at him, his eyes so full of wisdom and kindness. "I know not why. He is not in line to inherit." She rubbed her temples. "None of this makes sense. What am I to do?" She watched as his hands swallowed hers in a bastion of warmth and strength. "I should dismiss him at once," she added in haste.

Damien groaned and crossed arms over his chest. "Nay. He has too many of his own knights here. He will declare you mad and have you imprisoned in the tower."

Seraphina gasped.

Jarin gripped the hilt of his sword. "He's right. Your best course of action is to remain abed and feign your continued illness."

"For how long?"

"Until we discover the truth and bring the villain to justice. In the meantime, I will gather as many knights as I can on our side."

"And what if my sister returns? I fear for her."

Jarin exchanged a look with Damien, a slight smile on his lips. "Ronar can handle her."

"You do not know my sister." She huffed.

"You do not know Ronar."

Jarin continued to hold her hands, his thumb caressing her skin in a gesture that would have been far too forward under any other circumstances. As it was, she needed his comfort and strength. All the years of fear, uncertainty, and illness had finally taken their toll, and she longed to fall into this knight's arms and never leave. But that wouldn't be proper. Besides, he was merely being kind, performing his duty to God and king. Wasn't he?

"I'm so frightened, Sir Jarin," she whispered.

He brought her hands to his lips for a kiss. "Never fear, my lady. I will protect you." The care in his tone brought her gaze up to his, and she found him looking at her as if he would ransom a kingdom to keep her safe.

ᘒᙦᕬ

Killed his sister? The words echoed through the chamber, bounced off stone walls, careened off the vaulted ceilings, and fluttered the tapestry of a pastoral scene hanging just outside the Great Hall.

The Great Hall Alexia was forbidden to enter.

The Great Hall where a tragedy occurred—one that shadowed Ronar's face so deeply, it seemed he'd fade into the darkness beyond.

"What are you talking about?" she asked, fear rising at the look of utter despair in his eyes and the rage brewing just beneath the surface.

She took a step back. Her injured foot struck the floor, and she whimpered. Ronar had her in his arms within seconds.

"Put me down at once!"

He said naught, just carried her into the lesser hall and set her on a cushioned chair before a crackling fire.

The steward must have stoked the coals and left a tray of food and wine on the table, for she could smell the scent of roasted pork, garlic, boiled apples, and cinnamon.

Ronar, silent, solemn, poured himself a mug of wine and gulped it down, then poured two more, bringing them with him. He handed her a cup, which she took, suddenly uncomfortable in this man's presence.

Elbows on his knees, Ronar stared into the flames, gripping his cup as if it held the answer to the tormenting questions lining his face.

Alexia waited, sipping the spiced wine, trying not to stare at the man, but wanting so much to understand his pain, help him if she could. Doing her best to quiet her soul, she shifted to the Spirit within and prayed for sight, then waited, keeping her eyes open this time, her mind still. The swarm of dark shadows slinking and hovering around Ronar startled her at first. Her fear returned and she lost the sight.

There is no fear in perfect love, the friar had said.

Taking a deep breath, she tried again. No fear. Not when one existed in the perfect love of God.

The shadows arose again, specters from the underworld, formless, empty beings whose only goal was the destruction of man—to destroy his life and drag him into the dark prison in which they lived. The shadows spun around Ronar's head in a wild demonic dance—round and round until she grew dizzy watching them.

He gulped down his wine, then rose and poured more. The shadows followed him, braiding and coiling about him, attempting to bind him with invisible chains. Lifeless yellow eyes narrowed upon her, challenging her to intervene.

A brilliant flash drew her gaze beyond them where she spotted the light-beings, one by the window, the other by the door. Swords hung at their side.

She placed a hand on the Spear, snug in her pocket. Then swallowing the last traces of her fear, she waved her hand over the specters and whispered the name of Christ.

They vanished like the wisps of smoke they were.

"Did you say something?" Ronar took his seat again, shifting his shoulders as if a weight had suddenly been lifted.

"Simply that I wish you would tell me about your sister."

He took another gulp of wine. "'Tis a long, horrid tale."

"One which I wish to hear."

"You would not wish so if you knew…"

She waited. "Knew?"

"Knew that I am a vile wretch of the worst kind."

She wanted to say she could never think that of him, that he'd proven to be an honorable, godly man, but one didn't say that to their captor. Not when one intended to escape at the first opportunity.

He stood and waved his cup through the air, spilling wine over the side. "I grew up here at Rivenhall. In the castle you saw today. With my mother and father, the earl and countess of Rivenhall—Simon Meschin and his wife Madeline." He snapped his gaze to her, awaiting her reaction.

Meschin. Simon Meschin. The familiar name ricocheted through her mind. "Meschin is your family name, not

LePeine?" Though he'd said it before, she hadn't made the connection.

"Aye. I changed it for obvious reasons."

Obvious, indeed. Everyone in the realm had heard of Simon Meschin. He and the king had grown up together at court. When the king took the crown, he kept Simon by his side as a confidant, gave him an estate, and found him a bride.

She studied Ronar as he stared at the flames, the regal cut of his nose, his jaw shadowed with stubble, and his eyes so filled with fury and sorrow—this man she'd once deemed a mere knight who she'd then discovered was an earl, but who now, she learned, was one of the king's inner circle. "That makes you a very powerful man, Ronar."

He laughed bitterly. "Does it?"

"Your father died saving the king. If naught else, that means you have His Majesty's ear."

"Mayhap his ear, but not his loyalty. Not since Bishop Montruse arrived."

Several moments passed in silence before Alexia dared say, "I heard your mother died soon after your father."

"Six years ago." Ronar stared down at his drink, locks of hair falling in his face. "Some say 'twas a fever. I say 'twas a broken heart."

"They loved each other very much."

"Aye."

Rising, Ronar poured himself more wine and then sank back into his chair.

"I was eighteen, my sister fourteen, and we suddenly found ourselves with a vast estate to run, knights to command, and overflowing wealth sifting through our fingertips. To avoid painful memories, we moved here to the manor house, but instead of following my father's good example and becoming the man he taught me to be, instead of caring for my sister and being a godly and moral influence, I became a dissolute wastrel, drunkard, and scoundrel of the worst kind."

Alexia would not have believed it, save for Ronar's tone and the look of anguish on his face.

"How did I spend my time with my newfound responsibility and wealth? I hosted banquet after banquet, inviting all the local nobility and their fresh young daughters. As if that weren't enough debauchery, I attended the king's grand affairs in London, spent days, even weeks, at court in reveling and dissipation with no awareness of where I was or what I was doing."

Alexia swallowed. She had heard of many a young noble who behaved thus—had been vehemently warned of such by the friar. But she could not find it in her heart to associate such a libertine with the man who sat before her now—this King's Guard who held truth and honor above all else.

"Do I shock you, Alexia? Do you wish to hear more?"

"I am not easily shocked, Sir Knight." Though in truth, she wasn't sure she wanted to know more. Even so, she said, "Pray, continue."

"I ruined many a young maiden." He stared at her, assessing her reaction, his eyes glazed with wine. "It may surprise you the number of ladies willing to lose their maidenhead in the hopes of marrying an earl."

Alexia tried to hide her disgust, but some must have leaked onto her expression.

He huffed. "Forsooth, at last I see the disdain in your eyes." He rose and wavered slightly. "I will bore you no longer."

Rising, Alexia halted him with a touch. "Forgive me, Ronar. I have no right to judge you. I have many mistakes in my past as well."

He studied her. "I doubt that."

She pressed him to sit again, and when he did, she knelt at his feet. "God's forgiveness is not partial."

He rubbed his temples. "Just hard won, 'twould seem."

"What happened to your sister?"

"Do you truly wish to hear what a beast I am?"

Chapter 23

*R*onar knew he'd consumed too much wine. His head felt as heavy as iron, whilst thoughts whipped this way and that through his mind like trees in a storm. Worst of all, the shield he'd carefully forged around his heart was starting to crack.

All due to this beautiful lady who sat at his feet, gazing up at him as if he were a king and not the dissolute cullion he was.

Why would she not leave? Any decent lady would have stomped away in disgust when he'd first disclosed his true nature.

But she stayed, her initial disgust transforming into forgiveness, her revulsion into care.

Must be the wine. He rubbed his eyes. Or a wonderful dream.

That dream would definitely shatter when he continued.

"There was a man, a good friend who oft joined me in my celebrations. Lord Bromley." Ronar shifted his gaze to the fire, unable to look Alexia in the eyes. "He became infatuated with my sister, Idonea. Who wouldn't? She was not only lovely to look upon, but innocent and pure of heart. I forbade him, of course, to pursue her. Alack, I knew his motives were impure. He wished merely to bed her, get her out of his thoughts, and then move on to the next conquest."

Alexia lowered her gaze, as any decent lady would hearing such talk.

"One night I had another one of my lavish affairs here at the manor, and"—Ronar could barely say his name— "Brom and I were well into our cups. After everyone left, I must have fallen asleep in my bed, for I woke suddenly in the middle of the night and went looking for Idonea. I always ensured she was well and safe ere I retired." One thing he had done right. "I found Brom in her bedchamber."

Alexia looked up at him, her eyes moistening.

"I dragged him off my sister—much to her dismay—and challenged him to a duel. He had dishonored her and betrayed my trust. My good friend."

Alexia grabbed one of his hands. Her fingers were small, but their strength and warmth comforted him.

"We fought in the Great Hall you nearly entered, sword to sword. Through the entire battle, my sister watched from the side, screaming and begging me to stop."

Alexia ran a finger down the scar on his forehead. "'Tis how you got this."

He nodded. "A reminder of my foolishness. How could I expect my sister to behave any differently than what she had witnessed her brother doing for years?" He sighed. "I merely wanted to teach him a lesson. I wanted…I wanted… to hurt him as he had hurt me and my sister."

"And did you?"

"Aye. I sliced him up fairly well ere he ran off, bloodied and beaten, cursing both me and Idonea."

Silence invaded, save the crackle of flames and shift of fabric as Alexia moved slightly. "'Twas a fair duel, Ronar. Naught to be ashamed of."

Moments passed before he found enough of his voice to continue. Yet how could he even say the words? His eyes blurred, and he dropped his head into his hands. "She killed herself." There. He'd said it. Now the pain rose, the pain he'd so desperately tried to drown for four years—an agony that clawed his soul and threatened to grind it into dust.

She squeezed his hand. "What are you saying?"

"My sister. She swore she loved Brom and could not live without him, nor live with the man who had driven him away." He swallowed a burst of agony. "She jumped off a cliff."

Alexia's hand grew cold against his skin.

Surely now she would leave him to drown in his own despair and shame. Instead, she tightened her grip on his hand and laid her head on his thigh. No words were spoken. She merely remained, offering him the comfort of her presence.

He rubbed his eyes, suddenly ashamed of tears no knight should shed. Pushing her away, he stood and planted a boot on the hearth and an arm on the mantel. "So you see, my lady, I am no hero, no man of honor, as I pretend."

He heard her rise and stand beside him. "I'm sorry, Ronar. 'Twas an unfathomable betrayal from one so close." She touched his arm. "But you cannot take the blame upon yourself for your sister's death."

"Can I not?" He blustered back. "When I am the one who taught her to be immoral? Who placed no boundaries around her? Who left her alone with a man I knew to be a libertine? Why? Because I was besotted." Growling, he tore from her and walked away. He didn't deserve the woman's sympathy. Nor the look of care in her eyes. "I am pathetic."

"You did not push your sister off that cliff."

"I might as well have."

He turned and watched her hobble to her chair and felt guilty for his callous behavior.

"You made mistakes, I grant you. But you are not that man anymore," she stated, the softness gone from her tone. "The Ronar I know is honest, honorable, noble, and good."

"Humph. What do you truly know of me?"

"I know you are a man who follows his conscience, who knows right from wrong, who is kind and brave and who keeps secrets—even those of his enemies—to his own peril." Her eyes latched upon his, and he saw both anger and sincerity within them. "I know you seek the truth and God's will above all else. I know your people admire and respect you. That is all I need to know."

If he admitted it, her words touched a deep place in his soul. But he would not admit it. He *could* not.

"What happened then?" she asked.

Ronar picked up his mug to refill it, but realized this lady did not deserve any more of his besotted ramblings. He tossed it into the fire with a loud clank that startled Alexia and shot flames up the chimney from the wine. "I buried my sister, left the estate, and joined the Crusades." He returned to his seat and dug into his pocket for Saint Jude. "The bishop at Jerusalem gave this to me. Saint Jude, patron saint of lost causes." He gave a bitter chuckle. "The bishop said there was hope for my soul if I vowed to God and king that I would pay penance for every sinful act I committed, even if it took me the rest of my life."

"Ronar." She reached out to him, but he shifted away. "You don't need to pray to a dead saint nor pay for your sins. Our Lord Jesus Christ already did that when He was crucified. Why else would the Son of God have to endure such pain and humiliation?"

Scowling, he shoved Saint Jude back in his pocket. "More blasphemy from your book."

"God's Book," she returned. "For all to read and hear." She folded her hands in her lap. "There is no sin that cannot be forgiven if one truly repents and changes his ways, save the sin of rejecting Christ altogether. You cannot purchase your way to heaven, Ronar. None of us can."

Part of him wanted to believe her, but a larger part did not. There had to be punishment for what he'd done. 'Twas the way the world worked—crime, justice, punishment—a world God had created and set in motion.

"I will hear no more!" He leapt to his feet. Mayhap if he was cruel to this angel, she'd leave him as he deserved. "Begone with you." He waved her away.

She didn't flinch, didn't blink, merely rose on one foot and stumbled toward him, leaning her head on his arm. The sentiment disarmed him.

"How can you still be so kind?" he asked.

"You would push me away because you are in pain, but God would not have me abandon you, for He wants you to know He forgives you."

Once again, moisture filled Ronar's eyes. He brushed a lock of hair from her cheek and eased it behind her ear. "And what of you? Do *you* forgive me?"

"Forgiveness is not mine to give. I simply offer my friendship."

He eased a thumb over her cheek, as soft as it looked. Yet he wanted so much more. So much more he could never ask such a lady to give to a scoundrel like him.

She closed her eyes beneath his touch, a web of dark lashes fluttering over cheeks rosy from the fire. He should leave at once, but he found himself frozen in place, their bodies so close he felt her warmth, smelled the elixir of her scent. He wanted to kiss her. Not to satisfy any physical desire, but because he desperately needed her comfort.

She opened her eyes and gazed up at him with a coy smile. "Are you going to kiss me or not?"

When shock caused him to hesitate, she reached up and placed her lips on his.

❧❧❧

Alexia had no idea what madness had overcome her to behave the bold, saucy wench, but once her lips touched Ronar's, and he responded by wrapping his arms around her, pulling her close, and consuming her with his mouth, she didn't care.

"Alexia," he whispered, "Sweet, precious Alexia." His breath warmed her cheek as he ran fingers through her hair, dislodging her circlet and veil.

Heart thumping wildly, she gazed up at him, their eyes but inches apart, and what she saw within them sent a thrill spiraling down to her toes—love and desire and need all churning as one.

He claimed her mouth again, this time opening hers and tenderly exploring within. He tasted of wine and spice and sorrow, and she wanted more and more.

As if it had been dormant all these years, her body suddenly came to life. She returned his kiss, pressing closer against him and gripping the hair at his collar.

He tightened his embrace, encasing her in iron. His touch was gentle, loving, and yet, restrained...much like a wild animal trapped in a cage.

Oddly, she felt no fear. He whispered adoring words in her ears, and she wondered what it would be like to be loved by such a man, to be his wife, share his bed. The shame! *What was she thinking?* She wasn't thinking—couldn't think. She'd never kissed a man before, and she'd always questioned what the pother was about. But as Ronar began to trail hot kisses down her neck, her senses spun in such ecstasy, she feared she'd lose control at any moment.

A moan escaped her lips, and she clung to him, longing for more.

He stopped, gripped her arms, and pushed her back. His chest heaved and his eyes darkened as the air heated between them.

Had she done something wrong?

He smiled, planted a kiss on her forehead, and released her. "Forgive me, Alexia. I forgot myself."

Prithee, I beg you to remember! Catching her breath, she hobbled backward. "Of course." She'd behaved like a common hussy. And she would have done more if he hadn't stopped. Eyes filled with horror, she turned and limped away. She heard him start to follow, but she held up a hand. "Leave me be."

This time he did. She hopped up the stairs and was glad for the pain in her ankle as she made her way to her chamber, for it vanquished the desire still burning through her veins.

Slamming the door shut, she fell onto the bed and allowed her tears to finally flow.

Flow for this man who bore more pain than most could stand, this man who stirred her, soul and body, like no other. And flow for her own lack of control that, if not for Ronar, would have compromised everything she believed in.

Rolling over, she allowed her tears to dribble into her ears as she touched her lips, still on fire from his kiss. For such a powerful knight, he'd been so gentle, so loving.

"Holy Father, I'm so sorry." Hadn't the friar told her to control her emotions… that they would be the ruin of her?

She rolled back over and propped her head in her hands. A shaft of silver moonlight speared the narrow window and landed on the floral coverlet upon which she lay.

A bed on which Ronar had entertained many lovers.

She leapt from it as if it had the plague. Ankle throbbing as much as her heart, she lay down on the rug and fell asleep.

⁂

Was it Sir LeGode or was Drogo's lair colder and gloomier than usual? Mayhap 'twas just LeGode's foul mood, for as he crept forward, candle in hand, searching for the temperamental warlock, fear nearly choked him at the request he must make. Drogo's last reaction to the Spear played fresh in LeGode's mind. Another mention of the infernal object may send Drogo into a rage. And Sir LeGode did not want to be within range of any vile spells spewing from the warlock's fury.

Even though LeGode had promised Cedric to Drogo as an apprentice in exchange for the warlock's help in arranging the lad's marriage to Lady D'Clerc, he was sure there was a limit to that help. He feared he may have already overreached it. Now, taking a step forward, he coughed at the usual stench of rotten eggs, mold, and rancid meat.

"Lord Drogo?"

Wings flapped and a raven swooped down from a ledge above. LeGode shrieked and ducked out of the way but in the process disturbed a row of sleeping bats. Screeching, they took flight and spiraled up the black cone above him.

LeGode had long since overcome his guilt at the pact. 'Twas only for a year, and it would be good for Cedric. The lad hadn't a spark of ambition, and no matter how oft LeGode punished or berated him, Cedric remained a fluffheaded toad. Mayhap under the tutelage of Drogo's strength, power, and wisdom, Cedric would make something of his life.

Drogo *appeared* rather than entered the room. One minute no one was there, the next, his evil grin slithered over LeGode.

"You disturb me much of late," the warlock said, setting down the scroll in his hand. A spider as big as LeGode's hand crawled out from the center and scrambled across the table.

LeGode gulped. "I must cry your pardon, Drogo but 'tis urgent."

"Isn't it always?" Drogo arched a dark, crooked brow. "If you continue to need my services, you may soon owe me your grandchildren."

A foul taste flooded LeGode's mouth. "One last request, Lord Drogo, and all impediments to Cedric's union with Cristiana will be eliminated."

Drogo snorted and spun to examine various bottles sitting on a shelf, then took one and handed it to LeGode.

"What is this?"

"Just a little something I concocted for you. Have the lady drink it, and she will become consumed with love for your son."

"A love potion?" LeGode smiled. "Why didn't I think of that?"

"Because you are a pribbling maggot. Now, what is your request?"

LeGode bristled at the insult. "'Tis this Spear of Destiny. If I find it for the bishop, he vows to arrange Cedric's marriage to Lady D'Clere forthwith."

Drogo spun, his white robes flapping, his eyes narrow coals. "I told you I cannot see where it is. It belongs to Him," he snapped.

"But you sense it. You knew it was here in the castle." LeGode's heart pounded as he chose his words carefully. "Though my guard was unable to find it. Nor do I know who possessed it."

"Do you not?" Drogo shook his head and eyed LeGode as if he were a gnat.

LeGode searched his mind. "How could I? I never heard of the infernal thing until Bishop Montruse intruded on Luxley."

"And informed you that Lady Grecia D'Clere was believed to be in possession of it ere she died." The warlock tapped his long fingernails over the table and sighed.

"Alexia!" LeGode took up a rapid pace, anger shoving out fear. "Of course. Her mother gave it to her. That witch! All this time." He halted and faced Drogo's smirk. "We must find her. Then before I burn her at the stake, I will get the Spear and give it to Bishop Montruse." A sudden thought stole his joy. "How can we find her? *You* can! I've seen you do it before."

Drogo cocked his head. "Get me a piece of her clothing, a strand of hair, anything, and yes, I can and I *will* find her."

Chapter 24

*T*wo days passed. Two days in which, for the first time in her life, Alexia felt like a princess rather than a protector. Aye, the friar had always treated her with love and dignity, but from the moment he'd taken her into the forest, she'd been in training—physically, mentally, and spiritually. She'd had to learn to do battle, both with bow and arrow and without. She'd had to learn the secrets of the forest—how to climb, hunt, fish, and forage. She'd had to learn to receive and hone her spiritual gift of discernment. And most important of all, she had to learn the Words of the Holy Book, which the friar told her was the most powerful sword she could ever wield.

Hence, she'd never been treated like a cherished treasure, delicate and precious. In truth, she'd never wanted to be treated thus, as if she were weak, in need of protection, dependent on a man. She was Alexia D'Clere, God's warrior and Protector of the Spear, a woman who had defeated dozens of knights and sent many more running for their lives.

But here, in this place…with this knight—this man who carried her around as if she were a precious vase—her emotions swirled unbidden to places they'd never gone before.

Thankfully, neither of them spoke of the passionate kiss they'd shared. Nor did they speak of Ronar's past. In fact, Ronar had made her promise that for two days they would not speak of any of their trials or troubles. A respite from life, he had called it. What surprised her the most was how much she enjoyed this brief foray from reality—how much she looked forward to every minute spent in this man's company.

They took long rides through fields of wild flowers, and more than once, Ronar stopped to gather her a colorful bouquet. One day, he prepared a picnic beside a crystal blue lake. Another day, he took her to the top of the highest hill where a majestic view stole her breath. And each night they enjoyed their meal at the manor house with an abundance of wine and laughter.

After a fire destroyed two homes in the village, Ronar spent a day helping the people rebuild. Unable to assist, Alexia could only sit in the shade and try to stifle her rising admiration—to no avail—for this humble earl who worked alongside his serfs as if he were one of them. No wonder he had garnered their undying adoration and devotion.

Each evening as they sat before the fire, they spent hours discussing all manner of topics. From the legends of King Arthur, poems of Dante, and music of Jehan de Lescurel, to the king, what type of man he really was, and what the king's court was like. And together they chuckled at the pompous power struggles that oft made fools of wise men. She particularly enjoyed his humorous stories about his friends Jarin and Damien, some of which she'd have to share with her sister—if Alexia ever made it home again.

Alexia found Ronar to be educated, well spoken, gallant in every way, and growing more handsome with every passing moment—especially when he looked at her with that mischievous twinkle in his eye and a smile that bespoke of a growing affection that matched her own.

In truth, she found it difficult to believe the stories of his past. Alas, she could hardly believe he had been anything but the noble man before her.

Yet now at the dawn of their fifth day at Rivenhall, with her ankle feeling much better, Alexia feared her enchanted world was soon coming to an end. She must return to protect her sister, and Ronar was duty-bound by his king to find the Spear.

A Spear she felt even now weighing down her chemise as they broke their morning fast with eggs, bread, and fresh raspberries.

"Today, Lady Falcon, I insist you teach me your secret of archery." He winked at her like a naughty school boy.

She raised a brow. "Surely a well-trained knight as yourself knows how to shoot a bow and arrow."

"Aye, but not with your skill."

"'Tis more than skill, Sir Knight," she teased.

"Show me and we shall see." With that he rose from the table, hoisted her in his arms, and carried her outside.

"You've no need to carry me around anymore, Ronar. My ankle is healed."

"Mayhap, but I rather enjoy it." His smile, along with the look in his eyes, caused her insides to melt in a most pleasurable way. Something that had been happening much of late.

He placed her down in the courtyard and went to retrieve her bow and arrow. Oddly, though it had been strung over her shoulder more oft than not these last nine years, she hadn't thought of it once during the past week.

She watched him walk to the stables, admiring the authoritative gait that was uniquely his, the slope of his shoulders as if he carried a heavy burden, and the way the wind played among the strands of his brown hair as he disappeared from sight. He wore his usual leather boots, breeches, tunic and doublet, crisscrossed with belts that housed a sword and knives. Even here on his estate, she'd never seen him without his weapons.

Dark clouds swept in overhead, deepening the shadows, and sending a chill through her. An omen of things to come? She hugged herself and closed her eyes, sensing her angel nearby and something else—she spun around—something dark in the distance.

Not yet, Lord. Allow me another day.

Ronar appeared, holding her bow and quiver, his smile so bright, all her dour thoughts instantly swept away. He assisted her out the back gate and into a small, forested area beyond the manor wall, then handed her the bow and a single arrow.

"Pray, show me how you fire so fast and accurately that it seems you are an army of archers. And of course, while flying through the trees like a falcon." He grinned.

Snagging the bow, she gave him a look of challenge, then nocked the arrow and shifted it over the forest, seeking a target that would impress the knight. Why she cared to do so, she didn't want to ponder at the moment. But for some reason, 'twas vitally important to garner his respect.

Though she could oft tell from his eyes, she'd achieved a great deal of it already.

"The knot on the trunk of the pine."

He followed her gaze, squinted, and finally nodded.

Closing her eyes, she released the arrow.

Ronar bolted through the trees, returning with it in hand and a look of shock on his face. "You struck it in the center." He raked back his hair and huffed. "From at least thirty yards."

"Is that all? I must be out of practice." Positioning another arrow, she sought a target farther away. "That hawthorn tree. See the berries hanging from the low branch."

Seconds passed as he squinted in that direction. "I can hardly make them out. Aye, I see it now."

"The berry at the bottom."

He laughed. "Surely you—"

She let the arrow fly. With a snort of disbelief, Ronar plunged through the foliage to retrieve it. When he returned, he stared at her as if she were a ghost. "Show me your secret."

"It'll cost you, Sir Knight." She smiled.

His gaze dropped to her lips. "A kiss?"

"That would be *your* prize. What of mine?"

He gave her that smile that suffocated her senses.

Hogtoes! Was she that obvious? "'Twould seem you have too high an opinion of your charms, Sir Knight." Then fearing he'd see her rising blush, she handed him the bow and took a position behind him. "Hold it like this." The man was a fortress. She could hardly reach her arms around him to show him the proper grip. His leather doublet rubbed against her cheek, his warmth seeped into her skin, and his scent made her dizzy. What was wrong with her? She was no fawning maiden. *Gather your wits, Alexia!*

"I find I'm already getting much out of this lesson, my lady." He turned his face to look at her.

"Hush, Knight, and pay attention. See that pine cone stuck between two branches."

He nodded.

"Do not aim the arrow at it, merely keep the target in your sight. Now, stand sideways, feet spread, shoulders back, and pull the bow toward your ear lobe until the fletching touches it. You can use your cheek too, but you must use the same point each time. Do not touch the arrow, and keep your eye on the target."

His body stiffened as he pulled back the twine and sighted his target. The man was not unfamiliar with the bow. He released the arrow and struck the pine cone, splitting it in half.

"You make me a fool, Sir Knight, for you have no need of my instruction."

He turned so quickly she stumbled backward, and he caught her by the arms. "'Tis but ten yards, and the cone was large, not the size of a Hawthorne berry."

"Your form is good, your eye expert, you need but practice." She limped away from him, grateful to put distance between them.

"For all the practice in the kingdom, I could not hit a moving target at forty yards as you do. Nor with such speed and accuracy."

A burst of wind tossed Alexia's hair in her face, and she shoved it aside.

He studied her quizzically. "What is it you are not telling me, Lady Falcon?"

"Something you would not believe, Sir Knight."

"Try me and I'll grant you that kiss."

۞

Ronar chastised himself for bargaining a kiss with this lady, but he'd been staring at her lips ever since he'd carried her downstairs that morn.

But instead of abhorrence at his untoward suggestion, she laughed. "As I have said, what makes you think I desire another kiss, Sir Knight?"

"Mayhap your reaction to the last one."

She looked away, pink blossoming on her cheeks. "Vain goad. 'Twas your reaction you speak of. And I do not barter such intimacies."

"Then what favor have I to grant you?"

"My freedom." Her tone bore no humor this time.

An ache formed in his gut. "Have you not felt free these past days, Alexia? Free from the constant pain and trouble that plagues our lives?"

She gave a sad smile and nodded. "I have. And I am grateful to you for it."

Ronar approached and stood before her, longing for a glimpse of those lustrous green eyes.

His wish was granted when she raised her gaze to his, studying him with an intimacy that stirred a part of his heart long since dormant.

Then much to his surprise, she reached up and ran fingers over his jaw, delicate fingers, loving fingers. "I have felt many things this past week, Ronar, things which I never thought I'd feel."

He took her hand and brought it to his lips, never taking his eyes off hers, never wanting the connection between them to sever. Though she had attempted to braid her hair, fiery strands had loosened and now danced in the breeze over her bodice and down her back. Lowering her hand, he reached for one, longing to caress it between his fingers, but she moved away, chest heaving. And he couldn't help but be pleased to see his effect on her.

Hoisting the quiver onto her back, she took the bow and arrow from him, an impish gleam in her eye. "The trick is to learn to pull arrow after arrow from the quiver and fire them all in one fluid movement. Like this." Positioning an arrow, she scanned the forest with the expertise and intensity of a trained warrior. Then ere he could blink, she fired at something, withdrew an arrow, nocked it and fired again, then again and again—never stopping to aim or even breathe.

Smiling, she lowered the bow and gestured for him to examine her work. Thirty yards away Ronar found a series of shattered pine cones, some in trees, others on the ground, one on top of boulder. Shaking his head, he retrieved the arrows and returned to her.

"Most impressive, Lady Falcon. But how do you maintain such accuracy whilst flying through trees?"

She took the arrows. "Practice. Many hours of practice."

"I fail to see what would prompt you to practice from trees when the game you seek can be easily caught on the ground."

"Some game is best hunted from above."

"Like knights?" He cocked a brow.

She looked away and replaced the arrows in her quiver.

"But to your secret, my lady?"

"Very well." She smiled and scanned the forest once again. "That Birch nigh forty yards away."

Ronar found it then faced her just as she closed her eyes, pulled back the string, and released the arrow.

Closed her eyes? Impossible. Yet, moments later Ronar found the arrow embedded perfectly in the center of the trunk.

"You closed your eyes," he said, upon returning, still not believing what he'd seen.

"Aye, 'tis the Spirit that guides me."

"The Spirit?"

"Of God. He dwells within those who have received Christ."

He snorted. "God lives within mere humans?"

"His Word tells us thus."

Ronar frowned, disappointment threatening to unravel his joy of the past few days. "More blasphemy."

"More truth, Sir Knight. You said it yourself. 'Twould be impossible to shoot so accurately from such a distance while leaping from branch to branch. The Spirit guides me. He reveals things no human eye can see."

"What things?"

"Spirits, both light and dark, good and evil. Targets too far for me to hit with my natural eye."

He gave a cynical chuckle. "You see angels?"

She nodded.

"And I suppose devils as well."

"Aye. The Bible calls it discerning of spirits. I've had the gift since I was young. Even as a small child, I saw things in my chamber—beings of light who took me in flight over forest and lakes. My parents bade me keep silent, lest I be hailed a witch."

Ronar studied her, his doubts rising. "Then why couldn't you discern the evil within Sir LeGode? Why, after spending two years serving at Luxley, couldn't you discern who was poisoning your sister, or even *that* she was being poisoned?"

She released a long sigh and limped to sit on a fallen log. "To my shame, whenever I am overly nervous or fearful, I cannot see into the realm beyond ours, no matter how hard I try. My emotions overwhelm me, and despite my every effort, I cannot quiet them."

Something Ronar could well understand. After his sister had plunged to her death, rage and agony had consumed him, filling his head with whispers that bade him end it all as she had done, to throw himself in harm's way in battle or simply follow her off the same cliff. Something or *someone* had preserved him through those times, and he'd learned to barricade his feelings behind a shield of self-control.

Still—he shook his head—seeing angels and devils? He hated his own skepticism, but more than that, he hated the pain it caused in Alexia's eyes. "Tell me, Alexia, is there an angel here with us now?"

She pondered his request for a moment, then closed her eyes. Ronar watched as her breath settled and her lips began to move in silent prayer. After several moments, she opened her eyes and lifted her chin. "There are two here with us. My angel and yours. Mine stands to my left and yours is behind you."

Ronar turned but saw nothing. Not that he expected to. But he'd hoped to somehow validate this lady's claim, to prove she wasn't as mad as she sounded, that he hadn't fallen in love with a...*in love*? Indeed. He could not deny it now.

Alexia stood. "You think me mad. Mayhap even a witch."

He longed to erase the pain from her eyes, bring back the joy he'd seen just moments ago. "I don't know what I think."

"Ronar, you have the Spirit living within you as well. I've seen it. You merely have to learn to hear His voice, to recognize His leading." She glanced around the forest with an awe he'd not seen in her before. "There is a realm beyond ours, one you cannot imagine, filled with good and evil and battles and glory and"—she breathed a sigh and smiled—"endless wonders. 'Tis more real than this place and 'tis the destination of all when we breathe our last—some to the darkness, others to the light."

"You speak of heaven and hell. I know of these things."

"They are closer than you think. As are the beings who live in either place."

Truth beamed from her eyes. He wanted to believe her. To believe God gave powers to His followers, that Ronar had more than his sword and wits to defeat the darkness he so often sensed around him.

But 'twas far too incredible.

She stiffened and her gaze suddenly shifted back to the forest.

Dark clouds swallowed up the sun overhead, drowning the trees in shadows.

Ronar listened. His ears were well trained to detect any danger coming—men's breath, sword's screeching from sheaths, horse hooves. But there was nothing but the rustle of leaves and whistle of wind and chirp of—wait, why had the birds suddenly gone silent?

"What is it?" he asked.

Alexia tightened her grip on her bow and drew an arrow. "The angels have drawn their swords."

Chapter 25

*B*asket in hand, Seraphina entered the back gate of Castle Luxley and started across the busy courtyard. Some of the castle knights staved off their boredom by practicing with swords, others with ax or knife. Most, however, stood idly about, laughing and passing around tankards of ale. With the head knight so oft in his cups and LeGode spending most of his time brooding in his study, discipline among the men-at-arms had grown lax.

Keeping her gaze from them, Seraphina forced down yet another wave of dread. The chilling sensations had been coming more frequently of late, darker and more frightening than any she'd yet experienced. Danger still lurked in the castle, to be sure, but these forebodings were different, sinister, as if a black cloud hovered over Luxley and was about to descend.

So absorbed in her musings, Seraphina nearly ran into a page hurrying past with an armful of tunics recently cleaned by the laundress.

"Pardon me, mistress." His shout joined the clank of the blacksmith, neigh of horse, and grunt of pig.

She smiled his way and shook off her gruesome thoughts. 'Twas a rare sunny day, warm, with fresh breezes, ripe with the scent of herbs, pine, and spring flowers. Drawing a deep breath, Seraphina lifted her face to the sun and took her time across the courtyard. Cristiana had sent her to gather wild lavender that grew in the fields outside the castle walls. The lady swore that scattering the herbs across the floor of her chamber calmed her nerves and enabled her to breathe better. But Seraphina knew 'twas her mistress's kindness that had ordered her out on so fine a day, for normally she would never agree to leave Cristiana's side. In fact, she *hadn't* left her side, save to relieve herself, in many months, eating and even sleeping in Cristiana's chamber. Now, more than ever, she must remain with her, ever vigilant against anyone wishing to do her mistress harm.

Yet she had to admit, it felt wonderful to be outside the castle walls, feel the breeze through her hair and the sun warm her skin. Stepping around a chicken, she slowed her pace, delaying just a little longer her return to the stuffy chamber.

A slurred male voice blared over her. "Look what the sun brought out, the most comely lady in the castle." Other voices groaned in agreement. "Aye, come hither, mistress. Let's have a look at ye up close."

Seraphina dared a glance their way and found five knights dressed in coats of chain mail staring at her as if she were a roasted goose. She suddenly felt like a roasted goose as heat filled her chest and flooded her face. Ignoring them, she hurried to the kitchen.

"Not good enough for us?" The same voice followed her.

Another joined the first. "Why, you'd think a simple maid would be flattered to have the attention of knights of the realm."

"Yet she ne'er grants us even a look or nary a smile," another chimed in.

Was that all she was, a servant, a maid to the lady of the castle? A different kind of heat swamped her. 'Twas true, she supposed. Yet she hadn't felt that way in a long while. In truth, she'd never felt that way. Mayhap she'd allowed the D'Clere family's kindness to persuade her otherwise—to make her feel she was more of a friend, an equal, mayhap even a sister.

Nay, if she were any of those things, these besotted knights would treat her with respect, not like some common wench.

She heard them approach and rushed forward. But before she could reach the kitchen, one of them leapt in front of her.

"Alack, you forget your manners, Sir!" She stepped around him and proceeded as laughter bounded behind her.

Two more steps and she would be in the kitchen where dozens of people bustled about with their chores.

One more step.

A thick hand pinched her arm and spun her around. Four knights as big as trees surrounded her, crowding out the sun by their sheer size.

One of them fingered a lock of her hair. Another dared to touch the neckline of her bodice, his grimy finger sliding over the bare skin of her chest.

Dropping her basket, she leapt back and slapped both men away. "Pray, leave me be!" A brief scan of the courtyard revealed no rescuers in sight, just curious knights looking on.

"Come now, sweetheart. You keep yourself hidden away day and night. Surely, you must yearn for male attention."

"What I yearn for is you to behave like gentlemen."

"Grant us each a kiss, and you have our troth we will consider it next time."

"Or mayhap the time after that," one of them said, licking his lips.

"I'll grant you naught!" she snapped back, struggling in the man's grasp.

He tightened his grip. She tried to scream but found her voice had abandoned her.

"Looking for a fight?" A different male voice, deeper and more authoritative, intruded on the knights' laughter, instantly silencing them. The villains froze and turned to face

Sir Damien LaRage, anger stiffening his jaw, and a look in his eyes as if they were but rats he intended to stomp and be rid of.

Armor covered his upper and lower arms, bearing the crest of the king. Belts crisscrossed a leather breast plate into which were stuffed daggers, knives, and axes. His hand rested on the hilt of a sword strapped to his hip.

"We have no quarrel with you, LaRage."

"You will if you do not release the lady at once."

"She isn't a lady. Just a maid that thinks she's too good for us."

"I find I quite agree with her." Damien's eyes finally met hers, and she saw a smile of reassurance within them before he faced the knights again.

"You took a vow to defend women, not ravish them," he said.

"I remember no such vow." The man holding her chuckled.

"Me neither," another one said.

A third stepped forward, eyeing Damien in challenge. "All we ask is a small token of the lady's favor—a mere kiss—a gift she has no doubt given to many a—"

Seraphina never saw the fist coming. Neither did the knight. It landed across his jaw and jerked him backward so hard it seemed he was struck by a battering ram. He fell to the ground with an ominous thud. One of his friends drew a long knife, the other two swords. In one swift move, Damien shoved Seraphina behind him, drew his own blade, and quickly dispatched the first knight with a kick to the groin and a hilt-head thump on the skull.

Seraphina's heart seized. She should run to the safety of the castle. But she couldn't leave this brave man who defended her at such great risk to himself.

Or was it great risk? He went blade to blade with the second man while fending off the third with a knife and kicking the fourth man in the thigh, toppling him to the ground. He swung his sword so fast, Seraphina could hardly follow its movements, save for the sun's blinding reflections. He sliced the second man's thigh, sending him limping away, knocked the blade out of the third man's hand, and then picked up the fourth man beneath his chin and smashed him against the stable wall. "Touch her again, dare to even look her way, and I'll finish what I started here. Understand?"

Though a sneer rode on the knight's mouth, fear nodded from his eyes.

Damien released him, then turned to retrieve his sword from the ground. When he saw her still standing there, surprise and another emotion she could not place rolled over his face.

"Are you harmed?"

"Thanks to you, nay." She smiled and took a deep breath.

He made no reply, simply knelt, gathered the bundles of lavender and placed them back in the basket. When she slid her hand in the crook of his extended elbow, she felt the twitch of his muscles recently used to defend her honor. "You are my champion, Sir."

She sensed a hesitancy, even a nervousness in the large knight as he led her through the kitchen into the main hall. Servant boys dashed to and fro, preparing the tables for the noon meal while minstrels plucked their instruments in the corner as if naught of import had just occurred in the courtyard.

Yet much *had* occurred. This knight who walked so close beside her had just defeated four of Luxley's best knights! She smiled and could not deny the leap of her heart. 'Twas the stuff of romantic ballads—a fantasy she never thought would happen to someone like her.

"I do not know why the knights have become so bold of late." She broke the awkward silence between them, hoping he would answer. "I have never felt unsafe walking about the castle grounds."

"'Tis LeGode's doing. Something has him in a rage." He glanced around them before adding, "Lady Alexia D'Clere's escape, I would assume. Regardless, he calls none of the knights to account and allows the master of arms to drink himself into oblivion from dawn to dusk."

He stopped at the bottom of the stairs, and she took the first tread and turned to face him. Even with the advantage, he still towered over her. Black wavy hair crowned his head, while a mustache and well-trimmed beard circled a strong, well-formed mouth. His skin was a shade darker than hers, his brown eyes intense and somber, yet she sensed anger simmering within them.

And the way he looked at her now, not at all like the knights in the courtyard had looked at her, made her knees suddenly weak.

"They will not bother you again, Miss. I will see to it. And should any other man at Luxley behave in an untoward manner toward you, inform me immediately."

After the way he so easily dispatched four knights, she doubted anyone would dare bother her again. And for the briefest of moments, she relished in the feeling of being protected by such a man. "Why are you so kind to me, Sir?"

He started to say something, but hesitated, then taking her hand, he raised it to his lips and placed a kiss upon it. "I have taken a vow."

"So have Luxley's knights."

"I take mine seriously."

She half-hoped there was more to it than that. But what did it matter? Though the incident had been terrifying, it had reminded her that she was naught but a mere servant, a chamber maid. Her pedigree and education forbade her to even be labeled a true companion to the lady.

Noise drew their gazes to the hall where boys laid white cloths over the trestle tables, then covered them with steel knives, spoons, salt dishes, silver cups and mazers.

"You wish to leave Luxley," she said, drawing his eyes back to hers.

Surprise raised his brows, but he made no reply.

"There's a restlessness about you," she said shyly.

"I am not a man prone to idleness, Miss."

"Nay I wouldn't think so." She glanced down, knowing 'twas improper to proceed but unable to stop herself. "Yet there is something else, something that disturbs you."

His brow furrowed. "How do you know this?"

"Ofttimes, I sense things about people."

He rubbed his beard and nodded. "There is one I seek."

"Someone who did you harm."

Anger burst so suddenly in his eyes, her heart started to pound. "Someone who killed my mother and father and left me an orphan."

Though she longed to discover more, she said naught, and instead, boldly took his hand in hers.

The gesture brought a rare smile to his lips.

"I must away to my lady now, Sir LaRage."

"How fares she?"

"Better." A look of understanding passed between them. "She will attend the noon meal, and you can see for yourself."

"Then I shall see you there as well."

Feeling suddenly flushed, she withdrew her hand and started up the stairs. One glance over her shoulder told her his eyes remained upon her.

❦

Evil surrounded Alexia—dark, insatiable, evil. The hunter was seeking its prey with a ravenous hunger so cold and empty, it sent a shiver down to her bones.

"What is it?" Ronar asked again, drawing his sword and glancing over the forest with the eyes of a warrior trained to detect danger.

But this was not a danger one could sense naturally. Nay, this was something far beyond this world, something powerful, something that hunted without conscience, without limits.

Something that not only killed the body but dragged the soul to hell.

"'Tis evil," she murmured.

Ronar's eyes met hers. "I feel it as well."

Shock filtered through her at his statement. He returned his gaze to the trees as evening cloaked them in shadows. "Can you see it?" he asked.

Did he believe her? She swallowed, trying to settle her heart. Then taking a breath, she closed her eyes and sought the Spirit's sight, all the while whispering prayers in the Spirit for power and guidance. And *help*!

But only darkness prevailed. She opened her eyes, her nerves bound as tight as twine. "I cannot. I'm too frightened," she breathed out, hating the terror in her voice.

Ronar approached, gripped her arm, and started to lead her back toward the manor house. A growl raked across her spine.

The growl of a beast intent on capturing its prey.

A wolf, dark as the night, emerged from the trees, white fangs dripping, eyes blood red.

Ronar froze.

Another wolf appeared, and then another and another, caging them in a prison of sharp, salivating fangs.

She turned to Ronar and saw the terror in his eyes. *He sees them too.*

Sword before him, Ronar retreated, seeking an escape. Other wolves appeared, snarling and growling and staring at them with lifeless, malevolent eyes.

Alexia sought her breath. She had to calm herself. "Faith not fear, calm not calamity." The friar's words repeated in her head, along with a psalm she had memorized. *In God I have put my trust; I will not fear what flesh can do unto me.* But these beasts were not flesh! *Father, help!* Another Scripture blared in her thoughts: *For we wrestle not against flesh and blood, but against principalities, against powers, against the rulers of the darkness of this world, against spiritual wickedness in high places.*

"These are not real wolves, Ronar," she whispered. "We cannot defeat them with arrow or sword."

"Real or not, I cannot fight them all."

Indeed, at least twenty beasts surrounded them now, forming a circle of fangs and claws that closed in on them with every passing second.

The one who seemed to be the leader lifted his lips and uttered a howl that severed Alexia's heart. She slipped her hand into Ronar's and closed her eyes.

They were going to be eaten alive.

❧

Just as he had in Luxley castle, Ronar sensed the evil in these wolves…demonic beings…whatever they were. Terror as he'd never experienced in the fiercest battle turned his heart to ice. He had single-handedly battled a dozen warriors, led entire armies against enemy hordes. But how, by all the holy saints, could he defeat creatures from another realm? He turned to Alexia and found her eyes closed yet again. Fear clenched her features and heightened her breath. He clutched her arms and spun her to face him. "Draw your strength from within, Alexia. Not from what you feel, but from what you *know*. The truth you know. Feed your fear to the truth."

Something he had learned on the battlefield. There was always fear, but 'twas how one used that fear that made the difference.

Angry snarls stabbed the air as the beasts closed in.

Nudging her behind him, Ronar took a stance and swept his blade at the closest wolf. His sword struck something solid, and the wolf yelped and retreated. Not specters, after all! Real flesh and blood wolves. *With real fangs.* He didn't know which was worse.

Behind him, he heard Alexia's breath return, long and smooth and deep. He felt her push from him, heard the strain of her bowstring.

"Jesus," she uttered the simple name and let the arrow fly. It struck one of the wolves. The beast shrieked, leapt in the air, and instantly disappeared in a puff of black smoke.

Ronar could only stare, blinking, too stunned to move. Much to his shame, 'twas Alexia who continued the battle, firing arrow after arrow, the name of Jesus growing louder and bolder on her lips. Each arrow met its mark. And each wolf disappeared in a growl of inky smoke.

The remaining wolves grew only more ferocious, howling and salivating from devilish grins and eyes of fire. One of them charged Ronar, flying through the air, claws extended, mouth peeled back over pointed teeth.

He swung his blade, the name of their Savior on his lips. The beast's whimper faded in a sooty mist.

An arrow zipped past his ear, striking another charging wolf.

Pain tore through his right arm. He turned to find fangs embedded in his flesh.

"Ronar!" Alexia screamed.

Switching his blade into his left hand he plunged it into the wolf. "Jesus." The name emerged in but a whisper, but hatred like he'd never seen speared him from the animal's eyes before the beast disappeared.

Wheeling about, he swung at another and another, shouting the name of Christ.

Arrow after arrow sped through the air around him. Black smoke filled the clearing.

Then all grew silent…save the flutter of leaves, distant thunder, and the rasping of their breathing.

Both he and Alexia scanned the forest, turning slowly, weapons at the ready.

The wolves were gone.

He stared at her in amazement, his heart and mind awhirl with fear, shock, and thoughts he dared not entertain. "What just happened?"

But instead of relief, instead of running into his arms, anger darkened her brow. Slinging her bow over her shoulder, she stormed back to the manor.

"They found us."

Chapter 26

Unable to stomach the fine fare set before him, Sir LeGode rose from his place beside Lady D'Clere at the High Table and now stood at the edge of the great hall eyeing the mindless festivities. He'd arranged a veritable feast—salmon roasted in butter, pheasant baked in golden crusts, a pork fritter in mustard sauce, last year's plums stewed with raisins, cinnamon, and cloves and served with fresh cream. Endless jugs of beer were added to half-a-dozen precious wines brought from across the Christian world. Each course was accompanied by jugglers, acrobats, poets, or dancers.

Frivolous waste! He'd only ordered the entertainment to appease the bishop. Yet now the man's continued drunken laughter stole what remained of LeGode's good humor. Against his better judgment, he returned his gaze to the boorish man, who was shoving all manner of food in his mouth and laughing with glee at a skit wherein a goat chased a Saxon across the room.

Buffoon. Speaking of buffoons, where had Cedric run off to? LeGode had placed him beside Lady D'Clere for yet another attempt to charm the lady, but the dog-hearted clod had abandoned her after barely putting forth any effort at all. Giving leave for Jarin the Just to take his place. Which is why LeGode had left. He could hardly stand the flirtatious laughter and whispered affections flowing betwixt the two of them. *Vile knight!* Even now, his gaze landed on the lady as she leaned to whisper in Sir Jarin's ear.

LeGode fisted his hands. Why was she not sick in her bed? There was color to her fair cheeks and a luster in her eyes that hadn't been there for years. She'd even consumed her meal without so much as a hand on her stomach to indicate her illness.

He ground his teeth, restraining a curse. Had that witch Alexia told her the truth? Nay, for surely Cristiana would have had LeGode arrested at once. If only his knights would arrive. Not even the two remaining King's Guard would dare challenge fifty knights—LeGode's and the twenty he'd already brought over. In addition, many of Luxley's knights were loyal to him ever since he'd spread rumors of Lady D'Clere's madness.

Alack, her sudden recovery put him ill at ease. Her knights would not follow a woman weak in her bed, but they might follow a strong lady in command of her mind and body. Aye, Cristiana could easily put his long-laid plans to ruin—especially with that vain cockerel by her side.

Grrr! He wanted to growl, shout at the top of his lungs, stab someone with his knife. But instead, he smiled politely at a passing guest.

'Twas obvious Lady D'Clere had been warned about the potions. But LeGode had other methods. A smile began to form as plans took root.

That smile faded when Cedric appeared out of nowhere, glass of mead in hand. At the sight of his father, he spun to go the other way.

"Cedric!" LeGode shouted, bringing the lad sheepishly to his side. "I told you to stay beside Lady D'Clere, make an attempt at intelligent conversation, lavish her with praises… do *something* to gain her affection!"

Cedric seemed to shrink before his eyes. "I have tried, Father. 'Tis obvious she has no interest in me." He gazed at the lady in question. "See how she plays the coquette with Sir Jarin."

"Because you are not there!" LeGode seethed.

Cedric pouted.

"Never mind! Be gone. I'll figure something else out." Cedric happily skipped away, hooking arms with a jester, who spun him around, eliciting chuckles from the crowd.

LeGode shook his head and stopped a passing servant bearing a flagon of wine. "How much wine do you have left?"

"I'm almost empty, Sir. I was heading to the kitchens for more."

LeGode grabbed the flagon and stared inside. Enough for half a glass. A juggler who was tossing apples in the air dropped one, drawing jeers and cheers from the guests. The servant looked away for a moment, and LeGode reached into his pocket and pulled out the latest vial of poison Drogo had given him and emptied it into the jug.

"Before you refill it"—he handed it back to the servant— "be a good lad and pour the rest into Lady D'Clere's glass. She expressed how parched she was this day."

"Aye, Sir." After bowing, the lad sped off, and did exactly as LeGode had instructed him.

Slinking further into the shadows, LeGode reached in his pocket for the other vial, while he waited for the lady to take a drink. 'Twould be easier if she did. But whether she did or not—he gripped the vial tightly and smiled—he had another way to get exactly what he wanted.

※

Though Cristiana felt better than she had in years, she'd been hesitant to attend the noon day festivities for two reasons—one, the annoying attentions of Sir LeGode's son, who constantly buzzed around her like a pesky fly, and two and far worse, having to be polite to Sir LeGode, pasting on a smile and acting as if she didn't long to lock him up in the tower. Instead, she must wait, feign ignorance of his evil plans until Jarin assured her the knights were on her side.

But thankfully, a short while after their meal was served, both LeGode and his son left the table, granting her a welcome reprieve. One that grew even better when Sir Jarin took the seat beside her.

"Don't look now, but Sir LeGode is staring our way from the corner of the room." Jarin's eyes flashed mischief.

"I care not. I'm merely happy he left us alone."

"Rest assured, he won't do so for long." One brow rose in reprimand. "I told you to stay abed, my lady."

"Are you not happy to see me?" she replied coyly.

He smiled. "Quite the contrary. I am most happy to see you. And even more honored to sit by your side." He drew her hand to his lips for a kiss.

Warmth swirled within her at the look of affection in the strong knight's eyes. "Sir, I do feel a blush coming on. And from the looks of things." She glanced to the table just beneath theirs, where Seraphina and Damien sat side-by-side deep in conversation. "I am not the only one. No doubt your knightly training involved not only the art of war but the art of romance as well."

"Nay. With some ladies, it merely comes naturally."

"With some men, you mean to say, for I perceive you are naught but a libertine, a rather charming libertine, who has no doubt left myriad broken hearts by the wayside."

A spark of sorrow burned in his gaze before he responded. "I fear a fortnight ago your words would have rung true." He ran a gentle thumb over her hand before his eyes met hers once again. "But now, my heart has but one desire."

The sincerity in those eyes threatened to undo her. As it was, she could hardly quell the wild thump of her heart. *Nay!* She would not fall for his seduction—would not be listed among the many maids he'd chased around and bedded when he'd first arrived. The thought of which made her stomach sour.

She must change the subject. "No word of my sister or Ronar?"

A juggler dropped a ball, and laughter ensued as the minstrels began plucking a new tune.

"Not yet. Never fear. He won't allow her to return to danger. If I know Ronar, he already has a plan to save not only her but you and Luxley as well."

"And what of your plans, Sir Jarin?"

"I have convinced some of the knights to your side, but I must be careful not to approach those who will inform LeGode." He shifted a narrowed glance to the man in question. "I fear he has spread rumors that you are not in your right mind, that you cannot manage the estate."

Anger burned raw in her throat. "The snake!" Her gaze snapped to LeGode speaking with his son, who jerked away and began dancing with a jester.

Jarin shook his head at Cedric's foolishness. "With your sister gone and you so ill, many see LeGode as the rightful Lord of Luxley. They are accustomed to taking orders from him and demand the assurance of your health before granting you their fealty."

"Which is precisely why I appeared today." She raised her chin. "To show everyone I am no longer ill."

"'Tis a fine line you tread, my lady."

Against all propriety, she gripped his hand. "A line I am happy to tread as long as you are by my side."

"If only you would allow me."

"I have not dismissed you yet, have I?" She teased, but then grew somber. "I am most grateful for your protection, Sir Jarin. With my sister hunted, and my trusted steward poisoning me, I find myself quite alone, and oft very frightened."

A young boy approached and filled her cup with wine, and she suddenly wished there was no intrigue or danger afoot, and she was but a lady being courted by a handsome knight.

"You are not alone, my lady. As I have said, I will protect you with my life. You have my troth."

For some unknown reason, despite his good looks and flattery, despite the fact that he could charm a beggar from his last coin, she believed him.

Grabbing her glass, she took a big, long sip.

❧

Marriel la Lauendere mopped the sweat from her brow and waddled into the kitchen. Like every other day of her miserable life, she had spent hours down by the river cleaning clothes for all the inhabitants of the castle—beating, scrubbing, wringing, and hanging, until every bone in her body ached and she longed for food, a bed—and most of all a drink.

She made her way past the cooks and servants preparing the evening meal which, from the scents reaching her nose, consisted of meat pottage, stewed rabbit with onions and saffron, and something else that smelled quite sweet.

None of which was meant for her.

Nay, she'd have to wait and partake of the scraps left over after the lords and ladies ate. But for now, she'd be content with a sip of wine or ale. Well, more than a sip if she had her way. At nine and twenty and with a figure to match a pregnant sow, Marriel had long since given up her dream of marriage and children. Or any reprieve, for that matter, from the long hours of hard labor she'd endured since her father and mother died, leaving her alone in the world. The only thing that brought her any joy was her nightly spirits.

She searched the kitchen—full of stacks of dishes that awaited cleaning—for pitchers of good wine returned from the hall. She always found a few sips left at the bottom which she was happy to consume. No sense in wasting good drink.

But there was nothing tonight.

Passing into the pantry, she spotted a flask of wine set on a tray with fresh bread and cheese. The maid who was in the process of laying everything perfectly upon it, spotted Marriel and looked up.

"'Tis for Lady D'Clere. Sir LeGode ordered a special sour wine to help settle her stomach. She's taken ill again, I'm afraid."

Though Marriel had never had the pleasure of speaking to the lady of the manor, she'd oft heard of her long illness. "I'm sad to hear it," she said, though she meant not a word. She'd rather be ill and lying in a lavish chamber above with a bevy of servants waiting on her than spend day after day scrubbing dirty clothes. Poor, wealthy Lady D'Clere. Marriel could find no sympathy for the lady of the manor.

What she could find sympathy for was her desperate need for a drink. She stared at the flask of wine and licked her lips.

"Oh my," the maid exclaimed. "I've forgotten the yogurt. Milady loves her yogurt. What are you doing here, Marriel?"

"Looking for something to drink," she returned innocently. "'Twas a long, hot day."

"Aye, to be sure." The maid smiled. "There's some water and wine there in the barrel. Help yourself." Then off she dashed back to the kitchen.

Aye, bitter wine mixed with slimy water. Marriel eyed the pewter flask on Lady D'Clere's tray, then glanced toward the door. Before she changed her mind and with a speed that belied her wide girth, Marriel snagged the flask from its perch and drained it in one huge gulp. Spicy and delicious, just as she had expected. Wiping her mouth on her sleeve, she quickly ladled the watered down wine from the barrel into the flask and replaced it on the tray.

No one would ever know.

Chapter 27

*T*houghts and emotions awhirl, Alexia entered the courtyard, silently praising God for His deliverance. She'd never encountered such a ferocious demonic assault. And in truth, she hadn't been sure of her victory. Fear had gripped every nerve, every organ, until she could hardly breathe, hardly think of what to do. *Faith...faith.* She had needed faith! But alas, her fear had threatened to trample what little she possessed.

Potz! Why could she not learn this *one* lesson.

Ronar appeared beside her. "What in the name of all that is holy was that?"

As if the realization of what they had just done struck her all at once, her knees turned to porridge, the sky began to spin, and she stumbled, hating her display of weakness. Wrapping an arm around her, Ronar led her to sit on a bench by the stables. A lamp hanging on a post above cast a circle of light around them, reminding her that God was still with them.

Ronar took her hand in his, a gesture that calmed her more than she wanted to admit.

"*That* had naught to do with anything holy." She watched as he scanned the dark courtyard, his other hand fastened to the hilt of his sword. Ever the warrior. Did this knight never fail to surprise her? "You didn't tell me fighting demons was among your many skills, Sir Knight."

"I was unaware such a skill existed." He huffed. "In truth, 'twas learned quickly by your example and the necessity of my own survival."

The smell of roast chicken and baked pears wafted from the kitchen, tantalizing her taste buds but souring her stomach.

Bridon hurried out the kitchen door and made his way to them. "My lord, when do you require your evening"—horror streaked his hooded gaze—"You are injured, my lord!"

Alexia followed the steward's gaze to the blood staining Ronar's right sleeve. She had forgotten he'd been bitten. "We must tend it immediately." She started to rise, but Ronar tugged her back down and waved off his steward.

"Bridon, prepare the lady a bath in my chamber and retrieve another gown from Idon—the wardrobe. Then you may lay out our dinner in the hall and retire for the evening. We shall be in anon."

Though one judgmental brow cocked, the man nodded and uttered, "As you wish, my lord," ere he strode away.

Rising, Alexia tugged on Ronar, attempting to pull the massive knight to his feet, but it was like pulling a mountain from its moorings. "Your wound cannot wait. Come."

He didn't budge. "First, tell me what those fiends were and why we defeated them so easily."

"Easily?" Alexia continued to yank on him, but finally gave up and released his hand. "Mayhap for you. They were demons sent to kill us, I expect."

"But they had flesh and bone." He moved his arm and winced. "And *real* teeth."

"Aye, I am as surprised as you." Something she would have to ask the friar about later.

"Who sent them?"

"The bishop, LeGode. I know not. Someone with access to the powers of darkness. I have seen them before. Once last year, they surrounded and killed a traveler on his way to Luxley ere I could intervene."

"LeGode then. Not the bishop. I may not be fond of him, but he is still a man of the cloth." Ronar stood, placed her hand in the crook of his elbow, and started for the main entryway. "The name of Christ. You spoke it as you fired each arrow."

"As you did as well." She smiled.

"'Twas hard to deny the power it wielded."

"'Tis the most powerful name in all existence." That and the Spear in her pocket. "Without it, my arrows would have no impact on such otherworldly fiends."

"How did you know it would work?" He opened the large wooden door and led her into the entryway, dark save for a single candle perched on a sideboard.

"And these signs shall follow them that believe," she quoted from Scripture. "In my name shall they cast out devils; they shall speak with new tongues; they shall take up serpents; and if they drink any deadly thing, it shall not hurt them; they shall lay hands on the sick, and they shall recover."

This time Ronar did not cover his ears. Instead, he shut the door and simply stood there in the dark silence. Finally, she heard him release a sigh. "Simply saying His name? I cannot fathom it. Why do they not teach this in church?"

"Then what need would we have of priests?" she quipped.

"They are God's chosen."

Alexia bit her lip as Ronar led her to the foot of the stairway. "It pains me greatly to know that in the future, though all will have access to the Scriptures, people will rely on men once again and many of these men will not teach the power of the Spirit. 'Having a form of godliness, but denying its power,'" she quoted again.

"The friar has told you this."

"Aye. And I believe him." She turned to face him, barely able to make out his features in the dim candlelight. "I do pray he is safe."

He squeezed her hand. "I pray so as well."

"Now, Sir Knight. You must teach me more about controlling my emotions."

"Tush! What need? You did quite well today, Lady Falcon." He smiled. "Pray, what truth did you seek?"

"The only truth I know is real. That God loves me and will never leave me."

He nodded. "And when you sought that truth, what happened to your fear?"

"It lessened, to be sure. Yet I still felt it just a breath away, threatening to rise again." She cocked her head and studied him. "What truth do you seek when you are afraid, Ronar?"

He looked away. "Penance. That God will not let me die until I have paid the price for my sins."

Her heart sank, desperately longing to see him free of this torturous burden.

"Next time," he said. "Simply remember that the truth is always greater than fear's lie."

Turning, she took the first step but then faced him again. "I will do my best, Ronar LePeine, Sir Knight, Earl of Rivenhall, whoever you are today."

Without warning, he swept her in his arms and began ascending the stairs. "Today, I am your humble servant."

"We really haven't time for this, Ronar. Nor a bath, nor a meal. LeGode knows where we are. Surely, he will dispatch his knights forthwith."

"I agree."

He set her down before his chamber door.

"You agree with me? 'Tis a first. Does that mean you are to release me from captivity?"

He eased hair behind her ear. "And what an enchanting captive you have been. But let us not talk of such things. Not tonight. Let us enjoy a good meal, laughter, and wine one last time. And then we shall leave at first light."

Though she didn't want to admit it, that sounded absolutely heavenly. Had Ronar enjoyed their time together as much as she had? He'd had so many women, 'twas hard to believe he found her anything special. But how could she deny the look of complete adoration she now saw in his eyes?

"As you wish, Sir Knight."

His gaze lowered to her lips, and much to her shame, she hoped he'd remember their bargain for a kiss. But instead, he bowed and walked away.

Inside the chamber she found a large barrel full of warm water, a crackling fire, and a fresh kirtle and bodice. She couldn't remember the last time she'd bathed in water that wasn't cold and filled with fish, fronds, and frogs. Alas, she could have soaked in the sudsy warmth all night, save for her excitement of the evening ahead.

After drying and donning the fresh gown, she knelt by a chair, reached in the pocket of her chemise, and brought out the Spear. Candlelight shimmered over the aged steel, and she kissed it and drew it to her bosom. "Father, thank You for delivering us today from evil and for showing Your power to Ronar. Please open his eyes to Your grace and truth, and please protect us from the coming storm."

A storm she felt advancing toward her with ever increasing speed.

"Father, please protect Cristiana, Seraphina, Anabelle, and Friar Josef. Surround them with your warrior angels. Thank you, my King."

She rose, replaced the Spear, then pressed the folds of her emerald green skirt, relishing in the feel of the soft fabric and the way the gold trim glittered in the candlelight. A belt made of golden chains and embedded with jewels sat lightly on her hips and hung down the front of the gown. Though her hair was still damp, she'd managed to braid the strands around her face and pull them back with a golden tie. Gazing at herself in the mirror, she had to admit she barely recognized the lady staring back at her. She'd never felt as beautiful as she had this past week and as she made her way downstairs, a twinge of sorrow gripped her that her time here would soon come to an end.

Before she was halfway down, Ronar appeared, took the stairs two at a time and hoisted her in his arms.

"You really should stop doing that."

"Why?" He smelled of wine and lye and man, and she realized he had bathed as well. The wet tips of his brown hair curled at his collar, and his blue eyes beamed with the anticipation she felt in her own heart.

He set her down in the hall, and she was instantly assailed with the savory scents of chicken, onions, saffron, and something sweet. Pears? Steam rose from trenchers upon the candlelit table covered in a white cloth.

Ronar had donned a fresh tunic, doublet and breeches, but she could see the bulge of a bandage beneath his shirt sleeve. "Your arm!" She reached for it.

"Is well. Bridon tended it." He took her hand and led her to the table. "Come. Let us eat."

And so they sat and talked and ate and drank wine as if they hadn't just defeated a horde of demonic wolves and a troop of knights weren't on their way to capture them.

Somehow those things drifted into the background, merely tales of bad news from a land far away—a land that could never touch them here. All that mattered was this knight, this man with the broken heart and sad eyes, who gazed at her as if she possessed all the gold of Midas.

After the meal, they took seats before the fire as they had done the first night they'd arrived. Fond memories arose of that time only days ago that now seemed years for all she'd learned of him.

"Where will we go tomorrow, Ronar? Emerald Forest?" Or so she hoped. To find the friar and make plans to defeat LeGode.

"We make haste for London to see the king." He answered without looking at her.

"Nay!" She shouted. "I must discover if my sister is well and protected."

"She is. I trust Jarin."

"I do *not*." She sprang to her feet. "I don't know him at all."

He gave her an authoritative look that brooked no dispute. "You know me, and I trust him with my life."

Obstinate, arrogant man! "What can we do in London?"

"The king will listen to me…to us. I will request he send us back with his best knights to deal once and for all with LeGode."

"The king will believe Bishop Montruse. He will think me a witch and have me burned."

Ronar frowned. "It will not come to that."

"You do not know."

"What other choice do we have?" Ronar stood, his tone softening. "Storm Castle Luxley with one sword and a bow and arrow?"

She lifted her chin. "And God on our side."

He huffed. "I will not deny what I saw today, but surely God requires prudence and wisdom from his subjects, not foolhardy rashness."

Alexia swallowed down her frustration. "You sound like the friar."

"Wise man." Ronar tossed a piece of wood in the fire, sending sparks crackling up the chimney. "Let us not speak of this tonight." He reached for her hand. "Alexia, no more secrets between us. You know every detail about my life, and hence, I am surprised you still bear my company."

"I more than bear your company, Ronar. I enjoy it. *Have* enjoyed it immensely."

He caressed her fingers. "As I have yours. No more secrets, then? A pact between us?"

Alexia looked away. How could she make such a pact when she could feel the Spear this man sought for against her thigh? She was the Protector. She must not forget that. Regardless of the way this man made her insides turn to mush, he had come for the Spear—was duty-bound to bring it to the king. Doing so would earn him another rung up the ladder of penance he so ardently sought, no matter how misguided he was.

"No more secrets," she mumbled out. *Save one*

"Then let us enjoy the remainder of the evening." Releasing her hand, he moved to the table and poured them both wine, then tossed cushions before the fire and sat down.

Moments of silence passed as the wind whistled against the stone walls, the flames crackled, and a horse neighed from the stables. He sipped his wine. Firelight flickered over the firm line of his jaw and brought out the sorrow in his eyes. An errant strand of hair fell across his forehead, and he seemed so far away, she longed to bring him back. Rising from her chair, she knelt beside him and ran fingers over the scruff at his chin, turning his gaze to her. "Oh, that I could ease your pain, Ronar."

He grabbed her hand and brought it to his lips. "You have, Alexia. More than you know. I have never known a lady like you."

Feeling suddenly shy, she grinned. "Not courted any women who leap from tree to tree and shoot arrows down at you?"

He chuckled and shook his head. "As if that weren't exciting enough, I find you are so much more than that.

Godly, kind, generous, forgiving, courageous, fiercely loyal." He traced the line of her jaw with his finger. "And exceedingly beautiful."

Her heart swelled and she glanced down. "Cease, I beg you. You make me blush."

Placing a finger beneath her chin, he brought her gaze back to his, his eyes so full of affection, her breath escaped her.

Before she knew it, his lips were on hers, caressing her with warm, tender kisses that sent her thoughts spinning and her senses into ecstasy. And suddenly nothing but Ronar mattered. The taste of him, his touch, his scent. His very presence. He wrapped thick arms around her and pressed her against his chest.

Her heart pounded. Heat swamped her, and she couldn't get close enough to him, wanting more and more of him.

Gently, he laid her down on the cushions, continuing the kiss, going deeper with his need for her. His beard scratched her cheek. His strength surrounded her. And Alexia lost herself in him—utterly, completely lost. Something in the back of her mind told her 'twas wrong to be alone with him, lying atop pillows, receiving his kiss. *Wasn't it?*

He pulled back and gazed down upon her, his blue eyes burning with desire...and something else. "I love you, Alexia."

Too stunned to speak, she could only stare at him. *Love? Her?* Against her will, tears filled her eyes. One escaped and slid down her temple.

He halted it with his thumb. "Not the reaction I hoped for."

She embraced him, running fingers through the hair at his neck. "I love you, too," she whispered.

Once again, his lips found hers, and once again, Alexia entered another world where time and wolves and demons and danger ceased to exist. His grip tightened. His kiss grew deeper and more intense. But then he backed away, breathless, staring at her. He ran the back of his hand over her cheek, and she closed her eyes beneath his gentle touch. Suddenly she felt him lifting her body and rolling her over until her back was to him. Then wrapping an arm around her from behind, he laid down beside her.

His hot breath tickled her neck, making it difficult to settle the mad rush of blood through her veins, but it was his whisper in her ear that warmed her heart. "I will not dishonor you, Alexia. I love you too much for that."

With those precious words, this man made her feel more cherished, more loved, than all the passionate kisses in the kingdom. Slowly, her breath settled, her heart slowed, and she snuggled against him. Exhaustion weighed on her eyes, and she knew she was falling asleep in his arms. She knew 'twas most improper.

But she also knew she never wanted to leave his side.

Chapter 28

"*S*he destroyed my wolves!"

LeGode had never seen the warlock so furious. He took a step back lest a lightning bolt fling from the man's white-hot glance and strike him dead.

The stench of sulfur and burnt flesh rose like dragon's breath from the ever-present pot bubbling in the center of the chamber. Bats, unaffected by the furor brewing beneath them, hung in rows of black, dripping ink.

After several moments of Drogo mumbling and muttering and stopping to examine red coals scattered across a table, LeGode dared to say, "Can you not conjure up more?"

Drogo swung about, and LeGode could swear he saw smoke shoot from his mouth. "Conjure? Do you think it easy to pull such beasts from their feasting in hell?"

LeGode had no idea. Though he knew a *certain* beast he'd love to send to hell at the moment. He grew weary of this man's constant complaining and failures. Which reminded him. "The potion you gave me to ensure Lady D'Clere's affections bears no effect on her at all. She spends what little time she has away from her bed with that maggot, Jarin the Just."

Ignoring him, Drogo retrieved a scroll, spread it out on a table, and slid his long, black nail down the script therein.

"Forsooth!" LeGode continued, his anger growing, "Our laundress, a fat sow of a woman, has taken to following Cedric everywhere, proclaiming her love for him."

Drogo growled and glared up at him. "Because she drank the tonic meant for your lady, you half-brained lout."

LeGode grimaced. *Of course.* Could he not trust one maid—one well-paid maid—to do the simplest of tasks? He would see her released at once.

"We have bigger problems than the lady's interest in this knight at the moment," Drogo said, still reading the scroll.

"I quite agree." Capturing Alexia and the Spear for one. Then at last the bishop and this Jarin the Just could finally quit Luxley.

Drogo slammed his fist on the table. LeGode jerked as the warlock's eyes narrowed in fury. "She used the Spear against my wolves!"

LeGode restrained his laughter. "How could any Spear, especially the mere tip of one so old, defeat such hellish creatures?"

The warlock gaped at him as if he were an imbecile. "Because of where it has been. It is *holy.*" His lips twisted into a snarl as if the very word burned his mouth. "Know you naught of the battle we are in?"

The only battle LeGode was aware of was his struggle to acquire Luxley as his own. He shrugged. "Now that we know where she is, it should be a simple task to capture her."

"She is not alone," Drogo spat. "That knight is with her."

"*Ronar LePeine.*" LeGode had suspected as much, for the lady could not have escaped without help. "What is one knight against fifty? I will dispatch a troop right away."

"You fool! With the Spear in hand, they can defeat anyone or any*thing* we send against them."

Indeed? LeGode tapped his chin. Mayhap there was something to this Spear, after all, for LeGode had never seen Drogo so out of sorts. No wonder the king sought the relic as his own. With such an object, one could conquer the world. LeGode smiled. "Then how are we to steal it from them?"

Drogo fingered his long beard. "She must come to us of her own accord."

"Would that she were that dim-witted."

Ignoring him, Drogo held out his arm and whistled. A black raven appeared out of nowhere and landed on his hand. "What one thing would draw her back to Luxley?"

The raven eyed LeGode as if it wished to peck out his eyes. He swallowed. "Her sister."

"Then all you need do is send a message that her sister is dying."

"She won't believe it."

"Send someone she trusts. She *will* come. Those whose hearts are pure always put others ahead of themselves. Weak fools!" He shook his arm and the raven screeched and flapped up into the cavernous hole above them.

Someone she trusted. LeGode knew just the person.

❦

A chilled mist surrounded Cristiana. She rubbed her arms and took a step forward. Trees appeared out of the fog like subjects parting for royalty. Cold mud squished between her toes. She could see naught ahead of her, save misty shadows and a speck of light in the distance. Behind her, darkness pursued—a cloud of thick black rolling toward her, fierce, malevolent, devouring the forest as it went. A raven cawed. She hurried her pace.

Where am I? How did I get here? Her heart squeezed. Her mind spun with fleeting thoughts.

Still, the darkness came. And she knew if she didn't keep moving, keep fighting, it would swallow her whole, and she would be lost forever.

Shoving aside the misty curtain, she dashed forward. Her foot struck something hard. Pain sent her tumbling to the mud. Laughter barreled over her from behind. Tears filled her eyes. "Help me! Help!" She tried to get up, but the thick clay held fast to her ankle and tugged her back down.

"Nay!" She jerked from its grip and stood.

Up ahead, the light grew wider, brighter. A hand appeared from the center and reached toward her.

She stumbled forward. The mud turned to soft grass, the fog thinned, and birds serenaded her from above. Hope sprouted, and she picked up her pace, suddenly aware she wore naught but a night shift, her unbound hair fluttering about her.

She gripped the hand, strong and firm. Desiring to see her rescuer, she lifted her face—then her eyes opened, and her chamber appeared before her, distorted by her gauze bed curtains. Beyond them, Seraphina stood by the window.

A nightmare. 'Twas only a nightmare. She gripped her throat where her throbbing pulse told her 'twas much more than a dream. "Why am I still sick?" she muttered, drawing Seraphina to part the curtains and sit by her side.

"I have not taken my medicine?" Her lower lip started to quiver, and she pressed fingers against it, murmuring, "Mayhap, I am truly ill."

"Nay, milady. I do not believe that." Seraphina clasped her hands and scanned the chamber as if expecting a specter to leap out from the shadows at any moment. "We must pray for God's protection." Though from her tone, Cristiana doubted the woman believed He would come to their aid.

"And He will surely deliver us," Cristiana said as much to comfort herself as her friend.

Dipping a cloth in water, Seraphina dabbed it on Cristiana's face. "Here you are bringing me comfort when you are the one who is ill, my lady." She attempted a smile Cristiana knew was for her benefit alone. "However, I quite agree. We have much on which to pin our hope. Sir LePeine will protect Alexia, and soon she will return to reclaim

Luxley and defeat LeGode. In the meantime, we have your handsome knight Jarin to protect us."

"He is not *my* knight." Cristiana smiled and turned her head to the left. Even that small movement drained her of energy, but it was worth it to see the vase of fresh flowers on the table beside her bed. From Jarin the Just. He'd sent fresh ones every day since she'd once again been taken ill. She faced Seraphina. "And his friend is quite handsome as well."

Seraphina held a cup of wine to Cristiana's lips and helped her rise. "I will not deny it."

Though the maid's tone was devoid of emotion, Cristiana knew her friend too well, could sense the joy longing to burst forth on her expression—a joy that seemed out of reach for them both, especially in light of Cristiana's nightmare. Would either of them have the chance to pursue love ere the darkness consumed them?

Setting down the cup, Seraphina drew back the curtains and tied them to the posts. "Is there anything you need? Mayhap I could read to you?"

"Nay. I fear I'm far too tired. I will rest."

With a nod and a tender look, Seraphina returned to the window, leaned against the edge, and gazed out while Cristiana closed her eyes.

A giggle made her open them again, and she was surprised to see Seraphina holding a hand to her mouth. "What has you so amused?"

"'Tis naught." Seraphina giggled again. "Simply that the laundress has become quite taken with Cedric."

"LeGode's son?"

"Aye, she follows him around everywhere he goes. She was fawning after him just now in the courtyard, and yesterday, I saw her chasing him through the main hall. 'Tis quite amusing, though I suppose 'tis evil of me to say."

Cristiana's chuckle ended in a cough. "How does Cedric respond?" She hoped favorably. Then, at least the man would leave her be.

"That is the amusing part," Seraphina said. "He shouts at her to acquit him. Once, he dared push her away. Yet she continues her love struck pursuit."

Cristiana didn't have time to remark at the oddity when a rap on the door preceded Anabelle's pretty face. "Two gentlemen to see you, my lady. What shall I tell them?"

If they were the *two* gentlemen she hoped—which surely they were by the teasing look on Anabelle's face—Cristiana would be glad for their company, regardless of the impropriety. "Give me a moment, please." She was about to ask for Seraphina's help, but the lady was already by her side, propping her up on pillows and covering her night shift with the coverlet.

"How do I look?" she asked Seraphina.

"Even ill, you are a sight to stir any knight's heart."

Cristiana returned her friend's smile. If only she felt equally well, for the room began to spin and her stomach vaulted. She sank back onto the pillows as Seraphina opened the door and in walked Jarin the Just and his friend Sir Damien LaRage. Immediately, in the presence of such noble knights, all fears and morbid thoughts vanished.

Especially when Sir Jarin gazed at her as if she were a spring of water in the middle of a desert. "My lady." He approached, took her hand, and kissed it. His glance quickly took in the flowers at her bedside.

"Thank you for your kindness, Sir."

"Thank you for receiving us. I know 'tis most unseemly. And I see you are still unwell, hence we will not keep you. But I have urgent information." He shared a glance with Damien, who stood beside Seraphina at the foot of the bed.

Had Alexia been captured? Or worse? Cristiana's heart dashed against her chest as she stared at the knight, afraid to know and yet afraid not to. "Pray, keep it from me no longer."

"I am convinced they are now putting the poison in your food and drink. Hence, you must not partake of anything they bring you."

"But I still receive the vial of medicine each night."

"Which we pour out," Seraphina added.

Jarin nodded. "Aye, but LeGode is cunning. He is no doubt aware you are not drinking it."

Cristiana breathed out a sigh of relief. "That is why I am still ill."

"Aye. Henceforth, you must only accept food and drink from myself, Damien, or Anabelle. We will secretly send up enough for you both morning and night."

She reached for his hand, and he willingly took it and began caressing it with his thumb. "You are my savior, Sir Jarin." Oh, how she wished she were well so she could spend the day with this man, discover his secrets, feel safe by his side. But that was not to be. Mayhap never. "What news of my sister?"

"None. But that is a good sign."

The snort of horse, clank of metal, and shouts drew Seraphina and Damien to the windows, while Jarin remained by Cristiana's side.

"What is amiss?" Jarin asked.

"A squire leaves post haste," Damien commented, still staring into the courtyard. "Odd, but I saw that same squire leaving LeGode's study earlier,"

"Why would he send him out without a knight?" Seraphina asked. "And on a knight's charger?"

Damien rubbed his bearded jaw. "I know not. But whatever mission he embarks upon, it does not bode well for our cause."

Seraphina hugged herself. "Many things do not bode well. I have sensed"—she exchanged a glance with Cristiana—"I have sensed evil in this room. All around us." Her fearful gaze shifted to Jarin and then to Damien. "Last night I woke and could have sworn someone was in the chamber."

Jarin looked up. "With you and Lady D'Clere?"

"Aye. I heard wood creak, footsteps, and then a door grind open. But when I lit a candle and checked, it was bolted shut."

"From within?" Damien asked.

"Aye." She sank against the window ledge as if her strength escaped her.

Gently taking her arm, Damien led her to a chair, then shared a look with Jarin that made Cristiana's breath hitch. "What is it?"

"Is anything missing?" Damien asked.

"Missing?" Cristiana said. "There is naught of value here, save my jewels."

Seraphina nodded. "And they are in her chest as always. I saw them this morn when I replaced the ones she wore yesterday."

"I don't understand." Cristiana breathed out, fear pinching every nerve. "LeGode is already poisoning me, what else could he possibly want?"

Jarin continued to caress her hand, but his tone bore alarm. "Whatever they sought, it must have been of great value to risk getting caught."

Eyes suddenly wide, Seraphina rose and moved to her chest perched in the corner. Kneeling, she opened the lid and began rummaging through the contents, her search growing more frantic as she went. Finally, she stood and faced them, fear and confusion marring her features.

"What is it?" Cristiana asked.

"My swaddling cloth."

"What?" Damien asked.

No answer came from the maid, and Cristiana knew she was hesitant to relay her story. "'Twas Seraphina's when she was a babe and has sentimental value."

Seraphina sank into a chair. "Why would anyone want my swaddling cloth?"

❧

The sweet scent of pine and woman teased Ronar's senses, the rhythmic puff of angel's breath filled the air, and something warm and soft moved beneath his arm. Light formed a rainbow of gold and gray on his eyelids. He stirred. Memories returned of his evening with Alexia, the tender moments they'd shared, the kisses, her declaration of love. Had it been a dream?

He moved his arm. The woman beneath it shifted before her breathing deepened again. Nay. Not a dream. Yet so much better than anything he could have dreamed. Opening his eyes, he remained still, relishing the moment of her sleeping peacefully in his arms, as if they had spent a thousand nights together—the feel of her silky hair against his cheek, the warmth of her body pressed against his, her scent that drove him mad with desire.

Nay, 'twas so much more than that. He frowned, remembering the dozens of women he'd taken to his bed—their hope set on marrying an earl, his in but a few hours of pleasure. A few hours which never satisfied and left him wanting nothing more than to escort them from the manor and return to his bed alone.

Not this lady, this Alexia D'Clere, this Lady Falcon. Though he felt more desire for her than all the others put together, he didn't want to cheapen her by an act reserved for the sanctity of marriage, an act that sealed an eternal covenant between two people to love each other for all eternity.

Shame landed heavy on his heart. He had abused this wonderful gift of God, treated it callously and for his own pleasure. But no more. Lady Alexia D'Clere deserved to be held in the highest honor, and Ronar intended to do just that. At the right moment, and with the king's permission, he would ask for her hand.

She moaned, a low moan of pleasure that caused his body to react. He started to back away when she turned, opened her eyes a mere slit, and, upon seeing him, smiled.

That smile turned into a screech as she sprang to sit and leapt away from him, one hand on her chest, the other gripping her skirts.

"What have I done? What have *you* done?" Her green eyes raged.

Sitting there with her red hair flaming about her head, her eyes swollen with sleep, he realized he could get used to such a sight every morning.

"Your maidenhead is intact, Alexia." He stood and held out his hand for her. "I would never take such liberties."

"But we slept side by side." She glared at the rumpled cushions as if they had colluded in her fall from grace.

"Aye, a night I shall fondly remember." He grinned.

Her eyes narrowed, but he found a playful spark within them as she took his hand and allowed him to pull her to her feet.

Bridon entered the room, his gaze taking in the cushions and Ronar and Alexia's disheveled appearance. Uttering a huff of indignation, he turned to leave. Ronar didn't blame him. The poor man had witnessed far too much debauchery when Ronar had resided here.

"Bridon, would you have Cook pack bread, cheese, and dried meat. Enough for three days. The lady and I are embarking on a journey."

"Very well, my lord." The folds of his face tightened in an incriminating frown. "And when should we expect your return, if ever?"

Ignoring his biting tone, Ronar replied. "I know not. Have our horses saddled and ready to go within the hour."

The steward swung about, leaving them alone once again.

Alexia ran fingers through her chaotic hair, looking unusually nervous for the warrior she was. Had she meant what she'd said to him last night? That she loved him? Or had it been merely her passion speaking?

She went from fiddling with her hair to pressing the folds from her skirt.

He took those busy hands in his and brought them to his lips, staring at her over her knuckles. "I meant what I said last night, Alexia."

Her eyes lit and she breathed out a sigh. "As did I, Sir…Ronar."

Drawing her close, he kissed her forehead. "Then let us be on our way. I would not endanger you by remaining here another moment. Do you wish to wash or do whatever ladies do in the morning?"

"'Twill take me but a moment." She pushed away, turned and gave him a coy glance over her shoulder. "I will meet you at the stables anon."

True to her word, she reappeared in the courtyard not long after, wearing a fresh lavender tunic, laced up the front with gold thread and open at the sleeves. A beaded belt hung at her curvy hips and a matching headband circled her red hair that was braided and fell to her waist.

Ronar had never seen a vision so lovely.

She must have sensed his pleasure, for her face lit with a coquettish smile.

Even the stable boy stopped strapping on the horses' bridals to stare at her. Ronar spun to face him and cleared his throat, and the poor lad jerked his attention back to his task, face reddening.

"I would have worn your breeches, Ronar," Alexia said. "But alas, they were—"

The sound of a horse drew all their gazes to the front gate, and Ronar gestured for the stable boy to see who was coming. A moment later, the lad opened the gate and peered out. "My lord, a lone rider approaches," he shouted over his shoulder. "Fast. He bears no arms."

Ronar frowned, gripped the hilt of his sword, and took a stance before Alexia. "Allow him entrance."

A black charger soon galloped through the gates and reared up before them.

Pushing past Ronar, Alexia dashed toward the newcomer. "What is it, Hugh, where is your knight?"

"I have come alone, my lady, with an urgent message." He slid off the horse and dug through a saddle pouch. "They do not know I am gone."

Ronar ground his teeth together as foreboding trampled the joy of the morning.

Retrieving a piece of fabric, the lad held it out to Alexia.

Alarm fired in her eyes. She fingered the stained and worn fabric as if it were made of fine silk. "'Tis Seraphina's swaddling cloth. She would never part with this. What has happened to her? Tell me now."

"Nothing, my lady. She is well. But she bids you come right away. Your sister is dying."

Alexia gripped her stomach, her breath coming hard. "Dying? How can this be?"

"I know not, my lady. I am only instructed to bid you come post haste."

"Of course. Thank you, Hugh. Return before you are missed, and tell her I am on my way."

He nodded, his gaze skittering nervously to Ronar ere he spun around, leapt on the horse, and galloped off.

Alexia stood for a moment, caressing the cloth, her face ashen. Then turning, she started for her horse. "Come, we must return to my sister immediately."

Ronar took her by the elbow, hating himself ere he uttered the words he knew would destroy her love for him. "Nay, my lady, we will *not* go back to Luxley."

Chapter 29

*A*lexia jerked from Ronar's grip. "Aye, we *will* return to Luxley. Did you not hear the man?" She could hardly believe the look of defiance on the knight's face.

Especially after all they'd shared this past week!

"I heard," he said plainly, his jaw growing stiffer by the moment.

"Then you are aware of the urgency."

"All we know is what this squire has said. Why are you so quick to trust him?"

"Why are you so quick not to?" She shoved the cloth toward him. "Seraphina would never part with this unless she wished to prove to me 'twas her sending the message."

Ronar turned, grabbed the reins from the stable boy and dismissed him. "They could have stolen it."

"Nay. Only Seraphina, myself, and my sister know of its existence. Let alone its importance and location." She tried to settle her anger, but the terror raging through her only set it further ablaze.

He hoisted his packs over the horse's back and went to retrieve something in the stable.

She marched after him. "I cannot allow my sister to die. Especially not alone."

"Then we must make haste to London." Horses peeked at them from their stalls as the smell of hay, horseflesh, and manure enveloped her. "Once there," he continued, his tone softening, "we can acquire the help we need. If we go back to Luxley now, we will both be captured. You burned and I hanged. Then what good are we to your sister?" He grabbed a pouch and her bow and quiver and returned to the horses.

She snatched her bow from his hand, fuming. "What happened to the brave knight, the elite King's Guard? I cannot credit a man who trembles before a band of inept knights and a power-hungry steward." She attempted to grab her quiver, but he held fast.

His jaw flexed. His eyes grew cold. And for a moment, she thought she'd overstepped the limits of this knight's temper. But finally he released a sigh and attempted to take her hand in his. "There is a difference between bravery and foolishness, Alexia. Think. Think about what you are doing."

She moved away from him. "I cannot think. Not when my sister's life is in danger."

"Precisely. LeGode will not let her die. Not until she marries his son." He strapped her quiver to the pack on his horse.

"Alas, what if she already has?"

"Jarin would not have permitted it."

"You ask me to trust men I have no knowledge of."

"I ask you to trust *me*." He gave her a pointed look that bespoke of the intimacies they'd shared.

"You may be an earl, Sir Knight, but I am not your liegeman."

Grabbing the reins of her horse, he tied it to his saddle.

Not believing her eyes, she flung her bow over her shoulder and planted fists at her waist. "Then am I to be your prisoner again? After … after our declarations of love?"

"*Because* of my love for you, I will not see you harmed." He tied the knot tight.

Alexia tried one last appeal. "If you truly loved me, you'd allow me to see my sister."

"We *will* see her." He reached out to touch her face. "You have my troth. But only when we have victory on our side."

Retreating, she turned her back to him. Potz! She was no match for this knight. Not in this gown, with a sore ankle, and especially not without her arrows. Nor did she truly want to be. A pain like none she'd felt skewered her heart at his betrayal.

Alack, deep down, she knew he was right. Whether or not this was a trap, rushing into a castle filled with enemies who thought she was a witch might not be the wisest choice. Even if she could sneak into her sister's chamber through the tunnels, what could she do to save her if the poison had already done its damage?

She could be with her. Comfort her.

Which was more than she could do in London. What if Bishop Montruse had sent word she was a witch? What if the king didn't believe Ronar?

Terror gripped Alexia's throat so tight, she gasped for air and closed her eyes, seeking the Spirit within. Yet He was quiet today. Instead, she saw the friar's ever-calm face. "You worry overmuch, dear one. Remember the Scripture tells us to be anxious for naught, but in everything with prayer and supplication, with thanksgiving, let your requests be made known to God. And the peace of God will guard your heart." He had taken her hand and placed it upon the Holy Scrolls. "'Commit thy way unto the Lord; trust also in Him; and He shall bring it to pass.' Your anxiety and lack of trust will only cause you harm, dear one."

Alexia breathed out a sigh. She wanted to trust God. She just had no idea how.

The *Spear*! She had the Spear. She'd seen it defeat a dozen demon-wolves. Surely it could defeat whatever LeGode tossed her way. Mayhap if Ronar knew of it, he'd allow her to go. But she couldn't tell him that. After all he'd suffered, discovering she had the Spear all along, that she had lied repeatedly to him, might encase his heart in stone forever.

Her own heart felt as heavy as an anvil at the moment, for eventually she would have to betray his trust yet again.

She heard him approach from behind, felt his hands at her waist as he attempted to lift her onto her horse. But she jerked from his touch, slid her foot in the stirrup, and mounted the palfrey with ease. "I see I have no choice, my lord, but you will allow me my anger for now."

Ronar leapt on his charger and took the reins. "Three days there, three days back with an army of knights and an edict from the king to arrest LeGode for treason and bring him to trial. That's all I ask. Will you grant me that?"

Alexia nodded, hating herself for the lie.

❧

Alexia took the bread and cheese Ronar handed her and stared at them, unsure whether her stomach would accept much of anything at the moment. The fire crackled and spit sparks into a night sky splattered with twinkling stars.

"Ye best eat, Alexia. You'll need your strength for the rest of the journey. We made good time today, and with God's grace, we'll make London by nightfall on the morrow."

They'd traveled all day across rolling hills, through farmland and villages and thick forests that made Alexia long to leap from her horse into the trees. They'd only stopped twice for water and to stretch their legs—legs which now ached, along with her backside. After a day of such torture, she decided 'twas far better to fly through the treetops than ride horseback. Faster and less painful.

Her palfrey neighed from his spot beside Penance at the edge of the clearing as if agreeing with her.

Still, Ronar had never allowed Alexia out of his sight. Not once. Even when she relieved herself in the shrubbery, he was always too close for any reasonable escape. Which only increased her agony, for every minute she traveled farther away from her sister was another minute she could not rescue her.

She braved a bite of bread, if only to appease the knight who sat beside her, gauging her response—eyeing her as if she were, indeed, his prisoner. Wise man.

Ronar tossed a chunk of cheese into his mouth and stared at the fire. Around them, the buzz of crickets, warble of birds, hoot of owls, and especially the howl of wolves kept him on edge with his knife in hand. Sounds that had grown familiar to her during her years raised in the forest, she had no trouble hearing the slightest deviation—a human footstep, a breath, the stillness of night birds when danger lurked. *The presence of evil.* She felt none of those things this night, just the terror raking through her veins for her sister.

And the desperate need to be at her side.

That need battled against her desire to not betray the man beside her, not betray the love they had vowed. A love and intimacy she already felt slipping away with each passing moment.

The bread soured in her stomach.

"I cannot stop thinking of my sister," she uttered, fingering the slab of cheese.

Ronar handed her a pouch. "You must." And for a moment she spotted a shimmer of the same affection she'd seen in his eyes last night. "Pray for her safety and trust God," he added ere he turned away.

Smiling, she sipped the wine. "This from a man who believes God only listens to men of the cloth."

He tossed a stick in the fire and sighed. "I have seen many things, many strange things of late, that give me cause to think differently."

"That pleases me, Ronar."

He gave a sad smile and reached for her hand. "I wish I could please you even more, Alexia. I wish you weren't so angry with me."

Against her better judgment, she slipped her hand in his, then hated herself for the way his warmth and strength made her feel. "Then grant me my freedom, and allow me to return to Luxley. You can proceed to London without me." For if there was a trap awaiting them at Luxley, she couldn't bear to see him hurt.

He threaded his fingers through hers, gazing sadly at their intertwined hands. She felt his grief, his hesitancy, spill over her, and hope took root that he would grant her request.

Instead, he plucked a leather tie from a pocket of his doublet and wrapped it around their bound hands.

"What are you doing?" She yanked and pulled, but he tied it tight using his teeth and one hand before she could get free.

"How dare you! I thought you trusted me!" She attempted to rise, but he pulled her back down.

"Nay, I said I loved you. Trust?" He shook his head and gave her that devilish smile of his that if she weren't so mad would excite her. "I know you, Lady Falcon, and I believe you'd take the first opportunity to rush back to your sister and your own death."

She narrowed her eyes. He was right, of course. But she was still angry.

"Let us get our rest, for tomorrow will come soon enough." Then setting his pouch as a pillow, he tugged her to lay beside him and drew a quilt over them both. "I am a light sleeper, Alexia, so I advise you to accept your fate."

Fuming, she lay as still as she could until she heard the knight's breathing deepen. *Infuriating man.* No matter how wonderful it felt to cuddle so close beside him, she would be no man's prisoner. She picked ever-so-lightly at the leather strap around their wrists for what seemed like an hour. But the knot was far too tight to be undone without disturbing

Ronar. A knife would work. If she had one. If she could reach the one Ronar had stuffed in his belt. Hard to do when it was behind her.

She shifted slightly. Ronar moaned and gripped her arm with his other hand. "Be still," he muttered.

Alexia complied. But only until she was sure he'd fallen asleep again. It took another hour of gentle maneuvering, inch by inch, to turn herself and pluck the blade from his belt. Her movements brought forth occasional groans and complaints, but nothing to wake the knight completely. Then she waited, listening to the rustle of leaves and simmer of coals in the fire. Waited until Ronar was deep in sleep yet again, and his hand fell from its grip on her arm. She passed the next hour slicing through the tie. Just as she broke free, she caught his hand and laid it gently in the dirt then rolled ever so quietly away from him.

Rubbing her wrist, she stood and stared at him sleeping so soundly, so handsome, so honorable. And she hated herself for defying him. But she had no choice. Separating from him was the best way to ensure his safety.

Those who took company with a witch would die a witch's death.

"I love you, Ronar. Please forgive me," she whispered. Then retrieving her bow and quiver, she quietly mounted her palfrey and headed into the darkness, angrily swiping away her traitorous tears.

By night the following day, after driving her horse harder than she should, Alexia reached the edge of the Emerald Forest overlooking Castle Luxley. All was dark, save for torches lit by the front palisades. Exhaustion weakened her bones and weighed upon her eyelids, but she could not stop now. Though she desperately longed to find the friar and ensure his safety—though she needed to hear his words of encouragement and pray with him—there was no time, for her sister's life lay in the balance.

Sliding from the horse, she retrieved her bow and quiver and slung them over her shoulder, ensuring Ronar's knife was tucked securely in her belt. She thought to remove the palfrey's saddle and grant him his freedom, but she might have need of him to escape should things not go as planned. Instead, she gave him loose rein to forage for food.

Planned. Hmm. What *was* her plan? In truth, she had none. Ronar would call her a fool for reacting so brashly. The friar would agree and caution her to seek the Spirit's wisdom and not give reign to her feelings. Yet, she had tried to do just that during her journey. She had prayed, both in the Spirit and in the natural, shc'd sung praises, and she'd even demanded demons to flee. But all to no avail. Terror still drove her onward, come what may.

She caressed the horse's face and leaned against him. "Stay close, precious one. I shall return anon." Then drawing back her shoulders, she took a deep breath, and ventured into the fields. Within minutes, she had climbed over the village wall and, keeping to the shadows, had slipped easily through the sleeping town. Once at the back castle gate, she halted, ready to fire an arrow at something nearby to distract the guard, but she found him deep in his cups singing with another knight.

Easily—*too* easily—she inched behind him and slipped into the courtyard, dark save for torches lit by the stables. Her gaze latched upon the women's quarters in the distance. She had only to make it there, creep past sleeping maids, and then disappear into the tunnels that led to her sister's chamber.

Heart thundering, she proceeded across the yard. A chicken clucked from its nest. A dog howled in the distance. She halted, listening. Slowly, she retrieved an arrow from her quiver and inched forward. The hiss and spit of torch flames sizzled. A frog croaked.

Five more steps.

Shuffling sounds met her ears, the creak of chain mail and metal followed.

Two more.

"You there, halt at once!" Sir DeGay's voice boomed through the courtyard.

Instantly, twenty knights appeared out of the shadows like demons from a nightmare. Alexia's breath seized. She nocked her bow and spun around to face the tips of a dozen swords.

A man pushed through the knights. The light from his torch etched a maniacal grin on his face. LeGode.

"My dear. How nice to see you. We thought you might grace us with a visit."

She shifted her aim to his heart. "I could kill you where you stand, you misbegotten sack of refuse."

He smiled. "True. You may injure me with one of your arrows. But rest assured, your death would come swift and hard."

Alexia slowly lowered her bow and glanced over the men-at-arms. "Knights of Luxley, I and my sister are the rightful heirs to this estate. This traitor tried to murder me in my youth and has been poisoning my sister. I command you to arrest him at once!"

No one moved. No one spoke. Terror threatened to choke her.

"Obey me at once. I am Lady Alexia D'Clere, daughter of Baron Richard D'Clere."

Still nothing but a cough.

LeGode chuckled. "As you can see, they answer to me now." He raised his voice. "This woman is a witch. Take her to the tower!"

Chapter 30

*B*are-footed and dressed in naught but a thin chemise, Alexia paced the tiny chamber at the top of the keep. Five steps across, five back. Darkness forbade her from seeing the walls that imprisoned her in a circle of stone, but she didn't need the light. She knew every inch of this prison—this tomb she'd been cast into over a day ago. Taking another step, she bit her lip at the pain radiating through her feet, scraped raw from the icy hard stone.

Far above, through a single narrow window, she had watched the sun rise and span the sky, shifting a beam of light slowly across the chamber walls until it finally moved up and disappeared out the window again, marking the end of another day.

Fighting back tears, she hugged herself and began tracing the walls with her shoulder, round and round, feeling as though she were going mad. Mad with grief and guilt and terror.

The Spear was gone.

The maids who had stripped her of her attire had easily found it sewn into her chemise. No amount of pleading, commanding, or begging had convinced them to side with her against LeGode—so strong was the terror he inflicted. And now, she had not only failed to protect the Spear, but she no longer had its power to help her escape, to help her sister.

To help anyone.

Finally surrendering to her tears, she leaned against the rough wall and slid down to the floor. "I'm sorry, Father. I've made a muck of things. I've failed You."

She'd failed the friar and Ronar as well. They'd both been right. She'd followed her emotions, allowed her fear to keep her from hearing the will of God and from trusting that will. Otherwise, she would have sensed the trap that had been so craftily laid for her, would have known the evil that awaited her arrival.

"Foolish, foolish girl!" She dropped her head in her hands. "Why do I never listen?"

Footsteps echoed in the corridor. Alexia quickly dried her eyes as a strip of light appeared beneath the door. Pushing against the stone, she struggled to rise as the lock clanked and the door creaked open. A torch swept into the room, carried by a guard and followed by a shadow of a man behind it. Alexia blinked at the brightness.

"Remain there and close the door."

She recognized LeGode's voice ere he materialized before her as her eyes grew accustomed to the light.

"Well, look at the imperious Falcon of Emerald Forest now." He jeered. "Not so formidable without your bow and arrow." He laid a finger on his pointy chin and eyed her up and down. "Why, if I didn't know better, I'd assume you were naught but a serving wench."

"And you naught but an agent of hell," she spat and took a step toward him.

He smiled. "From the mouth of babes."

"What have you done to my sister? Do you intend to kill her?"

A malevolent gleam flashed in his dark eyes. "Do you take me for a monster? Nay, my son Cedric will marry your sister and inherit Luxley. If she behaves herself, I may even allow her to live. If not, well, all I foresee in her future is grave illness, I'm afraid."

She rushed him, her every intent to strangle that smile from his face. But before she could reach him, the guard leveled the tip of his spear at her chest.

She halted. "My sister will never marry that mewling bore."

The corner of his lip twitched. "We shall see."

She studied him as he fingered the ruby brooch at his neck. "What happened to you, Sir? What happened to make a man want to murder a child of only nine?"

He glanced over the chamber and sighed. "I couldn't very well have you and your sister divide the estate, could I? Not when I deserved it all. Hence, I got rid of the strong one. Or so I thought." He scowled at her. "Who could have known you would become the pesky Falcon?"

"All of this evil, all of this pain, just so you could inherit my estate. Is it that important to you? Is it worth betraying the friendship of my parents?"

"'Tis the way of the world. A man is measured by his status and holdings. Mine are poor through no fault of my own, save my birth and the king's greed. Why should my son, why should *I* suffer the disrespect of others while you and your sister inherit a barony? Bah! Two addle-brained women who have done naught to deserve it."

Alexia huffed. "And yet this addle-brained woman has evaded you for nine years."

He studied her then, his jaw shifting.

"Have you no fear of God?" she asked.

"There are other powers besides the Almighty's. *Stronger* powers. Ones that reward a man in this life and don't make him wait and hope for a promise that may never come in the next."

Alexia drew a deep breath and shoved aside her fear and anger as she sought the light and truth within. Shadows, bending and twisting, slithered around LeGode, their tiny yellow eyes flaming, their mouths elongated with silent screams. Chains formed around the man himself, starting at his shoes, winding up his legs, his belly, chest and then wrapping around his neck—thick, heavy chains that clanked with each step as he approached her.

"You are bound in darkness, Sir. You walk about in chains. But that does not have to be the end of things. You can be free."

"Begad, chains! I've never felt more free!" He laughed. "Free to finally receive my just reward."

The shadows slinking about him glared her way with eyes burning with such hate, she nearly fell backward. A spindly hand emerged from the darkness, a black craggy wisp that reached for her throat. For a moment—a brief moment—she thought it would strangle her, but then it disappeared with a puff and a growl as if it had met an invisible barrier. "'Twas you who sent those devilish wolves," she said.

He smiled. "Let us just say I have access to dark powers that would put your God to shame. Especially since you no longer possess the Spear." Reaching into his pocket, he held it up.

Golden light radiated from within the holy relic, causing it to shine even brighter than the torch. Her heart sank at the sight of it in the grasp of such evil, and she lunged to take it from him. But he leapt out of her reach as the tip of the guard's spear shoved her back.

"That does not belong to you, LeGode. It has naught to do with your greedy plans."

"Aye, but it does. If 'tis as powerful as they say, it will aid me greatly. If not, I will give it to the bishop, and he and his ill-bred knights can leave. Ah,"—his bushy brows rose above sadistic eyes—"save one, I would guess. Your lover who helped you escape. What spell did you cast on him to make him sacrifice so much, witch?"

"Love requires no spell. And I am no witch, as you well know."

"Yet Bishop Montruse has pronounced you as such."

"Without a trial?"

"He has no need to be sullied by your wicked presence when the evidence speaks for itself." LeGode dropped the Spear back into his pocket.

"Sir LePeine had naught to do with my escape. In truth, I have no knowledge of his whereabouts."

"Humph. I doubt that. If he attempts to rescue his lady love, he'll be hanged for treason. If not, then I suppose love will not win, after all."

"Regardless of what Sir LePeine does or doesn't do, love always wins in the end, LeGode."

With a snort, he turned to leave.

"What is to become of me?"

"Oh, my manners. I nearly forgot." He smiled in her direction. "Tomorrow at noon, you will be burned at the stake."

⊗⊘⊘

LeGode bounded down the winding stairs of the keep, his tunic flowing, and his mind and heart humming. Things were looking up, indeed, and his plans would soon come to fruition. Alexia would be dead, the bishop and his lackeys would depart, Cristiana would marry Cedric…

And the barony would be LeGode's.

Female laughter grated over his ears, an omen of disaster even before he found its source.

'Twas Cristiana D'Clere! Dressed in a lavish crimson tunic with a wreath of flowers on her head, her cheeks rosy, and her brown eyes sparkling, she sat beside that muckrake Jarin in the great hall.

How could that be? LeGode couldn't help but stare at them as he passed, his anger growing with each step. The knight held her hand and leaned close to say something to the lady, to which she responded with a nod and a smile. And such a smile! One reserved for the object of her heart. One LeGode longed to see her grace upon his son. Where was Cedric anyway?

And why wasn't Cristiana abed? After what he had ordered put in her food, she should not be able to hold up her head, let alone sit and play the coquette with that dastardly knight.

Both glanced his way. The knight's eyes narrowed, and the lady quickly averted her gaze.

Such disrespect! Such dishonor! Fury boiling, he took the corridor to the left and halted before the library where he knew he'd find the bishop either sleeping, reading, eating, or having his way with one of the serving wenches. The man had taken over the chamber next to LeGode's study on the pretense of needing to read the Scriptures in privacy.

Privacy, Bah! A place for his wenching and sleeping was more like it.

LeGode knew he shouldn't disturb him without being summoned, but he must get rid of Jarin the Just immediately. And he finally had the means to do exactly that.

After several knocks, an aggravated voice bade him entrance, and LeGode pushed the door open to a young maid scurrying out and the bishop adjusting his vestment. "What is it now, Sir?"

Disgust soured LeGode's belly at this man who dared present himself as holy. Merely more evidence of the weakness of the God he served. Biting back an insult, LeGode entered, reminding himself that this man had the king's ear and the power to destroy him if he so desired.

He fingered the Spear in his pocket. Oddly, he thought it would be bigger, sharper, or at least *cleaner* for something that held such power. But it appeared more something to be tossed out as refuse than a relic that could defeat armies.

Still, it would more than prove its usefulness if it could put this buffoon to flight.

"What do you want, Sir? You stand there staring at me as if you haven't a thought in your head."

"I came to...I came to..."

With a growl that would wake the dead, the bishop sank back into a chair, gave a tight smile, and folded hands over his belly. "Out with it, LeGode, or I shall have you arrested for driving a man of God to sheer madness."

LeGode swallowed, wrapped his hand around the Spear still in his pocket, then whispered. "I command you to be gone."

But instead of disappearing or fainting away dead, the bishop's face grew mottled with red. "What did you say?"

"Nothing." LeGode pulled out the Spear. "I have a gift." Useless piece of metal. He'd be happy to be rid of it if it would also rid him of this hypocritical weasel.

The bishop's eyes flew open. His bottom lip began to quiver as he slowly pushed himself up and approached LeGode with the first display of reverence he had witnessed in the man.

"Where? How?" He snagged it from LeGode's hand as if he weren't worthy to hold it.

"'Twas on the witch when we searched her."

Bishop Montruse stared at the relic for what seemed like an eternity, his eyes blinking, his mouth opening and closing with unuttered words, his fingers gently caressing it as if it held the secret to life itself.

"I have upheld my part of our bargain, your Excellency."

"So you have, LeGode." The bishop's eyes never left the spear. "God's truth, I didn't think you had it in you."

"And now you will convince the king to order my son and Lady D'Clere wed."

"Yes, yes, as you wish." The bishop waved one hand through the air.

LeGode pressed his luck. "And you and the King's Guard will depart Luxley forthwith."

"Of course. I am most anxious to present this to the king." Finally, he lifted his gaze to LeGode. "The witch had this? How did it not burn her skin?"

Because 'tis just a piece of metal, you lout. LeGode shrugged. "It matters not. We will burn her skin on the morrow."

"As she deserves." Still holding the Spear, the bishop moved to the window where a breeze brought in the scent of plowed earth and lavender from the fields. "It must be done in the village for all to see."

LeGode grimaced. "But, your Grace, I have discovered she is the Falcon of Emerald Forest, the woman who brought the villagers food. To avoid trouble, I recommend the courtyard."

"The Falcon you say? Humph. More reason to burn her as a lesson for all to see."

"I fear the people may riot."

"Riot! Ludicrous. They are peasants who cannot think for themselves. Nay. 'Tis best we use this witch as an example that we do not tolerate treason against the crown. Nor treason against God."

"I will order extra guards," LeGode offered just as the bishop's page entered with a tray of mead and cheese.

All too happy to leave this man's presence, LeGode smiled as he shut the door behind him.

Later that night, Bishop Montruse made no call for female company. Nor did he attend the evening repast, but instead ordered wine and boiled venison be brought to his chamber. When he had finished eating, he commanded his page to stoke the fire and help him disrobe, but then dismissed him so that he could study the Spear.

He could hardly believe it. The Spear that stabbed His Lord Christ! Right here in his very hands.

He always knew he was meant for greatness. Nay, he was no ordinary bishop. Not only had he attained the highest post possible for a man of his position—adviser to the king—but now that he had the Spear in his possession, he would be unstoppable. Soon he would become archbishop, and then God willing, mayhap even the next Pope.

With these dreams in his heart and a smile on his lips, Bishop Montruse set the Spear on the table beside his bed and fell fast asleep.

Sometime during the night, the Spear began to glow. A halo of light circled it, growing brighter and brighter until it lit the entire room as if the sun itself were rising in the chamber. A being of equal light gently lifted it from its place and carried it through the closed door.

Darkness surrounded the bishop again.

Chapter 31

*K*eeping to the shadows, Ronar slipped past the gatehouse and across the smaller courtyard of Luxley castle. The sentry hadn't questioned him when he'd hailed him from the tower above. He merely nodded his recognition and opened the gate. Either Ronar was walking into a trap, or word of his collusion with a witch had not reached the lower ranks of the guard assigned night duty.

Or mayhap they simply did not expect him to saunter through the front gate at two in the morning.

Now, if he could make it to the women's quarters and from thence into the tunnels, mayhap one of those secret passages would lead him close to the chamber he shared with Jarin and Damien.

The wind slapped dirt in his face, increasing his angst. When he'd woken at dawn to find Alexia had tricked him—yet again—a plethora of emotions twisted his gut—anger and frustration chief among them, along with the pain of betrayal. A pain he knew all too well. He had allowed himself to fall asleep because, deep down, he had trusted her to remain with him no matter how distraught she was at his decision. She had declared her love, and he thought that meant all lies and tricks were at an end. Fool! When would he learn? Now he had no choice but to go after her and pray she'd not already been caught.

He found the maids' quarters easily enough. Thank God the few women who tended the castle were fast asleep as he slipped inside, shoved aside the large wardrobe, and found entrance to the tunnels. He had no light to guide his way, but felt along the craggy stone, first right then left and then right again, up and up until his breath came hard and a chill shimmied down the sweat on his back. Finally, a tiny flicker of light appeared, and the stone transformed to wood. He pushed and entered a dark chamber.

Moonlight from the window made ghosts of white sheets draped over furniture and spun cobwebs into shimmering threads. An ominous weight of loss and sorrow made the air hard to breath. *The master solar*—Alexia's parents' bedchamber. Left untouched after her mother died, no doubt.

Passing quickly through the morbid place, he moved into the corridor, lit by sconced candles nearly depleted. He took a moment to determine where he was, then crept down the stairs—two flights and he found the familiar door to the chamber he'd shared with Damien and Jarin.

When he opened it and stepped inside, 'twas to a blade at his throat.

"State your business ere I slice you open."

Ronar smiled. "'Tis me, Damien."

The knife withdrew and a strong arm ushered him inside and quietly shut the door.

Flint struck steel, and the flame of a candle revealed his two friends wearing only linen breeches, faces puffy with sleep, and blades in hand.

"Ronar, what are you doing here?" Jarin rubbed his eyes.

"I should have known I couldn't sneak in on you two." Ronar gripped them both by the forearm.

"'Tis good to see you well." Jarin returned his greeting with a firm clasp.

Damien set down his knife. "LeGode and Bishop Montruse are searching for you. To arrest you for treason against the crown."

A ray of silver moonlight entered through the window, and Ronar moved to look outside. "'Tis LeGode who has committed treason by attempting to murder Alexia and poisoning her sister." The courtyard was empty. Good. His presence had not been noticed. "Have you seen Alexia...Lady Falcon? Has she arrived?"

"Aye," Jarin replied, and when he hesitated, Ronar faced him. "What is it?"

Damien lowered to a chair. "They caught her in the courtyard and locked her in the tower."

Ronar's heart crumbled to ash.

"They set a trap," Jarin added. "Told her Cristiana was dying. She walked right into it."

As Ronar had predicted. He closed his eyes and let out a deep breath, trying to settle his rising fear.

"She had the Spear, Ronar."

For a moment, he was unsure he heard clearly. Nay. Couldn't be. Alexia had vowed to him there would be no more secrets.

Ronar opened his eyes. "What are you saying?"

"The Spear of Destiny. Aye, all this time. 'Twas found on her person."

Could his heart stand another blow? Ronar pressed a hand to his chest as a palpable pain burned therein. His thoughts scattered to all the tender moments they'd shared, all the things he'd told her and no one else. His jaw tightened into a knot. She *knew* he and his men were searching for the Spear. She knew how much finding it meant to him, how much he longed to please his king. Yet she had adamantly denied knowing anything about it. And when they'd slept side by side, there it had been, mere inches from him.

Betrayal sank into Ronar's gut like a hard stone never to be lifted again. He leaned back against the wall and stared at the wooden floor.

"I fear she is not to be trusted, Ronar," Damien said. "I know you harbor affection for her, but she has done naught but deceive you, fire arrows at you, and play you for a fool."

Jarin rubbed his chin and shared a glance with Damien. "Now that the bishop has the Spear, we are ordered back to London on the morrow."

"What of Alexia?" Ronar stared at his friends.

"She is to be burned at the stake at noon."

Another punch to his gut. Ronar forced down the bile rising in his throat.

"I'm sorry, Ronar, but what can we do?" Jarin frowned. "The bishop has decreed it."

Bishop Montruse. God forgive him, but Ronar had not found the man worthy to make such a decree. Alexia was no witch. A liar, aye. Alack, a very good one. A liar who had caused him to defy the bishop, the king, and even God. Yet, were those not the workings of a witch? He raked a hand through his hair and longed to disappear into the wall behind him, melt into the cold, sharp stone and become so hard, no one could hurt him again.

Jarin approached and gripped Ronar's arm. "Leave at once for London and appeal to the king before we arrive with the bishop. Tell him you were merely pretending to befriend her while you searched for the Spear. He will understand."

But Ronar could not shake the vision of Alexia tied to a pole, screaming in agony whilst flames leapt around her feet. Turning, he gripped the edge of the window to hide the sudden weakness in his legs. Had she played him for a fool? Befriended him, declared her love for him, only with the intent to use him?

Just like his good friend Brom.

Yet…for what purpose? She didn't need protection, hadn't even asked for it. In truth, she'd done her best to avoid him.

He slammed his fist against the wall, ignoring the pain and the bloody mark it left. "How is she guarded?"

Damien snorted. "You aren't thinking—"

"Ten of Luxley's best knights stand guard at the door of her cell," Jarin interrupted, his voice full of anger and defeat. "Only LeGode holds the key. 'Tis impossible, Ronar. Even for you."

A torrent of fear swept over him, and he ground his teeth together, knowing they were right.

"Aye, I will leave," he finally said, pushing from the window.

"Wise." Damien rose. "We will see you in London."

Bidding his friends farewell, Ronar embraced them as though he would never see them again. Mayhap he wouldn't, for he had no intention of going to London.

Everything within him, every ounce of his being knew he must rescue Alexia. Witch or not, liar or not, he could not allow her to burn. What he didn't know was whether this need to save her came from his shattered heart, and hence, would most likely end in his death. Or did the Almighty wish her to be punished for her crimes? When it came to Alexia, Ronar didn't trust his judgment.

But there was one person who would tell him the truth.

An hour later, as Ronar rode Penance through Emerald Forest, he did something he rarely did. He talked to God. He asked Him for help to find the friar. An impossible task with so huge a forest and so little a man. *And a man who hid himself well.* But Ronar must find him before daybreak.

The scent of moss, loamy soil, and sodden wood wafted over him as the crunch and thud of Penance's hooves echoed through the misty air. Woodland creatures scurried about, stopping to peer at him in the patches of moonlight infiltrating the canopy.

Ronar was not one to cower at every shadow and sound in the darkness, but this night, something evil was afoot. Trees appeared from the mist like towering giants ready to pounce on him. Underbrush rose like thorny trolls determined to halt his progress. Vines reached for his throat and wrapped around his body. An owl gave an ominous *hoo hoo*, a raven cawed, a wolf howled—sounds that quickened his heart and slowed his pace. Gray shadows in the shape of men leapt between trees as moonlight spiraled down upon a world that seemed foreign to him.

Drawing his sword, he called the friar's name, only to hear his own voice echo hollow back to him.

Yet he kept going. He had no choice.

A figure stepped onto the path—too solid to be a shadow, too far to see his face.

"Who goes there?" Ronar said with a courage he didn't feel. "Announce yourself."

"Are you searching for me, Sir Knight?"

Friar Josef. Ronar released a breath and slid from Penance.

The friar stepped into a swath of moonlight, assessing Ronar with eyes filled with concern. "Where is Alexia?"

"That is why I have come. May we talk?"

"I thought we were." The friar gestured to a fallen log, whereupon—after many a grunt and groan—he lowered himself to sit. "Forgive an old man, but my feet are not what they used to be."

Ronar couldn't sit. He could hardly stand still. Sword still in hand, he glanced over the dark forest, no longer sensing evil. "Alexia is in the tower and will be burned at the stake on the morrow."

His words had the expected response. A gasp, followed by horror-filled eyes that soon blurred with tears. "Nay, this cannot be. How? I thought you protected her."

Guilt slammed atop Ronar's fear. "'Tis a long story, Friar. They claim she is a witch."

"A witch?" The friar gave an incredulous snort. "She could no more be a witch than the blessed Mother."

"Bishop Montruse is convinced."

"And you believe him?" The friar blew out a sigh, one brow arched. "Because he claims to speak for God?"

"Whom am I to believe? A man of the cloth or a woman who has lied to me repeatedly."

"Believe God, young knight. Seek His truth." He pointed toward Ronar's chest.

Sheathing his sword, Ronar knelt, picked up a stick and began batting leaves on the ground. "Mayhap this is God's will for her. She had the Spear all along. You *both* deceived me."

"So it is lost then." Despair weighed the friar's voice. "She hated deceiving you, Ronar. But she is the Protector of the Spear. 'Twas her God-appointed task to keep it safe from those who would abuse its power."

"Abuse?" Ronar returned angrily. "We intended to bring it to the king. Surely God's anointed should possess such a Holy treasure?"

"The king is but a man like you and me. The Spear should not be used for men's wars and struggles for power."

"What, pray, is its purpose then?"

"That is for God to decide."

Growling, Ronar rose and stared into the shadowy forest. "I don't know what to think anymore. You and Alexia have befuddled my mind with your heresies! Life was simpler ere I met you. I followed king and Church and earned my penance with good deeds."

The friar struggled to rise, then brushed off his cowl. "Follow God. 'Twill be much less confusing." He turned to leave.

"Where are you going?"

"To pray for Alexia. Only God can save her now."

More confused than ever, Ronar called after him. "What should I do?"

"Save her, of course."

"How can I? I am but one man against the bishop, Sir LeGode, and all the knights of Luxley."

Halting, the friar turned to face him. "Nay. You are one man *and* God."

❧

Alexia wasn't one to cry, but to her shame, she'd spent the last hour sobbing as if she were naught but a wee child. She cried for her failure to protect the Spear, the horrific fate awaiting her sister, for disappointing Ronar, the friar—and most of all, disappointing God. Some protector she was. God had given her such marvelous gifts of power and discernment, and she'd squandered them by allowing her emotions to control her actions instead of trusting Him. Now, all was lost. On the morrow, she'd be tied to a pole before her enemies as fire consumed her flesh bit by bit. She hugged herself. How much pain would she endure ere she fainted or died? Her skin grew cold and moist at the thought.

She glanced up at the dark window. Would that this night would end, and her sentence be carried out swiftly, for the endless waiting would be her undoing.

No longer did she hope for rescue. Ronar was most likely in London by now. She couldn't blame him. She'd deceived him too many times to expect his care. Or his forgiveness.

"Father," she wailed into the darkness. "I have failed You and everyone else I love. I deserve whatever punishment that comes my way." She swiped her tears. "Just please, please, save my sister. Do not allow her to wed Cedric. Protect her from the evil that lurks in this place."

A light appeared by her bare feet. The tiniest of specks at first. But then it grew brighter and brighter and wider and wider until it moved onto her toes and started sliding up her ankles and onto her chemise. She looked up to seek its source and found a man dressed in white, glowing as radiantly as the sun. His eyes met hers from a face firm but kind. His height reached for the ceiling, and the breadth of him was mighty. And though she'd seen such beings before and knew they were from God, she shrank against the stone wall in fear.

"Fear not, favored one." His voice was a soft thunder, authoritative yet gentle. He extended his arm toward her and opened his hand. There in his palm sat the Spear.

Her heart leapt for joy at the mere sight of it. She sensed he wanted her to take it from him, but her legs were unable to move. Finally, he placed it on the floor by her feet and backed away.

Would he take her with him? Unlock the door and release her as the angel had done for the Apostle Peter in the Scriptures?

"Take me with you," she dared to plead.

He merely smiled. "Nay. You have work to do, mighty warrior of the Most High."

Work? Mighty? All that remained was for her to die a torturous death.

She was about to ask him what work, when, as quickly as he had come, he turned and walked through the stone wall as if it were made of water.

A few minutes passed ere Alexia could breathe. Though darkness consumed the chamber once again, she remembered exactly where the angel had left the Spear. She found it quickly, sped to the door, grabbed the handle, and yanked with all her might.

It wouldn't budge.

She held the Spear up to it and commanded, "Open in the name of Jesus."

Nothing.

Favored one. She gazed up. "Then why do You wish me to die?" LeGode and the bishop would only discover the Spear in the morning. What was she supposed to do with it?

Her answer came within the hour when muffled voices sounded from outside her door, and the clank of the lock preceded the lovely vision of her sister. Two guards followed her in, one holding a torch, the other a sword. As soon as Cristiana saw her, she flew into Alexia's arms and began to sob. Forcing down her own tears, Alexia clung to her, breathing in her sweet scent, and never wanting to let go. But she had to, she had to be strong—for Cristiana's sake.

Taking her sister's arm, Alexia led her as far away from the knights as she could. "No more tears, sweet sister. 'Twill be all right. You'll see."

Face moist, Cristiana glanced at the guards. "Sir LeGode only granted me a minute."

"I'm surprised he allowed even that."

"I promised him I'd go for a stroll with Cedric." Her lips twisted in disgust.

Alexia brushed hair from her face. "I'm so happy to see you."

"I cannot bear to lose you, Alexia. What shall I do? I cannot go on!"

"You *will* go on, Cristiana. You must. God will be with you."

"He has not protected me thus far. 'Tis only been you."

"Because He sent me. He will send another." Placing a finger beneath her chin, she lifted her gaze. "You are stronger than you know, Cristiana. Remember when we were children and you escaped from our chamber at night and came to the aid of the widow Bane's sick child?"

"Only because you begged me to bring fresh nettle."

"But you did it nonetheless."

Cristiana swayed and Alexia wrapped an arm around her waist. "Are you still unwell?" Fear renewed.

Coughing, Cristiana leaned on her sister. "Aye, it came on me late today. I do not understand. I have been eating naught but what Jarin and Anabelle bring me." She pressed fingers to her temples.

"LeGode is too clever and has figured us out. You must tell Jarin. Promise me."

"Aye. But what does it matter? He will always find a way."

"Cristiana, you *must* believe. Believe God loves you and will never leave you. Therein lies your strength."

"*You* have always been my strength." Cristiana sobbed.

One of the guards cleared his throat. "Time's up."

Nay! These cannot be Alexia's last moments with her sister. She could not bear the pain. She embraced Cristiana, forcing down her agony, extending the moment as long as possible. *Wait*. The Spear! A gentle prompting touched her spirit. Pulling back ever so slightly, Alexia slipped the Spear into Cristiana's hand.

"What is this?"

"'Tis the Spear for which everyone seeks. It is yours now to protect." She closed her sister's fingers around the precious relic.

"The Spear of Destiny? I cannot…"

"You *can*. Mother gave it to me to protect, and now I pass it on to you, dear sister. You are now the Protector of the Spear."

"I can't even protect myself." Terror streaked Cristiana's voice.

"It will protect you. God will use it to guide you."

"But it isn't protecting you!"

"My time is up. 'Tis yours now."

"Nay nay nay!" Cristiana wailed.

"Shh. Be still," Alexia whispered, glancing at the guard. "Put it in your pocket and then hide it well. Seek out Friar Josef in the forest. He will tell you all."

"Now!" The guard with the sword approached.

Cristiana's terror-streaked eyes met Alexia's. She gripped the Spear tight just as the brute grabbed her arm.

Alexia squeezed her sister's hand. "Do not mourn me, sister. I will be in heaven, and we will see each other again."

The guard laughed. "Not where yer going, witch!"

As he tugged Cristiana away, light from the torch shone over Alexia's wrist. The mark of the Spear began to fade…slowly…slowly, growing fainter and lighter…until it was no more. One glance at her sister's wrist assured Alexia she had made the right decision.

The door slammed shut, enclosing her in a tomb of darkness once again. She rubbed her wrist, cold and empty now without the mark. She was no longer the Protector of the Spear. That could only mean one thing.

Tomorrow she would surely die.

Chapter 32

*A*lexia spent the remainder of the night and most of the morning in prayer. Despite her impending torturous death, God had filled her with a peace she hadn't expected. But it had been a hard won peace, for the demons of fear and despair had fought relentlessly to reign in her soul, to drag her spirit down into the muck and mire where they lived. Then she remembered Ronar's advice, and she sought the truth of God's love within. The truth of His Word she had read so many times and committed to memory. That all things work together for good for those who love God, that God loved her so much He gave His only Son to die in her stead, that this life was but a vapor, a shadow of things to come, and that if she remained steadfast to the end, such glories awaited her she could not imagine. She recited the Holy Words out loud and said the name Jesus so often that the demonic horde hovering about her had disappeared, leaving peace and love to flood her heart.

Thus, when five guards arrived to escort her to her death, she felt naught but anticipation for her move into eternity. Alas, mayhap a spark of fear for the pain she would suffer first. Yet even that vanished when the bishop in a flurry of crimson robes, golden crucifix swinging across his chest, stormed past the guards into her prison cell and burned her with eyes aflame with hatred.

"Where is the Spear, witch?"

She resisted the urge to laugh at his blustering countenance. "You took it from me, your Excellency. Do you not recall? Have you misplaced it?"

He growled and started for her, then controlled himself and lifted his chin. "Call for a wench to come search her." He shouted to one of the guards.

"Where would I hide it?" Alexia lifted her hands and glanced down at her chemise, so thin, it left naught to the imagination.

An imagination she saw spinning with lust behind the bishop's eyes.

She hugged herself. "Search me all you wish, but pray, let us proceed with the burning. I grow weary of the wait."

Something flickered in the man's widened eyes—shock, admiration? "Where is your fear, witch? Why are you not cowering before me, begging for your life? Do you not realize that a word from me would save you?"

"Do you not realize that if God wished me to live, no word from you would stop Him?"

He scowled. "Indeed. And He has ordered your death and sentenced you to hell."

"Has He? Then when you arrive yourself and don't find me there, you shall know the truth."

The sting of his slap radiated across her cheek ere she saw it coming. She welcomed the pain, and only lifted her chin higher, meeting his cold eyes staunchly.

With a flap of his robes, he raged from the room.

Within the hour, two kitchen maids came to search her, apologizing profusely, and offering her looks of pity as they removed her chemise and scanned her naked body like no one ever had. Enduring the shame, she remembered that Jesus had also been stripped naked during His hour of trial, and she suddenly felt comfort in the association.

After they left and Alexia was once again clothed, the guards returned, clasped her arms, and dragged her from the cell down the winding staircase, through the great hall, and across the courtyard. Squires, pages, and servants stopped to stare at her with horror. A few crossed themselves. As best she could, Alexia gave them looks of comfort and assurance as the guards led her through the front gate, across the bridge, and toward the village. So, she was to be burned as a spectacle to all. No matter. So had her Lord been. With His strength, she would endure it.

Down the muddy street and into the village square, the guards shoved her, finally halting before her death pyre—a stack of wood that reached her waist surrounding a thick pole. Her heart began to thump uncontrollably, aided by the shouts of the villagers she loved. Some reached for her, others stood sobbing—Gwendolyn, the widow, Forwin, the spicemonger, Gerald, the leather worker, among them. And of course, Wimarc, the butcher and his wife.

"We love you, Falcon!"

"God be with you, Falcon."

"Go with God, dear one."

She smiled, hoping to reassure them all was well.

But once they led her up makeshift stairs to the top of the woodpile, shoved her against the post, and tied her hands behind her, terror strangled her.

Lord, be with me, she whispered into the wind then gazed over the crowd that grew more and more agitated, growling and screaming and shouting until naught else could be heard. At the front, stood Sir LeGode, the ruby brooch at his neck glittering in the sun, a gloating look on his snarling lips. The bishop languished by his side, his page holding a canopy over him to protect him from the heat. And to his right stood Sir Jarin the Just and Sir Damien LaRage. Both knights bore stoic expressions, yet a twitch on Jarin's face and the anger in Damien's eyes spoke of raging emotions within. Behind them, rows of knights kept the crowd at bay with pikes and spears.

More shouts filled the air—prayers and blessings from the villagers followed by curses aimed at Sir LeGode and the guards. At least thirty additional knights stood around the perimeter of the square.

All this for little ol' her? She wanted to laugh but found her insides clenched so tight, she had trouble breathing.

Suddenly, without warning, Alexia thought of Ronar. And a sorrow she'd never known sliced through her heart. She loved him. And she would never see him again in this life. Not only that, but she had done the worst possible thing anyone could do to him—she had betrayed him. Just as his friend had done. She found her voice as she gazed up into a clear blue sky. "Father, please help him forgive me. Help him to love again. Help him to realize You have already paid the price for his sins. Open his eyes to see how near You are to him."

"She calls to the devil!" the bishop shouted. "Burn her at once!"

The crowd went mad.

A guard approached, torch in hand. Without looking up at her, he dipped the flame to the pile of wood at her feet.

❧

Ronar LePeine, Knight of the Elite King's Guard, crusader, and friend of the king, crouched beneath the window in one of the upper rooms of the Hornbuckle Inn. 'Twas the closest second story window to the market square where Alexia was to be burned. And the only one which faced her back.

Agony wrapped around his heart at the thought he might lose her, of the torturous death she faced. But he wouldn't allow his fear entrance. He couldn't. He had no time for fear or sorrow. And he especially had no time for mistakes.

He glanced over the raging mob. In the distance, two guards dragged Alexia atop a pile of wood, shoved her against a post, and bound her hands behind her. Sir LeGode, the bishop, and their knights formed an impenetrable wall around her, preventing the clamoring throng from rushing to her rescue. Shouts and curses filled the air as some of the villagers attempted to shove forward, but the knights forced them back with sharpened pikes.

Jarin and Damien stood beside the bishop, rigid and unmoving, though from this distance Ronar could not make out their expressions.

Distance. Aye, at least forty yards. An impossible shot. Especially for him. But 'twas the only plan that had a modicum of a chance.

His heart pummeled his ribs, his mind found no focus, sweat slid down his back. What was wrong with him? He was a trained warrior, an elite knight.

Yet… if he failed….

If he failed—he swallowed—he'd have to watch the woman he loved burn to death. Tortured at the hands of evil men. Aye, the bishop was evil. There was no other explanation. Which meant he was *not* appointed by God. Which meant not all men of the cloth were appointed by God, and not everything the Church said was from God.

Which also meant the penance Ronar tried so hard to achieve might all be for naught.

The friar's words were the only thing shouting in his mind that made sense. "Follow God alone, and you'll see He has already forgiven you."

Drawing an arrow from the quiver leaning against the wall, he positioned it, drew back the bowstring, and found his target—the ropes that bound Alexia's hands. Strung tight around both wrists, the bonds left less than an inch between her palms. Still, they blurred in his vision even as her hands melded with the pole. How could he shoot the ropes at this distance without slicing her hands? *Give me a shot, Father.*

Laughter cracked the air around him, vile laughter. Heard but *not* heard.

You'll never make that shot, Knight! Who do you think you are?

Ronar dared a glance behind him. No one was there. Just the cot, chest of drawers, side table and lantern that made up the small room. Then why did he feel like snakes were crawling up his skin? A shadow sprang from the corner then flitted across the chamber and disappeared. Had the wolves returned? Pulse pounding, he shook away the vision and reached in his pocket for Saint Jude. Surely, he would protect Ronar. Mayhap even help him make the shot. But the more he studied the statue, the more he realized 'twas just made of stone—a lifeless idol that possessed no power.

He tossed it into the corner. Besides, Ronar was no longer a hopeless cause.

Movement brought his gaze back out the window. One of the guards was lighting the wood.

Panic stung every nerve. He pulled back the string once again and took aim.

Go ahead. Shoot. You'll miss and kill her. Even her God cannot save her now.

A heaviness pressed on his shoulders, leeching away his hope… his faith.

Flames began to leap over the wood. The crowd stirred into a frenzy of screams and wailing.

"Nay!" Ronar shouted and quickly bowed his head.

"God, if You are here. I need You. I cannot make this shot, so *You* must. Please save Alexia."

The weight lifted, the air cleared, and Ronar took a deep breath. He sensed another presence in the room, a powerful one, a glorious one.

He drew back the bow, closed his eyes, uttered the name Jesus, and released the arrow.

Alexia's mind went numb. Flames reached for her feet. Unbearable heat swamped her, rising in waves that warped her view—twisting LeGode and the bishop into slithering demons and the crowd into a mass of writhing snakes. She could no longer hear anything but the hiss and crackle of the fire that would soon melt the skin from her body.

"Oh, Lord Jesus, help me." She bowed her head as the fire licked her feet and the pain began, searing, excruciating pain! "Take me quickly."

Her hands fell to her sides.

What? She stared at them, unbound, free, dripping with blood, and then looked up to the blue sky, waiting for an angel to swoop down and take her home.

But instead, commotion brought her gaze back to the crowd. Guards dropped to the ground, arrows piercing their legs and arms. A dozen knights surrounded LeGode and the bishop and whisked them away. More guards fell. Others drew swords and dashed across the square.

The fire burned her toes. *Pain! Pain! Such pain!* "Jesus, help! Hel"—air. There was no more air to breath. She gasped for one last breath, when to her right, the oddest sight appeared. Blankets, clothing, and quilts flew through the air and landed on the flames. Smoke curled upward. Sir Jarin and Damien scrambled atop, their movements awkward and...slow...so slow...as if the entire scene was happening in an endless nightmare. That must be it. The pain had sent her mind into a dream.

Rough hands grabbed her, tugged her down over the smoking cloth. *Hot hot hot!* Her feet landed in cool mud.

Nothing had ever felt so good. She coughed up smoke.

Hoisting her over his shoulder, Damien bolted down the street. Jarin right behind. The people of the village surrounded them. Cries of joy filled her ears. Hands reached for her.

Coughing, she sucked in more air.

Knights rushed toward them. An arrow struck one in the thigh. Jarin drew his sword and engaged two more.

"Get her to safety!" he shouted over his shoulder.

Picking up rocks and whatever they could find, the villagers tossed them at the oncoming guards. Still Damien ran. His boots slapped the soggy dirt. Mud splattered on her face as her head pounded against his back.

Alexia heard horses neigh and bridles jangle, felt herself hoisted atop a charger. The stable master handed Damien the reins and smiled at Alexia. Leaping behind her, Damien wrapped one arm around her waist, then nudged his horse out the gate.

They galloped across the field. Wind whipped her hair as young bean stalks whizzed past and the mayhem behind them faded into a distant clamor.

Only when they reached the cool woodland and her lungs filled with the familiar scent of oakmoss and cedar, did Alexia truly believe she'd been rescued.

Damien slowed his horse and glanced toward the castle. No one followed. At least not yet.

He slid from his charger and glanced up at her. "Are you hurt, my lady?"

She stared at this man who was all steel and roughness with eyes as hard as the chain mail he wore. "My feet pain me, but otherwise nay. Thank you." She hated the tremble in her voice and attempted to settle her nerves. "Where is Ronar? Is he—"

Before she could finish her sentence, the pounding of horses drew her gaze to two riders racing toward them, clods of mud flinging off their mounts' hooves. Damien started to draw his sword but released it as the two came closer.

Ronar. She'd know him anywhere, the commanding way he rode his charger, his brown hair flying in the wind, and finally when his face came into view, the smile meant only for her. Jarin rode by his side.

Before his horse came to a stop, Ronar slid off, took her by the waist, and drew her down into an embrace that was filled with laughter and tears and more love than she'd ever felt. He kissed her forehead then cupped her chin and gazed at her. "I feared I'd lost you."

Tears slipped down her checks. "I can't believe you came for me. Surely, I've died and gone to heaven."

Damien chuckled. "I doubt you'd find any of us there, my lady."

Ronar drew her close again, and she allowed herself a moment to feel safe in his strong embrace, to breathe in the scent of him, to pray this wasn't a dream.

"We need to go," Damien urged.

"Aye." Ronar nudged her back.

Alexia winced at the pain that only now returned amid the excitement.

Frowning, he lifted her atop Penance and examined her feet. "Forgive me, Alexia, I should have known. These burns will need tending. And these." He examined her hands. Bloody gashes sliced across both her wrists. In all the mayhem, she hadn't felt a thing.

"Excellent shooting, my friend," Jarin said.

Alexia stared at Ronar. "*You.* 'Twas you who shot my bonds?"

"I had an excellent teacher." He winked at her, then glanced at his friends. "And much help afterward."

"We assumed you'd try something." Damien's charger pawed the ground, no doubt sensing his master's anxiety. "We merely didn't know what or when."

Alexia's mind still spun with the shock of the day, for nothing made sense. "Where were you?"

"In a window at the Hornbuckle Inn."

"That's forty yards from...."

He smiled and leapt atop Penance behind her. "And I even closed my eyes."

What? Did that mean...? She hadn't the clarity of mind to consider it. "But now, you will be counted a traitor like me." She glanced at Jarin and Damien. "*All* of you will."

Jarin's horse snorted. "We may yet be able to convince the king that our cause is worthy."

Ronar wrapped his arms around her and took the reins.

"I'm sorry I lied to you," she whispered.

"It matters naught now."

Horses' thundering and shouts alerted them to a band of Luxley knights headed their way.

Alexia stiffened. "We can hide in the forest. I know many places."

"Nay." Damien stared at the advancing knights. "We should explain to the king what happened ere the bishop dispatches a messenger."

"I agree," Ronar said.

Alexia laid a hand on Ronar's arm holding the reins. "But what of my sister? I cannot leave her."

"If we go back, we will all be arrested."

"I do not wish to leave her either," Jarin said, drawing her gaze, and she saw sincerity in the handsome knight's eyes. "But we are of no use to her dead."

"You have my troth, Alexia." Ronar's breath warmed her neck. "We will return within a fortnight with the king's blessing to arrest LeGode and save your sister."

He didn't give her time to respond before the three knights prodded their horses forward into the thick forest. Before too long, they emerged onto the King's Highway. Over hills, across fields, past Inns and taverns, they raced, their speed and the wind preventing any conversation. She spent most of the time thanking God for saving her, the rest thanking Him for Ronar. She still had trouble believing that he not only forgave her but had risked his position, his reputation—his very life—for her.

Thoughts of her sister made her long to turn around, steal her from her bed, and take her with them. But that was naught but her foolish emotions speaking. Appealing to the king was the wisest choice, the only way to save Cristiana. Nay, from now on she would allow the Holy Spirit to guide her and not her whimsical feelings.

Besides, her sister had the Spear. Surely it would keep her safe.

So caught up in her thoughts, she didn't see the warriors galloping toward them in a cloud of dust and thunder. Not until Ronar reared up his horse so hard, the beast pawed the air in protest.

Damien let out a foul curse. "Bishop Montruse's knights! He sent for them nearly a fortnight ago."

"But they have no knowledge of what has occurred," Ronar said.

Jarin steadied his agitated horse. "Indeed. They will recognize us as part of the King's Guard and let us pass."

Sounds behind them drew their gazes to a band of at least forty Luxley knights charging their rear. As soon as they spotted the bishop's knights, one man broke rank and circled around, speeding toward the advancing army.

"Or not," Jarin added.

Trapped. Alexia's blood turned to ice. Outnumbered by at least one-hundred to four. They'd all be killed.

Or worse, captured.

And it was all her fault.

"What of the Spear? Do you have it?" Ronar asked, his tone desperate.

"Nay." She absently rubbed her wrist.

She felt him stiffen behind her, heard the warrior emerge in his tone. "Then, gentlemen, let us not go down without a fight!"

All three men drew their swords.

Grabbing her bow strapped to Ronar's saddle, Alexia resigned herself, for the second time that day, to her fate. For without the power of the Spear, what chance did they have?

Chapter 33

*E*ven as Alexia nocked an arrow in her bow, she refused to believe this was the end God had planned for her. Something deep within her told her it wasn't, that there was something yet she must do, some task yet unfinished. *But what?*

The knights before them and the ones behind started forward, trapping them between a press of swords that would impale them from both sides. Still, Ronar and his companions remained staunch, jaws tight, swords leveled, and eyes trained on their enemies.

Their horses grunted and thumped the ground, sensing the impending battle.

Terror tore through Alexia, scraping against muscle and nerve. Swallowing, she whispered a prayer, closed her eyes, and searched for the truth within—the peace, love and protection that came only from God, His love for her, His promises never to leave her, to be her rock, her refuge, her deliverer.

The words from 1 Samuel spilled from her lips, "There is none holy as the Lord: for there is none beside thee: neither is there any rock like our God."

There. She felt Him wrapping His loving arms around her. She sensed His smile and heard the words, *Open your eyes, my daughter.*

Alexia obeyed. Fear loosened its grip and scurried away. She drew in a breath and blinked—not believing what she was seeing. Beings of light, nay, warriors of light surrounded them—massive beings, some atop horses, some on foot, all wearing silver armor that glowed so bright, it transformed the green field to white. With their backs to Alexia and their blades pointed outward, they formed an impenetrable fortress around her and her friends.

Unbidden laughter spilled from her lips. Jarin and Damien gazed at her as if she'd gone mad.

Ronar shifted in the saddle.

Alexia lowered her bow. "I will call upon the Lord, who is worthy to be praised: so shall I be saved from mine enemies."

"Shh, woman. Have you gone mad?" Ronar said.

"Nay." She smiled. "Far from it." Before Ronar could stop her, she slid from the horse and pointed to the warriors of light. "Gentlemen, we are not alone."

Damien frowned. Jarin huffed. Ronar merely stared at her in silence.

Alexia lifted her face to heaven. "Open their eyes, Lord."

❧

'Twas not a good time for Lady Falcon to lose her mind. Ronar swung his leg over Penance and dropped to the ground beside her. He didn't know whether to shake sense into her or cover her with his body to protect her from the oncoming battle. If only he could. He no longer feared for his own life. 'Twas this precious angel's safety that threatened to rip his insides apart. Angel, indeed, for her heart, her every thought was for the welfare of others. She didn't deserve to die. Not like this.

She faced him, her green eyes sparkling with such love and peace, he almost believed there wasn't an advancing army nigh forty yards over her shoulder. But there they were. He could make out their determined faces, see the lust for blood in their eyes.

Alexia gripped his shoulders. "Open your eyes, Ronar."

He drew her close and pressed her head against his chest, fearing the worst—that the terror had caused her mind to falter. He heard her whisper a prayer into the folds of his doublet, and closing his eyes, he whispered one of his own. To spare this woman. *God, please spare this woman.*

When he opened his eyes, an overwhelming brightness made them slam shut again. 'Twas as if the sun had dropped from the sky and broke into a hundred orbs all around him. He dared another peek. Nay, not the sun. Men who glowed as brilliant as the sun, dressed in white and girded with shields, bucklers, and swords—large men who towered over Ronar and his friends, standing not twenty feet from where they were.

Begad, was this some new enemy?

Nudging Alexia behind him, he spun his sword before him, ready for whatever came. But the beings remained, forming a circle around Ronar and his friends. They neither spoke nor moved. Merely stood, swords at the ready.

Couldn't be. He rubbed his eyes and looked again.

Alexia smiled up at him and took his hand in hers. "I told you we were not alone."

His mind reeled. "What…what…?"

"God's angels. His warriors."

"What ails you, Ronar?" Jarin yelled down to him. "They are nearly upon us."

Uttering a groan of disgust at what he must perceive as sheer insanity, Damien raised his sword, ready to slice the first knight who dared attack.

Ronar shoved the tip of his blade in the dirt and raised his hands to them. "Be still. Do not charge."

"Are you mad?" Damien shouted.

Sliding from his charger, Jarin took a stance beside Ronar and followed his gaze to the angels. "What is it? What do you see?"

"You wouldn't believe me if I told you." Ronar smiled. "We must stay completely still. Move not a muscle. That is an order."

"Are we at least allowed to scream when they slice us in half?" Damien barked back with disgust.

Jarin held his sword out before him. "What does it matter? We are all going to die anyway."

With a huff of frustration, Damien dismounted and stood beside them. "Then let us die together."

Ronar flung an arm around Alexia and drew her close.

The knights were within ten yards of the angels now. Close enough for Ronar to see the detail of their faces. Not defiant, determined faces ready for battle, but suddenly confused faces. Alack, Ronar would even call them expressions of bewilderment as their eyes shifted away from their quarry and scanned the field as if looking for something.

Five more yards.

Jarin moaned.

The ground shook beneath the advancing army.

Damien growled.

Four yards.

Jarin and Damien lifted their blades high.

The stomp of hoof and clank of armor clamored in Ronar's ears.

His hand itched to pick up his sword.

Still, the warriors of light remained.

The knight leading the charge gave a signal to split, and half the knights went to the right, half to the left, circling around the band of angels.

Ronar could only stare in wonder. Alexia squeezed his hand.

Jarin and Damien remained frozen in place, blades leveled before them, faces tight with shock.

Turning, Ronar found the army circling behind them, the leaders greeted by Sir DeGay and Luxley's knights.

"They were just here. I saw them!" the captain shouted.

Sir DeGay's shaky voice returned, "Aye."

"How did this rock get here?" The commander motioned behind him to where Ronar and his friends stood.

DeGay scratched his beard. "Mayhap the shadows of the day deceived us."

"Nay, I saw them!"

"Where could they have gone?"

"Split up, men!" the commander bellowed. "Sir Graden, take the highway east, Sir Buxley, the west. I shall take my men north. You"—he pointed to DeGay—"take your men south back to Luxley. They couldn't have gone far!"

Ronar finally allowed his nerves to settle as he watched the knights divide and gallop away.

The angelic warriors sheathed their swords and instantly sped up to heaven in flashes of light, leaving the four of them standing alone in the middle of the field with only a breeze and the warble of birds as company.

"What just happened?" Jarin asked.

Alexia fell to her knees and raised her hands toward heaven. "He only is my rock and my salvation; he is my defense; I shall not be greatly moved."

Ronar glanced at his friends. "I think we've been serving the wrong king." Then dropping beside Alexia, he bowed his head and worshiped.

❧❧❧

Twilight lured the last remnants of sunlight through the trees of Emerald Forest, casting a golden hue over the leaves surrounding Alexia. And over the man who walked by her side, his hand entwined with hers. They walked in silence, serenaded by woodland creatures, the distance gurgle of a creek, and the sound of their boots crunching over twigs and pine needles.

She had come to cherish their evening walks this past week, the special time alone, sharing their thoughts, their dreams, and sometimes just quietly enjoying the verdant forest around them. Tonight was one of those quiet nights, yet Alexia sensed more than silent musing in Ronar. He seemed somber, and she wondered whether he regretted his sudden descent in rank from King's Elite Guard to outlaw…

From friend of the king to enemy.

After God had sent his angelic army to their rescue, Ronar had lost his desire to plead his case before the king. Instead, he insisted on finding the friar and returning to the hideout behind the waterfall where he could best plan how to defeat Sir LeGode. Of course, Alexia had been thrilled with his change of heart. In addition, Jarin had been more than willing to join them—prompted, no doubt, by a love Alexia now believed he held for her sister. The thought made her smile. But Damien had refused to give up, and after taking his leave, had galloped away to London as fast as he could.

"Why are you so downcast, Ronar?" she asked as they wove around a moss-laden boulder. "Is it Damien's news upon his return this morn that has dampened your mood?"

He chuckled. "Downcast? Nay." He glanced at her from the corner of his eye and smiled. "And if you mean the news that we are all wanted for high treason to the crown, why would that upset me?" His tone teased.

She jerked on his arm. "Be serious."

"I am." He squeezed her hand and gazed over the endless trees. "I take no concern for the label the king wishes to place upon me. Alas, I no longer wish to serve him. Not after what happened."

"You mean the angelic army?"

"What else?"

"Would that Jarin and Damien had seen."

"They saw the result. It is enough for now."

Moments passed as they walked in silence. A squirrel darted across the path with an acorn in his mouth, while overhead, a blackbird greeted them with a melodious song.

Alexia lifted the hem of her skirt to step over a puddle. "I wish the king had believed Damien's report and not the messenger the bishop sent ahead to defame you and your friends. I am sorry you lost a friend."

A breeze stirred the tips of Ronar's hair. "I wonder if he ever was a true friend." Fading sunlight angled through the trees onto his face, sharpening his jaw and deepening the blue of his eyes. "I may be an outlaw, but you, Lady Falcon are now labeled a witch throughout the kingdom."

"'Tis no matter. I am used to hiding. You are not."

"I'm a good learner." Halting, he faced her and lifted her hand for a kiss. "Besides, I find I enjoy thwarting the plans of men like Bishop Montruse."

He winked, his eyes full of mischief, and the look in them stirred a forbidden excitement within her. What maiden wouldn't be excited in the presence of this man? He wore his usual leather breeches, tunic, and boots, but his doublet had been replaced with one that bore no royal crest on the shoulder. Still, he looked every bit the knight as always, knives strapped to his belt and his ever present sword at his side.

But it was the light in his eyes that melted her heart. Not just affection for her. But a new sparkle which bespoke an inner joy, peace, and purpose no man could steal. And a destiny that would last forever.

He stroked her cheek and smiled. "What are you thinking?" His gaze dropped to her lips, and suddenly nervous, she turned a shoulder to him.

A lizard skittered up a trunk, reminding her of another more sinister reptile.

"Hard to believe the bishop would dare lie to the king—telling him 'twas you and your friends who stole the Spear."

Taking her hand, he placed it in the crook of his elbow and began walking again. "A month ago, I would have agreed, but Bishop Montruse thinks only of himself and what he can gain."

"Damien was fortunate to get away from London with his life."

"Aye, 'twas God's doing he was warned by a servant before his audience with the king."

She drew in a deep breath of the sweet scent of moisture, life, and hope. "Now he is here with you and Jarin—the three of you back together again. That pleases me greatly."

"Aye. In truth, I rather like being an outlaw. It has a sort of adventurous sound to it, does it not?"

She heard, rather than saw him smile. "Don't you dare become a rogue, Sir Knight. Not when you finally believe in the power and love of God."

"Never. I serve a different King now. A righteous One. And I intend to follow Him and do good for those in need."

She raised a brow. "Not because you must earn your penance?"

"Tush! How tiring that was." He chuckled. "Nay, I serve Him because I want to, because He is worthy." He sighed. "I cannot believe the Church deceives so many. Now that the friar is reading the Holy Scriptures to me, my spirit has come alive, and I cannot wait to see what God has for me to do. Such adventure awaits!"

True excitement rang in his voice, and Alexia could not be happier. "I, too, learned valuable lessons. I learned the Spear has no power in itself. 'Tis the Holy Spirit of God that is all-powerful. I also learned that I must walk by the Spirit, trust God, and not allow my emotions to dictate my actions. Faith cannot exist alongside fear."

"Good to hear, because I grow weary of rescuing you."

"Rescuing *me*?"

"Aye, multiple times."

"I never asked for your rescue, Sir Knight. 'Twas you who could not stay away from me, withal."

"That much is true, I fear." They stopped, and Alexia recognized the small clearing where Ronar had caught her the first day they'd met—the day she nearly shot him with her arrow.

She smiled up at him. "You know this place? This is where—"

He laid a finger on her lips. "I know exactly where we are." He shifted his stance nervously.

Shadows deepened as the last rays of the sun fled, and she could no longer make out the details of his face. "What is it, Ronar?"

Taking her hands in his, he knelt before her. "Lady Alexia D'Clere, will you honor me by becoming my wife?"

Alexia's heart thumped so loudly she could hear it in her ears. *Wife?* 'Twas the last thing she expected from him, especially considering the threat to their lives. "What on earth are you doing?"

One brow cocked. "I'm proposing. What do you think I'm doing?"

"You wish to marry *me*?"

"That's the general idea, aye."

Finally, his words penetrated her heart and joy exploded within. Dropping to her knees, she threw her arms around him and embraced him so hard they both went toppling backward to the dirt, laughing.

Flipping her on her back, he pinned her with his weight. "Somehow, this seems quite familiar."

"Aye," she returned. "'Twas the position I *allowed* you to enjoy for a brief moment when we first met."

"Allowed?"

"Seemed a shame to put such a mighty knight in his place so soon. You do recall what happened next?" she asked curtly.

No answer came. Just the press of his lips on hers. And once again her world dissolved around her. All that mattered was Ronar, the taste of him, smell of him, feel of him, and the intense love she bore for him in her heart.

Ending the kiss, he pushed back, breathless, and held her face in his hands. "I like that ending far better."

Alexia had trouble finding her own breath. "I quite agree."

He brushed hair from her face. "Are you going to answer me, Lady Falcon, or are you to pierce me with one of your arrows again?"

"I fear 'tis your arrow this time, Sir Knight, that has pierced my heart, for I am unable to answer anything but yes."

Reaching around his neck, she drew his lips down to hers once again.

Epilogue

*A*lexia couldn't wait to tell the friar the glorious news. She all but tugged Ronar along as they darted around trees and shrubs, mere shadows in the darkness now. But she knew the way by heart—a heart that was now bursting with joy. They reached the pond, dove behind the waterfall, and burst breathless into the underground chamber.

The friar was reading the Holy Scripture to an enraptured Damien and Jarin.

All three looked up.

"Did you know about this heresy, Ronar?" Damien remarked sternly, yet his expression was playful.

"Aye." Ronar took Alexia's hand and approached. "I suppose we should add it to our list of crimes."

"A growing number, I fear," Jarin said with a chuckle as he sipped his wine.

The friar laid down the scroll and approached, his face beaming. "What is it, dear one? There is a new glow about you."

If Alexia weren't a warrior, she'd shriek and jump, she felt so giddy. Instead, she merely replied with more excitement than she intended. "Ronar and I are to be married!"

"Wed?" Jarin set down his mug and rose to grip his friend's arm. "I knew it. 'Tis happy news."

Damien snorted and stood. "Marrying the Falcon of Emerald Forest? What will you do next, Ronar, hatch a bevy of little thieves?"

Alexia's face reddened as the friar gripped her, his eyes alight with joy. "God be praised! I knew it the minute I met Sir Knight." He hugged her tightly.

"Mayhap you could have informed me?"

"And have you run the other way? Nay. Not when your happiness was at stake."

She kissed him on the cheek, and he pushed her away, blushing. "A wedding!" He rubbed his hands together. "How glorious!"

As joyful as the occasion was, Alexia longed to add to that joy with good news from Jarin. Though she had desperately wanted to join the knight on his second visit to the castle that morning, she conceded 'twas safer if he went alone, in disguise of course, to discover how her sister fared.

She approached the handsome knight. "What news, Sir Jarin?"

He swept kind eyes her way. "Seraphina informs me that your sister is still ill but has been on the mend these past days. She will relay the message that you are safe, close, and will come to her aid soon."

"Thank you, Jarin. You could not see her?"

"Nay, LeGode has his knights everywhere." He glanced at Ronar. "No doubt he fears we will return."

"Wise man," Ronar said, exchanging a glance with Alexia. Then raising his voice, he addressed them all. "Now that Damien is back with the news that we are outlaws, 'tis high time we behave like them. I say we make plans to defeat LeGode and restore Luxley to its rightful heirs."

Jarin nodded, his expression firm and determined. "Count me in. I shall be thrilled to see that craven fiend in his place. However"—he arched a brow—"if we are to be outlaws, we need a name—something daunting to be emblazoned upon posters demanding our capture."

Alexia smiled. "I quite agree. A name that will put the fear of God into all who hear it."

"Precisely." He grinned.

Damien shook his head.

Glancing at Ronar, Alexia flattened her lips. "Knights of Justice, Knights of God...I know! Knights of the Eternal Realm."

Jarin nodded. "I like it. It sounds regal."

"And powerful." Ronar winked at her.

"We can call ourselves whatever you want," Damien scowled and crossed arms over his chest. "As long as it gets my name cleared so I can return to London."

"We shall do our best, Damien." Ronar gripped his friend's arm. "I know you have unfinished business there."

The friar fingered the crucifix hanging around his neck. "'Tis a good name. Aye, 'tis very good." He raised his fist in the air. "Hear, hear for the three Knights of the Eternal Realm!"

"Four." Alexia interjected vehemently.

Jarin's brow crinkled. "Women cannot be knights."

"This woman can and *will*." She grabbed her bow from the table.

"She has earned it." Ronar smiled her way, drawing his sword and leveling it before him. "Besides, I've learned that arguing with her is not worth the trouble."

Alexia gave a satisfied smirk and held out her bow.

"Very well." Drawing his blade, Jarin nodded toward Damien, who reluctantly drew his sword to join the others.

"Here, here, to the four Knights of the Eternal Realm!" he shouted, and all three blades and one bow clanked together.

The friar cheered. "Huzzah!"

"And as our first act of justice," Ronar said. "We shall defeat LeGode and return castle Luxley to Lady Cristiana D'Clere."

Alexia smiled. "With God on our side, who can be against us?"

Author's Note

After reading this book, it may appear to some that I have a problem with the Catholic Church. In truth, I take issue with most organized religion, Protestant or Catholic. Religion is manmade and because of that, it often falls short of God's idea of what church should be. That's not to say church is bad and we shouldn't attend, but only that we should check everything we hear, see, and learn against the infallible Word of God. Whenever I see something that either contradicts that Word or ignores parts of that Word, I feel obliged to speak out. For the best example of how church should be, I refer you to the Book of Acts in the Bible. May we all long to return to that simple way of doing and being the church that God intended. God Bless you all!

FOR A PEEK AT HOW I SEE THE CHARACTERS AND SCENES FROM THIS BOOK, CHECK OUT MY PINTEREST PAGE.
HTTPS://WWW.PINTEREST.COM/MLTYNDALL/PROTE CTORS-OF-THE-SPEAR/

About the Author

AWARD WINNING AND BEST-SELLING AUTHOR, MARYLU TYNDALL dreamt of pirates and sea-faring adventures during her childhood days on Florida's Coast. With more than seventeen books published, she makes no excuses for the deep spiritual themes embedded within her romantic adventures. Her hope is that readers will not only be entertained but will be brought closer to the Creator who loves them beyond measure. In a culture that accepts the occult, wizards, zombies, and vampires without batting an eye, MaryLu hopes to show the awesome present and powerful acts of God in a dying world. A Christy award nominee, MaryLu makes her home with her husband, six children, three grandchildren, and several stray cats on the California coast.

If you enjoyed this book, one of the nicest ways to say "thank you" to an author and help them be able to continue writing is to leave a favorable review on Amazon! Barnes and Noble, Kobo, Itunes (And elsewhere, too!) I would appreciate it if you would take a moment to do so. Thanks so much!

Comments? Questions? I love hearing from my readers, so feel free to contact me via my website:

http://www.marylutyndall.com

Or email me at:

marylu_tyndall@yahoo.com

Follow me on:

FACEBOOK:
https://www.facebook.com/marylu.tyndall.author

TWITTER:
https://twitter.com/MaryLuTyndall

BLOG:
http://crossandcutlass.blogspot.com/

PINTEREST:
http://www.pinterest.com/mltyndall/

To hear news about special prices and new releases that only my subscribers receive, sign up for my newsletter on my website or blog! http://www.marylutyndall.com

Other Books by MaryLu Tyndall

THE REDEMPTION

THE RELIANCE

THE RESTITUTION

THE RANSOM

THE RECKONING

THE FALCON AND THE SPARROW

THE RED SIREN

THE BLUE ENCHANTRESS

THE RAVEN SAINT

CHARITY'S CROSS

CHARLES TOWNE BELLES TRILOGY

SURRENDER THE HEART

SURRENDER THE NIGHT

SURRENDER THE DAWN

SURRENDER TO DESTINY TRILOGY

VEIL OF PEARLS

FORSAKEN DREAMS

ELUSIVE HOPE

ABANDONED MEMORIES

ESCAPE TO PARADISE TRILOGY

PEARLS FROM THE SEA DEVOTIONAL

CENTRAL PARK RENDEZVOUS

TEARS OF THE SEA

WESTWARD CHRISTMAS BRIDES

Made in the USA
Middletown, DE
12 January 2017